MW00615960

Babylon's

Fallen Star

By

Molly Miller

Big Sage Press

"Freedom is the Toughest Seed"

Copyright © 2021 Molly Miller

All Rights Reserved. No part of this book may be reproduced or used in any manner without the prior written permission of the copyright owner.

To request permissions, contact author at: MollyMiller@BigSage.Press

Paperback ISBN: 978-0-578-93711-3
First Paperback Edition July 2021
Cover Art by: Ben Ruppert of SapperSpy Designs LLC
Published by Big Sage Press in the USA
www.BigSage.Press

Dedicated with love to
Mike, Marcy, Glenn, and Ben.
You have been the midwives to my dreams, and I am so
thankful for you.

CHAPTER 1

Wolfe Homestead –Orein, Nevada

Rebecca could feel the damp breeze billowing in from the open window behind her. Sometime during the early morning, the weather had shifted from the stiff hot air that had filled her room and kept her tossing and turning when she had first gone to bed. It had been stifling in the house as wave upon wave of heat radiated from the ceiling. This, combined with Mike's deep humming snores, had kept her awake well past midnight. She had at one point given up on sleep entirely. Leaving their bed for the living room couch, Rebecca had watched mindless reruns on tv, the dialogue barely audible over the chug of the swamp cooler on the roof. Quiet as a freight train, it helped only to make the house muggy and smell faintly of public pool. Pure exhaustion finally forced her to climb back into bed to drift in and out of fitful confusing dreams.

Now the cool breeze almost sighed in relief as it filled the room she shared with her husband. It lifted the vinyl blinds and tickled across the bare skin of her back like chilled satin carrying with it the smell of wet earth, grass, and dewy sage. She opened her eyes to look through her lashes at the soft grey light filling their room, debating whether to let the chatter of rain beginning to fall against the walk outside her bedroom window lull her back to sleep or if she should get up and organize the kids for the day. She ran her hand across the sheets, closing her eyes again as she reached for the warmth of her husband's body.

Mike wasn't there, of course. She hadn't covered herself up in the night, he must have carefully draped the blankets over her chilled skin when he had gotten out of bed well before dawn. He was a tall man, her husband. Big and built along the same lines as the full-sized truck he drove, but it always surprised Rebecca how quiet he could be when he didn't want to wake her. He would have risen in absolute silence, dressed beside the bed pulling his heavy work boots on as he readied himself for yet another day. Her mind, detached from her body at rest in her comfortable nest, mulled these things over as she felt herself drifting back into sleep as gently as a floating leaf capsizing beneath the waters of a still blue pond. It could have been moments or hours before Mike was beside her again, shaking her awake.

"Becca." She took in a sharp breath, reevaluating the room around her before looking up at him. She could hear someone, most likely Louise, slamming cupboard doors in the kitchen and rattling the silverware in a drawer. Their teenaged daughter had not yet learned her father's skill for morning silence. Mike gave her a tight smile before leaning down to kiss her forehead. "There's runoff in the back pasture. I already moved most of the stock but there's still a couple of cows out there who wouldn't cooperate, and I have to go."

"I'll get them." She nodded closing her eyes again before forcing herself to sit up in bed, her bare skin suddenly tensing against the chill in the room. Mike kissed her again, this time on the neck as he let his warm heavy hand drop to her breast giving it a gentle squeeze before heading for the door. "Wait." Rebecca reached for the long night shirt she had tossed onto the bedside table in the middle of the night. "Have you eaten? Let me make you something."

"Daylight's burning, Babe." He gave her one of his crooked smiles and was gone.

Rebecca padded to the dresser across the room where she snatched up a worn-out pair of jeans from a drawer. Throwing them on under her night shirt she ran down the hall to the kitchen, her bare feet slapping across the hardwood floors to where Louise was unloading the dishwasher.

"Coffee?" Rebecca demanded of her daughter's surprised cornflower blue stare.

"He has it." Louise nodded, turning back to her work.

"I filled his thermos while he was out checking the cows."

Rebecca nodded, going through her mental checklist, marking off the order of the day and cursing her late start. "Breakfast?" Louise pointed towards the oven with a plate as the engine of Mike's work truck growled to life outside. Rebecca squeezed past her daughter to the oven, checking the timer. There were two minutes left. "Close enough." She sighed, grabbing a potholder from the counter with one hand as she motioned to her daughter to hand her a paper towel off the dispenser with the other. She pulled open the oven door to appraise the pastries baking inside. "Ham?"

"Chicken." Louise answered trying to avoid her mother's worried scowl. These were not Mike's favorite, but it would have to do. Ignoring the blast of heat from the oven lifting the tendrils of hair surrounding her face, she grabbed the closest loaf – a homemade version of a Hot Pocket complete with cheese and veggies – and wrapping it in the paper towel closed the oven door to dash out to the truck. Mike gave her a surprised smile as she knocked on the window, and rolling it down leaned out to give her another kiss as she passed him his breakfast.

"Beef?"

"Not sure." She lied. If she told him the truth, he might send it back into the house with her and she didn't want him eating out of the vending machines in the company yard again. "Lunch?" He pointed to the stainless-steel box in the passenger seat before dropping the truck into gear.

"Cows." He said, pointing to the back of the property as his truck crept forward.

"I'm on it." She nodded, turning back towards the front door. She waited on the stoop, waiving as his taillights disappeared down their long drive, then brushing gravel and sage burrs from the bottom of her bare feet stepped back into their long ranch style home. Her son Jack was in the living room, sitting in the middle of the floor wiping sleep from his eyes and trying to pull on his boots. "You're still in your pajamas son." She said, running her fingers through his hair as she stepped by.

"I want to say bye to Dad." He yawned.

"Dad's down the road." And when his sleepy little face clouded over. "We'll call him before the bus comes. Louise has breakfast for you." He brightened a little at this, though not much. He must not have slept well last night either. "Get dressed." Jack hmphed, changing direction back towards his room as Rebecca half walked half jogged through the kitchen to the mud room at the back of the house.

"I have to finish up outside." She called through the open door to Louise, who had started to place pastries on plates. Yanking a pair of cold socks from the dryer, Rebecca brushed a goathead from the hem of her jeans and began to pull them on. "Get Sammy up and dressed for me." Louise poked her head through the doorway to give her mother a flat stare and a deep sigh in protest. "Please?" Rebecca pulled Mike's heavy Carhart from the hook on the wall and stepped into her muck boots. "Get Sammy up and dressed and ready to go by the time I get back and I'll let you drive the Suburban down to the bus stop."

"Awesome!" Louise brightened, dancing in place. Rebecca smiled then stepped out the back door leading from their tiny mudroom to the yard. The rain came down in intermittent sheets, spritzing the dry sand and sage that rimmed the back yard and pastures, collecting in low spots and puddling against the concrete pad outside the open door of their barn. By nine the sun would burn through the clouds and by noon there would be no trace left of this morning's damp. Rebecca was able to coax the remaining two cows onto higher ground with a bucket of grain, their springy bald-faced calves trailing obediently behind. They lowed discontentedly as she led them through the thick sage of the upper field, a less established piece of land more brush than grass. But when they came over a low sandy hill and caught sight of the rest of the Wolfe family's small herd, Rebecca had to practically run to stay out from under foot. She watched as the cows loped off to bully their way past the other cattle into the bale of hay Mike had dropped at the edge of their creek earlier that morning.

Rebecca tossed the few remaining handfuls of grain off into the brush and made her way back to the wide gate dividing the two pastures. By the time she got back to the house Louise had the younger children fed and dressed and was eagerly standing next to the front door holding Rebecca's keys. Two-year-old Samantha ran over to velcro herself to her mother's leg, sing-songing her good mornings and making stripping out of muddy boots tricky. "Honey," Rebecca panted, "stand back before you get painted in muck." All the while Jack leaned against the front door with the sort of jovial dysphoria only an eight-year-old boy can muster.

"Louise says she's driving to the bus." He half laughed, half moaned.

"I am!" His sister shot him a sour look.

"You're not old enough." Jack shot back.

"Mom says I can!" Louise insisted.

"Mom's not the law."

"It's mom's car!"

"You'll go to jail."

"I will not!"

Rebecca washed her hands and scooped Sammy up into her arms, rolling her eyes at Jack's exponentially growing predictions of doom. "Ok guys. Jack, she can drive the truck as far as the bus stop. It will be fine. Louise, did you make sure that Sammy's car seat is strapped down tight? Go double check while I eat." Rebecca scowled as the first bite of her pastry produced fully cooked vegetables and crust, but icy gravy within the shredded chicken. *Poor Mike.* She thought spitting the lump of inedible food into the trash. *He'll buy another Snickers and be crabby by the time lunch rolls around.*

"Jack." She said, fishing her cell phone out of her purse. "Call your dad and find out how his morning is going."

Then to Louise as she shooed the kids out the front door, "We need to up the temperature on the breakfast loaves. They aren't cooking all the way through."

"Why can't we just leave the cows in the back?" Louise asked over the steering wheel as the massive SUV crept down their long drive and past their small herd now meandering around the front ten acres of fenced brushland. "Dad said they don't really mind the water."

"Keep it in the center." Rebecca reached over and helped her daughter guide the vehicle back to the middle of the drive as they bumped over a narrow bridge spanning the wide shallow creek that ran the length of their property. "They don't, usually. But this rain came out of nowhere and we aren't sure how much runoff the back pasture will get. The water soaks the roots of the grass and having the cows walk that pasture into a mudhole will kill it. We either move them or spend your college fund reseeding."

"I don't mind." Louise smiled as the Suburban chugged uphill towards the large double gate marking the edge of their homestead. "I don't even think I want to go to college."

"You're going." Becca fixed her daughter with a serious look as she hopped out to open one side of the gate, slamming the heavy truck door to emphasize the finality of her statement. She swung the gate wide and waving the truck through, watched nervously as Louise guided the vehicle to the edge of the county road ahead, nearly missing their mailbox. Her sigh was lost beneath the squeaking of wet brakes and the creaking of the gate hinges as she pushed it closed again.

"Mom!" Jack called from his seat in the back through the open window as she came to the driver's side door expecting Louise to put the SUV in park and climb down. She looked to where he was sitting, phone pressed against his ear, deep into conversation with Mike, "Dad says I can drive the tractor with him tonight." Rebecca could hear Mike's muffled "Maybe! … *Maybe* drive the tractor!" coming from the phone.

"Good job." She said, hinting to Louise to give her the wheel.

"You said I could drive to the bus stop." Louise scowled.

"And you did." Rebecca insisted.

"No." the SUV lunged a little as Louise shifted her foot on the break, then frowning mashed it down again. "This is the road. The bus stop is down there."

"Dad said I can drive the tractor." Jack taunted Louise from the back, continuing to ignore his father's emphatic maybes.

"Mom, you said the bus stop." Louise insisted. "You said."

"Fine." Becca tightened her lips, then as she walked around the vehicle and climbed back up in the passenger's seat she said, "You should be a lawyer. Therefore, you are going to college."

"This family could use a lawyer." Louise snorted, mimicking her father perfectly as the Suburban resumed its cautious creep down the county road.

"You're telling me. Ok, just a little more gas…" Rebecca gripped the dash as the SUV lunged forward, "Less gas. Less gas. Ok… good. Just stay relaxed."

"I am relaxed." Louise sniffed as she stretched her spine, straining to see further over the hood. "You stay relaxed."

"Louise." Rebecca's warning tone was a bit sharper than she intended.

"What Mom? I'm fine! See?"

"Don't get overconfident. That's how accidents

happen."

"Geez Mom, c'mon. I'm not going to wreck. Who do you think I am? Felicity?"

The sudden silence in the cab was as hot and thick as the heat in the house the night before as everyone, even Rebecca, waited to see how she would react. Louise had unintentionally picked at an old wound and Becca could feel Jack's eyes darting anxiously from his sister to herself and back again. Just as the silence was almost too much to bear, Mike's voice – tinny and electric from the phone - broke through "Yeay! Louisey's driving!"

Thankfully the school bus stop was only a quarter of a mile down the unpaved road from their mailbox. Mike's well-timed sarcasm had robbed the silence of its teeth though it still hung around them like a cloud of flammable gas awaiting a spark. Becca could tell Louise had immediately regretted letting the reference to her older sister slip but hadn't found the right words to apologize yet without simultaneously calling doubt down on her ability to drive. She would eventually just swallow her pride and make peace. Louise was like that. But the reference to her absent oldest child had stung Rebecca deeply and she couldn't trust herself to not return the apology with bad grace, which made her glad Louise had opted to hold out. Louise parked the Suburban well away from the wide v-ditch on the shoulder so Jack would have no problems climbing down from the cab. Rebecca stepped out and gave him a hug goodbye just as a large white Sheriff's crew cab truck pulled up behind them.

"Told you!" Jack hissed at Louise who was collecting her backpack from the foot space below Sammy's car seat, then breaking away from his mother ran to greet the young deputy who stepped out from inside. "Hi Mr. Yneko. Louise drove us from the house. Is Drew in there?"

"Hey buddy! Drew's in back." Max Yneko put his hand down to accept an enthusiastic high-five before opening the rear crew door to let his young son Andrew climb down.

Together the two boys tumbled away in a cloud of noise to join a couple of girls in matching polka-dot slickers standing under a tall pinion growing along the edge of the road. "Hey Louise."

"Hi Mr. Yneko." Louise returned sheepishly, then turned an apologetic face to her mother. "Bye. Mom."

Rebecca took in her daughter's expression for a moment then pulled her in for a tight hug. "Bye kid. I love you." Louise nodded her response and went to stand beside the others waiting for the bus, while Max Yneko walked up to join Rebecca at the front of the family Suburban. "So how did she do?"

Rebecca worked to keep her expression placid, her eyes never leaving her children as she carefully gauged her response. Max Yneko owned a smaller homestead further down the long dirt road stretching off into Federally managed land and Rebecca never could tell if she was talking to her neighbor, or to his badge. "Fine." She finally responded after a long silence. "Really well, actually… for a thirteen-year-old girl."

"You know." Max shifted his weight slightly in a way that made Rebecca want to step away, but she forced herself to stay rooted with her back against the grill and her arms folded across her chest. "She's almost old enough for a farm permit. Then she can help Mike around the place."

"How's Ane?" Rebecca turned to look up at the tall deputy, her face a stony mask. "Doing well?"

"Yes." Max nodded, taking a step or two back sensing the thinning civility in her tone. "Have a good one, Rebecca."

"You too Max." Rebecca watched him walk back to his patrol truck and drive away. Even managed a neighborly wave as he passed by.

"Mom?" Rebecca turned to find Louise at her elbow, tears glistening in her soft blue eyes. "I'm sorry. I should have stopped at the gate. I should have pulled over and let you drive." Her chin began to tremble as she spoke. "I'm sorry."

Rebecca let out a long breath, pulling her daughter in for another hug. "It's fine." She kissed the top of Louise's head. "Don't cry. It's ok. Dry your face, here's your bus."

Rebecca didn't need to go into town. There were a hundred things she and Sammy could get done around the house in the hours before the rest of the family came home. But the unintentional upset of the morning had left her feeling broken and agitated, and she just needed some time to put her head on right before getting down to the business of living. She climbed in behind the wheel, allowing the bus enough time to turn around at the edge of her property and come back down the dirt road, catching a glimpse of Louise's sorrowful expression through the window as it glided by. Jack and Andrew Yneko were sitting behind the driver lost in their own little world. Rebecca looked at Sammy in the rearview mirror, the toddler was staring apathetically out the window at the rolling sage and hills which tumbled down along the side of the county road away from her home.

"Hey Sammy." The toddler immediately brightened, a wide happy smile spreading across her peachy cream little face, her soft blue eyes so much like Louise's shining out from under an unruly mop of silvery blond hair. "Should we go get coffee?"

"I can have chocolate milk?" Sammy sang back.

"Yes, baby girl. You can have chocolate milk." Rebecca switched on the radio, turning the control from the FM dial to the Willie Nelson cd she kept on standby when she wasn't interested in commercials or talking heads. As Willie piped in, midway through the ballad of *Poncho and Lefty*, Rebecca guided her Suburban away from the side of the road towards town.

They pulled up to the window of the tiny shed that served as the town coffee shop and ordered, Rebecca absentmindedly reading the sign while the elderly gentleman inside made her latte. *The Coffee Pod*, it said above the company slogan, *We Ain't Starbucks*. With Sammy back in her car seat and gurgling happily away over her box of chocolate milk, Rebecca pulled her SUV back out onto Ore Carts Street, heading west to the state highway running through town.

Orein was an odd mix of aging apartment complex buildings, Victorian houses and saloons in the historic district, sump block commercial ag dealerships, Sears Craftsman Style cottage homes, and ranches. She drove past the empty fairgrounds, turning north onto Bridge Street spanning one of the larger tributaries feeding into the Leavitt River, and past the monument gate of a suburban community which had been abandoned by the builder halfway through development. The empty lots dotted the cul-de-sacs and streets like missing teeth in a boxer's smile. She rolled past hay fields, two gun clubs, a tractor dealership and Orein Well and Pump. She turned right onto Main Street between the Orein Ford Dealership and the Dollar General, past an open yard brimming with brown and white goats, then left again onto Basque Lane where she pulled into the parking lot shared by the Dairy Queen, Lester's Sports Bar, the Sack 'n Pack Grocery Depot, and Orein Feed and Saddlery.

"Geese! Mommy!" Sammy cried out with chocolate smeared glee pointing to the big grey feed store. "There's the geese store! We can pet them?"

"No baby, no geese today." Rebecca smiled as she pulled into a parking space and cut the engine. "They're sold out."

"Sold out?" Sammy cocked her head trying to make sense of this information.

"Yup." Rebecca stepped down from the driver's side and opened Sammy's door, pulling a pack of diaper wipes from under the bench seat to wipe the sticky mess from her daughter's cheeks. "Should we buy more cob and maybe some hot dogs?"

"Hot dogs! Hot dogs!" Sammy kicked her feet excitedly as Rebecca unbuckled her harness. "I like hot dogs!"

"I know you do."

The young lady behind the counter of the feed store smiled a greeting to Rebecca, fawning over Sammy while writing down the order for five fifty-pound bags of sweetened corn, oats, and barley and directing her to pull her truck around the back where "the boys will load you up." Rebecca thanked her as she paid, making sure to mention she would be running to the grocery store before loading her feed.

"That's not a problem." The girl smiled, speaking more to Sammy who had broken into a command performance of Itsy-Bitsy-Spider. "No it's not, is it cutie pie? Mommy can come back to pick up her stuff anytime until we close at five. After that we'll have to deliver it, won't we baby?"

They left the feed store, Sammy trailing a little behind as she stopped to inspect every crack in the aging asphalt before leaping over them in a massive feat of strength. She stopped only to beg for a ride in a grocery cart which had been abandoned at the corner of the Sack 'n Pack building then squealed with delight all the way in through the automatic doors. They stocked up on breakfast cereal, flour, sugar, Ritz crackers, ketchup, relish, and - to Sammy's delight - cheese filled hotdogs alongside the larger pack of all beef dogs Mike insisted tasted better than the ones made from pork and chicken. Rebecca was handing things from the cart to Sammy, who then tossed each item onto the belt when someone called her name from the head of the line. She looked up, suddenly recognizing Ane Yneko with her youngest son, Colt, in tow.

"Rebecca!" The deputy's wife smiled sweetly, handing a twenty to the cashier and leaning in to pet Sammy's hair. "I thought that was you."

"It's me." Rebecca forced a smile, inwardly cringing at this chance encounter.

"So!" Ane said looking over the items on the belt. "Hot dogs! You guys must be watching tonight."

"Watching…?"

"The comet. Max says it might be too overcast but

I'm still excited." She took a deep breath, appraising Rebecca's questioning gaze. "You know? For the kids." Taking in Rebecca's blank expression, Ane turned back to her cart and pulled a dog-eared copy of National Geographic from her purse to hand over. "It's going to be a close one. NASA says the big one is the size of an aircraft carrier!"

"The big one?" Rebeca looked down at the page which Ane had folded over featuring a high-definition illustration of a cluster of grey rocks beside other various objects – an aircraft carrier, a school bus, a VW Bug, a semi-truck, and a Mark Twain styled riverboat.

"Oh yea!" Ane's breathless enthusiasm was almost contagious. Almost. "They're going to split between us and the moon. It's supposed to be quite a show. We were thinking of roasting marshmallows with the kids tonight while we watched... you know, weather permitting... and it's going to be even closer than the one in 2018."

Ane suddenly swallowed down her excitement, stepping back from Rebecca's cart. "Anyway... I just thought with the hot dogs and everything. But..." Ane switched gears, growing a little somber. "Max said there was a little awkwardness this morning. I don't want you guys to think that just because... you know, what happened with Felicity that he's just waiting for a chance to.... I mean..." Ane furrowed her brow and took another step backwards, looking for the right words. "Max is really glad we finally have neighbors and he's not looking to make trouble. Anyway, I'm holding up the line and I'm sure you have things to do." She turned away leaving her magazine in Rebecca's hands and scooping up her son, placed him in the cart amongst her groceries as the cashier began ringing up Rebecca's items.

"Hey Ane?" The younger woman turned around, her large expressive eyes brimming with a mixture of wariness and expectancy. Rebecca walked over and handed her the magazine with a small smile. "I didn't know about the comet. Would you and your family like to come over to our place tonight? We have a fire pit, and camping chairs, and I can get more hot dogs."

"Or we can bring steaks!" Ane was working hard to contain her elation. "We have a bunch off our last batch of steers. And corn on the cob."

"And I have marshmallows at home." Rebecca replied. "What time are we supposed to be able to see it?"

"NASA says around ten at night. That's a little late for the kids to be up on a school night but we thought..."

"It's a special occasion." Rebecca waved her explanation off, "Want to come over around seven? That will give Mike some time to clean up after work, and get some stuff done around the house."

Rebecca paid for her groceries and pushed her cart to the Suburban, her emotions churning inside of her like a dust storm. She wanted – she needed – this thing between her family and the Ynekos to be over. It had been hanging across the fence line like a rancid hide for over a year now, and she needed it gone. She was still angry. She still harbored displaced anger at Max for the arrest and at her husband Mike for never dealing with small problems until they were massive problems. And she was still very angry at her daughter Felicity. She had been so angry for so long it almost felt like she was letting a piece of herself go. It felt like quitting. It felt like losing.

She sighed as she realized she still had to explain all of this to Mike. She pulled into the feed lot and handed the young man working the gate her purchase slip. He was loading the bags of grain into the back of her SUV when she noticed a large cardboard box tucked inside the attendant's gate hut with the words *Free to a Good Home* scrawled across the side. At the bottom of the box, using a tattered flannel jacket as a bed, a litter of black and white puppies slept pressed against each other for warmth. Reaching into the cab Rebecca picked up her phone from the cupholder where she had tossed it after Mike had hung up with Jack and hit the call button.

"Hey," she said when Mike picked up. "I think maybe it's time we got a dog."

CHAPTER 2

Woodview Heights Estates – Baptiste, Idaho

"Here comes trouble." Ashley looked up from her iPad to where her husband David was standing at the living room window munching on his acai bowl and appraising the front lawn. He turned to her with a wry smile, taking another bite and shrugging towards the world outside. "See for yourself." She stood up from her perch on the kitchen barstool and joined him at the window. Outside Abigail Messenger was standing at the foot of their drive dressed in her typical morning uniform – yoga pants and a tank top, the toe of her custom Nikes pressed against the edge of their lawn, her iPhone aimed directly down – presumably taking photos.

"Shit." Ashley muttered.

"The kids will hear you." David snorted into his spoon as he took another bite.

"She's going to see the sprinkler." Ashley sighed and walked back into the kitchen, picking up her iPad again. Then added "Besides, the kids are already out of the house. Megan wanted to take them to the planetarium in Boise. They won't be back until tonight. They have a special public show about the comet and then they're heading home tomorrow morning." She paused, looking up at the clock on the stove. "Shit, David. It's nine thirty. Are the sprinklers on? Is she still there?"

"Still there." He called from the window "And no, the timer must be off... oh, wait... here we go. Show time!"

Ashley cursed again as she ran barefooted back to the living room window. "Can she see you?"

"She hasn't looked up." David scraped his spoon across the bottom of his empty bowl, pulling out the last cluster of granola, then used it to gesture towards the pool of bubbling water forming at the far corner of their yard. "She only has eyes for that. How did she even know to be here this morning? Marco says he'll be by around noon to fix it."

"Joanna says she tips the guys on Marco's crew when they text her about things like this." Ashley sighed.

"That's a little Machiavellian." Dave scowled as they watched Abigail walk over to where the water from the broken sprinkler head was flowing into the street.

"Makes you wonder," Ashley growled, "if they're breaking them on purpose just to have something to report. That's our second broken sprinkler this year and its only August." then as Abigail raised her phone to take a picture, "Welp, there it is. We'll be getting our official fix-it report this afternoon after her damn yoga class." Ashley threw up her hands in exasperation and padded back into the kitchen. "You know, you give anyone the slightest modicum of power and they turn into a certified brownshirt."

"That's the truth." David followed her into the kitchen, rinsing his bowl and placing it in the top rack of the dishwasher as he spoke. "But it might be over soon. Word on the street says Noah Walker might be running a silent campaign to replace her on the HOA"

Ashley eyed him from over her Facebook feed, "You've been talking to Bear and Lisa again."

He shrugged, turning to lean against the sink, "They came into the office. They said they just dropped by to see if I wanted to grab lunch, but I think he was sounding me out on a case. Seems there's something brewing data safety related with a contractor working with the social security administration. It felt very interview like."

Ashley raised her eyebrows in mock awe, "Are you going to be an expert witness?"

"Tell me about the comet." He laughed, walking over to lean across the kitchen island where she was seated.

"Oh, so Mr. Experty-expert doesn't know everything?" She shot back in jest, her fingers already flying over the surface of her iPad to pull up an article she had been reading just moments before.

"Help a guy out." He sighed. "Your sister's kids are really into this stuff and I don't want to seem like I'm ..."

"Not a big enough nerd?" she interjected.

"Unlettered." He laughed. "Among my own people."

"Nerds." She sighed, her bright green eyes taking him in briefly before falling back to her device. He *was* a nerd. Deep down. Just an incredibly attractive one. Dave was lean and tall with sandy brown hair and bright hazel eyes, and a store-bought tan that made him look more like he belonged on a surfboard in sunny California than in the regional VP's office of a leading medical software firm. "But if it will keep you on the A list of your little nerd tribe, I think I have just the thing.... This is from Sci-Chai news..."

"Sci-Chai?"

"Science and Chai Tea." She rolled her eyes at him. "It's a nerd page for nerd mommies who want their nerd daughters to be even bigger nerds."

"Perfect!"

"After this article I can teach you how to build a breast pump out of nine-volt batteries and erector set pieces."

"Let's get back to the erections and breasts later." he quipped, then in his best Elvis voice "Lay some knowledge on me little mama."

"Tonight's comet is a rare X class heavenly body which means that there isn't enough data yet to determine its orbital path." Ashley read aloud, "Scientists will be tracking it for the next week but suspect that they will be reclassifying it in the "P" designation meaning it will have a return orbit – though its path must be extremely wide gauging from its approach and speed. The comet is not one but five bodies, the largest being just under three hundred and seventy-five meters in length..."

"Jesus." David breathed.

"Is that big?" Ashley looked up at him in surprise.

"That's pretty big."

"What is that in feet?" Ashley looked from her screen to her husband and back again. "Translate this from Nerd Latin to English for me."

"It's about twelve hundred feet." And then to her blank stare, "Remember that pub we loved in Boston?"

"The one with all the nets on the wall? The King-something?"

"Yes. Imagine walking from their front door to the front of the city hall building."

"Oh my God, that is big."

"It is."

"And you're a nerd for knowing that."

"I am but keep reading."

"Ok... so the biggest one is about three seventy-five... blah blah blah... and the smallest is approximately four meters wide and is expected to break up as it nears the sun giving a spectacular light show which can be seen through special telescopes."

"Not anything you would have in the back-yard kind of special."

"Darn." Ashley frowned. "I could do with a spectacular light show."

"So, she's a sungrazer."

"She?"

"They said it's going to be beautiful to watch. You're beautiful to watch. So, this comet must be a she."

"You know what?" Ashley put her iPad down and walked around the kitchen island to fold herself into David's arms. "You're a flatterer."

"It works for me though." He smiled down at her.

"And you are king of the nerds."

"And I have to get to the gym if I'm going to make my meeting on time." He looked at the clock on the stove, "I have about enough time to really hit it and shower before I have to be in."

"Fine." Ashley breathed against his chest. "Go be a big strong man. I'll just be here. Alone. Missing you. At least until about ten thirty. I'm going to stop by the gallery to see how things are going."

"Are we doing the thing here? Or are we going to the block party?"

"Ugh." Ashley pulled away and went back to her iPad. "Well. We have Megan and the kids in town. We should probably be social and let the boys hang out. But it means talking to Abigail. How can she not tell people don't like her?"

"Joanna likes her."

"True." Ashley narrowed her lips. "And that chick Teagan will be there, probably. She sucks up to Abigail. Wasn't she a stripper or something?"

"No, she's the lotto winner." He shook his head. "You're thinking about Lex Donati. But he didn't strip…"

"Thank God."

"He just owns a strip club."

"Gross."

"I gotta go."

She leaned her cheek into his kiss as he walked past her towards the utility room which sat between the kitchen and the garage. "Be home by six. That's when the barbeque starts. I would rather do this in the back yard with a bottle of wine, but we have to feed those children and rub elbows with the dregs of the neighborhood."

"We could sell this place and move." He said as he pulled his gym bag off the dryer and opened the garage door.

"And leave my travertine floors? I just picked them out."

"Then we wait a year."

"How's the transfer back to Manhattan looking?" Ashley, suddenly serious put her iPad down and fixed him with a hard gaze.

"I haven't heard anything yet."

"David." She pinched the bridge of her nose. "There

are other companies. We didn't have to get stranded out here."

"Gotta go." He gave her an apologetic look as he swung the door closed behind him.

Ashley sat in their expansive kitchen listening to the quiet of the house falling all around her, her eyes roaming listlessly over the spotless stainless-steel surface of her appliances to the polished surface of her granite countertops. She was still taking in her surroundings with a disinterested malaise when the sound of David's Dynamite Red Audi Spyder leaving the garage echoed back to her from the street. He hadn't been gone ten minutes when a new email notification came through on her device. She scanned it then pressed her facetime control, listening to the whirling chirp of the outgoing call as she waited for David to pick up. His face appeared in profile from the cradle where he mounted his phone on the dash, the angle highlighting his muscular jaw beneath his aviator-style Maui Jims, his hair whipping around in the wind as the roadster's deep growl filled her kitchen.

"What are you listening too?" Ashley asked.

"Elvis." David smiled, though he kept his eyes on the road.

"You have the worst taste in music."

"Hey mama." He laughed back, curling his lip up in Elvis like fashion.

"I was wrong. She got to us before work and yoga."

"She's got it in for you. How much this time?"

"Two hundred."

"That's a little steep."

"She says it's been broken for a week."

"It might have been. Did you notice?"

Ashley shook her head, "I really didn't."

"I'll call Marco after my meeting." Dave assured her. "We'll talk about it. If his guys can't handle mowing a yard without running down the sprinkler heads, maybe we hire a different crew. It was convenient to go with them after the purchase since they put all the landscaping in to begin with, but I think we need someone who doesn't report to the HOA"

"Sounds good to me." Then flipping through the display on her tablet she said, "I also have another factoid for you."

"Let's hear it."

"Between the years 1995 and 2017 there have been over three-thousand comets discovered by satellites, of these only five have been visible from earth."

"That is a neat fact. I'm going to lay that one on your nephews later and watch their heads explode in adoration."

"So long as you clean up the mess."

"Later beautiful."

"See ya handsome."

The screen went blank as he disconnected. He would be busy today. She might not hear from him at all until he got home. Ashley sighed and stretched, listening to her shoulders pop as she arched her back. She had just enough time to get in a morning shower and get dressed if she was going to make it to the gallery before Marco's crew showed up to fix the sprinkler head.

CHAPTER 3

Wagner RV Park – Pinefare, Montana

"Wait! Wait! Shit!" Sissy Wagner's voice shrieked from under the beat up old '95 Ram. "Shut it off!"

Len cut the engine as Sissy rolled herself out on the makeshift creeper, a jumbled mess of pallet wood nailed together on skateboard trucks. "Len," she laughed, her face a black mask of oil and dust, "I messed up. I have to start over. Either the gasket got pinched or I didn't put it on the threading straight…"

"Or you didn't get it tight enough?" He joked kicking her in the back pockets gently with the toe of his boot. She batted him away with the rag she had pulled from her back pocket to wipe her face.

"Either way. It's a damn mess under there. And I have to drain it again before I can check the filter. I have more of that 10W-40 in the storeroom of the RV office. Tell Shawna I need it while I clean this up." She smiled sheepishly back up at him, "Sorry it's taking so long."

Len spread his hands in an ambiguous fashion. "I'm just glad you have the time to do it. Didn't think she would make it into Libby with how rough she's been running, at least not without the obvious things taken care of. And God knows it's been a while since I've been able to get under there myself."

"I always have time for you, Len." Sissy's eyes crinkled at the edges, a lock of greying hair pulling free from the bandana she had tied around her head. Len returned her smile and walked back across the dirt road separating his tiny one-bedroom trailer from the back end of the Wagner RV Park, stopping momentarily to bend over -painfully- to fish a crumpled beer can out of a pile of pine litter and toss it in a recycling bin on his way back to the office. Sissy Wagner had been one of his oldest and dearest friends, he would have to find a way to pay her back for this kindness. Len had known Sissy and her twin sister Sassy since their last name was MacNeil. He had been seated with the family when Sassy married Morgan French, the local hotelier who half owned The Trapper. Everyone expected Sissy and Len would eventually marry. Instead, he was a groomsman when she walked down the aisle with Dicky Wagner right out of high school. Five years later he was a pallbearer when Dicky died beneath a massive widowmaker while working with the Mule Wash Lumber Company. She was the last of a handful of people clinging to this town, and a good mechanic – even if her grip on the wrench had a little less torque to it than it did back in '87.

He waived hello to Shawna who was reading a trashy romance behind the counter of the tiny store that took up the front half of the RV office. *Cat's away, mice will play,* he thought as he looked to the mop and bucket standing at the ready beside her chair. She waved him through to Sissy's inner sanctum, a shoebox of an office cluttered with invoices, catalogues, post-it notes and various RV parts – most looking as though they had fallen off along the roadside. He braced himself against the jamb of the storeroom, listening to his joints creak and pop in protest as he bent to pick up the two five-quart jugs of oil just inside the door, grunting as he forced himself back upright. Years of broken bones and sprains and bruises as a young man had left their mark on him. They had warned him as a young cowboy that he would end up stove-up but earning a paycheck seemed more important in those days. He regretted nothing but wished it didn't take a handful of Advil and a couple of beers to get to sleep at night.

He walked slowly back to his truck taking in the sights and smells of this lovely August morning. A large flock of white throated swifts chittered overhead as they swept between the tall pines rimming the park. Down the street he could hear the Blackman's blue tick bitch teaching her newest litter to bay. The warm sweet smell of waffles drifted to him from the open backdoor of Wagner's Café just kiddy corner from the RV Park office to the north. It mingled with the earthy scent of hot asphalt soaked in the sprinkling rain which had been loitering intermittently around town. There was the faint scent of oil and gasoline from his jeans, and the whisper of the breeze through the trees. Pain or no, it was a damn good day to be alive.

The faint moan of an electric guitar chirping out a few measured chords pulled his eyes to the top of The Trapper Hotel – the only building in town which stood five stories above the deck. He waved hello to a couple of Sissy's guests, a nice older couple with Texas plates on their MiniWin who had been in the park a couple of days. They waved back, trying to shush the two teacup papillons yipping and yodeling their own greeting as they turned miniature pirouettes at the end of their ribbon like leashes.

"Can they have a treat?" he asked as he passed by, and receiving a surprised "Yes!" he set down one of the cans of oil to fish a couple of sticks of homemade goose jerky from his shirt pocket, leftovers from his meager breakfast. He liked dogs, of all shapes and sizes. Always had, always would. He patted their silky little heads and smiled at their teensy yips which had become friendlier after the presentation of food. He hid his discomfort picking the can back up and carried on his way across the dusty park. By the time he reached his driveway Sissy had just finished replacing the plug on his oil pan and was sliding back out from under the old Dodge.

"Just in time." She smiled, then spit a tiny stream of tobacco juice behind his rear wheel before taking the jugs from him to fill the engine block with a long yellow funnel.

"So... you...ah..." He swallowed a moment, trying to hide his shallow breathing against the sharp pain in his arms and hands. "You going to the shindig at the Trapper?"

She chuckled a little at his use of the word shindig,

good old Len was becoming more and more like his old man every day. "Might could be." She nodded gently shaking the last drops of oil from one can before reaching for another. "What did we say from the pan? Its closer to eleven full quarts on this one, right? Hand me the other bottle you have in the cab." Then tipping the next jug up into the funnel she shrugged. "I would have to clean up a bit. But it seems like it could be fun."

"Daisy got that band out of Kalispell to come back out. It took her a week to convince them after what happened at the fourth of July." He jerked his head towards the Trapper standing stoically above the RV park. "Think she even paid extra and promised that Gyp wasn't invited."

"They were good." Sissy looked over her shoulder to the hotel where the crashing of drums and a few strains of *Brown Eyed Girl* had started up. "What are they called again? Rod and the... something mechanical."

"The Rocker Arms." Len laughed.

"Good band. Won't be long until they won't return Daisy's calls – Gyp Masters in the audience or no." She tossed the second jug down and took the one quart can he offered her, then wiping the funnel a bit with her back-pocket rag popped it open and sat it directly into the funnel upside down. "That Gyp. He was born to embarrass his people."

"Good thing not many of them are around anymore." Len mused, receiving a distracted "yup" in return as Sissy fished a fresh rag from her coveralls pocket and used it to remove the funnel from the engine then ducking down underneath, crawled under the new oil filter to further mop at it.

"Ok." She called out. "I'm clear. Keep it in neutral and kick it on."

"Scares the shit out of me to do this." He grumbled but did as she asked. Sissy may have grown her roots under the shade tree but still had a way of finding trouble when it came to engines, testimony told by the missing fingertips on her right hand where a fan blade pully had nicked them off twenty years ago just below the nail line of her middle and pointer.

"Just do it Len." She gently kicked him in the foot then held her breath as the massive engine roared to life, watching the smooth orange surface of the oil filter for leaks. She gave it a minute then pulled herself out from under the frame, a wide smile across her oil-streaked face. "You're all good." She beamed as he cut the engine.

"So, what went wrong the first time?"

"Uh... I uh, I didn't have it on tight enough." She scowled as she dusted off the front of her coveralls with her rag.

"I told you."

"Yea. You told me." She bent down to drag her big black drain pan out from under the truck, screwing down its lid before the semi-clean oil inside could slosh out. "I'll refill the two jugs you bought. Don't use them, Len. Seriously. I know it seems brand new and a waste but there's dirt and kitty litter in there now, I used the rest of that Tidy Cat to get up the mess. You don't want that in your engine."

"I can use it for my little lawnmower." He shrugged. "No need for it to go to waste."

"Len, you can't use this on your..." Sissy stopped, sighing at the deep hang dog expression Len offered her. "At least run it through a filter first. I'll have Shawna bring you one of those big bastards we put on the Class As."

"Sissy..." He turned away to hide his hot red cheeks. "You know I can't pay you for that."

"Well Len. I've been needing someone to fix that window in the men's room of the café for about a week now. How about we just make it even?"

He looked at her for a long moment, then nodded, knowing full well there wasn't a damn thing wrong with the window that scraping out some old paint and new caulking couldn't fix. He took in a deep breath and finally said, "Sure, we could do that."

"Good." She smiled thinly, gauging whether to ask if he wanted help pulling the oil out of the sun and into his battered old shed. As if sensing her dilemma, he muttered something about "handling it" then thanked her again for the help.

"That's what neighbors do, Len." Her dismissal of his thanks was not without affection. "I'm gonna go get in the shower, get this kitty litter out of my hair, then I'm going to go interrupt Shawna's library hour and crack the whip in there a bit. Want to swing by the café around five? I've got that minestrone you're so fond of on special today and we can lay down a good layer before we tie one on tonight. James French tells me Daisy was very enthusiastic about her new themed cocktail menu."

Len's stooped shoulders shook with laughter. "You should have seen her. Her eyes weren't even that bright eight years ago when she was voted prom queen! She's basically just slapped new names on everything. Cometpolitans, Major Tom Collins, Cape Canaveral Ice Teas…"

"That one at least sounds good." Sissy stopped laughing long enough to say.

"She has Morgan making them with coconut rum to give them a Florida feel, I guess. She's really dedicated to making that old place shine." They fell into a comfortable silence, watching as a large flock of snow geese V-ed overhead honking their encouragement to one another over the sound of Rod and the Rocker Arms practicing a few strains of *Take It Easy*. They would glide over the western horizon to join the larger body of geese congregating on Inch Lake where their population would get so large by fall that when they took to the skies their white bodies and black tipped wings would make the heavens look like a massive TV with the signal out and ants on the march.

"James French, huh?" Len finally said as the geese grew smaller in the distance.

"Oh yes. He came into the café with my sister and his two girls last week, full of news of how successful Daisy had been in bringing more tourists in for tonight." Sissy nodded. "You know that poor girl is going to work herself ragged trying to prop this old town up."

"Maybe." Len nodded. "But I expect we'll all boil in that kettle when it's on the fire."

"'Spect we will."

Five miles north from where Len and Sissy were enjoying their morning, Celia French sat in her blue Mustang parked in the narrow street running between the vacant Kroger and the Rexall drug store watching the parking lot of The Trapper Hotel and flicking the ashes from her Camel menthols out her driver's side window. She had dropped the twins off with her mother-in-law Sassy, giving the older woman a hug and a story about driving up to the library in Eloe. She could have just told Sassy she was looking for an extra shift at the Wagner Café but she knew all too well how fast word got around this little town. Even before social media, and email, and text messages, the slightest detail of her life could end up in casual conversation and she didn't need a contradiction from Sissy Wagner forcing her to make more excuses.

Besides, her plan would work out much better if James thought she was out of town for a few hours.

Celia had been there since eight, just sitting and smoking, and trying not to look at the Smith and Wesson sitting in her purse like a coiled rattlesnake. She sat with the butt of her cigarette crushed between her fingers, pressed against her chin, running the nail of her thumb back and forth across her jaw, her eyes narrowing every time a car drove past or the side door of the Trapper came open. She was straining to see – maybe even mentally willing – James' big black Ford

350 pull into the parking lot. She wanted him to come. Needed him to come. Prayed her will would call him out of the hinterland like a siren and pull him down to his doom inside The Trapper Hotel.

She could see it in her mind's eye, it would be smoky and sepia – like one of those film noir movies she loved to watch. Like *L.A. Confidential* or *The Black Dalia*. James would pull into the parking lot and let himself into the side door. She would give him a moment to make his pleasantries to his father, watch the windows like a hawk to see which one he finally went to. Count up from the bottom floor, and over to see which room. She would walk in through the front door, smile sweetly at Morgan behind the reception desk, use the stairs. Celia would climb up to their room, use the utility key she had stolen off her father-in-law's key ring, open the door as silent as a ghost.

They would be on the bed, tangled in each other's flesh. She would wait for Daisy to see her. Wait for her to scream. Then she would point her gun and pull the trigger. First him. Then her. And then herself. They would haunt the Trapper together, the three of them – James and Daisy trapped in their day of reckoning. Guests would feel Celia's horrible, cold presence on the stairs. Given time ghost hunters and mediums would come. They would talk to her, just outside the murder room. Someone would finally understand.

The side entrance of the Trapper came open with a bang jerking Celia from the depths of her mind. Daisy stepped out into the sunshine. She wasn't smoky. She wasn't in sepia. She was struggling to wrestle two enormous black plastic trash bags into the dumpster, a task made more difficult by her tiny stature. Celia choked down her immediate urge to rush over and help; watching instead with serpent's eyes as Daisy pressed herself against the side of the dumpster trying to gain some leverage as the trash bag shifted above her head, threatening to tear and spill into the parking lot. Daisy finally managed to get both bags into the dumpster and leaned against the side of the hotel to catch her breath. Then Morgan popped his head out of the door, Celia didn't have to hear him to know he was scolding Daisy for lugging around heavy trash "when she could ask for help".

He had been the same way for the short time she and James had lived with the in-laws while she was pregnant with the twins. Damn those Republican men and their arcane ideas of what a woman should and shouldn't do in their "delicate state". Daisy just smiled. That sweet sickening prom queen bitch smile. Let him hold the door open for her. Was probably apologizing. In Celia's head she could hear Daisy, in that soft satiny voice. *I know Mr. French. But it needed to be done. Oh yes please Mr. French. I would love a glass of water. It's hot, ain't it? Say, maybe we could use a little more help around here. Is James available?*

"No bitch. He isn't available." Celia muttered to herself, Daisy long gone behind the heavy metal door.

She looked down at the clock on her stereo, it was almost eleven. She would have had enough time to have gotten to Eloe and back by now. And she knew where James was anyway. He wouldn't be coming to the Trapper. She turned the engine over and backed the car up slowly, being sure not to rattle the gas too loudly and cause a scene. She backed up until the little alley way widened into Catman Street, then guided the car north onto Pollack. She didn't turn the radio back on until she was well out of town and on State Highway 39 – and then she cranked it up, her windows rattling away to Britney Spears' *Toxic*. Celia lit another cigarette and sang along. She was She-Ra... no, not She-Ra. She-Ra was a Reaganite. She was Xena, a warrior princess, an unstoppable force of nature. When the song was over she played it again, her foot dropping the pedal, riding all four hundred and seventy five horses under the hood like a wraith.

She would have played the song a third time but was suddenly struck with the vision of Daisy flushed with exertion and wiping her brow with the edges of her apron. She lit a new cigarette off her old one before smashing it out in the over flowing ashtray, sucking in that sweet menthol rush, her finger jamming the buttons until Beyoncé's *Single Ladies* came on, twisting the wheel as expertly as any NASCAR driver onto the thin strip of dirt road cutting through the timber up to the Mule Wash Ranch. She gunned the engine over hills and down washouts, fishtailing around curves until the pine suddenly gave way to pasture – cows belly deep in grass jerking their heads up from grazing to watch her fly past. She slammed on the breaks when the pasture rolled into farmyard, the rear of her Mustang whipping until it slid parallel with her open window, gravel and dust flying out in a rooster tail behind her.

Celia sat there for what felt like an eternity, gripping the steering wheel at ten and two and breathing through her nose in exhilaration, ignoring the cherry of her cigarette singeing her index finger. She could leave. She could just pack a bag and walk away. She could clean out the bank account. Go down to Vegas, to the Richard Petty driving school. James had said it wasn't a real school, just a paid "experience" – like a dude ranch – where tourists get to drive the cars a couple times around the track for huge fees. He said Richard Petty wasn't even there for the most part. But that had to be wrong. Sure, there's some truth to it. Of course, there is. But that was just on the surface. James was so into surface appearances. He didn't understand that NASCAR had to have their ear to the ground for new talent. Where else would all their drivers have come from?

She would show up. Some unassuming housewife from Montana. She would pay her thousand dollars. She would race the tires off that car and Richard Petty himself would stand up from his chair in the skybox. "Who the hell is that?!" he would demand over the radio. And she would be the biggest new thing in the racing world. No one would care that she was on the wrong side of thirty and had two kids. She might come back here, someday. To this place that held her down. This dry land she was stranded on when she was so obviously born a fish, born for the water. This cage built of mountains and rivers and cows and …

"Jesus Christ, Celia!" James' face was suddenly right beside hers as he leaned in the window and ripped her keys from the ignition. "I didn't buy this car for you to make a coffin out of it."

She watched him stalk away into the house, sweat drenching a large v shape down the back of his button-down shirt to his belt line. He had his sleeves rolled up over the henley he wore underneath, pushed up over his forearms, exposing coppery skin above the wrist line of his work gloves. Of course he hadn't come to the Trapper. It was August, there were colts to start and fences to mend and calves to move and the list went on and on and on, year after year, until you were old and tired and a husk of a person. Like some kind of life sucking merry-go-round.

Celia stepped out of the car and slammed the door, stalking him into the house. He stood in the kitchen pouring himself a glass of water from the tap, his wide brimmed cowboy hat hanging from the back of a dining room chair. She stood there with her arms crossed for a long time, waiting for him to turn around and apologize. Instead, he pulled loose the knot of the silk wild rag at his throat and took a long pull from the glass as he stared silently out the window.

"Give me my keys." She demanded hotly. He stood for a long time at the sink, never turning away from the window. "God damn it, James! Give me those keys right now! I have to lock the car." She threw her hands up at him in exasperation. He nodded, then pulling the keys from his pocket pressed the lock button on the fob. Outside her Mustang betrayed her by honking obediently as it locked.

"There." He said, pushing the keys back into his pocket. "It's locked."

"The window is down!" She insisted. "What if it rains?"

"I'll roll it up later."

"James! You give me my keys!"

"You could have killed yourself out there." He raised his eyebrows at her, a vein jumping in his jaw.

"Those are my keys! You have no right to keep them!"

"You could have wrapped that thing around a tree or slipped around a bend into a gorge."

"I won't be held hostage like this!" She shrieked stepping deeper into the room.

"A fence could have been down! What if cows were out? Have you ever seen what hitting a cow does to a car, Celia?"

"I don't give a shit about the fucking cows, James! Give me my keys!"

"Do you have any idea what that would do to the kids? To my parents?" He took a long, ragged breath. "To me? Having to pull your mangled corpse out of that car?"

"*Fuck you James!*" She was shrieking now, the rage exploding from her chest into her words making her own head ring. "*Give me my keys!* I have to pick up the kids."

"You are not driving the kids around in this state."

"In this state? *In this state!*" her voice shattered like glass before the force of her fury. "*What kind of a fucking state am I in? Give me my fucking keys!*"

"Why are you even here, Celia?" He sighed, leaning back against the sink. "Aren't you supposed to be in Eloe or Eureka or some damn place looking for a book?"

"Oh," her voice took on a taunting tone, "you got your mamma checking up on me?"

"No. I called home. You weren't there. I called around looking for you."

"Here I am. You can stop looking and give me my keys."

"Why are you here?"

"Do I need a reason to see my husband? You're my

34

husband James. Maybe I just wanted to say hi. But I don't anymore so give me my keys."

"No."

"I have to go pick up the kids."

"We aren't picking up the kids." He sighed, "I'm going to call my mom and ask her to keep them over night."

"I don't want her to."

"Too bad, Celia!" The mask of cool control which he had been maintaining finally slipped away, his voice barking and angry filled the ranch house like a bomb blast. "This is my place of work. I can't have you driving like a crazy person through the yard, mowing down tourists and old people and threatening my paycheck. Thank God this time no one saw you, but God damn it Celia I lose this job and we lose everything. The house. The truck. That damn Mustang. There ain't a ranch in miles that is hiring this season and you haven't taken any of the shifts at the café Aunt Sissy has offered. We'd be screwed. Now go get your ass in the truck while I tell Hank I have to leave for the rest of the day."

Celia stared hard at him, hoping his insides were boiling under her gaze. When he didn't even flinch, she stepped across the room and pushed him hard in the chest. "*I fucking hate you!*" she screamed, every fiber in her being seething.

"*Yea?!?*" He thundered back, easily swatting her aside and towards the door. "*Well go fucking hate me in the truck!*"

CHAPTER 4

Big Stakes Ranch – Outside Henderson, Nevada

The shrill breep-breep of the main line cut into the room, startling them all. Bobby paused for a moment looking up from his clipboard, nodding to Laura's questioning gaze. She sprang up from where she sat cross-legged on the large cowhide couch in the lobby, her brightly colored poncho style sun dress flowing behind her as she ran towards the little bull pen room that served as a reception desk. Bobby cleared his throat staring down at his clipboard, trying not to let his eyes follow her across the room or drift from her black ballet flats up the back of her leggings to where the hem of her dress and all that silky blond hair danced like ribbons in a breeze.

"Thank you for calling Big Stakes Ranch, this is Laura – how may I help you?"

"We'll just wait until she's done." Bobby shifted his weight, ignoring the hushed groans from the staff. This had been their third interruption this morning and the phones were just warming up.

"Excuse me?" Laura's incredulous tone drifted over from the front of the room. "No sir. This is not that kind of a ranch. We are a family establishment…. No, I don't have their number… I'm sure you can Google it on your own…. Yea, ok, bye then." The phone slammed into the cradle with a crunch that sounded like it may have broken followed by almost an immediate breep-breep. Bobby looked over to the reception desk where Laura was visibly pulling in a deep breath, centering herself before answering again.

"Thank you for calling Big…" she was cut off by the caller… "Oh yea, nice language sir. I'm sure you make your mama proud." She slammed the phone down again, the phone beeping loudly as she switched on the answering machine before walking back into the lobby to regain her seat on the couch surrounded by her coworkers. "Please continue." she said to Bobby, picking up the steno pad from the table beside her, her voice placid and cool, her face a lovely color of white and scarlet. She was a looker when she was happy, and stunning when she was mad.

"Everything ok?" he had to ask.

"I'm fine." She didn't look at him, but instead took a long sip off her mug of tea. "Just some drunk with nothing better to do with his time."

"Ok... so where was I..." the staff chuckled at this. "Right... reservations. This is inner company information, I probably shouldn't be sharing it, but I'm going to anyway because you guys are my top line crew and I know you can take the chips as they fall. As we all know the new owners are new to the hospitality industry and they haven't had many big events, so they don't really understand the importance of momentum during a given season..."

"They also don't understand the importance of a full paycheck." A slim middle-aged woman on the housekeeping crew sniped to the general agreement of the rest of the staff. Bobby held up his clipboard, signaling them to quiet down.

"I know, a week off has been a challenge. If it's any consolation their bottom line hurt too. It was a mistake, I advised against it, but it's done now. There's nothing I can do to go back in time and change their minds, but I know what will keep them from doing something like this again. We move on. We hit the ground running without a hitch. We really make this place shine and use this comet watching party to push new reservations. I want to be turning people down for rooms until winter. Cleaning crew, you did an amazing job at the break..." he was cut off by Hector coughing the phrase "layoff" into his fist followed by his fellow bartender Frankie sneezing "shut down" into his sleeve.

Bobby sighed, "Let's just get through this, okay? Anyway, I want you to dust up and put clean sheets on all the beds. Make sure the sinks and tubs haven't grown a film. Bartenders and food service, this is just a normal day for you. Get out there and do what you do best. Guest experience crew, we won't have any events until the cookout tonight. Pick your favorite job and lend a hand. I know that maintenance especially could use a fresh inflow of able bodies as we get the tent up and the dance floor in place. Admin, man the phones, help the crews when they need direction. All of you make sure to get great setup pics out through your social media channels. I want the fire marshal showing up with a worried look on his face because we're skimming legal capacity.

"The valet team won't be in until later." He looked over to the couch where his top guides had formed a little cluster in front of one of the empty fireplaces, "Jorge when the yellow vests start showing up, I want you to stop whatever you're doing and take a firm grip on their leadership. Those guys are dipshits and I need someone I can trust herding all those cats. Wranglers, we'll go over our bench points at the barn." Bobby looked down at the clipboard, not really reading, just looking for someplace to place his gaze that wasn't where his two remaining "wranglers" were standing next to each other, leaning against the wall of the lobby below a stylized painting of *Red River Drovers*.

"Everyone clear as to the mission? Good. Let's do this." As the staff broke off to their respective duties Laura stayed behind sipping her tea and making little check marks across her notes. "Miss Taylor..." he finally said when it was apparent she wasn't budging. "Have you got a minute?"

"I do." She nodded, not looking up from her steno pad. "Office?"

"Yup."

Laura flashed him one of her brilliant smiles, then got up from the couch and picking up her tea and the coaster it sat on made her way to the tiny office behind the receptionist's desk. He gave the lobby a moment to clear out, leaving only an elderly woman named Lupe using a vacuum to pull the traffic marks out of the massive southwestern rug in front of the receptionist desk. He passed the little bullpen to the office door, giving it a knock before walking in. Laura was sitting on the large desk he shared with two other managers – neither of whom had come back from the "break".

"Hi." She said quietly.

"Hi." He answered back, walking over to give her a gentle kiss.

"Ok... out with it. Where are Liam and Elle?"

Bobby sighed. "Liam called me while I was on the way in. He was hired by MGM and starts this afternoon. Elle is in Tahoe. She says she'll be back, but I really don't think she will. She kept putting me on hold, which tells me she's taking calls, which tells me she's already working and just not sure if she's going to like her new outfit."

"It's just you now?" Laura gave him a long hug.

"It's just me." He sighed.

"Who else?"

Bobby pulled back from her arms and looked over his clipboard. "Three from the cleaning crew. We lost Rosa and Mindy to the Mirage; those lucky bastards snapped them up no sooner than we laid them off."

"You mean gave them an unpaid break." Laura wrinkled her nose teasingly, earning a sour look in return.

"We're down two from food service," Bobby muttered, "three from maintenance, and the entire ostler crew."

"Ouch." Laura took his clipboard, flipping over the roster. "Oh no. Bobby. Tim, Alex, and Trisha left!"

"Yup." Bobby crossed his arms and let out a large breath. "Tim got a job with an adventure rafting crew in Colorado, Alex decided to head home to Sonora and spend some time with his family, and Trisha is out in LA teaching trick riding to a bunch of actors. Which leaves me with ..."

"Kip and Brody." Laura sniffed, handing him back his

roster. "Is it that they're just that loyal or no one would hire them?"

"I honestly have no idea." Bobby sat down next to her on the desk. "There's other things I noticed when I logged in this morning. The accounting software was still locked out, so I couldn't finish entering receipts from the first. I sent an email to the Baers letting them know."

"And?"

"All hell broke loose. I ended up on an email chain that was cc'd to some agency in New York and finally the Baers' attorney let me in. While the rest of you were getting ready for the meeting, I was speed scanning receipts from the gift shop." He turned at the hip to toss the clipboard onto the desk. "I think the Baers are selling Big Stakes. Which could mean nothing to us. Or it could mean everything. All I know is that if decisions about our jobs are going to be made from someplace as far away as New York…"

"Which is even further than Aspen where Levi Baer is." She grumbled, "He rarely comes down to see the place, or even checks in by phone."

"This ranch was an impulse buy for him. No one really expected him to move here." Bobby chuckled. "But if we really just hammer it this week, bring in enough business to make up for the shutdown, they can't ignore us or fire everyone and bring on a new crew."

"You should have never taken this job, Bobby." She sighed as he rubbed his temples. "It's not fair to you. It's not like an inn or a casino where you come in and manage the workflow and then clock out and go about your daily life. This has been your livelihood since you were a small boy. How many hours did you put in over the shutdown just making sure the stock was fed?"

"It doesn't matter."

"It does matter Bobby!" She insisted. "They do this to one of their amusement parks, the rollercoasters won't starve to death or fall over from dehydration so it's no big deal for the managers to just stay home. You slaved away all on your own keeping their stock alive without the hourly crews... and for what? To turn your salary into below minimum wage pay by giving the corporation more time than it's due? Only for them to turn around and sell out to some other corporation run by east coast stockbrokers and Yale graduates who for all their education wouldn't recognize the difference between a Hereford and a Hackamore?" She took a deep breath, then joined him sitting on the edge of the large desk, "Maybe you should think long and hard about going home to work your dad's place."

"It's still punching another guy's cows." He sighed. "But if this goes tits up? I may not have a choice. I can't work the casinos; I lack the temperament to be indoors that long. I can't go back to the rodeo circuit; the payouts are huge if you win but not as steady as I would like. Not if we're going to get married sometime this century."

She smiled at this, then said, "I don't know. I would live in a cardboard box with you so a one room horse trailer in the back of some state fairgrounds is actually quite a step up."

"I don't have a heeler anymore, remember? And there's always some guy who's got a faster horse and a better time." He shifted his weight a little. "Besides, we don't know anything yet. Not for sure. And while I still have this job I'm going to do it. That's what I promised the former owners before they sold out to Baer."

"So right away we have a problem." Laura said after a long pause. "If people are going to come, they're going to want to ride the ponies. It's not a dude ranch without the horsey rides."

"I've already called the university to replace the ostler crew." He nodded. "They're going to get in contact with our summer interns, see if they would like to get paid this time. Thought we could have them wear both hats for the time being."

"Good." Laura nodded. "I know at least Shane and Piper will show up. They both turned in resumes at the end of their term and HR just hasn't gotten back to us about hiring them. We can pay them out of petty cash until you get them on officially. But you still need at least one more wrangler."

"I know." Bobby pinched the bridge of his nose.

"Someone who knows horses, cattle, and people."

"I know."

"Someone who likes to flirt with the ladies. Keep them coming back."

"God hates me." Bobby shook his head.

"But I love you." Laura rubbed his back and gave him a little peck on the cheek. "I'll go make sure Kip and Brody aren't having a match fight in the hayloft or trying to tip over the bull. You need to call your brother."

Twenty miles away a pile of laundry laying wadded on a filthy bed burst out singing *I like big butts and I cannot lie, you other brothers can't deny, when a girl walks in...* "Hello" a voice thick with hangover gravel cut the ringtone off before it could get sprung. The pile of laundry shifted slightly as a bare arm emerged and searched the floor beside the bed like a miniature elephant trunk seeking a partially filled bottle of beer. "Who?"

Bobby walked around to the chair at his desk and sat down with an audible groan. "Dex... you know exactly who."

The pile of laundry sat up falling away to reveal a lean dark-haired man with a back full of surgery scars and a jaw line covered in scruff. He smelled one of the bottles he found, checking for chew spit before taking a big swig of the flat warm dregs. "Hey there baby bro! What's shaken bacon?"

"Hi Dex." Bobby pulled open his top drawer looking for something to kill the headache he felt coming on.

"It's a good thing you called." Dex pushed away from the bed, walking across the RV trailer he called home wearing nothing but a ragged pair of BVDs, waving out the door he had left wide open the previous night to Mrs. Davis watering the cactus patch outside her singlewide next door. "Hey there neighbor!" he called as the older woman gasped and struggled not to stare, then back to his brother "You would not believe the time I had up in Stampede. Buckle bunnies everywhere! It's like they set off a skank cannon and all I had to do was scoop them up off the ground."

"Lord..." Bobby slammed the drawer. This wasn't something a pill could fix. "Dex! I need to talk to you."

"So, talk." Dex jerked open his fridge and fished out a Coors Light, popping it open and taking a massive swig. "I'm just letting you know how my life is going. Not my fault you dropped off the face of the earth and settled down. How's Bethany?"

"It's Laura."

"Naw man, I'm pretty sure your girlfriend's name is Bethany."

"I'm pretty sure it's not."

"Have you checked her driver's license?"

"Dex, I don't have time for this."

"So, hang up."

"No! I ..." he whispered a curse under his breath. "Dex, man, I need your help."

"Say no more, little bro." Dex took another massive pull off his beer, draining it completely. "Let me brush my teeth and I'll be right there."

Bobby put his phone on his desk. Then he put his head on his desk. "God hates me."

Downtown – Phoenix, Arizona

"No. Mina.... I'm telling you. It's already done." Lucy slipped out of her Christian Louboutin Apostrophes and into her Jimmy Choo Traceys, appraising the effect in her full-length mirror. "No. We did it. We bought it. Hunter says all we have to do now is wait for escrow to close and then we can knock that wall out. Boom. It's a four bedroom. I just don't know if I'm going to keep the entry way here or use the one down the hall." God why? Why did she have to get the Naeem Khan dress in black instead of aqua? These shoes would have made the aqua. "No! I'm not expecting. You think I spend twelve hours a week at the gym to have another kid? We have it because we want it. We're getting more room, more space. And we didn't have to exile ourselves to the burbs to do it. It's going to be amazing. I'm already interviewing decorators."

She kicked the Choos to the back of her closet and dug out her Saint Laurents – bah, fucking tacky. Why did she even buy them? Back of the closet with you, ugly shoes. Where are those Guccis? "No, I have no idea… I hadn't even thought of that. But I'm sure Hunter has it… fine, hold on… Hunter!" oh thank God there they are. Wait. How did the Chanel sling backs get in here? And why wasn't her husband coming when he was called? "*Hunter!*"

In the living room Hunter Church smiled and shook his head, running his hand across his daughter Bella's hair. "Just a minute baby." He said, leaving her to play with her new telescope and walking into the master bedroom. "Yea, Lucy?"

"Mina wants to know where we're going to stay while they renovate the apartments and I can't find my Gucci pumps."

"I thought maybe we could go visit my folks. And if you're talking about the black strappy things, you tossed them out after we went to dinner with a couple of the analysts and you found out one of them had bought the same pair you had on eBay."

Lucy stared at him for a long moment, then "Oh, right." Then back to her phone. "I don't know Mina, I'm sure we'll just go back to Cabo. Whoever complained about an extra couple of weeks in Mexico, right? … No, we won't take

Bella! Are you nuts? That's what grandparents are for. Hey, you know that fringe dress I bought? What do you think of the Jimmy Choos with the crystal and the feathers with it? I think it might work…"

Hunter turned and walked back into the living room where Bella stood up on her tip toes trying to peer into the eyepiece of the telescope. "I can't see it." She pouted, her soft auburn braids framing her heart shaped face.

"At all?" Hunter sat back down on the ottoman beside her. "Well, what can you see?"

"My eyelashes." She turned and squinted out the window. "And there's a man in that building going like this." She lifted her little hand and did the best she could to extend her middle finger. "What does that mean, Daddy?"

"It means have a nice day." Hunter said looking into the telescope, gauging how far Bella had bumped it in her effort to see the sky, returning the gesture to the angry man on the patio of the building across the street as he turned the telescope back to the east. "Yea, you too buddy. Have a nice day."

"Oh, that's nice of him." Bella smiled and turned to the window waving her middle finger towards the other side of the street, jumping up on the ottoman beside her father as she did. "Hi! Have a nice day!"

"Bella!" Lucy came into the room, minus her phone and looking amazing as always. "Get your shoes off the furniture. Honestly. It's like having a little dog."

"Lucy." Hunter scowled. "She's fine. She wants to see the comet."

"Fine whatever." Lucy grabbed her purse from a table in the foyer and began transferring essentials into a crystal studded clutch. "I'm throwing it all out anyway. Hurry up and find your dirty snowball. I'm going to buzz the sitter up."

CHAPTER 5

John Mackay Elementary School – Orein, Nevada

Mike shifted uncomfortably in the molded plastic chair trying to surreptitiously read his emails under the folding table which had been set up by the PTA, keeping an ear to the school principal as he addressed the auditorium. He tuned mostly out as the general minutes of the previous meeting and a few budgetary items were addressed, using that time to flip through a report from the USGS forwarded to him by the corporate office in Houston and to review some of the engineer's schematics he would be using for his portion of the presentation.

"Now that we have some of the nit-picky details out of the way," The principal Joel Tavers, a short middle-aged round-faced man with salt and pepper hair, stood at the podium shuffling his notes. "And we would like to keep this brief – I'm sure you all have plans for tonight. I've been walking through the halls and looking over all the amazing comet exhibits the kids have put up." There was a spattering of chuckles from the crowd.

"I think my favorite one is …" he fished out a cell phone from his pocket and putting on a pair of reading glasses held it close to his face, "Twinkle Twinkle Little Comet by Kassie in Mrs. Troy's first grade class. You all can't see this too well..." he held his device out to the crowd, "but let's see if this old codger can get it to cast." He pushed a button and a scrolling icon appeared on a massive drop-down screen on the wall behind him. "And folks let's take a minute to thank Mike Wolfe here and the rest of the Copperhead Mining Corporation for donating the digital tools we use here in the gym and in the classroom. Their generous gifts have really made our curriculum more modern and interactive." Mike looked sheepishly around as the parents burst into applause, waving and feeling like an idiot. The classroom systems and computer lab had been funded by the district headquarters of the mining corporation; Mike had nothing to do with it and Joel damn well knew it.

"Ok here we go." Joel looked up at the screen which displayed a high-definition photo of a line art drawing of a comet which had been colored and covered in glitter glue and crape paper streamers. A child's incongruent hand had attempted to print the lines of a poem below. "It says, *My Poem: Twinkle Twinkle Little Comet. Twinkle twinkle little comet, Flying in the sky* – and I promise Mrs. Troy is going to eventually teach Kassie that sky is S-K-Y not S-K-E-Y-E, but the year is young," another loud chuckle from the crowd, "*You are very beautiful comet. Please don't smash my house.*" A little stick figure had been scribbled into the margins showing a happy little girl next to a square pink house. "That house looks very sturdy Kassie." he stated drawing more laughter from the bleachers "I'm sure it's going to be fine.

"Obviously the kids are excited. If you do not already have plans for this evening you are all welcome to join Mr. Gates and the sixth-grade science club as they will be tailgating in our staff parking lot. They will be making s'mores and hot coco and will be watching as Comet X2017 Y2 – or as John Roland in Mr. Robertson's class calls it…" the screen again flickered, this time showing a more sophisticated but still juvenile drawing of dinosaurs running in panic as a brilliant fiery comet screamed overhead "… The BIG One."

Mike watched as several of the parents wiped tears from their eyes as they laughed. He smiled, shaking his head. "Some of these are very ominous." Joel's voice broke as he chuckled along. "I know the teachers have been telling the kids that these comets won't come that close, but you can't really fault a ten-year-old for taking issue with the destruction of his good friends." The picture shifted again, this time showing a young boy with a bowl cut and an ear-to-ear smile holding up a plastic triceratops for the camera. The room hummed with parental giggles as an almost collective "awww" went up from the assembly.

"And just to show you that not all the children are predicting doom and gloom here is a beautiful drawing by Sam Aneyoshi," the image shifted to show a crayon drawing of a little boat on a wide-open sea, it was empty as water billowed peacefully around it, in the sky was a warm red sun off set to the right and to the left three brilliant stars in an almost triad formation, one of them with a long shimmery tail. A murmur of appreciation filled the gym. "Sam is in Mrs. Stone's sixth grade class and has drawn the comet as it will appear once it has passed Earth and continued its orbit towards the sun. The two upper stars are actually Venus and Mars, the lower one is X2017. Sam told me – which I found very interesting - that when it reaches this point of its flight, scientists will be able to accurately predict the remainder of the comet's orbit." The parents nodded to each other, humming out "Really?" and "Smart kid!".

"Folks..." the screen went blank, "I could show you a hundred of these and you would be impressed with every single one. Sure, they're art. But I also see them as a testament to all the hours of dedication our amazing staff has put in day in day out to engage your kids in the world around them. To connect them to current events and to reach each one of their thirsty little minds with the waters of education. Please remember this when the next bond issue comes up on the ballot. Yes, we have amazing partners in education who are helping us out with tech and connectivity, but we are still one of the lowest funded school districts in the state. I want to hire more amazing teachers like Mrs. Stone, and Mr. Robertson, and Mr. Gates, and ...."

Mike opened his text messages under the table, typing out a quick note home "PTA hasn't gotten to the mine structure portion of the agenda yet. Might be a little late."

The phone was a cold dead brick in his hand for a moment before buzzing back with Rebecca's "No problem. I already did the chores. Ynekos are here. Will save you a beer."

He didn't get home until eight. By then the kids – his three and the two Yneko boys – were chasing a horned toad through the flower beds in the front of the house while Becca and Ane were covering and taking in the food from the picknick table he had built on the west side of the house.

"Hi Babe." Becca looked up at him with a tight-lipped smile – she never really smiled anymore. He tried not to worry about it, but he couldn't ignore the empty ghost of what used to be the most dazzling thing he had seen in his entire life becoming her norm.

"Hi yourself." He said leaning in to kiss her cheek. "Sorry I'm late."

She shrugged nonchalantly. "I held a plate for you in the microwave. Make sure you take the foil off. There's potato salad in the fridge and if you want some Hawaiian rolls, I can leave them out."

"Beer?"

"In the cooler." She wiped her hands on a paper towel removing invisible mess. "You know what… you go sit with Max. I'll bring you your plate."

"I can do it."

"I know you can." Becca gave him another thin smile, her eyes never really warming. "But you've been working all day. Let me get it. Grab a beer and go be neighborly." He nodded and pulled a Sam Adams out of the cooler at the end of the table, walking over to where Max was sitting in a camping chair next to the fire pit.

"Hey Mike." A combination of the smoke from the fire pit, a full stomach, and beer had made Max's eyes a little glossy. "You made it home. How was it?"

Mike took the chair next to him, leaning way back and resting his scruffy Copperhead Mining Co hat on his knee. "Brutal. I had to meet with six – six! - state engineers this morning to go over the reclamation work out in Vya and Gerlach. And to go over the retrofit for the school. It was a nightmare."

"And then you got roped into the first PTA meeting of the season."

Mike chuckled. "That I did. You should have seen the office empty out after I suggested maybe someone could do it for me." Max nodded, taking a sip off his own beer.

"So how did it go?" He gestured to the area around him with the bottle. "I didn't really make it."

"Same old same old." Mike said, watching Louise cringe away from Colt who began to chase her with the now captured horned toad. "Your kids are awesome... blah blah blah... we need money ...blah blah blah... now here's Mike to tell you how we're going to fix the hundred and seventy-year-old mine shaft under the playground. Here's hoping it doesn't eat another school bus."

Max let out a long breath, "That was a shitty day."

"Yup." Mike took another drink. "Meanwhile the parents are looking at me like I personally dug the damn thing." Max started to laugh. "And then approved the plans to build a school over the top of it."

"You should see the way they look at you when their kid gets caught shoplifting."

"I bet." Mike deliberately kept his voice even, sidestepping that particular issue. If Becca had finally gotten to the point where she could have the Ynekos over again he wasn't going to be the one dragging up the past.

"Well look at you two." Ane provided rescue by walking over and sitting down next to her husband in a vacant chair. "You would think you were high school fishing buddies."

"I believe we could have been." Mike gave her a little smile, as he looked to where Becca was crossing the yard from the house balancing his plate in one hand and a couple of fresh beers in the other. "If I had grown up in Pioche. I'm fairly certain we could have."

"Damn California transplants." Max's wide smile belied his deadpan tone.

"I just went wherever Uncle Sam sent me. I didn't pick it." Becca handed him his plate and a fresh beer, settling into the last open chair. She called for Louise to bring the quilt off the couch for the kids to sit on as the sinking sun set the sky above them ablaze with luminous shades of scarlet, honey and salmon against a rich open field of cobalt. Mike ate and laughed, petted the horned toad before it "escaped" his grip and dashed off into the uplifted silvery hands of sage. Then he refreshed everyone's beers before settling in to construct s'mores and tell ghost stories as they waited under a brimming moon for the arrival of X2017.

Top of the Trapper Hotel – Pinefare, Montana

Daisy Yarnell whispered some directions to Shawna Lee who had agreed to work the event rather than party: Circle a little more with the champagne. Make sure to upsell the other cocktails. Don't be afraid to mention the appetizer menu if someone looks a little *too* tight. Rod and the Rocker Arms had just started playing *Sweet Home Alabama* when she spotted Verdi Groger leaning up against the southern wall of the roof top balcony, swirling an olive in her "Startini". She greeted a few of her guests, thankfully more out-of-towners this time than there had been for her 4th of July roof-top BBQ, before moving through the crowd around the dancefloor to say hello.

"I love what you've done with the place." Verdi said in her thick Queens accent as she waved a perfectly manicured finger at the string of outdoor lights that formed a sort of canopy around the outer edges of the patio. "Very … uhm...

grown up looking."

"Thank you." Daisy sensed the underlying insult but refused to rise to the bait. It had to be hard being an outsider trying to run a business in a backwoods little town, and she had always heard that New Yorkers were unintentionally rude but kind underneath their gruff exteriors. "We put a lot of work into the place over the past couple of years and I believe this ol' gal is starting to come back into herself."

Verdi just raised her eyebrows and nodded, taking another sip off her drink. "And the martini's ... oh, sorry Daisy... the *Startinis* aren't bad either. Keep this up and I might someday be able to tell my own guests they don't have to cold camp on their boats for the night because there's a decent hotel right in town."

"Are you having fun, Verdi?" Daisy's hospitable smile was starting to hurt her cheeks.

"I am." Verdi nodded, brushing a length of her coal black hair behind her ear.

"Did you bring Brenden? We have a little group of kids in the presidential suite with a clown and later Pete Sanders is going to teach them about the comet and take them out on the balcony..."

"Oh! You have a presidential suite? How nice." Verdi's smile dripped with sour honey. "Which president stayed here, I wonder?"

"We've named it in honor of President Cleveland." Daisy's smile faded. "He was the one who signed Montana into statehood."

"No." Verdi sipped her drink. "In answer to your question. I left Brenden at home tonight. He'll be watching the comet from our dock. Less light pollution. Better view. It's just me tonight."

"Oh, well that's a shame. But I'm sure he'll have a great time." Daisy took a deep breath, steeling herself for what she was going to ask next. "Verdi," she lowered her tone and stepped closer, if only to shield herself from meeting any other eyes while she talked. "I've been meaning to find a chance to ask you..."

"No time like the present." Verdi shrugged, popping the olive into her mouth and placing the empty glass on the ledge.

"Do you..." Daisy paused, organizing her thoughts, "and I'm not meaning to pry. You can tell me if it's none of my business..."

"Oh, I will."

"Yes, I'm sure. But ... do you find it ... difficult to balance running a business and being a mother?"

"Why?" Verdi's face took on a narrow feline smile as she leaned an elbow onto the balcony, her large amber colored eyes sparkling like talons. "Have you found some big strong man to help me out? Some son of the wild frontier to chop my wood and wrestle the bears that haunt my door?"

"No." Daisy gasped, her voice dropping to a whisper. "I would never presume..."

"That's a shame. I could train him to use the bathroom and love Pound and Updike..."

"No, no, Verdi. You got me all wrong."

"...I would have to teach him to read ... that would be a challenge..."

"No. I'm just asking if you feel like you have to sacrifice some of one thing to do the other..."

Verdi's eyes took Daisy in, coldly assessing her the way one might a sculpture, or an insect. Finally, she blinked, her placid not quite smile returning to her face. "Not at all."

"Oh." Daisy looked down at her shoes, then took a deep breath and picked up Verdi's empty glass. "Another?"

"Please."

Daisy said a rather unkind thing under her breath as she walked away, then immediately scolded herself for being so uncivil. Taking the glass to the bar she asked Thomas, another hired local who by luck happened to be rather talented with the bottles, for another Startini then looked at her watch.

It was 9:30. In fifteen minutes the band would wind down to softer ballads and Morgan would dim the lights so they wouldn't interfere with comet gazing. She had fallen in love with the Rocker Arms' versions of *Earth Angel* and *In the Still of The Night* and had begged them to play those songs while the comet was overhead. She looked over to where her business partner Morgan French was mingling, swapping stories with Sheriff Buck Petty and his wife Marie, making sure to include a couple from out of town who were staying in the Wagner RV Park. He was great. Well, of course he was. He had run the Trapper with her father for all those years she was growing up among the house cleaning carts and stealing cookies from the kitchen. She was going to be fine. She wasn't alone.

She smiled, thanking Thomas for the drink and turning back towards Verdi ran her hand across her still flat belly as if she were simply smoothing her dress. "We're going to be fine." She said as much to herself as anyone. "We have good people who love us."

Camelback Country Club – Phoenix, Arizona

The gold-plated elevator doors swished open before them as if guided by the disembodied spirit of an eighteenth-century doorman announcing their arrival to court. Lucy slipped into the upper room a few paces, making her pause to take her husband's arm look effortless and organic. She knew she had taken all the air out of the room, but it would ruin the effect to act like she had noticed. She smiled sweetly at Hunter, her feather like false lashes tickling the curve of her high cheekbones, every bit the adoring wife and picture of young love.

"You smell amazing." He whispered into her ear as

he adjusted the cuffs of his Canali shirt beneath his Hermès suit jacket and kissed her cheek.

"I better." She whispered back. "It cost you two-hundred an ounce."

"Worth every penny."

"Ok tiger. Simmer down. Here comes the boss."

"Hunter!" Eugene Vaughn – of Vaughn, James and Cole Attorneys at Law – stepped forward leading his wife Nancy through the parting crowd. Nancy was draped in Gucci from head to foot with the most daring backline in the room. "Right on time. I was just singing your praises to Mr. Goodwin our newest client."

"I hope you didn't lose your voice on the chorus." Hunter returned his firm handshake, adding a manly clap on the back. "That's what we pay the choir for."

"Lucy!" Eugene leaned in to give her a peck on the cheek. "As always we stand in worshipful transfixion. You remember my wife Nancy of course. C'mon over and say hello to the new money."

Luke Goodwin turned out to be none other than the older less photogenic brother of Hank Goodwin, the state senator. He was a round man with thinning hair but sharp eyes which missed little in the air around him. He sat on the veranda – their private party had leased out the top floor of the equestrian pavilion which had not one, but two terraces done in tasteful southwestern adobe – he was on the one furthest from the dance floor and bandstand but apparently closest to the sommelier. He was dressed simply compared to all the fash lazing about him. The best the current season could offer drifted past him like seedpods on a desert wind. But Goodwin wore only a black blazer with slacks, Lucy suspected Hart Schaffner Marx, and a white starched shirt which reeked something low like Calvin Klein.

Lucy batted her eyes as he took her hand tenderly in his own when introductions were made, accepted gracefully a glass of Chateau Mouton when he offered, and made it her night's goal to be charming despite his horrific slip-on dress shoes. He had – after all – excellent taste in wine. And at least he wasn't wearing the off-the-rack polo shirt and pleated slacks that seemed to be the assigned snowbird uniform for the region. And he wasn't very handsy. God, she hated that. Just the one gentle shake in greeting and then kept his paws to himself. She nodded along with the conversation while inwardly she was cringing at the thought of him in Birkenstocks – with socks! It didn't matter though. He could wear a purple pegasus costume and she would still be polite. If he was in this room, he was worth millions.

Somehow the men had turned the conversation to cars. She made quick eye contact with Nancy whose nod was so slight as to be imperceptible and they both excused themselves for a trip to the powder room. They walked together, chatting like old friends until their husbands disappeared behind a sea of partners, junior partners, associates, clients, and the always tragically costumed paralegals before breaking off to their own sides of the room. *Poor souls, the paralegals*, Lucy thought making a bee line for the bar. They were like backwards Italians. Italians, the ones actually from Italy, on a whole dressed impeccably but their hair – *Lord, their hair!* -it was as if they forgot how a mirror worked once they got to their eyebrows. Paralegals were that in reverse. They wore two hundred-dollar updos and fashion forward clips but pared it with cheap mall manikin hand-me-downs cut and pasted in sequins, lyrca, and knit. If shitty fabric were cocaine, the paras were in the process of being rolled out of the back seat of their best friend's car in front of the doors of a cross town emergency room.

She had time for one Gimlet and a stroll around the room before she had to be back at Hunter's side. And then it was water from here on out. Cheery is attractive, sloshed is not. She made her order, then asked the bartender to send water with a lemon twist to whichever table ordered the "Ritini" slipping him a fifty to be sure he remembered. It wasn't a request he was unfamiliar with, though he did spit some jovial bullshit about it being bad luck to toast with water in your glass.

And it was bullshit. Her luck was just fine. Just look at her.

She made her rounds, saying hello to the other wives, really enjoyed the smoked salmon and caviar canapés, and eventually made it back to where the men had shed their suit jackets and were talking card tricks... or hammers... who cares.

"Ah, the belle of the ball has returned to us." Eugene's cheeks were bright red and sweating as they stood as she approached. He could do with a little water right now himself. "Where has my Nancy gone?"

"I believe she is in the corner talking to Mrs. Cole and Mrs. James." Lucy accepted the chair Hunter held out for her, and his jacket when he offered though she was in no way cold. It made her look powerful, like a force of nature, to be out here with the men, braving the elements, casually sipping her drink while they laughed. "I'm sure she will be back in just a moment."

A white coated waiter approached the table, asked if they would like anything special for the toast. "I'll have a Ritini." She said, ignoring Hunter's knowing smile.

"I don't believe I know it." The waiter gave her a confused look.

"It's some fancy thing she discovered in Rome." Eugene said a bit too loudly. "It's all she ever drinks anymore."

"Your bartender knows it." Lucy assured him. "He just made me one and it's amazing... but gone."

"And for you, sir?" To Hunter who smiled slightly and leaned back in his chair.

"Make that two." *Good boy*, thought Lucy. *He's catching on.*

"You make them sound so tempting." Eugene shook

his head. "But Mr. Goodwin and I have dedicated ourselves to Dionysus this evening and will remain with the red.... Or if he would like to switch it up?"

"I believe, actually," Mr. Goodwin sighed, "considering the occasion of the night, the rarity of it, we should perhaps enjoy something more befitting. I noticed on the menu you have the '88 Perrier Jouet Belle Epoque?"

"I believe we have three bottles, sir." The waiter nodded.

"Excellent." Mr. Goodwin smiled. "I'll take them all. Mrs. Church might I tempt you with just one glass for the toast?"

"Mr. Goodwin." Lucy smiled, suddenly deciding she liked Mr. Goodwin very much. "You may."

CHAPTER 6

1004 Yellow Jack Place – Baptiste, Idaho

"Hi baby girl!" Mary Beth Church waved to her husband Rob from the end of the driveway, urging him to come over. He nodded, but obviously misunderstanding, turned back to his conversation with Bear Thyme. The men were currently admiring the new pool table in Bear's third car garage, the addition thus completing the room's transformation from workshop to game room. "I'm so glad you called. I haven't heard from you in a long time."

"Nana, are you going to watch the co-mit?" Sweet little Bella's voice almost brought her to tears as Mary Beth pressed her cell phone closer to her ear, drinking in every syllable.

"Yes I am." She smiled parroting back Bella's mispronunciation of the word *comet*, "I am watching the co-mit. A bunch of us are having a block party. We have kids riding their bikes, and we have sparklers... have you ever played with a sparkler?"

"No." Bella sounded unsure, as if in a past life she may have but that was a hundred years ago and she couldn't clearly remember. "What's that?"

"They're sticks you hold on to and you put a little bit of fire at one end and they shoot sparks that look like stars." Mary Beth covered the receiver and waved again to Rob, mouthing *I have Bella on the phone!* Rob's eyebrows raised as he excused himself to jog down the driveway to join his wife.

"Like birthday candles?" Mary Beth switched the call to speaker so Rob could hear.

"Yes sweetheart, just like birthday candles." Her husband's face split into a wide smile as Mary Beth responded. "Just like the candles on a cake only you can run around with them and draw pictures in the air. I have Pop Pop right here, Bella. Do you want to say hi?"

"Hi Bella!" Rob leaned in closer to the phone. "How are you?"

"Hi Pop Pop!" Bella was breathless with excitement. "I'm watching the co-mit. Daddy bought a television scope so I could see it."

Rob met Mary Beth's gaze as they stifled their laughter at her halting attempt at larger syllables, "He did? What a nice daddy you have. I'm so glad he had you call. Your big cousins are here, and someone is talking about bringing out the slip and slide."

"A slippery slide? That sounds fun. My mommy and daddy went to a party. Mommy took her Oscar de la Renta clutch and her Jimmy Choos"

"Oh yea, *those* she knows how to pronounce." Mary Beth whispered darkly, earning a shush from her husband.

"They went to a party?" Rob kept the conversation rolling. He agreed, but this had been their first phone call from Bella in over a month and he didn't want to miss a moment of it. "And you got to stay home and watch the comet through your telescope."

"Yes." He closed his eyes at her little lisp, trying to imagine what she must look like walking around in the apartment with a phone pressed against her little cheek. He hadn't seen any new pictures of her either since Lucy had blocked Mary Beth on Facebook and he wondered how much she had grown. "Daddy says it's a work party and those are no fun. Mommy had Sarah come over and we ordered a pizza."

"I like pizza." Rob put his arm around Mary Beth's quaking shoulders and pulled her in to his side. He had no idea who Sarah was but God Bless her if she wasn't his favorite person in the world right now. "What do you have on it?"

"Cheese… an' pineapple… an' ham… an' bacon…"

"Pineapple on a pizza!" Mary Beth put on a tone of dramatic shock.

"Eww yuck!" Rob played along, laughing.

"Pop-pop!" Bella giggled, "It has olives too."

"Oh well then I guess it's ok."

"I have to go. I think the co-mit is coming soon."

Mary Beth looked panicked, like she would breakdown and start tearfully begging her granddaughter to stay on the phone. "Ok Bella." Her voice cracked. "I love you little one."

"I love you too Nana. And I love you Pop Pop."

"I love you Bells." Rob helped Mary Beth to wipe a tear from her cheek as she made kissing noises into the phone. "Bye -bye."

The phone was silent for a long minute and they almost hung up when a young woman's voice came over the line "Hello?"

"Hello. Who's this?" Rob took the phone while his wife did her best to dry her eyes.

"This is Sarah Anders. I'm the nanny."

"Sarah," Mary Beth gasped, "Thank you so so much. This phone call… it made today feel just like Christmas."

"Yea…. About that." The young woman took a deep breath, "Could we maybe not tell Lucy and Hunter about it? It's none of my business, whatever's happening. But she took your names off the emergency contact sheet. I know I shouldn't get in the middle but… The thing is I really need this job. It's not just the pay but I'm at ASU and this is helping me get my hours in for my degree…"

"What are you studying?" Rob asked out of mild curiosity.

"Early childhood development. I just got out of a lecture on how important it is for a child's psyche to feel like they are bringing knowledge to the tribe, it makes them feel connected and she's so excited by the telescope and the comet I think she needed to share…"

"Your secret is safe with us Sarah." Mary Beth nodded at the phone, pinching her nose to dry it instead of sniffing.

"Absolutely." Rob agreed "And Sarah... thank you. You have no idea how much this means to us." They said their goodbyes just as their older daughter Tammy walked by with Lisa Thyme while a pack of kids screamed by on their bikes enjoying the freedom of the open road. She took one look at Mary Beth's face and rushed over.

"Oh my God, Mom. What's wrong?"

"Absolutely nothing." Mary Beth shook her chestnut locks, her large brown eyes brimming with unspent tears. "Tonight, was great but now it's perfect. I just got a call from Miss Bella Church." Tammy smiled and gave her mother a hug, while Mary Beth did her best to not break down. "The nanny snuck her around the fence for a moment. It was like she was right here."

"C'mon Mom." Tammy said leading Mary Beth towards the Thyme's garage door. "Let's let you powder your nose and get you a glass of wine."

Rob rejoined Bear Thyme at the end of the pool table, thanking him for his hospitality as he pointed the way into the downstairs bathroom. They talked about their college days and work and kids, slipping back into easy conversation as they watched a few of the older neighborhood boys organizing a game of touch football in the street. He let his eyes drift up towards his back fence where Yellow Jack Place met Blackjack Oak Parkway – smiling slightly at Noah Walker's massive Yukon parked blocking the entrance to the cul-de-sac. "Did he really put a snorkel on that thing?" he asked jerking a thumb towards the top of the gentle hill.

"He did." Bear handed him another beer from a full-sized fridge behind the pool table. "He says it's shit-hit-the-fan ready now. Between that and those fancy tires I don't think even the National Guard could take him down." Bear was referring to the non-pneumatic tires which had been last month's modification to the family vehicle, an expensive set of wheels which used honeycombed high-density polymers to support the weight of the truck on the road rather than air. "It's spooky watching them fold over a curb and he pays a little more on the gas mileage, but he says it's worth it come the end of the world. Have you seen his garage?"

"I haven't."

"You got to see it." Bear laughed, jerking his head to indicate that Rob should follow him over. "It will blow your mind."

They crossed the lush carpet of grass that stretched out in front of the houses heading up hill towards the parked truck, the only indication they had passed onto the Walker's property being the variation in mow lines left in the lawn. The entire community was "open" with the exception of the tall Navaho white vinyl privacy fencing which separated the back yards from the front. Each lot was nearly a half-acre, much larger than other neighborhoods Rob and Mary Beth had owned in, but then again, the house footprint was too.

Noah Walker was sitting in an Eddie Bauer camping chair just around the edge of his casita attached to his four-car garage. The men watched as his oldest son, Jefferson, made a picture-perfect counter run past Ferris Michaels, the young man in his late twenties who owned the large pseudo -colonial near the edge of the developed lots on Blackjack Oak. Finding his way blocked by Ferris' friend and neighbor Derik, Jefferson stutter stepped back a half a pace and lobbed the ball effortlessly to his younger brother Beau waiting in the "end zone" beside their father's truck.

"Hey there, neighbors!" Noah smiled underneath his ball cap and Ray-Bans looking like he could be just as comfortable at the working end of a fishing pole as he was in his own front yard. Rob hadn't been sure about the Walkers who had built their "modest" four car, two story plus basement Prairie style home just kitty corner from he and Mary Beth, and admittedly had more than a few reservations when the two flagpoles went up in the yard – one of which flew the large yellow Gadsden Flag to the left of the Red, White, and Blue. But two years of over the mailbox conversations and a couple of tools lent back and forth had helped to answer his qualms. Noah – despite his rough exterior, a combination of tattoos and neatly trimmed salt and pepper goatee – was a genuinely likable guy. As were his wife and kids – all six of them with one on the way. Mary Beth had quipped that this next one would spring from the womb with a polite "Good morning Mr. and Mrs. Church." before asking if it could mow their lawn.

"Hey Noah." Bear was obviously at ease with the Walkers, something which spoke volumes to Rob about the nature of their family. "Good grief the arm on your kid."

"Yup. He gets it done." Rob watched as a flicker of pride crossed Noah's face before disappearing again. Another thing he liked about the Walkers. They weren't a boastful bunch despite excelling at seemingly everything they put their hands to. He looked up as Noah's wife came out of the house with a tall glass of lemonade and handed it to her husband with a cheerful smile.

"Oh no thank you Jen." Bear demurred as she brought a cup his way, indicating the beer in his hand. "But later I would not say no to one of your brownies."

"How did you know I was making those?" She blushed a little, placing a tender hand on her husband's shoulder.

"Good news travels extremely fast." Rob offered. "Especially around here."

"Well, I will take that complement. Thank you. And I will make sure you two have a few left aside." Then she turned to the street where her boys were getting ready to set up another play. "Boys it's getting dark. Make sure Whiskey and Tango are fed before the sun sets."

"Ok mom." Beau called from the curb then turned back to the game as Jefferson waved his acknowledgement.

"Oh, speaking of which – Bear – I made a new batch of the duck meal and venison this week and I have some extra for Scotus if you like." When he nodded enthusiastically, she leaned down and kissed Noah's cheek with a request that he help get the bag over to the neighbors before walking back inside.

"She makes her own dog food?" Rob was astounded.

"Oh yea." Noah smiled and nodded. "She's happy to share the recipe though I think she should hold onto it and open her own business. I swear if I needed a new shirt that woman could bake it for me."

"Hey Noah." Bear shifted his weight a bit, "Rob says he's never seen the garage."

"Is that right?" Noah took a sip off his lemonade, then stood up from his chair. "We will have to fix that." The sudden wail of a blaring horn from up the street cut in just as the men were about to walk inside. They looked to where Abigail Messenger had stopped her big black Range Rover at the junction of the two streets and was furiously smashing the palm of her hand into her steering wheel.

"Should... we..." Rob looked to the other two for direction "...at least see what she wants?"

"I'm not her dog." Noah's tone was so off hand he could have been commenting on the color of the grass or a rock in the driveway. "She can climb on down from there and talk like decent people."

She did, in fact climb on down, and was about to bang on the Walker's front door when Noah opened back up. "Hello Abigail. Have you come to join the block party?"

"No. I have not." Rob and Bear listened as her refined but angry London accent cut into the room from where she stood on the front porch. "I have come to address the issue of your vehicle parked in the middle of the road. I could have it towed, as you well know! Instead, I am here. Haunting your doorstep."

"No. You can't."

"Pardon?"

"You cannot have my truck towed." He crossed his arms and leaned casually against the doorframe, waving to Beau acknowledging yet another perfect catch.

"That vehicle is blocking access of traffic!"

"I know it is." Noah nodded. "That's the point. See we are having a block party. And being as all the people on the block are already here, we decided to restrict access to residents only. Now the kids could play and ride their bikes in the street."

"A block party?" Rob could hear the irritation and distain oozing from Abigail's voice. "I don't believe you submitted a request for a block party to the Hoa" The final word she pronounced hoe-ah. "Had you done so I would have, regretfully, rejected it."

"Oh, I'm sure you would have. Good thing this isn't something we need to submit to the H.O.A." Noah emphasized the letters in the acronym slightly, making Abigail seethe.

"Anything which happens in this community…"

He cut her off, "Is not necessarily under your control, Abigail. As it turns out the covenants, conditions, and restrictions of Woodview Heights Estates are silent on the issue."

"I could still lodge a noise complaint." He had given her pause and she was grasping. "With the police."

"It's a free country Abigail. You can call anyone you want." He shrugged. "But then again, they can ignore you."

"They will not ignore me."

"Noise violations do not register as a disturbance until they are well audible beyond the boundaries of the participants property – as you can see we have Matt and Derik playing football with my kids so even if we were being loud enough to be heard from the back end of Blackjack it wouldn't matter until about ten at night. We'll all be watching the comet by then. You should grab a blanket and come join us."

"But you are impeding traffic!"

"Which would be a problem," he nodded, "if I hadn't applied for a permit from the city to do so."

"A permit?" Rob and Bear looked at each other in amusement as Abigail's voice raised to the pitch of a train whistle.

"Yes, a permit." Rob could tell Noah was trying hard not to laugh himself. "They're little permission slips you get from the city that says…"

"I know what a permit is you vile hick!" Abigail snapped.

"Now there's no need for name calling Abby." Noah put his hands up. "You are welcome to join us if you're going to be civil. But if you refuse, I could trespass you from this party for the next forty-eight hours."

"Forty-eight hours?!?"

"That's when the permit expires."

"I would very much like to see this permit."

"It's taped to the truck window Abigail." Noah couldn't contain his soft laughter any longer as he pointed to the truck, "On display at the barricade per Baptiste City Code."

"Ah-ha!" Abigale sounded triumphant "The truck! Which is parked in the street, impeding traffic, improper to your CC and Rs."

"Don't you mean the currs?" Rob chuckled at Noah pronouncing the acronym as a word.

"*You know what I mean!*" Abigail exploded, her tone so hot Jennifer poked her worried face out of the kitchen giving Bear and Rob a scolding smile as they doubled over in silent laughter.

"Sorry Abigail, but you are wrong there too."

"The CC and Rs clearly state that all vehicles must be garaged" pronounced ghare-augged "when they are at home."

"Read it again, Abbs." Noah clipped. "They specifically state 'At no time will a vehicle belonging to a resident remain in the driveway of a given residence for longer than a ten-hour period.' As you can clearly see that isn't my driveway. That's the road. It is a public easement which is under the authority of the city council, the very people who signed my permit."

"But…" Rob could only imagine the shade of red Abigail's face had turned as she stammered for a response, finally reaching only, "This isn't over, Mr. Walker."

"Actually, Abigail… it is." Noah reached into the back pocket of his Wranglers and produced a folded slip of yellow paper. "As this is my party – mine being the name on the permit on the barricade – I am now officially trespassing you from this gathering until the permit runs out." He handed her the paper, which she opened, reading in disbelief. "There's a couple of things you need to note on this trespass order. They are very important to you. First, you will notice I have included a guest list…"

"This is almost the entire community!" She shrieked.

"It is, and you also need to take a look at the time stamp at the bottom near the city clerk's name on the permit as you leave. It says 9am. Now the letter of this trespass order states that you may not come within the confines of the barrier nor may you harass participants which are invited to this party at their place of residence. I want you to look across the street where Dave and Ashley Lindon are having a cocktail with Mrs. Wheeler on her front porch. They are party participants." He held up his hand to stop her from interrupting, "You are going to return to your home. Crack a nice bottle of wine. You are going to write a nice apology email to the Lindons for the chickenshit sprinkler violation you wrote them at 9:30 am because… as you can see… you were trespassing and engaging in harassment."

Abigail looked down at the time written into the trespass order, "You wrote in 9am? You *pre*-trespassed me from your party?!?"

Noah sighed. "Normally we would have been told by

the city council that we had to wait until you actually attempted to disrupt our gathering... but as it turns out there are over seventy-five recorded instances with Baptiste Police Department where you have called over non-enforceable issues this year ranging from people walking their dogs too close to your yard to complaints which the chief believed to be pure cranks..."

"Do all you bloody Yanks scurry around like rats to protect each other?" Abigale hissed. "Or have I completely lost my mind?!"

"I can't speak to your mental state Abby. I'm not a shrink. But I can assure you that there was no conspiracy on the part of the Lindons." He gave her a noncommittal shrug. "Sometimes stuff just works out. I didn't want to have to use this order, which is why I am handing it too you instead of pasting it to your front door as constructive notice. I was hoping you would find a way to get over whatever issues you have with your neighbors and come watch a comet go by with us. But your attitude and your language have made that impossible. Now, get off my porch and off my block before I call the sheriff."

Bear and Rob watched through the curtains as Abigail stormed over to the Walker's Yukon barricading the block. She snapped a picture of the permit on her phone before climbing back into her Range Rover and gunning the vehicle up the street, the sun glinting off the *Namaste Bitches* decal in her back window. They looked to Noah in amazed silence. Abigail had grown accustomed to cowing her neighbors and using her position on the HOA board to command obedience. She had been elected prior to the Walkers moving in; only partially because no one else had the time to spend completing the administrative tasks required, but mostly because it was generally thought that by appeasing her in what should have been a largely ceremonial position she surely would be kept occupied and out of everyone's hair. Never before had they seen someone withstand one of Abigail's screaming jags, so notorious they had been nicknamed "the full English fry-up," though none dared even whisper it while Abigail was in earshot.

"So." Noah turned from the closed door, a small smile playing at the edges of his otherwise relaxed expression. "You wanted to see the garage."

CHAPTER 7

As the dark of night veiled the face of the earth, it was as if the entire planet fell into expectant silence. The eyes of her inhabitants all turned to the heavens awaiting the comet's arrival. Seconds ticked by in silence as the pale, dispassionate face of the moon shone down, a thick blanket of constellations twisted overhead behind her. Mothers looked to fathers in disappointment, fearing their children would miss the passage of the falling star. Worried the experts had been wrong. That there would be no vision in the sky tonight. Then, like a cinder taking light on a stand of dry brush, the comet flickered to life above them – a speck at first, but growing and churning as it left the space between Earth and Mars suddenly burning to glorious life and dominating nearly the entire visible sky. It ate up distance, hungry for speed, its pheasant's tail of light streaming out behind it like a bridal train.

For sixteen and a half minutes it traversed the sky, a brilliant gash against the moon, burning through the firmament rimmed with green and azure light. In Idaho, Mary Beth lifted little Chris Walker into her lap so he could dance his hands above his head as if he could catch the comet's tail. In Nevada, Jack Wolfe and Colt Yneko gave a collective "wow!" while Sammy snuggled fast asleep in her mother's arms. In Arizona, little Bella cried excitedly to her nanny "It's here! It's here! I can see it!" while across town her parents stood among a silent crowd on the polo pitch marveling at the comet's beauty. In Montana the lights dimmed on the top of the Trapper Hotel as Rod and the Rocker Arms stood gazing into the night sky, their instruments mute in wonder. Daisy held Sassy French's hand while a chorus of excited children's voices echoed up from the balcony below.

In Henderson a more boisterous crowd of party goers cheered and whooped, hoisting their glasses into the blackness above them, startling the remuda awake in their stalls. Laura, caught up in the moment, ignored the company's official policy on employee fraternization and wrapping herself in Bobby's arms watched him as he watched it. Dex almost missed the comet as he and a busty peroxide blond had ducked behind the event tent stretched over the dance floor and outdoor bar to compare scars – both real and imagined. James French caught sight of it through the living room window, leaving his makeshift bed on the couch for the open yard outside his cabin watching as the comet disappeared over the tree line to the vast wilderness beyond. And alone, a tiny figure outlined in the dark at the edge of a wooden dock, Brenden Groger watched as two comets passed him by – one above and one reflected on the inky surface of Inch Lake.

Then, like a whisper in a wind, the comet breached the horizon and was gone.

The band inside the tent at Big Stakes Ranch burst out with a cover of Brooks 'n Dun's *Boot Scootin' Boogie* calling their audience back into the party while Rod and the Rocker Arms played *This Magic Moment*. Inside the Camelback pavilion the bandstand chimed in with *Unchained Melody*. In Baptiste, Teagan Brooker surprised her neighbors by draping a massive sheet across her two-bay garage door and playing the movie *Space Camp* from a wireless projector. She topped this by wheeling out a rented movie theater style popcorn machine from her one car garage. Across the neighborhood Abigail Messenger stood in the darkened window of her upstairs bedroom glaring at the gathering through a pair of field glasses, opening her second bottle of wine about the same time Len walked Sissy Wagner up the porch stairs of her little bungalow behind the café, accepting her warm hug goodnight, hat in hand, his mouth shut firm against forty some odd years of feeling.

CHAPTER 8

Comet Day +1
1003 Blackjack Oak Parkway – Baptiste, Idaho

"I don't understand how you aren't seeing this from a logical and reasonable perspective." Abigail was pacing her living room, her phone on speaker in one hand and her homeowner's handbook in the other. "It was obviously against our association by-laws and he should be punished."

"Ms. Messenger," Bob Tyler, the attorney who managed the Homeowner's Association, was on the other end of the line, as was Tim Hume the regional construction manager for Semaphore Builders Inc. and Bruce Tolman the construction superintendent. "I'm sorry you're so upset about this but please try to see this from our perspective. The block party wasn't against any of our restrictions. Mr. Walker is correct. Silence on an issue is a form of permission."

"But I am the HOA president!" She was very close to yelling. "They didn't even ask my permission. Can't you do something?"

"That's what I'm trying to explain. We don't have any real legal right to do anything." Bob paused. "And considering the trespass order and the city permit – as a measure of keeping our board out of a neighborhood dispute, I'm cancelling all the fixit orders you wrote on the 13th and the ones which came in this morning."

"There's no way he has the legal grounds to enforce that. Those fines keep our organization solvent!"

"We should be solvent based on dues alone." Bob chose his wording very carefully. "The fines are a means of deterrent only. To keep people adhering to the CC&Rs. If you pursue this, and Mr. Walker takes us to court – we could end up insolvent very quickly. This is Idaho. Civil court justices around here tend to side with the owners of the property rather than the corporations which manage the common grounds."

"But he lacks any real force of law!" Abagail didn't know if she wanted to laugh or cry. "He was bluffing! He's just trying to bully me around."

"It's too big a risk." Bob insisted. "Civil litigation is time consuming and expensive, and in the end we could lose. We would go through a long drawn-out procedure just to end up paying Mr. Walker's attorney fees, he could sue not just the HOA but you personally. And when this gets really ugly – because it will - there are a million things which the homeowners themselves can do to reduce or even avoid paying their regular dues in the meantime."

"And just from our perspective, Abigail." Tim's voice cut in, "We're trying to sell homes here. No one wants to live in a neighborhood that they feel has tyrannical control over their lives."

"You Americans and your notions of tyranny!" Abigail snapped. "You're all just fundamentally ungovernable. It isn't civilized."

"Hey Tim." Bruce's voice sounded hollow and tinny as if he also had the speakerphone on. "I have to meet with the dirt-work guy in fifteen minutes and I wanted to head over to lot fifty-one and take some measurements on the pad before he gets here so we can get better numbers on billing hours. I have to go."

"No wait! Bruce." Abigail stamped her foot. "I still need to talk to you about the switch faceplate in my powder room."

"Submit a service request." Was Bruce's quick reply as the phone made an audible click.

"Uhm hang on there a minute Abigail." It was Tim. "Those fit and finish issues are only warrantied up to the first year after purchase. If you have an issue with your faceplate, you'll have to fix it yourself."

"You expect ... *me* ... to change the faceplate on my

light switch?" Abigail dropped her copy of the CC&Rs onto her sofa, so she would have her hand free to cover her eyes, as if she could somehow shut out how very not her way this entire conversation was going.

"Maintenance is one of the many joys of homeownership." Tim sounded apologetic. "I have a meeting to get to myself. Talk to you guys later."

"No Tim! We have to fix this HOA issue!" But it was too late, he had already hung up. "Bob, are you still on at least?"

"Uhm ...yea." He sounded distracted and she could hear him typing on his computer. "Ms. Messenger... I just got an email from Mr. Walker and I might have to call you back..."

"What?!" Abigail was dumbfounded. "Don't hang up. What is it about?"

"Well..." he seemed reluctant to say, but finally sighed... "You haven't been actually entering people's properties, have you?"

Abagail could feel the blood draining from her face. "...no... I ... not really. I just ... "

She heard Bob curse softly under his breath. "Abigail. Let me stop you right there. Don't say anything else. Not to me, not to anyone. I need to remind you that the authority of the HOA extends only to the outside of a property which is readily seen from the walk or the road. Otherwise, the individual lots are private property and you may not enter."

"For heaven's sake, Bob! She's feeding strays in her back yard." Abigail thundered. "We are a community. This absolutely affects all of us. Don't lecture me about your ridiculous notions of private property, you will thank me when we aren't hip deep in filthy feral cats."

"There are pictures Abigail." His voice was measured.

"Noah Walker may not photograph me without my permission!"

"He didn't. This is security footage from the house." He took a breath. "There's more. The photos apparently have already been circulated among the neighbors. There's a petition to remove you as HOA president and hold a new election."

"No." Abigail whispered, her throat suddenly dry.

"I have to tell you," Bob's voice held a serious tone, "even if they hadn't signed, these are absolutely grounds for removal. We – the HOA board – must operate with as little personal impact to the homeowners as possible. We make sure the lawns are mowed, the common areas kept up, and the property values maintained. That is all."

"You can't remove me, Bob." Abigail insisted. "You can't."

"If I don't remove you, the neighborhood could vote to fire my firm from the board, and I would lose a lot of private clients." He sighed. "And any firm coming behind me will make taking you off the board their first order of business. I'm sorry Abby but I've got to end this phone call."

The click of the phone left Abigail Messenger screaming her indignation to her empty living room.

Il Risorante Ponte Romano – Scottsdale, Arizona

Hunter walked directly up to the maître d's desk making no eye contact with the people waiting on the little row of benches for an open table. The girl behind the counter – a pretty little redhead wearing a tag that said "Natalie" – gave him a sweet smile and asked if he had reservations. "Actually, I think my party has already been seated. I'm here with Eugene Vaughn."

"Mr. Church?"

"That's me." He leaned over the front of the little

station flashing her a winning smile. "Unless of course my father is here. He isn't, is he?"

"I don't think so." She giggled, blushing deeply as she grabbed a passing waiter. "Marco, will you please take Mr. Church to table twelve?"

"Right this way sir." Marco led him through the dining room and around an ornately carved wood bar to a quieter corner of the restaurant away from the open concept kitchen. He thanked Marco, slipping him a ten as Eugene and Mr. Goodwin stood to greet him.

"Boss." He returned Eugene's enthusiastic handshake, and Goodwin's more reserved one. "Luke. Good to see you again."

"I trust your wife recovered well from last night?" Goodwin smiled warmly as Hunter took an empty seat at the table.

"I believe she's at the spa today doing just that." He said picking up the menu and giving it a cursory glance. Then to Eugene. "How is Nan?"

"Asleep last I saw." Vaughn also glanced at the menu, then put it back down. "But that was six this morning before my run. No doubt she's out and about by now."

"That was quite a party you folks threw. Thank you for the invitation." Goodwin also laid the menu down, and almost immediately Marco was at his side. "I'll have the citro branzini, salad, and a bottle of prosecco for the table."

"The Santa Margherita or the Mionetto, sir?"

"Is the Margherita fresh?"

"Yes sir. Not quite a year."

"That one then."

Ever dependable Vaughn ordered the aragosta linguini, also a salad, insisting the meal be placed on his tab; Hunter ordered the gamberetto marsala, bucked the trend by ordering bagnun and a bottle of Aqua Panna with a lime twist. They made small talk for a while, enjoying the wine, until Goodwin became quiet for a bit before saying. "I suppose we should talk business, after all you have – both of you – been more than chivalrous with me and your time. I suppose it's time to ruin that all with work."

Eugene chuckled a bit, placing his napkin in his lap as Marco placed his plate in front of him. "What Mr. Goodwin and I were talking about before your arrival Hunter, he would like you to take over a large portion of a personal project of his, advise him in legal matters and get some of your staff ..."

"No." Goodwin's interruption wasn't sharp, but it was firm. "No staff. These issues, Mr. Church..."

"Please, call me Hunter."

Goodwin's face flickered a smile, "These issues, Hunter, they are of a rather personal nature. They aren't illicit by any means, but I would appreciate a very tight circle of knowledge. I would prefer that a majority of your work is completed at my home. I know its unorthodox, but you will have your own office and private entrance, state of the art technology and private server, and a secure landline to keep all calls off the cellular networks. I would only expect you to work one day a week, during which I will pay the full amount you are expected from your firm plus a bonus. And in the event you have a court date or some other requirement of your time, you will still be paid so long as my goals are achieved."

Hunter and Vaughn exchanged glances, Eugene's face suddenly still and unreadable. "This sounds serious. It must be if you are willing to pay so high a price for secrecy."

"Let's call it privacy." Goodwin shifted in his seat. "My brother is a United States Senator, as you must know. Though you've both been far too polite to mention it. The state of politics these days, how polarized it has become... just horrible! I don't think we have seen the like since Caesar was murdered on the senate floor. If word of this project to slip out, it would be first misunderstood and then perhaps weaponized into something nasty meant to harm him and his very important work. There is also a slight concern for public good. Were I anyone else? My project would be ignored as an odd hobby. But being as I am a member of a politically connected family – it has the prospect of frightening some people. I don't want that. To be responsible for panic in the streets."

"It isn't criminal?" Hunter gave Luke Goodwin a heavy look.

"No. On my honor. It's perfectly above board."

"Is it military?"

"No. Though I would ask that you treat it as though it were the same as top secret intelligence." Goodwin cleared his throat. "Your wife, Lucy, she is a charming, lovely woman. But I must ask you not even discuss this with her."

"I never discuss my clients with my wife." Hunter took a sip of his water, sitting back casually in the chair though his mind was busy decoding Goodwin's body language. "That's just the nature of my work."

"There is one more thing." Goodwin rested his fork on the edge of his plate for a moment, looking at Hunter intensely, "I would need you to start today. As soon as we have finished this lunch, in fact."

"That soon?"

"I have reason to believe this project is time sensitive. We really haven't the luxury of waiting."

Hunter was silent for a moment, taking it all in. "One condition." He finally said, "I have a parachute. If at any time I feel as if this project is not in my area of expertise, or it sails into unsavory waters – I'm out. With pay. You retain the protection of my privilege, but the firm receives its due plus a percentage."

Goodwin nodded, mainly to himself, and then offered his hand. "Agreed."

"Good then." Eugene smiled, as Marco took his salad dish, replacing it with his main course, "Did you bring the Maserati?"

"I did."

"Good. You and Mr. Goodwin will take the company

car to your new office. Leave your keys with the service and they will get your car home for you."

Goodwin was silent as to his mysterious "hobby" for the remainder of dinner and Hunter sensed that pressing him for information would only make him more closed off. He had dealt with overly circumspect clients before. It usually meant there was a considerable number of skeletons in the family closet, typically involving some social shame or an embarrassing proclivity. It could be the odd mistress who needed to disappear with a new name and bank account after refusing an abortion, a not quite platonic relationship with a golfing buddy or old college roommate, an occasional drug dealer who needed to be taken out of county lockup on a minor charge before they started making deals with the district attorney.

He was certain that Goodwin would take him into confidence once Eugene Vaughn's back was turned. Guilty men – especially those at Goodwin's age (and stage of life judging by his general physical shape and rabid oenophilia) – loved to confess. By the time the meal had finished and Vaughn had placed the call for the car service, Hunter was convinced that two things were true – Goodwin was dying, and he wanted to sweep some embarrassing personal details under the carpet of history before he did.

Hunter was wrong, though, in thinking a font of personal knowledge would come bursting forward from his new client in the car. Goodwin said only that Hunter should call his wife to let her know he would most likely be late home this evening – not that unusual in the legal field and news which Lucy treated with emotionally removed support. His job, after all, kept her hip deep in luxury shoes and social standing. Then the remainder of the time in the car Goodwin chatted politely about local history and landmarks as they slipped by the tinted windows. The car wound its way through the Entertainment District turning east on Camelback Road to North Hayden and then Chaparral, finally mounting the Pima

Freeway northbound – but still Goodwin was a bubbling brook of cocktail conversation with deeply hidden depths.

When they finally arrived at a private airfield in the satellite community of Carefree, Goodwin finally let loose a small balloon of information "Oh, yes." He said. "I should have told you. My house where we will be working is near Saint George, Utah. With the right winds it should take my pilot about twenty to thirty minutes to get there, and then another forty by car. I realize this must be torture, not knowing your goals and purpose with this task," Hunter was wise enough to offer a nonplussed shrug at this. "but I really can't say much with your driver, or mine, or my airstaff present. I promise, or at least I hope, in the end you will understand."

He wasn't surprised to find the plane – a Challenger 350 – already fueled and ready to board. He was surprised to see that the stewardess already had a bottle of Aqua Panna poured out into a crystal highball glass with a lime twist. Goodwin apparently never missed a detail. "I never drink on flights." Goodwin smiled as Hunter made himself comfortable in one of the plush leather seats with his drink, he himself taking the long couch towards the tail of the plane. "I think perhaps the sudden climb in altitude and the pressurized air just makes the alcohol unbearable. My head swims." The stewardess asked if they were comfortable and receiving an answer to the affirmative smiled and disembarked to stay in Carefree. The pilots waved from the cockpit before closing the curtain separating the cockpit from the cabin. "If you don't mind, Hunter, I think I will close my eyes for a bit."

CHAPTER 9

The Acropolis - Red Mountains, Utah

The "house" as Goodwin had called it turned out to be a seventy-five hundred square foot compound high in the Red Mountains outside Ivins, Utah accessible only by four-wheel drive – a trip which they made by a luxury Land Rover along a winding rocky single lane road. Built along the design of a Roman Villa, complete with a thick outer security wall and outer courtyard garden, the color and shape of the house mimicked the hematite sandstone of the buttes around it so as to be nearly imperceptible even from the air. The Range Rover pulled up to the wall, dropping them off beside a heavy blast proof gate guarded with a keypad. Hunter watched as the car disappeared in a trail of rust colored dust as the gate swung shut behind it.

"We walk from here." Goodwin said, surprisingly spry for how round he was. "I want to give you the full tour. We will start with the inner yard."

"These security measures…" Hunter turned and pointed around him. "The gates, the walls, the cameras, they all look military."

"They're better." Goodwin's tone was off hand as he pressed the buttons of the keypad and the door popped open from its frame with a heavy clunk. "My brother put me in touch with one of the contracting firms he knows. One of the corporations which builds embassies, state buildings, prisons, that sort of thing. Very expensive but well worth it. By now your code should have been entered into all the security programs." He handed Hunter a laminated card from his wallet. "I took the liberty of using Bella's birthday. To make it easy to remember. Getting in once you've entered the incorrect code is … well it won't happen."

He pushed the door open to reveal an inner courtyard which consisted primarily of an elongated pool filled with brightly colored koi and various plants. "Once a week or so a housecleaning team comes up. They weed the food gardens and clean the pond. We only use crews which are in the process of deportation so they work a couple of weeks in a row, we give them a little money for their trouble, and then they are whisked out of the country where they can't pose an immediate threat."

"Ok." Hunter stopped for a moment under the shade of a breeze through which had been made green and leafy by grapevines coiling over its wooden beams. "There's no one here. You have to tell me what this is about. Deported people just end up right back in the states like a revolving door. That's not even close to a usable security plan. Unless by deported you mean they aren't alive on the other end." He looked around at the inner court, at the fish skimming the top of the water, listening to the hiss of a tiny waterfall built into a stylish monument of rock. "That's not what you mean... is it?"

"Oh God. Nothing as ghoulish as that." Goodwin gave him a small smile. "I simply mean that when it happens these people will be nowhere near this location to compromise it."

"When *what* happens?"

"When the world ends."

Hunter followed in stunned silence as Goodwin led him around the pond to a narrow gravel path leading behind the waterfall to a hidden pair of elevator doors. The older man smiled sheepishly as he pressed a call button, then waited for the car to arrive, indicating that Hunter should follow him in as the doors slid open. "I suppose we should start at the very bottom." Goodwin mumbled, almost to himself as he pressed a square button labeled "C". The ride down felt as if it lasted for hours, neither man speaking until the doors opened again to reveal a massive dome like room cut into the very rock of the mountain.

"This is our cistern." Goodwin smiled proudly, leading Hunter out of the elevator onto a massive metal platform overlooking the water. "We use an oil pumping system to feed this lake. The engineers drilled into an aquafer that runs under the mountain." Hunter followed him out onto a catwalk spanning the room, looking down into the deep black depths below. "Water comes in here and in turn is fed through the entire complex. On a level above this is our private armory, fully stocked with enough rifles and rounds to keep a battalion of Marines well supplied for a couple of years. And just outside that going further into the mountain we have a below ground pistol and rifle range. But what you really must see is the supply room!" Hunter followed Goodwin across the catwalk to a door which led to a staircase, and beyond that a tunnel like room the size of an aircraft hangar stacked from floor to ceiling with meals ready to eat.

"These are only for the direst of circumstances." Goodwin made a face. "They are absolutely disgusting. You would have to be near death to want to consume one. But they will keep one from eyeing his neighbors as a potential source of protein."

They walked to the opposite end of the storeroom to another door leading to a mechanical bay – what Goodwin called the guts of the building – complete with a large bank of utility style inverters. "The electric system is a work of genius. All the tiles on the roof and a good portion of the drive pavers are solar collectors. We have none of those garish arrays and panels you see in fly over country. The ones in the ground are specially engineered to support the weight of vehicles, and they look just like stone. The battery system is housed through here," Goodwin opened a large metal door revealing a large square room which housed rows of sleek white and black batteries, each about the size of a small refrigerator.

Then closing the door again, he pointed across the opposite side of the room to another platform, this one rimmed in thick glass with a large control panel overlooking a deep bay housing several large tanks and a pair of massive generators. "But as you can see, we still have our backup power and fuel supply just in case these fail. We had to make those walls of very thick concrete as the generators are quite loud. The noise in this room would be unbearable if we ever had to use them. They're the same models used in hydro-electric damns but with a semitruck engine turning them over instead of water flow. Over there," He pointed down into the bay to a closed door beside the tanks, "is the plumbing station housing water pumps and controls for the house, garden and fishpond. And past that is our air filtration system, the bigger filters are up on the roof, but we have a secondary system down here just to be safe and to keep things flowing correctly."

They left this room taking a flight of stairs off the platform, walking through a long concrete living space built above the generator bay. It was about the size of Hunter's penthouse apartment complete with two bedrooms, a living room, dining area and kitchen, and a small security closet filled with monitors from which the entire compound could be viewed. "We've hidden all the practical measures down here. We're about two thousand feet from the surface, accessible only by the elevator which we took down and a stairwell which I do not recommend unless you are in impeccable shape as it is about twice the height of the Eiffel Tower. I even had them build resting rooms every quarter of the distance just to make it manageable."

He led the way back into the elevator, talking as the doors closed and they ascended back up to the courtyard. "We've utilized a lot of mining technology here – as you can see the elevator is rather utilitarian but there's none of that pesky changing cars and so forth. And the shaft itself has a ladder niche so should the car stop working at any time you simply pry the doors open by means of a lever inside of the call box, reach out and climb down to the closest resting room.

There are – of course – similar though less comfortable style accommodations under each of the two servants' wings with a connecting corridor meeting this elevator halfway down."

"Servants wings?" Hunter wrinkled his brow as the doors came open with a metallic ding. "But I thought you didn't have a regular staff here."

"Oh yes." Goodwin nodded leading the way back around the pond and through a beautifully carved oak door into the house itself. As he spoke Hunter took in the sprawling living room, counting three fireplaces each with their own set of chairs and couches making it look more like the lobby of a luxury hotel than a home. "We're deep in Mormon Country here so many of the families have prepared for disaster to some degree or another but there will always be one or two incautious souls who will require food, shelter, lodging. In return they may cook, clean, provide security, grow food, or complete any one of the many tasks it will take to keep this place running. We will be like an ark, providing shelter and safety until the government can get the system up and running again. Now through here is the kitchen fully stocked with all the actual food. And through that door is a stairwell leading to a wine and storage cellar with more provisions. It too has a network of tunnels which reach several parts of the compound as well as a service dock outside the outer gate.

"Upstairs are my quarters – my bedroom and study, several bedrooms for guests with en suite showers as well as a full library and formal dining. There's a dumb waiter just there beyond the fireplace." He pointed to a massive hearth that held a roasting spit large enough to cook an entire hog against the far wall. "It leads to the dining room and hall."

"Your portion of the house is through here." Goodwin walked back across the lounge towards a staircase Hunter had not noticed as they had come in. It rose to a small gallery and a large oak door, also secured by a numbered pad. "If you would please – enter your code."

Hunter punched the numbers into the pad, noting that for all his efforts Goodwin had missed Bella's birthday by a week which told Hunter he had gotten the information from May, Hunter's own secretary. He would have to talk to her about informational diligence but would not be too strict in the event it was actually Eugene Vaughn who had asked for it.

The door came open with a mechanical click revealing an open vestibule which flowed into a comfortably sized parlor and beyond that another curving staircase as well as a large den. A slim door built into the back wall beside a large fireplace told Hunter there would be servant's passages built into this wing as well. Up the staircase was a formal dining room and a small terrace. A long corridor led to a thirteen hundred square foot space which Goodwin called the master bedroom. It had its own sitting room, library, full bathroom with both a tub and a spa shower, and a couple small rooms which looked suspiciously like valet berths. Further down the corridor were four other slightly smaller rooms.

"There's room here for a nursery." Goodwin gave him a shy smile. "And of course, Miss Bella will have her own room. Just due to the construction they can't all have windows, so I thought this one could be for your nanny." he opened the door to a large windowless space with a small bathroom off one side and a bedroom off the other. "I trust she is single and will not require a larger family apartment."

"She is…" Hunter looked at the rooms and then at Mr. Goodwin. "I'm sorry. I'm not quite understanding. I thought you said I would have an office."

"Oh! Yes… it's back this way." Goodwin practically sprinted back towards the dining room stairs.

"No." Hunter said falling just a few steps behind. "What I mean is that this? This isn't an office. This is a house. I've seen smaller brownstones in New York City."

"Yes. I know." Goodwin called over his shoulder as he padded down the stairs to a hall at the back of the den which opened to yet another staircase leading to the ground floor. "But I can't have you put as much work into this project of mine as I'm asking and just leave your family to starve – or worse."

The bottom of the staircase opened up into a large office with French windows, a beautiful oak and leather desk in the center and several banks of built-in file cabinets against the inner wall – also in well-crafted oak. "This will be your workspace; it has its own water closet and a digital intercom built into the desk which will reach every room in the house. And this door here," He opened a large door behind the desk "This hall leads first to the garage in the outer court and further on to the stables. There are no horses here as of yet, but here in your desk is a master key for that door. It's the only one on this entire compound which will work without electricity and is hidden in the back of the tack loft behind several bales of straw. The contractors insisted on building at least one, though I was reluctant…"

Hunter held up his hand, the pieces all falling into place. Goodwin had been truthful about his "hobby" – anyone else storing provisions and setting up an emergency home would just be considered one lone crank with some extravagant ideas. The older brother of a United States Senator using private contractors building a doomsday compound in the desert for himself, a few trusted advisors, and "staff" – the optics would be damning to say the least. There would be whispers of mental instability even though anyone who spoke to Luke Goodwin would know right away that he wasn't insane. Perhaps a bit odd, but not insane. Up until arriving at the house Hunter wouldn't have even considered him "eccentric". He did a quick assessment of the mental profile he had built on Luke Goodwin's brother – a notorious war hawk who chaired a couple committees including a joint one on intelligence. Which would bring questions as to what Luke Goodwin knew that the general public did not.

"Luke." Hunter finally said. "What exactly are you preparing for?"

Goodwin's smile clouded a little as he watched his new attorney finally catching up. "Well, that's just it. There's no way to know. It could be an attack on the US – nuclear or something else. Cyber-attacks in particular are capable of killing millions if they hack the right parts of our system – the electric grid, our water, even hacking our stock market could cause more damage than simple mayhem. It could be a shift in political stability, an unforeseen natural phenomenon, it could be a viral pandemic. That's why I have the medical filters on the roof, to make sure the air inside stays clean. It's also why," he paused for a moment, his expression reminding Hunter of Bella's face whenever Lucy caught her picking her nose. There was an awareness of the social implications to this project, but no real heartfelt shame. "we have a full medical bay on the other side of the kitchens."

"A medical bay." Hunter had to sit down. He walked to a leather settee below the bank of windows and sank into it.

"Yes." Goodwin sat beside him, watching his face intently for any hint as to what the attorney was thinking. "It is almost the exact mirror image of your own wing, but it also has a cold storage space adjacent to the wine cellar, a small surgery, and a patient room. This is one of the things I need you to do for me. I'm horrible at personnel research. I find it incredibly tedious. I need you to find us a physician who can fit the do everything bill. Depending on how long it takes for things to get back to normal – whatever the disaster may be – we will need someone who can deliver babies, set bones, deal with traumatic wounds, remove the odd appendix – and all while keeping our home a complete secret.

"There are other requirements as well. He needs to be a family man of the utmost character. Someone with children or at least a wife." Goodwin sniffed. "I find from my research that people with skin in the game are more motivated to make their communities work." He paused for a moment, then sighed. "I believe I may have given you too much to think about. If you would like to opt out of this project you may do so. My jet will take you home and I trust that you will not reveal these details to anyone."

Hunter thought about that for a moment. Then he looked around at the office, mentally calculating the amount of money which Goodwin had put into preparing to rebuild society after some terrible unknown disaster. Everything was state of the art and luxurious. The desk alone must have cost upwards of five thousand dollars, not counting the digital integrations of the small tablet computer built into the top. "Ok." He said at last nodding. "I can do this."

"You can!" Goodwin was ecstatic, happily dancing in place on the couch. "You'll see! We will make this place the cradle of civilization! We will have other tasks to tackle once we locate an adequate physician, but for now let's focus on this. I have some leads which I have compiled in the top drawer of your desk along with a credit card which I want you to use to purchase whatever supplies you need. But first let me show you the gold vault."

"You have a gold vault?" Hunter looked at Goodwin who had already risen and was walking towards the door. "You have a gold vault … here?"

"Of course I do." Goodwin gave the younger man a wry smile. "You didn't think that in the event of a total collapse we would be reduced to trafficking in deer meat and chicken feathers, did you? Please Hunter. We aren't savages."

CHAPTER 10

Comet Day +15
1002 Yellow Jack Place – Baptiste, Idaho

"The Russians?" Rob Church's voice was incredulous. "Like not talking heads and pundit rhetoric but really? The Russians."

"Or the Chinese." Noah responded, pulling the lever on his Dillion reloading press, advancing shells to the next station where they were in their turn belled, given a charge, a slug, and crimped before falling into a small plastic container with a dull clink. "And we have a couple of our so-called allies in Europe who haven't been as friendly as of late. It's just a matter of time before they start making decisions for the good of their own agenda and to hell with what's good for us. You can't fault them for looking out for their own, we do the same. But you can't ignore it either."

He looked over to where Rob was sitting on one of his leather couches holding a tall glass of Jennifer's sweet tea and shaking his head. Bear Thyme sat on the opposite couch nodding in agreement, leg crossed at the ankle his empty glass on a side table which had been built out of an empty munitions box. They were in Noah's fourth garage, a space he had converted into an informal den decorated in the very highest of tacticool fashion complete with a large black and white 'Join or Die' flag hanging over the workbench along the far side of the room. In the days following the comet party Noah's garage had become the informal clubhouse for a good portion of the men in the neighborhood. Tonight, he was hosting a poker game while Jen and the wives settled into the dining room for margaritas and Bunco. The game wasn't supposed to start for another thirty minutes but Rob and Bear had come over early to admire the new gun-safe in the corner of the room.

"Aren't you worried that someone could break in here?" Bear had asked. "Wouldn't it be safer in the house?"

Noah had just offered his typical shrug. "Maybe if I were going to be keeping my guns in it. But since I'm just taking out the shelves and putting a conductive cage on the inside it's not that big of a deal. Besides it's a good decoy. They break in, grab the safe, can't open it here so they have to drive it off – that takes time, makes noise. More time for the police to arrive, more time for my family to get safe, and in the end they just get replaceable car parts." This had been the start of the current conversation.

"What exactly are you prepping for?" Rob asked as Noah finished the last of his shells and taking a sip off his own glass of sweet tea started to pack them in a small plastic ammo box.

"It could be anything." Noah looked up for a moment while he worked. "It could be something as simple as a house fire. Teaching the kids to be aware of their surroundings, help each other to get to safety no matter what part of the house they are in. In that situation, for me, it's locating the source of the threat and clearing the ammo out of the house so rounds aren't cooking off when first responders arrive." He closed the box and shook it slightly. "It's larger things like being involved in the community, making sure brush and defensible spaces are maintained even if it means long hours volunteering for highway clean up. This keeps our house safe from things like floods and brushfire, helps keep emergency service budgets from being hit so they have the tools and the people they need when they need it. Its teaching the kids practical skills like horseback riding, hunting, car maintenance, first-aid. Those are things you put in your back pocket, kind of a mental Swiss army knife that will help them all through life.

"And it's bigger picture worst case scenario stuff like having food stores, knowing where your fresh water sources are, having the information and tools you might need to clean water and avoid disease." Noah worked at putting his reload supplies away as he spoke. "We keep the kids vaccines up to date. We have a family meeting every two weeks where we encourage the kids to identify a possible threat in the world around them. We let the littlest ones go first because they need the praise from the group and the older kids need to feel included in the executive process. Last week Chris taught us how to defend ourselves from alien invasion, Peyton reminded us what to do in case the dinosaurs came back, and Beau and Jefferson helped us come up with a workable solution to city water being cut off indefinitely. You boil it down to the basics, the things you really need – food, water, health, security, shelter, transportation – and you look at how those things can be threatened and how you can adapt and overcome."

"It's more of a mindset." Bear said, thinking about his family and whether or not he even had a working fire extinguisher in the house.

"More or less." Noah put the ammo box up on a shelf above the workbench then joined the other two men on the couches. "Jen keeps a huge garden in the back. She won't grow anything ornamental. Everything has a practical purpose. We make it a point to get to know the neighbors, teach our kids to be respectful and polite towards their elders. You never know what a kid will pick up just mowing a neighbor's lawn. Last week Mrs. Zhou taught Beau how to identify two types of edible weed native to this area that were growing in her flower beds. Rob, you actually taught Jefferson something the other day when he was riding his bike."

"I did?" Rob tried to think about the last time he had seen the sixteen-year-old. "You mean his bike chain? All I did was help him put it back on."

"Nope it was more than that." Noah smiled. "You helped him get the chain back on and while you were doing that you chatted with him about that boat you're building in your garage. You thought you were just making small talk but now my son knows the difference between clinker and carvel hulls. You sparked his curiosity. He came home and ordered a bunch of boat building books off the internet. He's expanding his knowledge base in a practical area because of a two-minute conversation with you. It could turn out to be a general interest, it could be a hobby. But it falls in the category of transportation and is inherently useful."

"My wife would love to hear you say that." Rob smiled. "She wants me to open an actual shop, build them professionally, keep them out of the garage. I keep telling her – honey, I'm retired. I just want to build them one at a time."

The doorbell rang, it's muffled chime in the house accompanied by a small beeping from the intercom on the garage wall. "Oh good." Noah stood up and checked the security display above the intercom's flashing light, "The techies are here. Let's get this game started."

The techies were Derik Pratt and Ferris Michaels, two guys who had made their fortunes building a quant in their dorm room at UC Stanford which they later sold to Ferris' father's financial firm. The golden egg that project laid was reinvested with Michaels and Waverly Capitol Group and continued to churn out more gold every quarter. With that money they semi-retired to their McMansions in Baptiste, where they spent their days developing gaming software and engaging in a friendly one-upmanship as to which new car or gadget they could bring home next.

Ferris looked to his wife Alla beside him, noting the anxiety on her cousin Zia's face as she stood beside Derik. The girls had not been as well received as Ferris had hoped. Suburban neighborhoods are insular by nature, each resident tending to treat neighbors as acquaintances while they went about their busy lives. It wasn't an active ill will, just encapsulation in one's own personal sphere. One year ago, when Alla had come from Daleke, a tiny village about a hundred miles south of Kharkiv, introducing her to the neighbors had gone well. They asked questions about her fiancé visa process, when was the wedding, a few even attended the tiny ceremony down at the courthouse – the Walkers being among them. Abigale Messenger did not, but did attend the celebratory BBQ afterwards where she spent her time drinking wine and asking Alla awkward political questions about her childhood. His new bride was – is – about the least politically minded person Ferris had ever met.

However, when Zia showed up two weeks ago, something in the neighborly dynamic had changed. He had heard the uncomplimentary talk of Kiev invasions, mail order brides, and accusations of prostitution around the gym in the clubhouse when the real housewives of Woodview Heights Estates thought he was out of earshot. When it was let slip that Zia was Alla's cousin, Derik had fielded unintentionally unkind jokes about how he would someday have to stop "buying the same model" as Ferris. Most of the gossip seemed to be coming from Abigale Messenger and her surrogate in neighborhood politics Joanna Ross. Teagan Booker never seemed to say anything directly, but she certainly hadn't gone out of her way to be friendly or make Zia's entree into neighborhood society any easier.

The detached attention had made Zia retreat from attempting to make new friends outside of their own tiny circle, and he had heard her and Derik arguing on several occasions over whether she should just go home. They hadn't officiated their marriage yet and Zia, being a bit old fashioned, had maintained her residence in the casita rather than joining Derik in the main portion of the house. She was homesick and lonely, but when the Walker's had extended their invitation to join them for game night, she had been wary.

"Maybe..." Zia shifted uncomfortably in her new heels, "Maybe we should go home?"

"It will be fine." Ferris gave her a confident smile and was about to ring the doorbell again when Jennifer Walker opened the door, the warm light of the house spilling out onto the porch.

"Hi! Sorry." She said breathlessly as she pulled the door wide open with a welcoming smile. "The blender lid wasn't on right and now I have margarita mix all over my counter. Are daiquiris ok instead?"

Derik looked to the shy smile that had perched on Zia's lips as she said thank you and let Jenifer take her little mink stole. At this moment he would have nominated the Walker's for sainthood, much less HOA president. Alla gave Jenifer a little hug in greeting, handing her a bottle of wine. Zia also brought a gift, a small stoneware fox resting on a flat hollow base, its little stylized nose pointed up as if howling. "It's beautiful!" Jennifer exclaimed. "What does it do?"

"It is for ..." a flash of frustration crossed Zia's brow as she sought the right verb conjugation. "baking pies. The fruit steams out of the fox, and he whistles a little. This keeps your bottom crust crunchy."

"This is so thoughtful." Jennifer pulled her in for another hug. "I will use this all the time. Thank you."

Jennifer soon had the two cousins settled into her dining room beside Mary Beth Church and Lisa Thyme where they were greeted enthusiastically. "We've wrecked the ritas." Mary Beth chirped indicating a pile of dish towels in the sink. "Have you two ever played Bunco?" Lisa asked patting the two chairs beside her. "Alright you men, down the hall to the cave with the rest of them!" Jenifer sang giving Ferris and Derik a good-natured shove in the direction of the garage. "Women folk only."

Derik took one last look at his fiancé, watching Zia's shoulders relax as Lisa started going over the rules of the game and showing the two newcomers how to play. "I don't know about you." he said as they reached the end of the hall, "But Noah Walker has my vote."

"It's gonna be a landslide." Ferris nodded as he opened the door to the garage.

"Hey guys." Noah waved from the poker table behind

the twin couches where he, Rob, and Bear were sitting. "Ready to lose some money?"

"Yea, fat chance." Ferris laughed back as he and Derik found their chairs. No sooner had they sat down when the doorbell rang again.

"Very cool." Noah said checking the display. "Looks like the Zhous made it. You guys watch it around old Feng. That guy could bluff you out of your skivvies. And it looks like Teagan Booker is with them." He went back to the table. "Jen will be happy about that. She's been trying to get Teagan to join the hen party for over a year."

"Hey... uh..." Derik tried to sound as casual as he could as he stacked the chips Bear had passed him in order. "Do you think the Rosses will make it?"

Noah sat down, passed a box of cigars around the table, and clipping the end of his own replied, "The Rosses will be invited when they stop being such insufferable pricks. It's the Lindons who are on the fence, may or may not show."

"Wait – they just came out of the house. All the lights are off." Joanna stood in Abigail Messenger's living room just far enough from the window to not be spotted from the street. Abigail jogged in from the kitchen with an open bottle of wine to stand beside her, watching as David and Ashley walked across their lawn to the sidewalk.

"So now we see whose side they're on." She half whispered handing Joanna's husband Travis the beer she had in her hand. "What the hell are they waiting for? They're just standing there in the street like a couple of idiots."

Travis shrugged, taking a sip off the beer and placing it on the coaster beside them. "They could be weighing their options. Just don't make any sudden moves. They can still see you through the blinds."

Abigail gave him an appreciative look then put her arm around Joanna's shoulders. "It must be so nice to have such a knowledgeable man around the house. Is there no end to the practical knowledge he holds?"

"There isn't." Joanna agreed. "But then again, he needs it. His job is very dangerous. He's had to develop almost a sixth sense about people."

"Dangerous?" Abigail turned her questioning eyes to Travis. "But I thought you did something with public lands?"

"It's riskier than you would think." He slurred a little, leaning back into the couch where he was sitting, crossing his leg at the knee. "You have cowboys who don't want to listen about their cattle. Hunters who don't want to listen about game. Indians who don't want to listen about anything. The odd lost hiker you have to go find because they were too stupid to stay on the trail. We pay billions of dollars a year maintaining good usable hiking paths but every season some dope wants to wander off away from the beaten path. It's like running a daycare sometimes, dealing with the general public."

"Did you say cowboys?" Abigail's eyes went wide with shock. "People still think that's a thing?"

"Oh wait, she's waving." Joanna interrupted, straining forward at the neck trying to get a better view without walking closer to the window itself.

"Oh my god." Abigail laughed. "Is she waving at us? She looks like a fool."

"Abigail, look." Joanna pointed towards the other side of the yard where Dan and Tammy Allen had immerged on the sidewalk from behind Abigail's garage, Tammy waving back as the Lindon's crossed the street to meet them at the corner.

"Well." Abigail turned from the window to sink down into the couch next to Travis. "That settles that then. Tammy is off to play bingo or bonkers or whatever at the Walkers.

Joanna and I watched Rob and Mary Beth walk over there after dinner. It's like a bloody cult these wretched people."

Joanna turned away from the window, a wicked smile on her face. "Abigail. You're right. They're all over at the Walkers."

"And?"

"Well, who's minding the children?"

Realization slowly and triumphantly crossed Abigail's face. "Hand me my phone!"

Noah half laughed and half groaned as Feng Zhou raked the chips from the center pile towards himself and stacked them neatly in his bank. "Did I tell you about this guy?"

"I only play the cards as they come." Feng shrugged, though his wide smile didn't fit the casual tone.

"Alright Dan." Bear shook his head reaching for his beer. "Deal."

"So, not to ruin the night." Dan said as he collected the cards and began to shuffle. "But I hear you are going to be running for President of the Homeowners' Association."

"Yea, I've been thinking about that." Noah leaned back in his chair. "I put my name in because there needed to be at least one person interested in the post or the property management team could just pick from their last pool of applicants." Dan had finished shuffling and started to deal one card at a time, Noah picking his up as they fell. "As far as I know that would be Joanna and Travis Ross. Not much of a regime change there. But just through conversations I've had and really thinking about it, I'm wondering if I'm really the best man for the job."

"I think you would do ok." Ferris said as he picked up his own stack of cards.

"But do we want just ok?" Noah insisted. "I think we should settle for nothing shy of excellent.'

"And just who do you think would be excellent?" Rob asked, trying not to scowl at his own hand.

"Well, Rob." Noah put his cigar down in the ashtray he and Bear were sharing and gave Rob a serious look. "I was actually thinking that you would fit the bill quite nicely."

"Me?"

"Yes you." Noah nodded, glancing down at his hand and then tossing his bet into the middle of the table. "Think about it. Really think about it. You're an attorney."

"*Was* an attorney." Rob shook his head, making his own contribution to the pot. "I'm retired."

"Fine, but you know the law. You know real estate." Most of the men around the table nodded at this. "You have the time I don't between work and family – you can really get the job done right. No one can say that with your own home and your daughter and your grandkids up the street that you aren't invested in this neighborhood. And besides…" Noah smiled as he discarded five cards. "People like you. You like them. You're not looking to scratch your ego. You just want to be an asset to your neighbors."

Before Rob could even think about formulating his answer to this, or to meet the expectant looks of the other men around the table, Tammy burst into the garage with a frantic look on her face and her cell phone pressed against her ear. "Dan! The police and fire department are at our house."

"What?!" Dan stood up then looked to the men around the table.

"Go." Noah said standing up from his chair, "We can come back to this. Feng do you need to go check on your house?"

"Yes. I think I will." He stood with a grim but knowing look on his face, followed closely by Bear Thyme.

"C'mon guys." Rob said, nodding to Ferris and Derik. "Let's go see what we can do to help."

He and Mary Beth grabbed their coats, rushing out the door behind their daughter his eyes falling on Bear who was on the phone, presumably with his 14-year-old son Tyler. He was being very measured in his words, but Rob could see the muscles on his jaw twitching. "Bring Scotus into the house and double check to see if all the doors and windows are locked and the alarm is on. Mom and I will be over in a little bit."

Zia and Derik were right on Rob's heels, walking up the street towards Blackjack Oak Parkway even though Zia was saying something about "papers". He stopped just for a moment as Derik tapped his shoulder. "You were an attorney?"

"Yes." Rob nodded, his gaze wandering to where the hint of red and blue lights flickered over the faces of sleeping houses. "I was a federal prosecutor for about twenty years, and had a private practice for twelve more after that."

"Zia doesn't have her ID on her." Derik sighed. "She's legal. But she didn't bring them to the party. Is this going to be a problem?"

"No." He shook his head. "But if she's really worried you two are more than welcome to wait at my house. Sometimes police officers read nervousness as criminality and that's not going to do her any good. "

"I'll stay with Zia." Alla volunteered. "You men go."

"Go into the back yard through the side gate." Mary Beth said, pointing to their house on the corner. "We left the sliding door unlocked. There is lunch meat and milk in the fridge and cookies in the hound dog jar on the counter. Just help yourself to whatever you want." The two women nodded and kicked off their heels so they could run across the greenway separating the houses on each block.

"Milk and cookies?" Rob said to his wife as they walked faster to catch up to Tammy.

"Not now." She hissed back squeezing his hand as they led Ferris and Derik up the street behind Noah, Dan and

Bear. All the neighborhood girls had opted for a slumber party at the Allens' and they came around the corner to see not just one, but three sheriff's units and a fire engine parked in the front of the house. Noah and Bear were engaged in a lively discussion with what must have been the patrol sergeant while a flock of little girls in their pajamas watched as a fire crew exited the wide-open front door. Rob could hear one of them shout "All clear" to the officer before they started putting away their gear. He came up behind Bear and Noah, a little out of breath as Tammy, Jenifer, and Lisa sorted their own broods out from the group to give everyone tearful hugs.

"What happened?" Rob asked as they reached Noah and Bear standing cross armed in the yard as the Sargent apologized to Tammy who looked like she was using all her strength to keep her cool.

"They said a neighbor called 911." Bear answered, his eyes never leaving the face of his ten-year-old daughter Jane clinging to her mother, her little bare feet stained from standing in the grass and the front of her My Little Pony nightgown drenched with tears. This had been her first sleep over and she had been thrilled to be included with the big girls, now she was pleading to go home. "Said they had been walking their dog and saw smoke coming out of the windows."

"Son of a ..."

"Rob. Look." Mary Beth cut him off pointing down the street behind her where Abigail Messenger and Travis and Joanna Ross were standing in the driveway drinking glasses of wine and watching the show.

"I'll do it." Rob said, turning back to Bear and Noah. "The HOA board. I'll run for president."

"Good." Noah said as his young daughters Lila and Macy left their mother to run across the lawn to where he stood.

CHAPTER 11

Comet Day +100
Meeting on Proposed Water Rights Extensions.
Room 203 of the Abigail Wilson Community Hall – Orein,
Nevada

Thom Jensen, one of the five county commissioners seated at the table commanding the room raised his hand for order. "I understand that everyone here wants to be heard. And we have opened the mic specifically, so you may all address your concerns. But we can't have these kinds of unproductive cross arguments, we just don't have time. Please, respect your fellow citizens and let each other speak. If you wish to counter an argument – by all means join the line behind the podium and voice your opinion. Now… please continue Ms. …" He looked down at his notes reaching for her name.

"Garza." Dalisay's voice boomed over the speakers as she leaned into the mic. "And thank you. All I am saying is that the world is changing. This whole idea of cowboys and cattle farming and the myth of rugged individualism is keeping our community from the kind of progressive growth which it so desperately needs." The room around her erupted again, some shouting counter opinions, some insults, some just shouting. "My husband…" she stopped for a moment, collecting her thoughts over the din, "my husband is a blackjack dealer in Reno. He has to commute over an hour just to earn his paycheck…"

"No one is forcing him to commute." Tim Barring's deep voice echoed from the back of the room. "You and yours could just move to Reno."

"But what about the other families like us in this community? We could use those jobs." A steady chorus of boos threatened to drown her out even with the help of the mic. "And now you are saying that the request to extend the permit for the Comstock Townhouse complex is probably going to be denied because the county lacks the current water resources when the answer is so simple. Cut off the ranchers and the farmers and make this place the population center it really wants to be."

"No one wants that here bitch!" some woman's voice carried out from the back.

"Hey. That's enough!" Marvin Ghidossi, the commissioner from district five, boomed out. "Deputy Yneko, find out who that was and escort her from the room. I will not have that kind of course language used in this meeting."

"Get your fucking hands off me!" A round faced Native American woman wearing a Water Rights are Washoe Rights T-Shirt shrieked, trying to pull her arm from Max Yneko's grasp as he half marched half dragged her towards the doors. "I have a right to be here! You people are talking about taking more water from the reservation for your fucking skyscrapers and …" but the rest was lost as the doors slammed shut behind them. The five councilmen covered their mics to confer with each other before Don Parks, the representative from district three, spoke into the microphone in front of him.

"Do we have any other members of the Orein Valley Native Community here?" Don asked as a spattering of hands went up in the back. "Ok. Please, if you have something which you would like to contribute find a place in the line. We know this is an entire county issue and we want to hear from you as well. Please continue Ms. Garza."

Dalisay looked at the hardened faces around her. "If we just make the ranchers move, we could have all the water we needed…"

"My family has been ranching this land since before this state joined the Union." Tim Barring stood up this time. "You cannot deprive me and mine of our property and our way of life just because you want more asphalt and brighter lights. There are places like that. And it ain't here."

"Ms. Garza." Loretta Bravo, the councilwoman from district two addressed Dalisay through her microphone. "Thank you. I think we have heard what you have to say."

"Next speaker please." Counselman Negewen from district three waved the line forward.

"Uhm Yes. Hello. I'm Kat Thurston." A woman in her mid-sixties with stringy long greying red hair and a tie-dyed Grateful Dead t-shirt stepped up to the podium. "And I have to say that some of what Ms. Garza said I agree with." Groans broke out from around the room. "But I agree too that this project is not what our beautiful valley needs. We don't need more people here. We need fewer. I think we forget that we – human beings – we're just visitors here. We are just passing through this eternal earth and we treat it like we own it. No one can own this land. No one *should* own this land. But I agree, the cattle ranchers and the farms - look at the damage they've done by removing native plants and species. This land was perfect just as it was before we ruined it all, and we should attempt to return to that harmony. We should adjust our way of life, embrace xeriscaping and recycling. Consume less. Give more back."

"I would like to remind those here." Counselman Negewen was seated sideways in his chair, his leg crossed at the ankle and his notes in his lap, but as he spoke into his microphone, he turned forward to give Kat Thurston a very serious look. "Grey County has enshrined the right to farm within its charter. We are not here to discuss whether or not the current ranchers or farmers should be permitted to maintain their water rights but rather if the county should allow an extension of the Comstock Townhouse project permit as has been proposed. If we agree that means that the county will have to reassess land values and propose bonds county wide in order to build the needed support systems not just for the construction but for the increase in residents. That's money which we might not get even if we do grant the extension because the voters of this county might not appreciate the higher taxes."

"I would pay any taxes it took to return this beautiful valley to her natural state." Kat interrupted him. "I would give everything I own."

"I'm sure you would." Counselman Negewen sighed. "And if you can convince your neighbors to join you, I invite you to put such a measure to the counsel by regular means. But that is not the purpose of this meeting. Do you support the extension, yes or no?"

"No, councilman." Kat's face was red as she scowled at him from over her glasses. "I do not."

"Thank you for your time." He turned back in his chair. "Next speaker please."

"Hi I'm Tom Bishop. I own Thunder Bar over on Red Light Row." A burly man with a shaved head, his massive arms covered in tattoos came up to the microphone. "I'm also a volunteer firefighter with Orein Second Station. I don't have a lot to say, except that I don't think the townhouses are a great idea. We're already close to max carrying capacity for water table consumption in this area and if any of you remember the Bullfrog Fire out of Twain Canyon -I worked that one and it was a bitch to put out. There was a large amount of damage that could have been avoided, not just to the few historic cabins that were out there but to the hillside itself because we couldn't get water to it fast enough and the winds weren't working with us to get an adequate break.

"USGS is saying that area along the upper shelf of the canyon will most likely slide the next good rain we get because we lost so much juniper up there." Tom paused, giving them all time to mull that information over. "Right now it looks fine because it's got a heavy load of snow, but if we get a quick melt that's just as bad. That means floods and mud down here in the valley. We were flying in tankers from Washoe Valley and Tahoe and they just weren't getting here in time. Putting a bigger load on the water table isn't the answer so I say no to really any further development."

"Thank you, Mr. Bishop." Counselman Jimmy Olsen from district one nodded at him. "And thank you for your service to our community. Next speaker please."

The meeting continued on this bend, finally breaking up around five when Counselman Negewen called adjournment, almost immediately he was thronged by concerned cattlemen who owned some of the smaller spreads in the Orein Valley. They had gone into cattle production because it had been a lifelong dream and they especially didn't like the tone of some of the discussion tonight and needed reassurance that they weren't going to wake up in the morning with a county water man on their front porch looking to cap their well heads. Mike looked at Becca where she sat with Sammy sleeping in her lap, Jack had laid his head against his sister's arm and was snoring softly from under his little wide brimmed black felt cowboy hat. He was proud of Louise for not complaining or shoving him off, she was really starting to show a lot more maturity these days. He reached down and ignoring the cramp in the small of his back lifted Jack into his arms and led his family out of the doors in the back.

"Hey Mike." Tim Barring caught up to him at the stairs, walking beside him as they made their way down towards the lobby of the community hall. "I was hoping you would show up tonight. Saves me the drive out to find you. I understand you've taken some days off from the mine?"

"Same as I did last year." Mike nodded. "We just finished our vax'n brand. Have some fall cows I want to be home to keep an eye on. Might just make that my regular rotation as I'm getting some pretty good results. I don't go back again until after Thanksgiving. And then I'm not really getting any days away from the Copperhead until May when the kids have the big state stock show."

"I remember those days." Tim's eyes went a little misty as the years rolled back in his mind. "Your kids doing any dairy this year?"

"I keep telling Louise she should." Mike turned and gave his daughter walking just a few paces behind a meaningful smile. She had been doing that of late, silently shadowing him and absorbing his conversations like a sponge. "But she's got this little two-year heifer she's been finishing, hoping to grab some ribbons. Louise only has eyes for the sponsors dinner and auction."

"Well, if she's looking to branch out, I have a couple of does in milk I need off the feed bill which I would be willing to exchange for a little heavy lifting." Tim's tone was so offhand Mike almost didn't recognize the underlying message. Becca on the other hand did.

"What kind of lifting?" She asked, her tone light but her eyes glittering. She had been admiring Cathy Barring's little herd of American Alpines for some time now and would move heaven and earth to get one dry, much less two in milk.

"Just the usual stuff." Tim said as the group left Abigail Wilson Hall and stepped out into the parking lot heading towards Mike's big black Ford Super Duty. He spoke while Mike buckled Jack into his booster, taking the sleeping boy's hat off to lean him against the baby seat in the center of the back bench while Becca strapped in Sammy. Louise stood by quietly hanging on to every word. "I need someone who can cut out the calves or run an iron. The crew I hired last year is out working some bigger place in Oregon, I'd ask Dex and Bobby up but they have their hands full just trying to keep the dude ranch they're running down in Henderson from going tits up. Coy and LeAnna have their own spread in Idaho and have the same issue I have finding people who know how to run an iron and a Newberry knife. Maggie's in Anchorage with her husband, they can't make it down right now, and Byrd would like to forget the Nevada sand in his blood." Tim leaned against the bed of the truck shutting his mouth firm, feeling he had already said too much.

"I don't know Tim. Sounds like you might need my

whole A team here." Mike pulled a can of Copenhagen from his back pocket and packing it against his palm, offered some first to the older man before taking his own. He had been out to the Barring's place for their Fourth of July celebration, it was well over five-hundred acres cutting back into canyons with prime pasture irrigated naturally off the marshes formed in the bends of meanders off the Leavitt River – not counting the additional two-hundred-acre area behind their property line the Barring's grazed on lease from the Bureau of Land Management. That was a lot of ground to cover, and a lot of head – the Barring's had over three hundred. "Becca can punch and rope with the best of them if your wife doesn't mind hanging on to Sammy while she works."

"Oh, she won't!" Tim chuckled a little bit. "You might have a hard time getting your tot back though. She's like one of my good nurse cows. If she gets to holding a baby, she loves it like it's her very own and begrudges the eventual separation."

"Louise here is clean with the nutter." Mike affectionately pinched his daughter's cheek. "And Jack can almost give a vaccine without sticking himself first." Tim laughed at this. "And I can help you with pens and irons so there's at least a three crew we can give you." He was silent for a moment, debating if he should horse trade up a bit. And then arriving at a decision said. "I tell you what. I'll take your two goats but I need something else too. I've got five open heifers now and I'll have another ten next September. Think you might be able to supply them with a gentleman caller as well?"

"You've got beefmasters, right?" then to Mike's nod. "If you don't mind a grade out with my Limousine ..." his voice trailed off asking Mike to fill in the blank.

"I don't. I'm just looking at market weight, not papers."

"I could bring over Showtime. He throws a sound calf. He can get a bit stinky in the pen but he's a one minded man when it comes to the ladies."

"Well Tim. I think we have a deal."

"All right then." Tim smiled and held out his hand. No sooner had Mike taken it to seal the deal a low guttural rumble filled the air, seeming to come from everywhere – the sky, the row of slippery elm along the front of the parking lot, the ground beneath them.

"What on earth?" Tim looked around and suddenly both men were thrown to the ground. Mike hit the pavement hard knocking the wind from his lungs. He thought he saw Tim smack into the side of the truck on his way down. Somewhere behind him Louise was screaming, and Becca was calling his name over and over again begging him to tell her he was alright. The earth bucked and rolled as the rumbling grew louder, and Mike watched as the tires of his truck lifted slightly on its suspension while the asphalt beneath them jittered, rocking the cab.

People ran from the community hall, falling on the walk outside as the ground beneath them swayed. Mike crawled over to where Louise was lying flat on her stomach just inches from the gnashing tires, her mouth covered in blood from a split upper lip, the driver's side door swinging wildly above her head. He stood, riding the asphalt like a giant wave and pressing his back against the door to keep it open as he scooped Louise up from between his legs and helped her to scramble into the cab yelling for her and Rebecca to buckle up.

More screams and car alarms sounded as the foundation of the meeting hall cracked with the sound of a blast, the windows of the northside blowing out into the parking lot and the west wall crumbling in a cascade of brick and plaster. He grabbed the first aid kit he kept under the driver's seat and half walked half stumbled to where Tim was crawling blindly away from the truck, his face a mask of blood. Mike sat down in front of him, and ripping a bag of saline from the kit and popping the cap at the end used it to flush the gore from Tim's head so he could locate the wound, binding it with gauze while the world danced madly around him. The slippery elm crashed to the ground and a massive crack formed in the parking lot. Across the street the school building sank into the earth like a ship into a boiling sea as the beams and supports of the ancient mine beneath it snapped like matchsticks.

"We're next!" Tim cried out as they watched the library behind the school swallowed up by the earth, followed by a row of Victorian houses behind. Across town the bell in the tower of Saint Michaels, the oldest original structure in the valley, clanged wildly as the building swayed and rolled like a dinghy in rough seas before it too fell into the earth.

"No." Mike shook his head, holding and lashing the bandage as tightly as he could. "The mine doesn't come out this far. It stops under the school and cuts north towards the Sheriff's station and then under the old McGill ranch."

"Hank McGill was a drunk son-of-a-bitch who left his wife swimming in debt with two hundred head of scrawny cows." Tim responded. "That place can go."

Then just as suddenly as it had started, the quake and the rumbling fell into almost ear-splitting silence leaving the pale November sky to blacken as fires sprang up in town like candles held by mourners at a vigil.

"Mike." He looked up from where he sat, holding Tim Barring to his chest like a rescue swimmer. Becca stood over him with a couple of the shovels he kept in the back of the truck, the side of her face starting to bruise and swell where the initial shake had tossed her from her seat like a ragdoll, her face striking the dash. Behind them Sammy was squalling for her mother, refusing Louise's comfort as Jack whimpered with fear. "Mike." She said again, her voice as calm as if she were waking him from a nap in his hammock, but her eyes burning with urgency. "We have to put that fire out, and shut off the gas to the building. And we have to try to get people out."

"Do you have a shovel for me?" Tim asked looking at her hands clinched like iron rings around the handles.

"No." she said gently. "I have a front bench in the truck where you are going to lie down until an ambulance can get here. Louise is in the back with the kids, she's going to look out for you. Keep you awake until they show up."

CHAPTER 12

Comet Day +101
Trapper Hotel Bar - Pinefare, Montana

"The Ring of Fire erupted with fury late yesterday evening in what experts call a massive tectonic swarm." The TV above the bar at the Trapper Hotel was turned to a cable news station and was up louder than usual as several of the town's residents had gathered there for breakfast and a view of the outside world. Sissy Wagner had shooed her usual crowd over and was currently helping wait tables, listening in between orders and running plates. Few residents of Pinefare owned television sets, and of those who did few had a cable connection.

Those who were willing to pay out the monthly fees still came into the Trapper for their morning news so as not to be left out of the friendly gatherings over coffee and bacon. The town relied on the Trapper as a sort of informational and cultural hub, and at the heart of it all was Daisy humming away behind the bar keeping plates moving from the kitchen to Sissy's tray. Morgan had kept a news stand in the lobby since the eighties which did marginal business, but it was Daisy who brought in the flat screen TVs and cable networks during the renovation. This was where the people of Pinefare gathered to watch major news events, Presidential Inaugurations, Stanley Cup Finals, and Miss America pageants.

Late last night the ground had tremored, the only small earthquake in the region even the older residents could remember, and the HAM radio channels had lit up. An aquifer had bubbled to the surface on the Mule Wash Ranch washing out a portion of an old logging road up on Inch Ridge as it cut through snow and ice like butter. It hadn't caused any real damage but the wash, dry for at least the past fifty years not counting the occasional spring runoff, was now a full-fledged creek flowing swiftly on its nearly forgotten course joining the Flatbow River which filled Inch Lake just north of town. South along the edge of State Highway 39 running towards the City of Wein and its corresponding dam, truckers reported a massive sinkhole opening up inside a fallow field of wheat and in almost shark like fashion eating up the dirt towards the shoulder.

"I think that might be the old landfill." Len Hall's voice had buzzed over the airwaves, awakened from his rest by the gentle sway of his trailer in the quake. "They covered it over sometime in the late thirties."

"Over the course of twenty-four hours," the pretty blond reporter on the news vanished, as footage of various locations began to play though at times the picture fuzzed and pixelated while the signal adjusted, "there have been massive earthquakes in Greece and Coastal Italy, followed by new eruptions of the Kilauea volcano in Hawaii and the Aleutian Islands in Alaska. This area hasn't seen any notable activity since the June 2017 eruption which shut down commercial air travel. In the early morning hours residents of Karuizawa and Miyota, Japan were awakened to the sound of municipal alarms, scientists there have stated the nearby Mount Asama is showing early signs of impending eruption. Evacuations have been ordered for this and several other locations.

"The US Pacific Warning Center has issued alerts for the Philippine Islands as well as the tiny islands of Palau and Colonia as they have been tracking several large earthquakes off the coast of Taiwan. No stranger to tectonic activity, there were several quakes overnight in the State of California – a 5.2 was registered along the San Andreas outside of McKittrick just before midnight and five minutes later a smaller 4.3 quake shook the residents of Palm Springs. Earth scientists are more interested in the larger earthquakes which have registered on smaller fault lines not thought to be very active. The small mining town of Orein, Nevada experienced a whopping 6.5 on the Richter scale, a quake which devastated many of the main buildings in town. The quake originated deep within the Opal Mountain range but scientists from the University of Nevada at Reno say this particular quake was so devastating because of older mines which honeycomb under the town. Five casualties and multiple injuries are reported. Further north the USGS station in Flathead County, Montana registered a smaller quake in an area which was not thought to have an active fault zone. In a phone interview resident Geologist and National Park Ranger Peter Sanders described the event."

A cheer went up from those gathered in the Trapper as mugs were raised to toast Pete, who smiled sheepishly from the bar where Daisy was serving him a steaming platter of biscuits and gravy. His voice came over the tv, hollow because the station had conducted the interview over the phone. "We think this may have been a smaller fault which has newly formed. We're waiting for the University in Bozeman to give us their assessment on magnitude as we don't have a monitoring station close enough to give us a good reading. Just feeling it from personal experience I would guess it to be with in the two and a half to three and a half range. One of the interesting occurrences following the quake itself is a renewed activity of alluvial sources which we had thought completely dormant."

"That's it?" Pete joked. "I was on the phone with them for about half an hour."

"We're small potatoes." Sissy patted his back in an almost motherly way as she walked by. Pete was one of her favorite transplants, he fit right in with the rest of the town's residents and worked hard to be a member of the little community.

"Alright local he-rod." Gyp Masters yelled out from the back, his voice already rough around the edges with whiskey and dripping in sarcasm.

"Shut the hell up Gyp." Sissy sang sweetly. "And drink your coffee." He glowered back at her but had learned through hard experience not to cross Sissy Wagner if he wanted to eat at her café. Hers was about the only table left in town which would host him, Daisy only letting him back in by Sissy's kind request, and Lord knew neither he nor his wife could cook anything other than canned SpaghettiOs and, on the days they were straight, maybe methamphetamines.

"South America too has had its share of geological activity." The anchor continued from the screen, "With 7.2 earthquakes registering in Quito, Ecuador and La Paz, Bolivia; a 6.5 in Esquel, Argentina and a 6.2 reported off the Peruvian coast." The screen was suddenly filled with a large floating icon announcing Breaking News followed by a heavy ominous tone. It dissolved again as the reporter reappeared, "We are now receiving breaking news from across the globe. An hour ago, a 7.1 earthquake struck Erzurum, Turkey, toppling structures. Early estimates say casualties could be in the tens of thousands as an entire block of apartments near their business district has collapsed. A similar earthquake has also occurred in Shamakhi, Azerbaijain where there are also high numbers of expected casualties. A tsunami warning has been issued now for the Northern coasts of Queensland, Australia as several large earthquakes are being reported in the Coral Sea. Evacuation efforts there are being hampered by unexpected interference with electronic communication devices …."

"Hey!" Nate Petty called out from his usual table near the large window overlooking the RV Park and Flatbow River. "That's about the same time all the HAMs cut out and my cell quit working."

"You don't have reception, Nate?" Daisy looked at him from over her register as she rang Mamie Blackman up for her breakfast.

"I have some." Nate shrugged, "But it's not working as well as it should. My calls are dropping, and when they finally get through reception is spotty. Twitter is down. What the hell is going on?"

"What if something happens?" Mamie said quietly to Daisy. "What if we need to call the hospital in Whitefish and we can't get through?"

"It's just a little interference." Pete looked at her consolingly. "It should clear up soon. I wouldn't worry."

"Ok folks." Daisy used her remote behind the bar to turn the screen on the wall off. "That's enough bad news for one day." There was a general grumbling of agreement as people returned to their plates while Sissy and Daisy made their rounds making certain every cup and belly were filled.

"What do you suppose is going on?" Len asked, turning in his bar stool towards Pete, nodding his thanks to Daisy for the refill.

"We live on an active planet is all." Pete smiled. "Alone these activities are major local events, but you package them all together like the news does and it seems even more ominous. I wouldn't worry too much."

"But how about our fault?" Daisy asked, arching her spine against the tightness in her back. Her clothes had become uncomfortable as of late and it wouldn't be long before she couldn't hide her growth any longer. Morgan had already noticed and confronted her, but in the end agreed to keep her secret for her as long as he could. Sissy Wagner kept eyeing her suspiciously every time she came behind the bar to refill the coffee pot, so that would not be much longer.

"Oh, he's just a shallow little guy." Pete flashed her a smile. "He won't hurt anyone. But we do get our own monitoring equipment now, which will be fun to play with. And the USGS has given me the go ahead to run a raffle of sorts here to name it."

"We get to name the fault?" Sissy came behind the bar and dropped off a stack of menus.

"Yup." Pete nodded taking a sip off his coffee. "I was actually going to ask if you and Daisy would work together on collecting suggested names and votes. Put up a display or something. Usually, they run these things in the newspaper."

"But we don't have one." Sissy nodded. "I could find some room on the café specials board. And Daisy you have the newsstand in the lobby. Remember when Morgan used to put the headlines up on the whiteboard in the back? That would make a good place to list the names people suggest." Pete paid for his meal, waving goodbye as Daisy collected his plate. The two women bussed the tables together, spreading the word among their diners and offered slips of paper and pens in the event someone had a name right off the top of their head. As they stepped into the kitchen with a stack of plates, Sissy took Daisy's load from her and dropping them off at the dishwasher station before waving a quick hello to Lodi Blackman working the grill. Then, grabbing Daisy by the hand, practically dragged her into the kitchen office, closing the door.

"Alright Missy." The older woman crossed her arms, a stern look on her face. "Which one of these nit-wits got you in this mess and what are you planning to do when you can't tie your apron anymore?"

Daisy's eyes brimmed with tears as she gave Sissy a desperate look. "Is it that bad?"

"No." Sissy shook her head. "But you forget my mama was the midwife around here for years before people started driving into Whitefish. My sister and I used to make the rounds with her be it logging camp or cattleman's wife or the occasional outlaw cat house. I say you have about a month left and everyone is going to know. And you know how tongues wag in this town. Now, who's is it and what is he planning to do to help you out?"

"I haven't told him yet."

"You haven't... Daisy! You can't keep something like this to yourself! It's not fair to you, it's not fair to the baby. It's not fair to the father."

"It's complicated Sissy." Daisy sighed as she sat

down on a stack of pickle buckets, then immediately stood back up as the waistband of her jeans cut into her painfully. "And besides, I haven't really had the chance. He's not been back into town. And I don't have a number for him."

Sissy did some mental calculations, arriving at "The fourth of July. That good looking bronc rider who knocked Gyp's front tooth loose when he relieved himself on the bandstand. Well shit, girl. You sure picked a showstopper." At this Daisy broke down and started to cry. Sissy gathered her in for a motherly hug. "Now, come on. None of that. Everything is going to work out. It would have been a nightmare had it been one of the local men as all the good ones are married and the rest are about as useless as tits on a fence post. You have a good life here, Daisy. And a lot of love to offer. And lots of people who love you. This baby may be from the wrong side of the sheet but he won't be the first one born in this town, and certainly not the last. Does Morgan know?"

Daisy nodded as she blew her nose. "There's one other thing." She sniffed, collecting herself for a moment. "It's twins."

Sissy sighed, sitting down on a pickle bucket. "That is a problem. I hate to say it Daisy, but we got to tell Sassy if Morgan hasn't already."

"I know."

"Because we all know who is going to be the prime suspect when that little nugget gets out."

"I know." Daisy sobbed into her apron. "Sissy. He's been like a brother to me. This is going to ruin him in this town and it's not even his fault."

"Well now calm down." Sissy Wagner stood up, smoothing the wrinkles out of her jeans. "We'll boil that kettle of fish when the time comes. In the meantime, stay in here and fix your face. I'll finish the breakfast service."

The Acropolis - Red Mountains, Utah

"Yes." Hunter leaned back in his chair to put his feet up on his desk, opening the file on his lap and skimming the contents. "That's right it's a fully funded private concierge practice." There was a slight pause as he waited for the response on the other end. "No. Nothing like that. We're not looking for someone to rubber stamp a scrip pad. We're looking for someone to actually practice medicine for a small group of clients... Well right now your patients would consist of one elderly gentleman at his home and later provide a general clinic for his staff. You wouldn't even have to leave your current practice just give us a few days every month. During that time we provide steady pay, some very attractive fringe benefits, all travel expenses... I have a presentation I would like to show you about this if you have time.... Uh yes, let me look at my calendar."

Hunter paused for a minute, clicking through his schedule on the screen. "Yes, we can absolutely do this after the first of the year. Yes, the twelfth is perfect. In fact, let me host you in Las Vegas. It's close enough that if you like what we have to offer we can take the company jet to our location for you to take a tour. Yes. Las Vegas. Which of the casino's is your favorite? We'll put you up in the penthouse all expenses paid...." He stopped as the voice on the other end once again took on a skeptical tone. "Well Dr. McCrory to be quite honest we have a copy of your resume and we are extremely impressed. We work with a couple of groups who help veterans transition into the civilian workforce and your name came up in discussion."

That part was a flat out lie. Goodwin's brother had pulled a stack of military service records for them to go through after Hunter had suggested that the only place they were going to find the kind of well-rounded doctor Luke wanted would be someone who had spent his time in a MASH unit. "The Bellagio? Absolutely. Give me about an hour and I'll fax over all the travel information and your flight confirmation. Yes. You too. Goodbye."

He hung up and took a breath before he tapped the intercom notification on the small computer tablet built into his desk. It had been flashing for about a half hour, but he had been ignoring it while he finished some calls. "Hunter?" Goodwin's voice came through the tablet, he sounded stressed.

"Hey Luke, sorry about that. I was on the phone."

"Not a problem." Goodwin's voice echoed up from the desk. "Do you have a moment now?"

"I do." Hunter gathered a couple of files as he stood up from his chair. "I have some news for you anyway."

"Wonderful." Some of the gloom lifted from Goodwin's voice. "I'm in my study."

Hunter walked out of his office and through the little parlor which attached his apartment to the rest of the building, down the gallery and across the large open salon to the grand staircase which led to Goodwin's personal chambers. The study was a large open room with a hearth and several overstuffed chairs outside a bank sized vault. Hunter remembered having to catch his breath when he saw the amount of gold and jewelry Goodwin had been quietly squirreling away. The riches in the vault didn't even register a tenth of what the family was worth, but it was a considerably sized physical manifestation of the billions of numbers stored digitally across several national and international banks. He stopped short of the door and knocked.

"Come in!" Goodwin called from the other side and then as Hunter opened the door, "You don't have to knock. You are welcome in any room of this house."

"I just want to respect your space." Hunter smiled as he closed the door behind him. Goodwin was sitting on a large leather couch to the left of the door, a roaring fire in the hearth warming the marble tile on the floor. "I had a roommate in college and believe me! I learned to respect privacy just for privacy's sake."

Goodwin gave him a harried look, spinning his own tablet around to reveal a newscast describing a massive earthquake somewhere in the Nevada wasteland. "Have you seen this?" and when Hunter shook his head the older man sighed. "That could have been it. The big one. We could have been caught with our pants around our ankles and our cheeks smeared with... well, never mind. I have information, but you go first. What's your news?"

"I have three candidates," Hunter said, taking in Goodwin's obvious agitation, "but none of them want to meet until after the holidays." Goodwin scowled as he pulled his reading glasses from his shirt pocket and took the files which Hunter offered him. "Doctor Gou out of Massachusetts won't be able to meet until February."

"Did you dangle Vegas?" Goodwin gave Hunter an exasperated look. "The Chinese love Vegas."

"He's from Texas where he went to college on a baseball scholarship." Hunter responded, "And yes. I did."

"And still nothing sooner?"

"Nope."

"Damn. Ok then February. And the other two?"

"Doctor Corker out of Illinois will meet us on the first. I think he sees this as a free New Year's trip to Vegas for the wife."

"And we have the official story down?" Goodwin paused "No prepper news? No tour of the *full* facility?"

"As far as any of these candidates are concerned, I'm representing a chain of luxury retreats catering to the discerning billionaire."

"Excellent." Goodwin looked at him over the top of his glasses. "That, Hunter, was a stroke of genius. Then come any sort of event we just send the security team and the jet and presto! Our doctor is on site. And the third?"

"Doctor McCrory out of Kansas City." Hunter said.

"We meet with him on the twelfth of January. Now he is a little different from the other candidates as he isn't married. But he's young – thirty-eight – and healthy and I'm certain given the right circumstances the family situation will work itself out naturally."

"Well…" Goodwin looked unsure.

"Luke. It isn't an issue. His performance reviews are stellar, he did two tours in Iraq and another in Afghanistan, I really like this guy." He smiled. "Besides, we're taking him to Vegas. Worst case scenario I drag him through the strip clubs and have him pick out a model. Something with good gas mileage and leather seats."

"Ha. Ha." Goodwin said dryly though a hint of a smile played at the edge of his lips. "I trust you, Hunter. This is absolutely something you can handle."

"Good." Hunter said. "I just have to finalize his travel package and it's done. What's your news?"

"Well, while you have been toiling away rowing the ship by yourself, this happened." Goodwin picked up a remote and turned on a flat screen tv above the fireplace mantle. It was already tuned into a major news network, areal footage of a small town in Nevada which had been all but destroyed by a massive earthquake. "There have been a swarm of these events over the past twenty-four hours." Goodwin sighed. I need you to check back in with the USGS, make sure we haven't the same liabilities here. Also, I want you to talk with that researcher out of Dartmouth again… Tamir… something."

"Tamir Sang." Hunter nodded. "You're wondering about that paper connecting tectonic activity with solar interference in the magnetosphere." Over the roughly three and a half months Hunter had been working with Goodwin he had become well versed in every possible contingency which could end life on earth as they knew it. Every conspiracy theory, every paper published on the internet by crackpots and doomsayers, every religious text from the Bible to the Pali

Canon to the Poetic Edda. If someone was wearing a sandwich board that said the end was near – it was his job to know their dogma by verse. He even had his favorites from the Sweet Meteor of Death which just sounded exciting to the rise of a mutant version of the Nipah Virus becoming airborne and wiping out 85% of the world population."

"Yes. Him!" Goodwin nodded a bit too enthusiastically.

Hunter gave the older man a serious look, "When was the last time you slept?" and when this question was waved off, he asked, "How about the last time you've eaten? Have you at least had lunch?"

"I have not." Goodwin muttered darkly.

"Would you care to dine with me?"

"I … uh…" Goodwin stammered as he looked around, obviously taken back by the invitation as Hunter collected his files and headed back towards the door. "

"Let me finish Dr. McCrory's file and I'll join you here?" He said gently as a small smile broke through the shadows weighing down Goodwin's face. "I'll have the steak this time I think."

"Very good then." Goodwin nodded reaching for his tablet to place the order with the kitchen as Hunter left the room.

The restructuring of The Acropolis from super-secret hyper-lux doomsday bunker hadn't just been for the benefit of screening medical candidates. Hunter had gone through his first afternoon in his office getting his feet wet in the work and realized there were no restaurants within good driving distance. Refusing to live off whatever canned goods which Goodwin kept in the kitchen pantry or worse – the MREs stacked in the basement – he had convinced Goodwin to hide the vestibule elevator behind a thin veneer of sheetrock which could be easily smashed down in case of emergency and to form an LLC which would allow them to take on a small staff. They had hired a chef and two live in housekeepers who stayed in the "servant's wing" on the ground floor beneath Goodwin's apartment – the warren of interconnecting hallways between the walls also covered over and hidden from plain view along with the door connecting his section of the house with the stables outside the outer wall.

As far as the staff were concerned Mr. Goodwin was an eccentric hotelier who rarely had guests at his personal B&B, and thanks to a large built-in bookshelf on a heavy-duty sliding hinge not even the maid had seen the vault. Life was far more civilized now, and he had noticed a change in Goodwin to match. His urgency had subsided as he really began to enjoy his home, rather than feeling absolutely disconnected from the outside world. Hunter planned to finish his task of bringing on the "spa physician" as the job title was written and then suggesting that perhaps Goodwin purchase some actual resorts to act as income and further legal camouflage for The Acropolis itself. Small B&Bs and Inns, or maybe a dude ranch, to keep this location from sticking out on a tax document were prime candidates. And who knew – Goodwin might accidently make a little money back to replace all that had hemorrhaged in The Acropolis' construction.

When he arrived back in his office the intercom light was flashing again.

"Hey Luke." He said tapping the tablet.

"Chef wants to know if you want the foie gras and caviar hour d'vours as well?"

"Tell him yes." Hunter signed off making a mental note to suggest over lunch that Goodwin build a gym in one of the wings. Lucy would not appreciate the softening of his waistline if this kept up much longer.

CHAPTER 13

Comet Day +150
Flyboys Bar and Grill – St. George, Utah

"Flooding?" Hunter dipped his roast beef sandwich into the little brown ramekin of au jous, watching as the bread greedily sucked up the slick of oil across the top. "How bad?"

On the other end of the line in the middle of their living room Lucy ran her toes over the marshmallowey fluff of her new angora rug. "Well, it's been raining for days, typical. They say the Gila is up to the point that they're shutting down roads and parts of the highway."

"The Gila?" Hunter took a bite of his sandwich and chewed for a bit before he answered. "Baby if the Gila is flooding that's all the way out in Buckeye. It's nothing but farmland out there. They could use the water."

"Okay." Lucy scowled, the irritation creeping into her voice. "But yesterday they had to shut down parts of the 60 and the 10 because the Salt River was full. Even the airport closed." She pouted slightly. "I couldn't even get to Cabo if I wanted to."

"It's monsoon season in Cabo too, sweatheart." Hunter said, taking another bite.

"God! Do you have to do that right in my ear?" Lucy hissed. "I couldn't even get into Scottsdale to hit up Saks or Barneys…"

"Oh no!" Hunter laughed, "Not Barneys! Say it ain't so!"

"Isn't." Lucy groused, correcting him. "All I'm saying is you've been away, and I've been stuck in the house. We didn't even spend New Year's together. I'm just sick of the mileage. Come home."

"I can't. I really wish I could." He sighed. "I have

enough time for this sandwich while they're going through preflight and I'm off again."

"To Las Vegas." She sighed "That place is so fucking tacky."

"I know." He dipped a french-fry into his ketchup. "When I'm done here, I promise we'll take a week off and go somewhere nice. How does Fiji sound?"

"Wet." She walked into the bedroom and slumped down on the side of the bed. "And diseased."

"Ok, how about Monaco?"

"I don't really feel like hitting up the Mediterranean this year. Remember how dirty the beaches were?"

"Ok. Where would you like to go?"

"We've done Paris, and Rome…" she looked at her nails, inspecting in detail the perfect polish on her French tips. "I could do Barcelona for a week."

"Barcelona it is."

"I love you."

"I love you too." He put the french-fry in his mouth. "Put the munchkin on the phone."

Lucy groaned slightly, then pulling the phone away from her ear shouted into the living room. "Bella. Bella!" and then rolling her eyes as her daughter bounced into the room handed her the cell phone "Your daddy wants to speak to you."

"Hi Daddy!" Bella said excitedly. "Are you coming home?"

"No baby. I'm sorry. But hey, I thought we could go to the zoo when I get back into town."

"I like the zoo! I want to see the big cats this time. Can we?"

Bored listening to her daughter's side of the conversation, Lucy stood up from the bed and looked herself over in the mirror. Prada never let her down, and always complimented her exquisite figure. Always. Especially this crepe de chine in billowy white just skimming her at midthigh.

Not so high as to suggest she had a price, but not so low as to suggest she couldn't be had. She listened to Bella droning away, her ratty tangle of auburn hair bouncing just as often as she did. It was almost too much to bear. She blew kisses into the phone for Hunter as Bella demanded, saying byes and I love you, but her heart and mind were on that vixen staring back at her in the mirror. That woman was powerful. That woman was young. There's no way that woman has had a child my gawd she looks amazing.

"Sarah?" Lucy called as she made a quick adjustment to her lipstick and walked out of her bedroom door and stepped into the Manolo Blahnik Doit Rosette caged sandals she already had waiting in the foyer. "I have my cell phone. Please don't call. I mean obviously if you have to go to the hospital – but otherwise I'm just not available. You'll understand when you have kids just how important these nights away really are for your sanity. Anyway – credit card is on the counter. Order whatever Bella wants. Stay off the freeways if you go anywhere, stay out of the warehouse district, and I'll see you tomorrow sometime around lunch. I don't know. Maybe three-ish."

"Bella." Sarah called softly to the little girl who had resumed her place on the couch after hanging up the phone, already dressed in her pjs and settling in to watch a marathon of Disney Princess movies. "Come say goodbye to Mommy."

"Don't get up sweetheart." Lucy waved her daughter back down to the couch. "Seriously Sarah, she'll crumple the dress. Bye baby. Mommy loves you. Bye Sarah. Have fun." Sarah waited until she heard the ding of the private elevator opening and then the whoosh of the doors closing again before turning from the door. You never knew when Lucy was going to come breezing back in after an eyelash curler or a different pair of heels. Once the door to the elevator had closed however it was a safe bet she was well away. Sarah felt a tug at her sweatpants leg, she looked down and smiled at Bella's heart shaped face and smoothed the silky waves of the little girl's beautiful auburn locks with her hand.

"Sarah." Bella whispered, her eyes darting to the door. She too was used to her mother's sudden returns. "Can I call Nana and Pop-pop again?"

Sarah bit her bottom lip, thinking. "Let's give it a few minutes. It's not too late yet and they could be having dinner."

"Ok." Bella looked so disappointed Sarah wanted to cry.

"Hey. Should I order a pizza?"

"Can I have a salad? Mommy says pizza is making me too fat."

"Oh Bella. Sweetheart." Sarah scooped her up off her feet and held her close. Some days she would just love to knock that Lucy Church right out of her fancy heels and square onto her flat little ass. "Honey. You couldn't be fat if you tried. Look at you. Light as a feather." She lifted the little girl up in the air as if she were doing a barbell curl, giving her raspberries on the tummy with every set. Bella erupted in giggles begging "Again! Again!" every time Sarah took a rest.

"We don't have to have pizza if you don't want it." Sarah finally said sitting her down. "What would you like instead?"

"What's the place with the really big fish sticks?"

"Do you mean Lighthouse? The one over by the zoo?" Bella nodded. "You want the same thing we had last time? The fish and chips? With the fruit cup or the Jell-O?"

"Jell-O!!" Bella threw her arms in the air and did a little happy dance.

"Ok. Let me see if they're on the delivery app. If not, we might have to order from somewhere else." Sarah pulled her phone from her back pocket and scrolled through her home screen to find the app, thinking that there had been enough time for Lucy to have gotten into the car waiting downstairs. "Then after I order, we can call your grandparents." Sarah rocked on her feet as Bella threw herself onto her leg, hugging it close with unbelievable strength. She was only four and small for her age, but when her heart led the way, she could be mighty.

"I love you, Sarah."

Sarah hugged Bella back, bending down to give her a little kiss on the nose. "I love you too kiddo." Sarah's heart felt like a thousand knives had just gone through it. How was she going to tell Bella that this week was going to be their last one together? She would need the time off for finals, and then there was commencement, and she was moving on. She blinked back tears as she found the Lighthouse Grill listed on the app on her phone.

1002 Yellow Jack Place - Baptiste, Idaho

The knock echoed through the house, heavy and authoritative. Jenny came to the door wiping the dish soap from her hands with a kitchen towel while Macy and Payton covied at her heels, just inside fourteen-year-old Beau held baby Aaron – all faces curious to see who was at the door.

"Travis." Jenny's voice was calm and pleasant. "How are you?"

"I'm fine." He said looking over her shoulder into the house. "I just dropped by to remind you that this is a census year. I'm the resident federal officer in the neighborhood and I'm just reminding my neighbors that participation in the U.S. Census is federal law and you will be expected to comply."

"Are you reminding all the neighbors?" Jenny leaned against the frame of the door, blocking his view inside her house and staring him directly in the eye.

"No. Not all." He returned her gaze but cocked his head towards the flags in her yard. "Just those who have exhibited certain attitudes. Ones which might think themselves above the law."

"Travis." Jenny smiled sweetly at him. "I know very well why you are here. You are here because you know my husband and a few of the other men in the neighborhood are on a hunting trip and you think you can show up here and rough up his family a little. See if I call him, ruin his good time, make him come home to rescue me. And I understand that you think because I stay home, raise my children, and bake cookies that I'm a soft target." He opened his mouth to protest but she held up her hand to stop him. "Now I'm going to go back in my house and finish my dishes. Then I am going to make a call, but not the one you want. I'm going to call the office where you work and I'm going to lodge a complaint."

He smirked at this. "And when no one there gives a shit? What are you going to do then?"

"Then neighbor to neighbor let me tell you." Jenny lowered her voice, "You darken my door again you will regret it. Be careful not to slip on the ice on your way back down the walk."

Travis was still standing there his mouth agape as the door slammed in his face.

Connor Creek, Oregon

Noah looked down from the outcropping of rock to where Whiskey and Tango were leashed to a stand of aspen, whining plaintively against their muzzles. They could smell the big cat no doubt and were getting anxious. "Ok son." He said in a low even tone as he turned back to where Jefferson was lying prone beside him, the scope of his .308 DPMS AR-platform rifle trained on a stand of trees. "Just easy air."

"I know." Jefferson's voice was calm, controlled, as

he took a deep steadying breath.

"Now, double check to make sure it's a tom."

The barrel of the rifle moved minutely as he followed his father's instructions, slowly scanning the tawny animal as it hunched over a large log pulsing its claws through the rotting bark and snow. "I've got berries on the vine."

Noah looked to where Bear lay beside Jefferson, tucking his head into the crook of his arm to keep from laughing. Rob, Dave and Dan were just below on a little shelf and hadn't heard the quip as they slowly passed a pair of binoculars between them to get a better look at the cougar.

"Ok. You know what to do."

The barrel of the rifle moved back by a matter of centimeters as Jefferson reset his crosshairs over the crook of the cougar's forelimbs. Then he hooked the second knuckle of his right index finger firmly around the trigger. He released a long steady stream of air and squeezed.

"Direct hit!" Dan whooped from below as Whiskey and Tango did their level best to bay through their restraints.

"Well done son." Noah clapped Jefferson on the shoulder as Bear lifted his binoculars to watch the flurry of snow beyond the fallen log. "Now all we have to do is hike down there and find him."

Big Stakes Ranch – Henderson, Nevada

"Alright Dex!" Bobby called from the tail end of the squeeze shoot. "Let her out."

Dex climbed the heavy gage pole fencing on the side of the chute then reached down to pull the handle letting the massive cow come bounding out of the chute and into the round pen with the rest of the herd.

"Laura!" Bobby called out above the chorus of

disgruntled moos to where the slim blond sat astride a blue-eyed paint named Silo. "That one too! On the truck."

Laura nodded and clucking her horse into gear set about the work of cutting the big black cow out, encouraging her into a side pen where Jorge was working the gate while Hector and Piper used their horses as a blockade against the rest of the herd.

"Well, that's the last one." Bobby sighed. "We've got nothing left to cull if we want to be the least bit productive next year."

"They've got good weight on them." Dex said from his perch watching as Laura, Hector, and Piper moved on to the task of releasing the development head from the pen and driving them back out onto the fenced pasture. "Hey, who knew your bartender could vaquero like that."

"I did." Bobby's eyes scanned the dry yellow sage and buffalo grass outside the pen. "It's why I hired him. You'd be shocked to see Leticia from housekeeping get out here in the dirt, nut the hell out of some calves, and then switch hats and get back to dusting. Nothing but top hands around here. I won't accept anything less." He sighed, "Six split hooves, two sets of worn molars, and fifteen on the truck just because they're at their personal peak.... And no word from corporate on a replacement budget."

"I hear it's flooding in Phoenix." Dex turned to watch Jorge using a prod to encourage the culls up a platform and onto the waiting semi.

"Lucky bastards. We could use the water." Bobby sighed. "The one thing I miss from home – other than mom and dad."

"Rain?"

"Snow." Bobby sighed. "And those stupid snowman cookies mom used to sneak into our gloves when we did this with dad."

Dex let out a long breath in agreement.

Thunder Bar – Orein, Nevada

"Is this everyone?" Sheriff Ely Lane looked around at the small crowd, a hint of sadness in his tone.

"Tim and Cathy Barring are in the parking lot." Max Yneko replied, "They have Maggie and her husband with them, but we don't know how long they're in town this time."

Sheriff Lane nodded, then waved hello to Tim as he came in dusting the snow from his hat and coat in the doorway before begrudgingly allowing his daughter Maggie to guide him to one of the many empty tables in the bar, the big scar running from the side of his eye to the top of his scalp still red and angry. "All right, all right, I'm not a damn baby." The older man grumbled as Maggie fussed over him before taking her seat.

"Anything from the bar?" Tom Bishop asked.

"No." said Maggie as Cathy took her seat next to her husband, patting another open chair indicating her son in law Josh should take it.

"Coors." Tim replied earning a nod from the big bartender and a glower from his only daughter.

"Ok. First order of business." Ely said taking a seat on the edge of one of the bar tables where he could be seen by all gathered. "How many of you are holding votes for spouses and neighbors and do you have the paperwork?" Few hands came up. "Ok. There's not that many of you. Let's just read them out and I'll take the absentee slips when we're done." He pointed first to Jacob Lowery who was sitting beside his wife Gertie. "Jacob, who are you here for?"

"I'm representing Schertz Ranch. Mary won't come into town this close to the mine and Calvin won't leave her."

"Ok." Ely nodded, pointing to another hand. "Jake, who are you here for?"

"The Thurstons. They have some specific things they

want read."

"Of course they do." Ely's comment drew a few chuckles from the crowd. "Mike, I assume you are voting for Becca?"

"I am." He said.

"Your girl Louise could have watched the kids, she's old enough." Ely said with a smile.

"They have our kids with them." Ane Yneko spoke up from the side of the room. "Becca was kind enough to stay behind with them. Keep an eye on things." Ely nodded at this.

"Well, that seems to be it."

"Sheriff." Tim Barring tried to stand up, but thought better of it and stayed down – wincing slightly. "I would like for Maggie and Josh to be included in the vote. The sale of their land up north just went through and they put in an offer on the Roger's place this afternoon."

"Normally I would say no, but..." Ely sighed and crossed his arms, tucking his clipboard against his chest. "We all know the state of the market right now." Heads started nodding. All across the Orein valley "For Sale – Price Reduced" signs had sprung up like goathead with very few buyers looking to take a chance on the little town swallowed by the mine. Even the development corporation which had been dreaming of townhomes and apartment complexes dotting the iron-stained hills had pulled out for greener pastures.

As winter and tragedy choked off the supply of tourists, shops up and down the remaining historic districts in town had shuttered, "Space for Lease" signs hung from display windows like signal flags on the mast of a beleaguered ship. Aunt Rose's Candy Factory was the first to close after sixty-two years in business followed by the little photo studios which specialized in ole'timey tin type recreations where tourists could dress up as saloon girls or cavalry soldiers and mug stone faced for a fifty-dollar black-and-white photo.

Finally, the historic saloons and inns that counted on a steady flow of local business to make ends meet had locked their doors as the exodus had dried that well up too.

"Has the offer been accepted?"

"Not yet." Josh spoke up. "We put it in at the close of business. Just the way it worked out. We're still waiting to hear from the sellers."

"All right." Ely said thoughtfully, "All in favor of letting the Masters vote?" All but one hand went up, Ceciliee Goya's. Of all the residents she was the least hit by the loss of the town. She worked as an underwriter in Reno for a large insurance firm and lived predominantly off her alimony.

"What?" she demanded of the withering stares which came her way from the rest of the room. "Their offer wasn't accepted yet."

"It doesn't matter." Ely pinched the bridge of his nose. "The ayes have it. The Masters are permitted to vote. First order of business. New zoning for the town. Copperhead Mining Corporation has determined that every part of the town which was going to settle after the earthquake, at least for now, has. That means Red Light Row and Ore Springs Road are safe for habitation. The rest of the homes and businesses from Mark Twain east to Silver Canyon are to be condemned."

"What?" Ceciliee squawked from the back of the room. "That's my place! My son is home with my elderly mother right now! Do I need to go get him? And what about my horse?"

Ely turned to Deputy Yneko who nodded and immediately walked out the door, then turning back to Ceciliee he said "Max will go get them right now, so you can stay here. But yes, this means that you should find a place to stay tonight and we can escort you back in the morning with the remaining residents to pack their things. Mike if you could explain."

"These shafts weren't built to any uniform

measurements and were given just enough support to hold them up. Back in 1850 this wasn't too much of an issue, but it's been over a hundred and seventy years of ground percolation and shifting stresses. This quake was just too much for the structure to take. And to be honest – we don't know when or if we will get another good shake like that. Red Light Row and Ore Springs are fine because they're built over a solid shelf of bedrock that hasn't been touched, but there are old vent shafts and some exploration tunnels cut out all over from Mark Twain on. They wouldn't collapse as deeply as the main part of town but there's still a chance they could go. Copperhead doesn't think that the mine should be saved, or could be remediated safely. They're recommending a strategic demolition."

"Which brings us to our second order of business." Ely spoke over the murmur of dismay. "As you know our current post office is right in the middle of that area. The federal government does not have a new location to build a facility on, and they are now refusing to even consider keeping an office here unless we reincorporate. Based on our loss of population we are most likely not going to get a new building, but they might consider taking over one of the empty places over on Main Street. Either way if we don't have a charter, they aren't even going to talk to us. So, if you have any statements or proposals to put into a new charter now is the time to speak."

Jake Sanders stood up, rebalancing on his prosthetic leg, smiling a little sheepishly as he cleared his throat, "The Thurstons have asked me to present this statement to the group. Our fellow citizens, how fortunate are we that nature in all her wisdom has seen fit to grant us a new opportunity for rebirth! With a single stroke she has wiped away hundreds of years of white supremacist colonial occupation of native lands…"

"Jesus tapdancing hockey-sticks!" Ely broke in. "Sorry Jake but we can't be subjected to this right now." He walked over to the man and took the piece of paper and skimming it, "blah blah blah – greenways and solar energy – blah blah – oh for Pete's sake she's quoting Marx."

"All in favor of ignoring the Thurstons?" Tom spoke from behind the bar and this time every hand in the place emphatically went up.

"You're a good man for looking out for a neighbor Jake." Ely sighed patting him on the back as he sat back down. "But in this particular case we're hoping the Thurstons move on to pinker pastures. Anyone else?"

"Well." Ane said, "There is one thing which Kat Thurston got right." The room fell dead silent as she stood up, her hands shaking a bit under their scrutiny. "We are fortunate. We're all fortunate to be alive. We were all in the Abigail Wilson Community Hall. And thanks to providence and our neighbors everyone here got out alive. Sure, we were battered, and bruised, and terrified – but alive. Think about how much worse this could have been if more people were home, or the kids were in school and the library open. We've lost buildings. And neighbors. And friends. But we're still alive. There's a scripture I keep thinking about – Mike, it was actually Rebecca who read this to me the other day – it's the 30th Psalm. 'Oh Lord, you have brought me up from the grave, You have kept me alive that I should not go down into the pit.' – If we are going to have a new charter, I think that verse belongs within its opening clause." There was a murmur of general agreement.

"Ok. All in favor of including the Psalm in the charter?" Slowly one hand after another came up until they were all raised. Ely gave a little chuckle. "Y'all know the Thurstons are going to be hotter than alfalfa about this one."

"Guess they should have shown up." Tim Barring quipped.

CHAPTER 14

Northern Las Vegas Airport - Las Vegas, Nevada

Hunter thanked the air hostess for the water and the Advil. She smiled, the motherly expression of concern strange on her young face. When she asked if they needed anything else and Hunter said no, she wished them a safe flight and exited the jet to remain in Las Vegas. He looked over to where Doctor McCrory was laying on the long sofa style club seat with a hot towel draped over his face. Last night had started early with dinner and drinks at Prime in the Bellagio, and had ended somewhere around the baccarat tables at the Stratosphere hours after midnight. When the limo arrived to pick them both up the next morning they were as ragged and worn as a cocktail napkin stuffed in a hooker's purse.

"Hey?" Hunter rasped leaning his head back, thankful for his Raen sunglasses. "You ok over there?" Receiving only a grunt in return, he closed his eyes as the Challenger 350 taxied out and left the ground bound for St. George.

Edith Thomas School of Child Development, Room 306 - Tempe, Arizona

Sarah's mind wandered from the adjunct's lecture yet again as she found herself sketching little flowers in the margins of her notepad, thinking about the future. She couldn't help but worry about the coming weeks. Lucy had, in her usual fashion, reacted to Sarah's news that she would be moving on to find work outside the Church household with disinterest. But had also delegated the task of finding her replacement to Sarah, which was a massive undertaking. Two years ago, Sarah had simply taken the job through an internship posting with one of the caregiving agencies in town. When the internship had ended, Lucy had offered to hire her privately. She could just place another ad but Sarah had grown deeply attached to little Bella and wanted her to have the best possible care after she left.

The Churches had been very good to her, working with her school schedule and the pay was amazing. She had less free time than her peers with regular part time work as Lucy kept a very active social calendar, but Sarah had all of her bills and the portions of her tuition not covered by scholarships paid with cash to spare. She thought about the reading parties she and Bella would have, dressed up in fancy hats under a tent of sheets – she with her textbooks and Bella snuggled up against her side with her Doctor Seuss or a thick book of fairy tales looking over the pictures until dropping off to sleep. She felt she was abandoning Bella. She felt a sadness that couldn't be lifted by the excitement of new possibilities and advancements in life. She thought about the years of research and work she had put into her degree. Had she really done that just to spend the rest of her life as a nanny? And what about when Bella was old enough for Lucy to send off to some boarding school on the east coast or even Europe? Lucy had made it clear this was the path she wanted for her child, and Mr. Church rarely countered his wife's domestic decisions.

She was still lost in these thoughts as the people around her began packing up their books and notes to head for the door.

Copperhead Mining Equipment Yard
Treasure Peak – 10 miles North of Orein, Nevada

Jake Sanders pulled the massive articulated truck alongside the fleet of skidders and hydraulic shovels parked behind the long lengths of construction fencing topped in barbed wire. He took a minute to adjust the cuff of his prosthetic through his jeans, rubbing where the nude-colored socket met his lower thigh, before climbing down from the cab. It wouldn't be long until he would need the leg replaced or at least the socket refitted over the titanium pilon which ran from just below his knee to the top of his heavy steel toed work boot. He didn't want to take the time off work to head all the way into Reno just to sit in line at the VA, but needs must when the devil drives. And the sooner he took care of it, the better chance there would be of having the new cuff broken in and ready for the open of August muley season.

He climbed up the stairs of the office trailer and let himself in, sitting down in the chair opposite Mike Wolfe's cluttered desk as his boss finished a phone call, enjoying the muggy heat of the electric convection blower on the floor warming his skin. Mike wrapped up his call, something about a grading project being put off until February out at the Gerlach site. The Copperhead Mining Corporation had taken on the retrofitting and reconstruction of the old Hot Shot Mine here in Orein as part of an operations deal they had made with Grey County officials in exchange for a permit to open up a new section of their copper operation further south near Watchman Mountain. Somewhere along the line favors were traded and Mike ended up having the remediation of a second mine – the Bull Horn – up in Washoe County dropped in his lap as well. He hung up the phone with an audible breath and leaned back in his chair.

"Hey Jake. How goes it?"

"How goes it with you." Jake said, tapping his sunglasses rhythmically on his leg, the hint of a smile on his face.

"More of the same." Mike leaned back in his chair

with a sigh, "Some hippies are already threatening to stage protests outside the Gerlach gates. We tried explaining that removing the mercury from the lower shafts was actually better for the water and the environment but all they see are corporate trucks. It's just Burning Man mentality. Everyone wants to bitch about how horrible we are – paying people in to do a dangerous job no one else wants to do.

"So far, the bong smoke hasn't delivered a better action plan then chanting idiotic slogans, so here we are. I had to send Patrick and Jude in after some stupid chick who tried to do a one woman sit in last week and got lost. That was a mess. She ended up in the damn hospital. And you want so bad to feel sorry for her, but you can't because she did it to herself. I hate the Gerlach job. I don't know what Houston was thinking taking it on." He sighed. "How about you? How's the east cut-in going?" Jake and a few others had been tasked with cutting a path into the Hot Shot pit off the far eastern bedrock so that some of the debris could be removed from the bottom and a demolitions team could get in to finish stabilizing the remains of the old mine.

"It's going good." Jake nodded taking an object out of his front shirt pocket, then set a golf ball sized silvery dalmatian spotted rock onto the top of Mike's paperwork. "Found that."

Mike looked at him, raising an eyebrow as he picked up the rock, and inspecting it for a moment grinned as he tossed it back. "Great find Jake. Looks like the Hot Shot boys missed one. I assume you want to know if you can keep it, and as far as I'm concerned, I never saw it."

Jake made a face Mike couldn't quite read. "Well thank you Mike. That's very kind of you. Now what would you like me to do with the rest of it I have in the back of the truck? Gonna be hard finding a shelf big enough to display fifteen tons of silver ore for my nieces and nephews."

"Fifteen... tons?" Mike's jaw fell open.

"Yea, as we got down to about the five-hundred-foot

mark we hit a vug. Pretty sure we got most of it but then we went down another fifty feet and the rock changed color again. Started getting these odd streaks of gold in it." Jake winked.

"Holy shit." Mike breathed. "I gotta call Houston."

French's Cabin on the Bear Reach outside of Pinefare, Montana

"Alright great run." James walked up to where his daughter Becky was sitting astride her little palomino, patting the horse's neck as he spoke. "I like that you're taking it a little slower through the snow. But I think you might be trying too hard to stay in your old track. Right now, we have the benefit of the marks but when you get in the arena in the summer, we won't have that. Stick to your fundamentals – eyeline at the side of the barrel, lift to the next as you complete the turn. I know you can get closer if you get your head out of trying to reproduce your last run." Becky lifted her eyes from her father to the three barrels in the practice arena behind him. She finally nodded, taking it all in.

"Okay." He said stepping back from her horse. "How about you give me two more good runs and then help me set up the calves for your sister."

"Okay Dad." She bit her bottom lip in thought. For an eleven-year-old she was just as serious as any pro when it came to chasing cans. Same went for her twin sister Brynne when it came to calf catching. How he ended up with a pair of Rodeo killers was beyond him, but the girls had been stacking ribbons, buckles, and trophies up on their shelf next to their shared Breyer horse collection for the past two years with no signs of slowing "Come on Biscuits!" she clicked to her horse, "Let's do it again."

James walked over to the arena fence where his

mother was standing, her face calm but her nails digging trenches in the wood. There would never be a time when Sassy French saw a child astride a horse and wouldn't somewhere in the back of her mind be thinking about the worst imaginable possibilities. It was good though. It's what made her a good horsewoman and an excellent coach.

"She's doing great mom." He said reaching over the fence to pat her back. "They both are. You've done good."

"I know." She said, acknowledging his reassurance that the girls were going to be just fine, snow and ice be damned.

Movement in the corner of his eye pulled James' attention to where his father Morgan had just pulled up in his old gold and silver Chevy. James looked at the sky, it couldn't even be eleven in the morning yet.

"Hey, Dad." James said, his tone filled with dread. His father never drove up this far without a good reason or bad news.

"I tried calling. I figured you were out here." Morgan's gaze followed his granddaughter as she thundered down the arena, turning Biscuits around the barrels as smoothly as if he were on rails. "There's trouble in town."

"Is it Celia?" James asked receiving a grave nod from his father.

"She tried to run Daisy down with her car." James was prepared for a lot, but not for that. He stood there dumbfounded for what seemed like an eternity, finally able to muddle out the words what? and why? "I spoke with your Aunt Sissy. She says one-minute Celia was taking orders at the café and the next minute she just walked out the door. James... Celia has some very real problems. I know you love her son, but right now your love is keeping her from getting the help she needs."

"Daddy!" Becky's voice cut through the frozen air around him, the innocent joy in it adding more weight to his chest. "Did you see? Daddy, what was my time?"

Connor Creek, Oregon

Dan sat doubled over at the waist, tears stinging his eyes as he laughed. Noah leaned his head over the canvas back of his captain's chair trying to catch his breath while Bear, Rob, and Jefferson howled from their own seats around the glowing fire.

"I didn't have the heart to tell her." Dave gasped as he regained his breath. "I mean it was a funeral! Just not the appropriate time to mention it."

"Well did she notice?" Bear wheezed.

"No!" Dave nearly stopped breathing he was laughing so hard. "And it just kept getting worse! I've got my arm around Ashley, she's crying. Her granddad is in the coffin and I'm just trying to be supportive. And her mom is on the other side, and every time she blows her nose she's leaning on me and the whole time I'm trying not to even look. It was a disaster. Hands down worse scenario I've ever been through."

Their laughter joined the smoke from their fire drifting through the trees, a flurry of snow sprinkling down now and then to catch the weak winter light. Jefferson looked around the circle of men, then to the field dressed carcasses hung in the trees out of the reach of scavengers, to where Whiskey and Tango were taking playful swats at one another under the branches of a large pine. He looked again to his dad, who catching his eye gave him a knowing smile and a slight nod before taking another sip off his coffee.

"It's too bad Feng missed this trip." Bear shook his head. "He's got a story or two."

"So, you're really going to eat those?" Rob nodded to the cats hung in the tree after a pause in the conversation, looking to Bear and Noah, incredulous curiosity filling his face.

"Hell yes." Bear nodded. "Jenny has a great sausage recipe. Taught it to Lisa last winter. You'd be surprised how good it is with eggs. Besides, not the worst thing I've ever eaten. I remember this time we were out on float and ..."

He paused as a loud popping noise drifted into camp on the wind. Rob looked to Noah who shrugged and stood up looking around their camp then shrugged again. Tango and Whiskey stopped playing and moved closer to the fire, whining softly, their floppy ears fanning out as they cocked their heads back and forth trying to understand the sound.

"That's not a fire, is it?" Dave whispered standing up as well, unable to locate the origin of the sound.

"I'm not sure." Bear said as the noise stopped momentarily before starting up again, this time sounding much closer. "Think we should check it out?"

"It's not a fire." Noah said. "It's too wet to burn anything that hasn't been..." he stopped as a second popping noise followed by a hissing sound echoed up the road behind them. "What the hell?"

"Dad." Jefferson's voice tremored slightly. "Look."

He was pointing to the sky where miles above them a large commercial airliner had been passing silently overhead, bound for some far-off northern place. They watched it seemingly frozen in midair as the slate-colored sky turned shades of pale green and pink around it, the sunlight glinting off its aluminum body like the scales of a tiny fish caught in an angry churning sea. The popping noise came again, echoing deeper in the woods, further away but they could not tear their eyes from the beleaguered aircraft. Seconds seemed like hours as it hovered there, it's nose finally giving into gravity and turning back towards the earth in a graceful arch.

"It's not going to hit here." Dan breathed. "They'll be in the trees on the other side of the mountain."

Bear's voice sounded numb. "It doesn't look like he has any control over it."

They watched as the plane came down, dartlike at first, but at the mercy of crosswinds the massive fuselage began to drift sideways pulling the airplane into a lazy spiral. They heard it finally as it drifted over the tops of the trees circling their campsite – not the screaming of engines struggling desperately to escape the earth but the cold empty whisper of wind slipping over its helpless wings.

"We should call someone." Rob shook his head as if he were trying to shake from his mind the horrible image of the airliner falling. He pulled his keys from his drab green parka, walking over to his silver Jeep Grand Cherokee parked just beyond the tents.

"What's wrong with the sky?" Jefferson asked, his face pale and his eyes wide.

"It could almost look like Arora Borealis." Dan said. "But that's impossible. We're too far south, aren't we?"

"Sometimes." Noah sounded distracted, he was staring at his watch, tapping the face. "Jefferson. Show me your wrist, son." Jefferson held out his arm, his father furrowed his brow then tapped it's face too.

"I don't understand." Rob called from the Jeep behind them. "My fob isn't working."

"Doesn't matter." Noah turned to him, "The phones won't work anyway."

Over Wittwer Canyon, Utah

It was the silence that woke him, not the faint hint of smoke and melted plastic lingering in the stagnant air. Hunter opened his eyes and lifted his head slightly, straining to hear the low conversation of the pilots muffled by the curtain separating cockpit from cabin. He pressed the button to bring his seat back upright, but it remained unresponsive. Pushing himself up into a sitting position, the fog of sleep rapidly falling away from his mind, Hunter looked into McCrory's steely gaze.

"Something's wrong." The doctor pointed matter-of-factly towards the front of the jet. As if in response, the curtain moved aside and copilot Shane Cooper yelled back to them from the cockpit.

"I need your attention!" His voice was calm but firm, cutting through the fear Hunter could feel welling up within him. "We have experienced a dual engine failure and we have no electrical or hydraulic power. The airplane is still controllable, but we will be making an immediate emergency landing. I need both of you to move to the forward cabin seats and strap in!"

Neither of the two passengers hesitated in following the copilot's command, all the while pilot Adam Carls called into his headset, "MADAY, MAYDAY, MAYDAY, any station, this is N5102-Alpha in emergency descent. We have no engines, no power, copy?" Then waiting a beat, he began again, "MAYDAY, MAYDAY, MAYDAY, any station copy?" Carls then hissed "It's fucked. Everything is fucked."

"What happened?" Hunter looked to Steven who stared back, his expression remarkably calm as he pointed out the window. Hunter turned to look outside, his stomach lurching as the plane suddenly shuddered and lost altitude, the strange green tint to the light filling the cab matching his queasiness. Above them the sky almost seemed alive as ribbons of swirling green, yellow, and pink flowed like water over head. "What the hell is that?" Hunter leaned closer to the window, trying to make sense of what he was seeing.

"Ok you two!" Cooper shouted back to them. "Brace for impact!"

Hunter tucked his head between his knees, catching a glimpse of brick red mountains and sand canyon walls looming closer through the cockpit window. And then the world became a swirling tumble of rock and sand and the sound of aluminum ripping open like a cotton sheet.

CHAPTER 15

Edith Thomas School of Child Development – Tempe, Arizona

Sarah took the stairs rather than the elevator, though it would have only been a single floor ride. Especially today, she wanted to slow things down. She was needing perspective, thinking space, wanted to stretch these moments out to avoid this afternoon. She had almost stepped onto the center landing between floors when the lights above her flickered rapidly. She paused to look up, then quickly turned her head away as the bulbs charged before flashing out in a series of loud, glass shattering pops.

Surprised yelps from her fellow students echoed through the halls followed by some self-conscious laughter as the smell of ozone filled the air. The building wasn't dark without the overhead lights as it had been built with long windows and an open floorplan to let in as much natural sun as possible, but there was something off – almost sickly- about the muted sunshine coming in.

The girl on the stairs ahead of her held her phone up to her ear. She had been talking loudly about her weekend plans but was now saying "Hello? Hello?" She looked to Sarah's questioning face and shrugged. "My phone's dead."

Someone on the ground floor shouted. "Look at the sky!" Sarah raced down the stairs, seeing first the crowded arcade style commons through the wide windows where nearly every student and professor had stopped to stare up. The low flat clouds hanging over the campus were alive with color as waving streams of rainbow hues dipped and swirled. Sarah's hands were on the bar to open the large double glass doors and step outside when a frantic professor's assistant came running from the southern hall.

"Help! Please help! Professor Dollis is having a heart

attack!" a crowd gathered around her, murmuring concerned questions. "I don't know. I don't know" She cried. "The lights went out and he just collapsed. I tried to call 911 but none of the phones are working. They're all down. My cell is dead. I don't know what to do." A security guard pushed through the crowd telling everyone to go about their business before walking down the south hall. Sarah looked back outside, at the lights dancing over her like a rolling flag. She knew Professor Dollis. He had been out all the previous semester recovering from pacemaker surgery and had just started teaching again. She shifted the weight of her backpack and opened her purse, pulling out the iPhone the Church's had given her for Christmas. It was dead, as was the little tablet computer she had been using to follow the lecture notes just moments before. The door opened in front of her and she jumped, looking up into the serious face of Lance Weber, a junior year engineering student who she had tutored in a capstone sociology course last fall.

"You startled me." She breathed, trying to understand why the phones would be down.

"Sorry." He smiled shyly. "I was waiving from outside. I don't think you saw." He was cut off by a deafening boom that rattled the windows, and then panicked screams as two more bomb like blasts shook them. As Sarah watched a black plume of flame and smoke climbed into the sky just past the campus buildings to the south east.

"What was that?" Sarah screamed ducking down as the panicked crowd scattered in complete chaos.

"It was the airport." Lance looked at her, a grim tight-lipped frown on his face. "I need you to come with me." Lance took her by the hand, leading her in a half run through the crowd across the commons towards the large library at the north end of the campus.

"Don't worry!" He shouted back to her over more panicked screams as another explosion sounded in the distance. "They'll stop falling in the next five to ten minutes.

The towers don't let them stack up too deep and most of the pilots coming in will try to avoid the populated areas." He opened the door for her then took the lead again, pulling her deep into the darkened lobby and off to a side door which would avoid line of sight from the main desk. He pressed his finger against his lips, indicating she should be quiet as across the room she heard security and library staff searching rows of shelves for the odd cluster of students to shoo out. He ducked behind a reference shelf pulling her down beside him, the voice of a security guard calling out "Ok. We're clear. Everyone out."

There was a shuffling of feet and the doors banged closed, the rasp of a key in the lock and then silence.

"We shouldn't be here." Sarah said, suddenly apprehensive.

"Trust me." He said, pulling a glowstick out of his bag, snapping it and shaking it to life before handing it too her. "You're going to want to be here."

He led her into the basement, the automatic energy saving lights remaining dark overhead instead of flickering to life as they passed the motion sensors. Moving forward guided only by the light of the glowstick it felt more like descending into a massive tomb than walking through a college building. At the end of a section they turned, and Sarah could see the multi colored glow of other chem lights just ahead. Lance motioned for her to walk in front of him where a small circle of people were standing around a desk in a study alcove. They turned as she approached, their expressions of excitement and fear made macabre by the long shadows cast by the dim light of the sticks.

"Guys, this is Sarah." Lance said. "Is this all of us?"

One of the members nodded, a young woman Sarah thought she recognized. "Tyler wasn't on campus today." She seemed worried. "He's all the way out in Tolleson."

"Don't worry Leia." A tall young man with narrow Asian features patted her arm. "He knows the plan. He'll meet us at one of the rendezvous points."

"Sarah, this is Leia Majors – she's in the ag science program." Lance said, then going around the group introduced the others. The taller man next to Leia was Kennedy Li, an engineering student. Next to him Lottie Williams, a young woman in her fourth year of the nursing program and beside her Mae Lu who was working on dual majors in history and anthropology. The last two members of the group was a young man named Jessie Smith a forestry management major and Mathew Renner a student in the school's astronomy program. All introductions made, Lance turned to the group and said, "Ok. We're going to need to read Sarah in."

"Read me in?" She looked around at all the others and then asked, "Aren't you worried we might get in trouble when the lights come on and they find us down here?"

"The lights aren't coming back on." Mathew adjusted his glasses, more as a nervous habit than out of need.

"What?" Sarah couldn't help but laugh at the finality of his tone. "Of course, they are. A flash flood probably knocked out a transformer. Or whatever those explosions at the airport were hit something critical. But they'll get it fixed. Even if it's a terror attack, the lights always come back on."

"It wasn't a terror attack." Lance said. "And the lights aren't coming back on. Matt, tell her."

"You remember the comet that came by last August?" Matt asked as he pulled his backpack up from the floor, removing a large black binder which he placed on the table.

Sarah nodded. "I watched it with the little girl I care for."

"We believe that it may have impacted the coronal surface of the sun and induced a massive ejection of plasma which has now hit and flooded Earth's magnetosphere." Matt looked at her as if this were self-explanatory, his face falling into a ghastly mask of long shadow when she returned his expression with a blank stare.

"You're going to have to slow that down for her."

Leia sighed. "She hasn't been here for any of the scenario runs."

"Scenario runs?" Sarah knew parroting back their words in question form sounded ridiculous, but there was nothing else she knew to do.

"We're kind of a club." Lance said. "We meet every Tuesday at someone's dorm, we trade off. We watch podcasts and footage from previous emergency situations, run preparedness scenarios on how to cope with different situations. Every Saturday we have pizza and play paintball or go hiking. Anyway, this was one of the scenarios we've been studying since the comet came by."

"It wasn't just a sungrazer." Matt jumped in opening the binder and showing her a chart of the comet's projected path. "It was a cluster of comets heading towards the sun during a period when we had an elevated number of solar storms – they're a buildup of energy on the outer layer that fire off mass amounts of plasma into space. Impacts or even just comets breaking up across the corona help to give these ejections an added push. Usually, the magnetic field of the earth just tosses these things aside. We get some radio frequency or satellite disturbances. But it's not a big deal. However..." he turned the page to show her a stylized diagram of the earth's magnetic field, a shield extending around the planet and tapering out into space away from the sun. "sometimes they hit and their energy syncs with the magnetosphere and it floods. That's why we are seeing Arora Borealis in Phoenix. It's why every electronic device on the planet has stopped working. It's why the power isn't going to come back on."

"This has happened before." Mae stepped in, taking control of the binder and flipping to a section in the back which held photocopies of old newspaper clippings and some personal diaries describing northern lights occurring suddenly over a trapping camp and a fire in a telegraph office. "The last one was in 1859, at the time the only technology which could be damaged were primitive battery arrays. The wires captured and conducted that energy back to the offices where they were overcome, and the offices burnt down."

"But these days." Lance said. "We have electrical grids and electronics everywhere. Our grid acts as a massive antenna directing the energy through our transformers and substations blowing them out. Your phone is dead right now because it has received such a massive energy dose just from the charge in the air it was overloaded. Now yes, we could rebuild these structures that have been damaged... but that's going to take years. The large power transformers the grid relies on, it can take up to five years just to build a single one. We will need hundreds if not thousands. Most of them are built in China and can take six months to install – not counting transit. Those estimates are from a world where everything is functioning normally. We now live in a world with no electrical grid. The factories which make them won't function. The staff which they use to build them are going to be worried about other things than building transformers."

"Other things?" Sarah took a ragged breath as the pieces fell into place. "Other things like living."

Leia nodded. "Our entire food network is dependent on transportation. Cities consume food which is grown and shipped from around the world. It is planted and harvested with heavy equipment – which won't run. It is shipped in trucks, trains, planes, boats – that won't run. The average family only keeps about three days' worth of food in their house. When that's gone, there's going to be angry mobs outside of empty stores. The few personal gardens people keep won't produce enough food to feed them. And that's just here where its warm. No one is gardening in the snow. People won't have food. Many people won't have water. It's all going to come crashing down."

"Without power we won't have air conditioning." Sarah could feel her knees going weak. She needed to sit down. Lance helped her sink to the floor, pulling a bottle of water out of his bag. "Lance," she croaked. "Remember when you had to get through that class on specialized care in city populations? You talked about the importance of heating and cooling in modern houses. I even used it in a paper of my own." She sniffed taking a drink off the bottle. "We build houses to be clean, you said. But we don't build them to keep us warm and cool without technology. All this time I thought you were talking about the beauty of human progress. We don't have to worry about big fireplaces to spit cinders onto the carpet. We can have big beautiful windows and let sunlight in, because we don't have to worry about keeping cool. Do you remember?" He nodded. "You know who are the first people to die in emergency situations when shelter is no longer adequate? The old and the young."

"Guys." Kennedy stepped further into the group. "We have to get moving. We are running out of time."

"Out of time?" Sarah looked from one face to another.

"It's hard to explain." Lance sighed. "It's complicated. In a nutshell, cities eat themselves once people start to get desperate. Society breaks down. The more people you are around the more dangerous it gets, the harder it is to survive – be it from violence or infectious disease or starvation – large gatherings of population don't do well in times of crises."

"And to make matters worse." Kennedy said. "The government typically tries to keep people contained. Pen them in. Put them in emergency camps. Which is just another place to starve once the people holding the keys die off or walk away."

"So." Lance took the water from Sarah's hand. "We're leaving. We'll have to find some way of getting out of the city, find someplace safe – someplace a little more habitable."

"This area?" Mae sat down next to her. "The population never rose much higher than fifty thousand until the fifties when central heating, cooling, plumbing, and food transportation made it possible."

"There were some advances in medicine too." Lottie Williams leaned against the desk with a sigh.

"Can we not do this now?" Mae scowled back at her.

"I'm just saying."

"Well say it some other time."

"Fine."

"Fine." Mae snipped, then turned back to Sarah as if nothing had happened. "This area is going to reset. There's not enough water, it's too hot, we can't suddenly learn how to farm again. We don't have the time. Too many people will be dead first. If we are going to survive, we need to leave before they can shut down the roads. Before anyone else knows to go. In these kinds of situations, the people who make it are the ones who recognize they are in danger early and take steps to get themselves to safety."

"What we want to know is," Lance looked at his hands shyly, rubbing them together nervously "will you come with us?"

"What if the power comes back on?" Sarah looked at him seriously.

"Then we feel stupid and head right back."

"No... really. If the power comes back on, we come right back."

"Of course." Lance nodded. "C'mon. You saved my life with those study notes. Give me a chance to return the favor."

"I will." Sarah said after a long pause. "But on one condition. I get to bring a couple people with me."

Matt looked unsure, but Lance nodded immediately. "Of course. I know you have family here."

"They aren't family." Sara said. "But one of them is close."

"Where are they right now?" Mae asked

"Downtown." Sarah saw the look Matt flashed to Lance, who then assured the group that he would take her, and they would catch up soon.

They grabbed their backpacks and made their way out of the library using the emergency fire exit, the alarm never sounding. As he was leaving, Matt stuffed a rock into the striker plate to keep the door from locking behind them in the event they needed to get back in. The other's split off heading towards the dorms through the slowly growing crowd of students. The initial explosions seemingly now over, people came into the commons to watch the sky and the smoke billowing upwards.

"Aren't we going together?" Sarah asked as they all went their separate directions.

"We know where to meet." Lance said as they walked past the department of psychology building heading north on McAllister Mall. Earlier panic had given way to small games of soccer and picnics as an almost carnival like atmosphere began to form. A couple of leggy blonds in jeans and ASU tank tops walked by, smiling at Lance.

"Hey." One of them called over her shoulder to them. "Free ice cream in the hall. They have to give it away or it will melt."

Lance kept walking, nearly dragging Sarah towards University Drive. He finally turned to her and said. "Look. This is uncomfortable. But we have to think by different rules than we normally would."

"I know." Sarah nodded, even though there were still parts of her brain screaming that everything would be fine. The lights would come back on. It's just a power outage. But the lights dancing above her head in the sickly green sky. The lack of sirens screaming as the airport burned in the distance. The lack of a safe authority figure showing up to tell her it was okay. All these things told her that inner voice screaming that normalcy would return soon, was wrong.

"No. I mean right now." He turned and looked her in the eye. "It's going to be uncomfortable right now. If we are going to meet everyone and get to where we are going on time, we need transportation that doesn't rely on electricity." He sighed. "We're going to have to steal a couple of bikes."

They found a stand of unguarded bicycles outside the University Club; a pair were leaning against a full rack tethered on loosely locked chains to a concrete pylon. Lance looked around to see if anyone was watching and then lifted them one by one over the top of the pilon, coiling the dangling chains around the seat post. As they pushed off from the curb, Sarah pulled up alongside him.

"This is why your parents pay your tuition?" She asked, smiling weakly. "So, you can just look at a bike and see the obvious way to steal it?"

"I pay my own tuition." He smiled back at her as they turned right onto South Mill Avenue, swerving around cars that had stopped functioning in the middle of intersections and perplexed motorists looking at the sky. "A better question is, did their parents pay that much in tuition for them not to even know to put the chain through the tire?"

They peddled past Hayden Flour Mill and Giuliano Park, crossing the left-hand bridge while the Salt River churned and boiled beneath them. "Matt thinks the flooding is related." Lance said. "There have been historic amounts of rainfall this year, even for monsoon season. He thinks the quake swarm we had back in November is related as well."

"I know why we are going downtown," she shouted ahead to him as he dodged around a fire truck that had craned itself onto the sidewalk, the crew standing around while one of them tinkered under the hood. "But why did the group not leave together."

"People are followers by nature." He said as she came back alongside him. "Especially when their norms are being disturbed. One or two people walking in a given direction, no big deal. But the whole group of us going together – people might fall into line thinking we're going to take care of them. And when we don't, it would cause trouble."

"Where are we going?" Sarah panted slightly. She

hadn't been on a bike in a few months, and her legs were starting to burn.

"North." Lance said. "Well first we're going to follow the Salt east… backtrack it to just before the dam. From there the Verdi, north. We don't want to leave the water. It's as much a guide as it is a resource." He slowed as they got to Washington Street, his heart pounding as they made a left-hand turn past a jackknifed beer truck avoiding broken glass on the road. Sarah could see flames and smoke in the distance at the golf course where it looked as if one of the airliners had crashed. There were no fire engines, no cop cars, no emergency response at all. "We have to take fifty-sixth!" He shouted back to her, passing her the water bottle which had been left on the bike. "We want to avoid the airport."

They stopped for a small rest when they reached Van Buren, gasping for breath as they finished off what remained of their water. "Lance." Sarah looked at him seriously. "What are we going to do for food?"

"Matt has a couple cartons of MREs." Lance panted. "He has one of those tow behind trailers for kids. He and Tyler both bought them and stocked them up, but with Tyler out in Tolleson we don't know if he's going to come to campus to get it or just meet us at our first campsite, so we probably only have Matt's. We're going to load our food on to there. And then we have to scavenge. I know it's poorly planned. But it's the best we got. This was all kind of a hobby, really."

"How far north?" She asked as they pushed off again peddling for 52nd street and the freeway onramp.

"We have to get out of the desert." He said as they pushed onto the Red Mountain Freeway. By this time most motorists had already abandoned their cars, and only a few were left walking the lanes in disbelief. They cut neatly through the mid-morning commute frozen in time around them, the sun starting to climb toward its zenith. "Or at least the low desert. We're lucky its winter. It would be far too hot to do this in summer. There's going to be some parts where we have to hike overland to get to the Colorado. We're really playing it by ear. If we push ourselves, it should take us maybe three days to make the Flagstaff area."

"Lance." Sarah gasped as they passed over the Grand Canal, swerving around a woman who had crumpled onto the asphalt sobbing. "One of these people I have to get. She's a little girl. She can't push it. She's never really been out of her penthouse other than to go to the park or on family vacation." He gave her an odd look but said nothing.

They stayed on the Red Mountain Freeway, crossing the interchange where it became the Papago. Their lungs straining with effort to push up the 7th Street exit. Here they had to stop for a moment to navigate a collision where both cars had caught fire, and without any sign of emergency response the drivers had eventually just walked away to let them burn. They saw one lone police officer on foot, standing in the middle of Garfield attempting to calm a screaming woman who was sitting on the curb. As they crossed Pierce Street on 7th they were suddenly joined by an older Hispanic man on a bike, who easily kept pace with them though Sarah was pedaling faster and harder than he was.

"Hey." He said to her, taking a long pull off of the Modelo he had balanced on the handlebars. "You're going to give yourself a heart attack. Try a different gear." And with that he swooped away up Filmore as though nothing at all were wrong. Sarah couldn't help but feel a little resentment towards him but tried changing the gears on the bike seeking an easier ride. Reaching East Van Buren they took a right, Lance dropping behind to let Sara lead the way. As houses gave way to businesses and businesses to skyscrapers, they finally found some relief from the sun. Turning onto 3rd they passed the basilica then right again on Monroe, moving up on to sidewalks now and then to avoid cars blocking the narrowing road and people milling around. Sarah stopped as they reached the corner of Monroe and 1st, leaning up against the cool concrete face of the skyrise building and gasping for air.

"Are you warmed up?" She asked Lance finally.

"For?" He panted back.

"We have to climb all the way up there." She pointed straight up to the top of the building. Lance looked at it, then back at her.

"I'll stay here and guard the bikes."

CHAPTER 16

1002 Yellow Jack Place – Baptiste, Idaho

"Thank you." Teagan took the cup of coffee Jenifer Walker had poured from the enamel camping percolator which she set back down on her cast iron stove. "I can't believe my house got so cold so fast. I thought if I just burrowed under my blankets, I would be ok. With Samson and Delilah on the bed with me I was a little warmer, but I couldn't even go down to the kitchen to get food, everything there had to be cooked... I don't know what I'm going to do."

"You're going to be ok." Jennifer rubbed her back comfortingly as they looked out the window of the upstairs family room, watching as the smoke from Lex Donati's house lifted like a black veil into the sky. The fire had started in the garage, the melted ruin of his ninety-thousand-dollar Jaguar iPace just visible in the charred husk that was left of the walls.

"How long do you suppose it's going to burn?" Teagan asked.

"Until it runs out of fuel." Jenifer turned back to the stove and put another quarter of wood inside. "Or until enough of the snow melts to smother it. We're lucky. We're lucky Bi noticed it in time. We're lucky Noah had the gas shutoff key in the garage. We're lucky it's too wet for the flames to spread. We're lucky for snow days keeping the kids at home. We would have had to go get them. That would have been a huge task considering." The baby cried from the other room and Jenifer walked across the hall to gather him out of his crib, returning to settle down on the sofa to check his diaper and put him to her breast.

"They're back." Teagan turned from the window. "Should I let them in?"

"Yes." Jenifer nodded, mentally saying a prayer for her son Beau as she watched Lila and Macy keeping little Peyton occupied with his building blocks. She kept praying until the sound of feet coming up the stairs told her she would have to provide some answers for some very scared people, and fast. Then she prayed for Noah. That God would protect him. That angels would guard him and Jefferson. That they would find their way home somehow.

She readjusted her nursing shawl over her shoulder as the Michaels came into the room followed by Derik and his fiancé Zia. "We knocked on all the doors." Ferris Michaels said, pulling off his gloves and warming his hands on the stove while Alla and Zia took off their snowy coats, and hanging them over the back of a rocking chair sat down on the sectional beside Jenifer to share a wool afghan. "The places where people are home – it's just Tom Percy, Tammy Allen, Mary Beth, Ashley Lindon, the Rosses, and Abigail. The Zhou s have a fireplace. They've taken in Janice Wheeler's dogs. I guess she had a doctor's appointment in town and must have gotten stranded. I'm hoping, really hoping, she's ok."

There was a general murmur of agreement. Janice Wheeler was the neighborhood grandma, never minded the kids playing in her yard, was a fixture on her front porch on warm afternoons waving hello to her neighbors. Everyone who met her, loved her immediately. "We've turned off all the gas to empty houses." Ferris continued. "And the places where they would let us."

"So, everyone except Abigail and the Rosses." Jenifer was keeping mental notes.

"Yup." Ferris nodded, taking a seat next to Derik on the couch. "They all say they have some things they want to tend to and then they will be coming over. Tom Percy is going to walk into town to see what's happening there. Tammy is beside herself; her oldest daughter is in Boise for some science club thing. They were staying overnight at the university hotel and had a tour scheduled for today."

"Ok." Jenifer nodded, thinking. "When Beau gets back, we'll brainstorm to see what we can do to help. In the meantime, go back to your house and go through your food stores. Do you have any coolers?"

He and Derik exchanged uncomfortable looks then shook their heads. "We aren't really outdoor types." Derik said. "Otherwise we would have gone hunting with the others."

"Well, we are lucky for that." Jenifer said with a soft smile. "Because otherwise we wouldn't have you here to help us." She took a breath, organizing her thoughts, "So, your perishables. Pack them in garbage bags and take them out back, fill the bag with clean snow and then cover them over. If we don't get a warm spell that should keep it fresh enough to eat. Somethings will probably freeze overnight. It's ok. As long as the food doesn't rot, we can still find ways to cook wilted vegetables and greens. Are you staying here or across the street?"

"The Zhous have offered us their den." Ferris said. "We're all camping out on their floor until further notice. Lisa, Tyler, and Jane are taking their guestroom. But Mary Beth said that she and Tammy will bring the kids here if you're ok with the company."

"I am." She said, switching squirmy grunting Aaron to her other breast under the shawl. "If you wouldn't mind taking the bed out of Macy's room and putting it in Lilia's we can push those beds together and the girls can all sleep there. Tammy and Mary Beth can take Jefferson's room which leaves Teagan and Ashley – if they don't mind sharing Beau's bed. He can take the sleeper in the loveseat downstairs. Do you mind Teagan?"

"No." She shook her head. "If Ashley doesn't."

"If she does, we'll figure it out." Jenifer adjusted her shirt as Aaron dropped off the breast to sleep. "But either way I think that's everyone safe and warm for the night."

There was a moment of silence as they all took that

information in. "You..." Derik finally said in a low voice. "You really don't think the power is going to come back on?"

"I'm going to hope for the best." Jennifer chose her words carefully. "But I'm going to be ready to stay alive in the event of the worst."

She prayed again for Noah. She prayed he would sense she was thinking of him. Prayed he was alive.

Fox Creek, Western Oregon

They trudged through the snow in a line, Noah taking the lead with Jefferson, Rob, Dave, Dan, and Bear in the rear and the two dogs Whiskey and Tango bounding in their tracks behind them. Despite the wind and the cold, they had started to sweat under their heavy layers of jackets and snow pants, thermal underwear and warm socks. Jefferson's face had gone pink under the weight of his pack, but he kept up a good pace not wanting to fall behind his father. Noah stopped for a moment looking up at a transmission line poking out through the trees and the long, charred gash spanning the large bucket like object strapped to the top of the pole where the arms formed a T.

"That was the popping sound we herd." He said when everyone had caught up, the men taking advantage of an opportunity to rest. They had taken stock of their camp, unloaded their vehicles, and filled their hunting packs with nothing but the essentials. While they worked Jefferson had spent his time cutting down their kill from the trees, stripping each big cat of hide and meat with his boot knife leaving only the bones behind. He rolled the meat into the hide like a bedroll, using a spool of thin nylon cord to bundle them up in neat packages that could be tied off to the top racks on their packs.

Each man carried his kill, his rifle and ammo along with his bedroll, and whatever tool he could strap to his belt. Jefferson carried the tent for himself and his father, Rob carried his and Dan's, Bear had agreed to share with Dave for the sake of lightening the general load so the Thyme's large four-person family tent was left behind at camp. This was a sacrifice which allowed him to carry extra food and the campfire set. They each had their own first aid kit, an extra set of clothes, and their own canteen. Dave was glad he had let Rob talk him into buying a set of snowshoes before leaving Baptiste, but after the first mile of the hike down the side of the mountain to fox creek he had wished he had brought his Nordic skis instead.

"How did that happen?" Dan asked, watching thin wisps of smoke curling from the dimly glowing charcoal eating away at the pole above the transformer.

"The overload must have cracked the casing." Noah said. "They fill the transformers with mineral oil to keep them from overheating, but the energy surge going through the lines could have pushed it past boiling putting pressure on the weld." He looked down at his map and then to the compass he held, and then to the sky. "We're lucky this happened in the middle of winter. Had it been summer the trees might have caught and the fires would have cut us off from the river. It looks like this line extends all the way down into the next valley."

They had left their dead and useless vehicles between the trees behind their camp. They had also left their chairs around the smothered fire, and all the perishable food inside the coolers. Noah had tucked the two mason jars of Ole Smokey whiskey down at the bottom of his pack with his clothes along with a few other valuables he had taken from the truck and a small roll of cash. "We have about another two miles to the Snake. We should probably set up camp there, eat something, get some rest. It's a long walk to Annex and the bridge if we can't find someone with a boat to give us a ride."

"What's your deal, Noah?" Dave asked as they stared back downhill following the edge of the creek over rough rocks and saplings and brush and snow. "Are you some kind of former special forces government black ops guy? How do you know how to do this?"

Noah smiled, despite the lead weight in his heart that held his thoughts of Jenny, their new baby, and the rest of his kids. "No." He shook his head. "Bear's the military man. Did twenty years – was it?" He called over his shoulder to the larger man bringing up the rear. "Bear? I forget. In the Navy."

"Twenty-four." Bear called back, his words coming in plumes of steam.

"Twenty-four." Noah shook his head. "Lucky guy. My folks wouldn't hear of me joining after college. Threatened to cut me off if I did. At that time, I had just met Jenny and was worried she wouldn't like me if I didn't have the right car. I didn't know her very well back then. If I had, I would have broken my father's heart and shamed the entire family and still got the girl."

"Grandpa Levi didn't want you to join the military?" Jefferson gave his father a confused look. "But he always makes such a huge deal about veteran's day."

"Yup." The single flat answer was all the information Noah offered and for a moment they all just trudged in silence, their wide snowshoes whisking through the deepening snow.

"So where did you learn all this?" Dave finally asked.

"Mostly hunting guides, some of the guys my dad hired too. Lots of former military there in the oil business." Noah replied as he climbed over a fallen pine blocking their path through the narrow draw. "But books and magazines too. And experience. I've been hunting since I was younger than Jefferson. Experience is the best teacher. It's not black magic. Hiking, finding your way through the woods, taking care of yourself so you don't die. The information is out there."

Dave thought about this, as the group continued in silence.

Big Stakes Ranch – Henderson, Nevada

Laura walked out onto the wide reception porch shaking her head "no" to Bobby who was standing in the yard surrounded by the handful of staff who had made it into work that morning. No. No power to the HAM radio in the manager's office. No power to the rooms. And no – no power to the pump house back behind the dining hall.

"Well, that's it." He sighed. "Those of you with family nearby pick a mount. Gear them up for pavement and go check on your loved ones. For all we know this is just our lines and everything will be back up and running by tonight." There were some skeptical nods as several people left the little group heading to the barn where the guest remuda was stabled. He lost Lupita from the kitchen crew, Hector, Jorge, and Piper. Only Dex, Laura, Lectica, Kip and Brody remained.

"We got problems." He started.

"You're telling me." Dex broke in with a half-smile.

"That's not helping now." Bobby glowered at his brother. "We have work to do otherwise these little problems are going to get big right around sundown. We have twenty head of horses and sixty cattle who are expecting to be fed and watered. The feed isn't such a problem, but the water is. Without power our pumps don't work. Without our pumps, water doesn't come out of the ground. We have to start thinking creatively and the snark isn't helping."

"I think," Laura offered gently "Dex is just pointing out that we have to be wrong about it being a downed line. Even the entire grid going down doesn't kill the backup generators. It doesn't turn phones to expensive paperweights in our pockets. It certainly doesn't turn the sky green."

Bobby glowered at the ground, he hated Laura taking Dex's side in an argument. He hated it even more when Dex was right. "Well, what do you think it is?" No one had an answer. "Ok. So can we just solve this one issue first?"

"Hey guys." Brody had turned to wave goodbye to Hector. As the young bartender rode through the big outer gates, Brody spotted another rider approaching. "Look who it is!"

The big black quarter horse came through at a trot, Devin Harding from the D-Bar H down the road on his back. "Hello at the house." He called out waving to Bobby.

"Hey Devin." He cracked a smile as the tall rail thin man in his mid-fifties swung down from his mount to shake his hand. "How about this weather."

"Yea, it's somethin'." Devin waved hello to the others, then smoothing the greying whiskers of his mustache with a thumb and forefinger said, "It's like this at least five miles in each direction. I have a guy riding out up the 515, cars are stopped there like toys on the floor. There are families on foot trying to find water. We've got about thirty people at our place about ready to pass out from shock. Others just wandered off along the highway heading towards the city. It's going to be a disaster. One of the guys we have is a State Trooper, his radio is out, so it doesn't look like emergency services is going to be helping."

Bobby nodded grimly, "We got about the same here."

"Well… I was going to float an idea past you. I know your people and stock are going to need water. We have one of those old wind generated pumps on our place but unless we put someone up there to turn it all night, it's not going to keep up."

"What did you have in mind?"

Devin pointed south east towards a jagged set of hills to where a massive water tank stood out against their side just above the soft lush green of a golf course. Bobby shook his head, hating the simple logic of the plan. "You're going to get me fired."

"For what? Taking care of company stock?" Devin smiled. "Besides, you've always known that if Big Stakes lets you go you can come work for me."

"We're going to get arrested."

"Not while the phone and the radio are down." Devin cocked his hat a bit. "It's our water anyway, Bobby. This clown stole it off the table to keep their greens green while the creeks that fed our pastures went dry. That tank is gravity fed. All we have to do is liberate the flow. Other than that, the closest source of water is Lake Mead."

Bobby let out a long breath. "It will be slow, might take all night for it to get here."

"In the meantime, we collect our head and play through." Devin's smile was devilish.

"Fine." Bobby said after a long thoughtful pause. "Have your guys cut the fences on your side, I'll send Kip and Brody to get them down on ours. I'll have Laura follow you out on the big buckboard, we've got a basement full of bottled water and some food in the cold locker that needs to be eaten before it spoils. She can pick up your refugees and bring them back here hayride style. We don't have power, but we still have the room and the means to feed people." He paused. "Hey Devin. What do you suppose we do if this isn't just a temporary situation?"

"Well, there are some things we can do to get the water out of the wells without the electric pumps." Devin ran his thumb over his chin. "Get water back to the houses. That's our immediate problem. We have our feed laid up for about six months. We can stretch that out to eight if we have to. There's always a solution."

Bobby nodded, then turned around to the group. "Dex. Saddle up. You, me, and Devin are going to go piss off the neighbors."

Lowery Canyon Road / County Road 605 - Orein, Nevada

Mike tucked his hands into his armpits wishing he had grabbed his gloves from his truck. He had been on the phone with Houston talking about the political significance of Jake's find when the lines had gone dead and the sky outside the work trailer took on the appearance of a low flame on a gas range. When he and Jake both tried their vehicles, they couldn't even get the starters to click. They had spent the rest of the day hiking up to the jobsite making sure none of their equipment operators were stuck inside the pit leading down into the Hot Shot and then he sent everyone home on foot.

Three of his guys who lived in Reno had to stay in old town, Sheriff Ely let them into the Ruby Boot Saloon to find rooms in the old hotel upstairs. The Ruby Boot had become a shelter of sorts for people who lived in the condemned sections of town and had refused to leave. After that he swung by Jake Sander's place to make sure the equipment operator had made it home. After talking with Jake for a while, Mike began the long walk home.

He skirted a stalled out big rig, it's driver nowhere to be seen, and kept walking until the sound of hooves clicking across the pavement made him turn around. Max Yneko came riding up on a sleek chestnut mare, a big boned roan saddled up and ponied behind. Mike greeted his neighbor as a wave of relief swept over him, warming him from the inside out.

"The Thurstons said they saw you heading out this way." Max called as the horses drew up and he handed the reigns of the roan to Mike. "I figured you might be heading home and could use a ride."

Mike swung up into the saddle and shook Max's hand. "You figured right. It's slow going on foot and I need to see how Becca and the kids are holding up. Who's is this?"

"He belongs to County Search and Rescue." Max said, pulling an extra set of gloves from his saddlebag, and handing them to Mike. "We've been keeping these two in the stables behind the station for them. I figure you can hold onto him until we get things back upright."

"I appreciate the loan." Mike said putting on the gloves. "I really do."

CHAPTER 17

Downtown – Phoenix, Arizona

Sarah leaned against the door of the Church apartment, sweat rolling down her face and her legs shaking, threatening to buckle. She sagged there red-faced and panting for a long time before she pulled her keys from her bag and finding the right one turned it in the lock, knocking as she opened the door. Lucy was standing in the kitchen staring across the living room at the lights swirling in the sky outside her windows, but turned as Sarah came in.

"Oh. You're here." She said with little emotion. "I thought you had class until four. What time is it? Is it four? Nothing is working. The power went out a while ago and everything is dead. I need to get to the Apple Store today, there's something wrong with my phone. I'm so tired of this bullshit. If you pay good money for something, it should work. I can't call the car service to drive me. Hey! Let me see your phone!"

"It's not working either." Sarah said though she handed the device over anyway. "No one's is. The power is out. It's …" she tried to think of the right words. "It's gone."

"The power is gone?" Lucy laughed. "Really. I think you've been spending too much time with Bella. You're starting to sound like her."

"We need to go, Lucy." Sarah panted as she reached for a glass in the cupboard, turning on the kitchen sink. The pipes groaned and rattled a little bit, but no water came out.

"Yea. There's no water either." Lucy sighed. "I went down to the concierge; he says there's no water pressure past the third floor. Can you believe that? All the people who paid to be up here. No water. I don't know when they plan on fixing it."

"They can't fix it, Lucy." Sarah leaned against the sink, her mouth dry and sticky. "We need to take Bella and go. I have some friends; we're going to look for some place safe to stay. I came here to get you two."

Lucy gave her a defiant look, then walked over to her leather couch and sat down. "I'm not going anywhere."

"Don't you feel the air, Lucy?" Sarah walked over to her, ignoring the woman's glare directed at her shoes nearly touching the angora rug. "It's still and its hot. In a few hours it will be unbearable. You can't keep Bella up here."

"There's a fire over there." Lucy pointed towards the airport. "I'm pretty sure as soon as they have it out, they'll get the power fixed."

"Yes! There's a fire. A plane crashed. Several planes crashed. No one is putting them out. Think about it. Have you heard any sirens at all? Any emergency vehicles? The power is gone."

Lucy thought about this for a long moment, then said. "Well of course you wouldn't hear the emergency vehicles. This place is far too well built. We don't need to have our evenings bothered by the constant mewling of police sirens in the Warehouse district."

"Let me take Bella." Sarah pleaded. "If you won't go, let me take Bella with me so she can be safe."

"Oh my God Sarah." Lucy hissed. "You're really just working my last nerve. I need you to take care of Bella so I can walk down to the Apple Store and scream at whatever high school dropout they have hired to run the desk. My. Phone. Isn't. Working." She sat there for a moment in silence, tapping her bare toes against the rug, her arms crossed tightly against her chest.

"Please Lucy." Sarah got down on her knees as hot tears rolled across her cheeks. "Please let me take Bella somewhere she will be safe."

"Fine." Lucy spat. "I'm going to leave. Lock the door behind you."

A sudden thought cut through Sarah's relief spurred on by the tugging doubt she still had at the back of her mind. "I'm going to need a parent release form. Like the one you signed when I took Bella to visit my parents in Boulder. Just in case I need to get her treatment in a hospital or anything."

"Exactly how long do you plan on being gone?" Lucy's voice was incredulous.

"Just until the power is back on. Then we'll come right back." It wasn't a lie. In fact, it was exactly the deal Lance had made with her. "And the camping gear. We want to borrow that too."

Lucy let out a long put-upon groan. "There's a stack of the release forms in Hunter's desk. Bottom drawer on the left behind all the family documents. The key to the storage area is in there too. Hurry up and get it so I can sign the damn thing and get out of here. I'll have to take the fucking stairs. I am not doing that in my new Valentinos. I'll be in my room changing."

Sarah followed Lucy into the bedroom behind the kitchen, then went through the adjoining door into Mr. Church's home office while Lucy stepped into her walk-in closet to rummage through the boxes of shoes stacked to one side, cursing softly under her breath. Sarah found the key to the desk under the leather blotter and opened the drawer, flipping through the folders marked deeds, will, birth certs, and Bella. Finding the release form, she took the time to fill it out in its entirety, walking it in to Lucy to sign. Huffing in irritation Lucy snatched the pen from Sarah's hand and scribbled her signature at the bottom, pulling on a brand-new pair of high-top sneakers which probably cost as much as Sarah earned in a month.

"The street will ruin them." Lucy moaned looking at herself in the mirror, turning her feet from one side to the other before grabbing her purse off a shelf. "It's so filthy down there. Alright. I'm off."

"Don't you want to say goodbye to Bella?" Sarah

prodded, hoping Lucy would stop and take the time to consider what was really happening around her.

"She's napping. I don't want to wake her." Lucy said curtly, disappearing into the living room. Moments later Sarah heard the slam of the front door followed by the banging of the door to the stairwell as it closed. She walked back into the office and took Bella's birth certificate and a small plastic ID card from the file, then replaced the key under the leather blotter

She found the little girl hiding under her bed, crying. She pulled Bella into her lap, comforting her and asking about the lights in the apartment. From Bella's answers she was able to determine that the little girl had crawled under her bed after the lightbulbs had gone out in a series of loud bursts and the following explosions from the airport had rattled the high-rise windows. Sarah could tell from the pale pinkness of her lips and the ashen color of her face that besides being terrified, the little girl was probably slightly dehydrated from the heat building up in the apartment.

"We're taking a trip." Sarah said as she helped the five-year-old out of her pajamas and into a pair of knit pants and a t-shirt. She opened Bella's closet, looking for the box marked "winter clothes" she had put in there after the family's last ski trip up to Flagstaff. In it she found two thick wool sweaters, socks, gloves, and a little designer snow suit. Taking a Neman Marcus bag from Lucy's closet she dumped the contents out on the bed and began folding the warmer clothes and some other essentials into the bag including Bella's toothbrush, toothpaste, her hair brush, a rain slicker and Bella's cashmere stuffed bear.

Grabbing another bag, this one from Saks 5th, Sarah packed up as much food as she thought the bag could carry without breaking. A box of cereal, several cans of soup, a half empty box of Oreos, and as many of Mr. Church's single serving protein shakes as she could get in. She thought for long minute on the small amount of food she could find, then dashing back into the office opened Mr. Church's desk again – this time taking the emergency cash from the top drawer along with his 9mm Smith and Wesson and a box of shells. Putting these in the Neman Marcus bag on top of Bella's clothes she pulled a bottle of Fiji water from the fridge and encouraged the little girl to drink while she stuffed the remaining bottles into the Saks 5th bag.

"Sarah." Bella's eyes had started to brighten a bit as Sarah handed her a slice of cheese and some grapes before putting those too in the food bag. "Where are we going?"

"On an adventure." Sarah smiled down at her as she upended her backpack onto the kitchen countertops, dumping out her binders and books to make room for another box of cereal, more protein shakes, and a few changes of clothes for herself from the back of Lucy's closet – including her Bogner Snow suit and a pair of North Face Snow Hiking Boots in pristine condition. She didn't need to check if they would fit as half of her own wardrobe at home consisted of cast-offs from Lucy's previous season. "There's room in here for your fairy tale book. Do you want to get it?" Bella nodded, skipping off to her room to retrieve her leather-bound copy of Grimm's Complete Fairy Tales. Certain they were as ready as they would ever be, Sarah wrote a quick letter and left it in Mr. Church's desk before gathering up the bags in one hand and taking Bella's hand with the other led the little girl out of the stifling apartment to the stairs.

It felt as if it took hours to reach the bottom of the stairs, Bella complaining a little about the climb down and asking repeatedly why they couldn't take the elevator. When they reached the bottom, Sarah found the doorman behind the concierge desk and asked him for his help getting some items out of storage. He gave her a look of dismay but agreed and the three of them went back to the stairwell to descend into the basement.

The penthouse storage lockers were nearly as large as Sarah's studio apartment near the college and on the upper level of the basement for convenience. She opened the lockup and asked the doorman to carry out Lucy's mountain bike and take it up the flight of stairs. "I'm going to put the rest of the camping gear together and then I'll help you with that." She pointed to the little canopied trailer Lucy had purchased for Bella last summer so that Sarah could take the little girl on rides through the park. It had been used twice, mostly due to the look of irritation the doorman was giving her now at the thought of muscling the trailer up the stairwell.

As soon as he had disappeared behind the heavy door Sarah worked fast, pulling down the aluminum framed hiking pack Mr. Church had purchased when his firm had sent all of the junior partners for a team building seminar in the Western Sierras. She took a quick stock of what was in the pack, a first aid kit still in its shrink wrap, a large plastic water bottle with a built-in carbon filter, a folding shovel, a small hand ax, a fire-starting kit, a gortex jacket, and a hammock tent coiled neatly in a nylon bag. She quickly stuffed the clothing from the Neman Marcus bag into the backpack, stowing the handgun and shells just as the lower-level door squeaked open announcing the doorman's return. Stuffing the whole lot into the trailer Sarah pulled from the top while the doorman lifted from the bottom as they struggled to make the light trailer fit up the narrow staircase. He helped her to attach the trailer to the bike in the lobby, asking if there was anything else he could do for her.

"Yes." She said, settling Bella into one seat of the trailer and the bag of food, her school bag, and the snow boots into the other. "You can go. No, not back to your station. Leave the building. Go home. Get your family. Leave the city." She handed him a twenty-dollar bill from the emergency cash as she hoisted the hiking pack onto her back, asking the doorman to hold open the big glass doors. Bella squealed in delight as the bike left the lobby and Sarah turned south on the wide sidewalk to where she had left Lance waiting beside the stolen bikes. He was gone, but the bicycle she had ridden from the campus was leaned against the wall, a paper note flapping in its spokes. She reached down and unfolded it, reading the words in Lance's neat hand. "Couldn't wait. Had to make the rendezvous. I'm sorry."

"Is that from your friend?" Bella asked as Sarah's heart leapt into her throat. They were alone. He had left them. They were on their own.

"Yes Baby." Sarah answered in a shaky voice, tucking the note into her pocket as she collected her thoughts. "Are you ready to go?"

"Yes please." Bella sang out from the trailer as Sarah started to pedal, her legs screaming in pain. She couldn't stop now. There was no going back now. She kept on 1st Street, intending to turn east onto Washington until something she had driven past in her car a thousand times sprang into her mind. She stayed on until Washington and then took a right, nearly colliding with a man in a business suit who was simply standing in the middle of the road staring at the ribbons of color swirling in the emerald sky.

At the corner of 3rd and Washington a large crowd had gathered outside a large convention center; most of them were city police officers, sheriff's deputies, and firefighters, but a few others in civilian clothes. They were listening to a man standing on the convention center steps shouting out different municipal priorities as she continued by, slowed by the trailer. She caught a glimpse of the train yard as she crossed 12th, it was engulfed in flame though she couldn't see the source. She stayed on the sidewalk until 19th, where an ambulance had jumped the curb and smashed into an auto shop wall blocking her path. It must have been responding to a call when everything stopped because there was a clear lane behind it all the way to the Interstate.

As she crossed under the freeway overpass, she noticed a few young men huddled up on the concrete reinforced walls. They shouted at her, whistling, one of them throwing a beer can that rattled to the pavement behind her.

She would have to get out of the city, into more suburban areas, places which were looking to maintain their sanity and weren't reveling in the chaos. She kept on Washington until 27th nearly gasping with joy as the big sump block building came into view, the stencil style painted sign above the door reading "Army Joe's Surplus Store" in big black letters.

The security gate was down but the door behind it was open as she pulled the bicycle to a halt in front. She climbed down from the bike, her legs rubbery from peddling and rattled the gate until an older man with a round belly stood cautiously to the side of the door, a shotgun in his hand.

"We're closed." He said flatly, his eyes scanning the road behind her.

"Please." She held up her hands to show him she meant him no harm, stepping aside so he could see Bella in the trailer. "Please. I need some supplies."

"Like what kind of supplies?" He lowered the shotgun slightly but didn't come any closer.

"I need food. The stuff that won't go bad."

"MREs?"

"Yes!" She nodded. "As many as we can fit on here. And a map. I need a map of the state if you have it."

He looked at her thoughtfully then pointed to the side of the building. "Come around back."

Sarah nodded, then getting back on the bike she peddled around in the direction he had pointed stopping in front of a large corrugated yard gate painted the same color as the building. A whistle echoed from somewhere in the building and the gate opened just wide enough for the bike and trailer to pass through. Upon entering she found herself surrounded by men, all heavily armed and wearing flak jackets, one of them a uniformed sheriff's deputy. Behind a massive military style truck curious women and children peeped out at her, worry etched in their faces.

The older man stepped into an open doorway leading into the business, he looked her over for a moment then said, "We don't have a lot to spare, but we do have some."

She pulled the wad of cash from her pocket, holding it up. "I'll pay. Whatever you can give me. I'll pay for it." He nodded then cocked his head indicating she should follow him in. Sarah pulled Bella from the trailer, holding her hand as she complied. Inside the store were endless rows of shelves stacked with various goods: camping stoves, water filtration systems, combat boots, folded flags, navy blankets, and various odds and ends Sarah didn't recognize. He pointed to a stack of boxes with the words Meals Ready to Eat on the side. "You can have some of these but with your little one in tow you might be happier with the HDRs. I also have some BP-5s if you want." He laughed "No one here will eat them so they're going cheap."

"I..." Sarah could feel tears stinging her eyes as the weight of the day crushed down on her shoulders. "I have no idea what any of those things are." She sobbed.

"Hey. Don't do that. Don't cry." The man looked at her, pulling a bandanna from a rack and handing it too her to dry her face. "Your baby is watching. She's looking to you now."

"Bella's not mine." She sniffed as she wiped her eyes. "I'm her nanny."

He scowled for a minute, his eyes flitting to the back door as if he was debating whether or not to call for his friends, "Where are her parents?"

"Bella's dad is in Vegas, and when I showed up to get them Bella's mom decided to go to the Apple Store." One of the men, the deputy, had stepped into the building behind her. He was standing there silently his arms slightly crossed as if appraising her.

"Do they know you have the girl?" He finally asked. Sarah nodded, pulling the release form from her back pocket and handing over for the man to read. He looked it over and then handed it back with a shrug. "The fucking Apple Store." He muttered under his breath and then stepped back out into the yard.

"Let's give you the HDRs and see what else we can scrounge up for you." The older man said.

They helped her load the trailer with a mixture of Humanitarian Daily Rations and Meals Ready to Eat, taking the mylar packs out of the boxes and using duct tape to strap them into small bundles so they would fit together around her other supplies. While they worked a few of the other children came out from behind the truck to watch, Bella smiled shyly at them waiting for Sarah to give her permission to play then giggled loudly as Sarah nodded, running off to join them in a game of hide and seek among the heavy equipment in the yard.

"Alright Miss Nanny, let's see what you have in the bag." The older man – the other men called him Big Jim – handed her a warm Gatorade as he pulled the pack from her shoulders and opened it up. "When was the last time you had something to eat? Oh holy shit." He gave her a disapproving look as he pulled the handgun from her pack. She had forgotten it was in there. "This isn't a loaf of bread." He said sternly, checking the weapon over. "And one in the chamber. Jesus Christ. Tim!" He shouted across the yard to one of the younger men manning the gate. "Go inside and get me one of the Kydex 101s." then to Sarah, "Do you have a belt on?" she shook her head "And a belt. I'm guessing a 28. Do you know how to use this?"

"I know where the safety is, and how to aim." She admitted bashfully. "I spent a day at the range when Mr. Church bought it. I think he had a bad client he was worried about at the time."

"Did you hit the target?"

"Yes." Sarah looked down at her shoes. "I scraped up the back of my thumb, but I eventually hit something that looked important on the target."

"Well, that's going to have to do." Big Jim sighed as Tim came out with a holster and the belt. He spoke as he laced the belt through the holster, "That scrape on your thumb is called idiot burn. It comes from not holding the handgrip properly. A gun is like any other tool, you have to keep your hands on the operational parts and away from the mechanical parts. You wouldn't stick your hand on the fan blade of a running engine, would you?" Sarah shook her head as he handed her the belt and holster, earning a gruff smile from Big Jim. "Same concept."

She put the belt around her waist, the now holstered gun feeling heavy and somehow alive at her side, while Big Jim finished taking inventory of her pack. He passed more instructions to Tim who dashed back into the store to collect a few more things. In a couple of minutes, Tim emerged with a box which he handed to Big Jim who repacked her sack. "All the right brand names," he muttered, "but none of the stuff you actually need. I put sunscreen in there, you two don't want to burn. I also put a compass in the front flap with your map. There's a basic survival guide in there too, and a breakdown fishing pole, some twine, two bars of soap, some little bottles of shampoo – you have to stay clean in the field - lots of fishing line, a stack of chem lights, some duct tape, a camp cook set, two baklavas to keep the elements off your face and neck – use them, and more carbon filters for your water bottle. Also, I gave you a Bible. You need to read it and your survival guide every night."

He led Sarah to a table behind the big truck where a sort of potluck meal had been laid out, then he invited her to eat as he asked her about her route and where she planned to go. He advised her against backtracking to follow the Salt River through the city but to instead make use of the freeway systems to cut directly across. "You've already lost a lot of time, and you need to make up for it." They talked about her day, the strange clandestine meeting in the library, the stolen bikes, Lucy's reaction to the situation, Lance being gone. The men around the table exchanged glowering but knowing looks, but let Sarah keep talking. There was something cathartic in relating the details of the ride, the people, the gathering of officers at the city center – this too provoked a nonverbal conversation from the group – and the crashed abandoned ambulance.

"Are you all planning on staying here?" she asked, looking around counting four families plus Big Jim, Tim, and the deputy, then smiled to Bella sitting at the end of the table spooning a large helping of macaroni salad into her mouth.

"No." He shook his head. "We have a team bringing back some mules from Camelback, probably won't be back until after dark. We're heading out before first light unless something happens, and we have to bug out. If you and Bella would like to stay until then we can make you up a cot in the back of the shop. We would ask you to just fall in with us, but I don't think that thing will keep up with the mules and we didn't plan for any additional riders."

"I'll stay the night." Sarah said, feeling the deep ache in her bones. "But I need to find my group. They have a plan to get us out of the desert where there's water."

"And where do you think you will go once you're out of the desert?"

"I don't know." Sarah sighed. "I've only thought this far. Bella's grandparents live in Idaho, but without a car that feels like it might as well be on the moon. I would like to get her back to her family. I just don't know." She could feel her head drooping, the combination of food and exhaustion working to shut her down.

"Well. You aren't going to get Bella anywhere this tired." He said. "It's getting dark, let's get you two bedded down for the night."

"How much do I owe you?" She asked reaching for her pocket.

"Well, I'll take thirty for the belt and holster." Big Jim smiled as he stood up from the table, speaking as she and Bella followed him into the loading bay where merchandise had been hastily moved to the edges of the room to make space for a line of cots, each with a pillow and an army blanket. "We'll call that the idiot fine for tossing a loaded weapon into a bag. There always is one. This time it's just money. Next time it could be lost supplies or even a life. The rest of the stuff you've already paid for."

"No." She shook her head, looking down at the wad of cash she clutched in her sweaty fist. "I didn't."

"You brought us something more valuable than money." He said. "You told us the time and place of the municipal meeting – that gives us a safer rout out of town and tells us which departments are organized enough to cause trouble. You also told us about the ambulance. There will be invaluable supplies on that rig and right now it's unguarded. Tim and Deputy Merris are leading a team to go recover those right now. You two need sleep. You have a big day tomorrow. So, pick a cot and hit it."

Sarah felt as though she had barely shut her eyes when she was being shaken awake again. She sat up, the change in the light in the room telling her that she had been out for hours. During the day the aurora had tinted everything green, but the light was pale. Now it was early morning, closer to midnight, and the bright greens and reds weaving through the sky were bright enough to be downtown street lights on the Vegas strip. She looked up at Deputy Merris standing over her cot as the sound of Bella's purring little snores filled the empty room around her. Everyone else had gotten up, dressed, and were ready to head out.

Merris stood there considering her for a moment before he said, "If you're getting out, now is the time. When people wake up and the lights are still out it's going to get wild." He paused, as if considering his next words carefully. "If you're dead set on following the river, don't be afraid to lose sight of it. If the speed of the water picks up, or you see an increase in litter moving on the surface, or if it gets murky out of nowhere pull the bike as far away from the bank as you can get it and head up hill. We don't know how our waterways are going to act now that no one is manning the spill ways and dams. Don't enter canyons you can't climb up the sides quickly with Bella, flash floods will sound like thunder... if you hear it without a cloud in the sky... run." He pressed a small object into her hand. It was a small medal on a chain depicting Saint Christopher carrying Christ over a river. He bent down and scooped up Bella from the cot beside her then said, "There were epi pens on that rig you told us about. I put a couple in your backpack. People who use them after being bitten by a rattlesnake have a better chance of living."

"Thank you." Sarah said, tears welling up in her eyes. "I can't thank all of you enough."

He nodded, carrying Bella to where the bike and trailer were parked placing her carefully in the second seat beside the gear while Sarah pulled her hiking pack on despite the screaming pain in her muscles. Bella mumbled something in her sleep, then turned over to rest her head awkwardly against the restraint straps. Deputy Merris closed the canopy over the trailer, shook Sarah's hand, wished her luck, then walked out the gates to join the others with the mules. Big Jim said his goodbyes as well, reminding her to stop once she was out of city limits to use the sunscreen and the baklavas. He gave her a fatherly hug as she mounted the bicycle, then waved her through the big corrugated gate.

She ignored the protest in her legs as she peddled. Waving goodbye to the people mounted on the little band of mules gathered in the middle of Washington Street as she continued her journey east towards the Hohokam Expressway. From there she would head north to McDowell Road, take that east all the way to the Beeline Highway North. But that would take hours of peddling. As the sky writhed like a pit of rainbow-colored vipers above her head, words written by Robert Frost whispered through her mind.

CHAPTER 18

Sheriff's Lockup – Pinefare, Montana

James French sat in the hard wooden chair with his back to the narrow hall leading along the face of the cells staring at his wife Celia as she sat on the long concrete bench that served as both seat and bed in the tiny cell. When he had first come in, she had been singing – the tune was something high and mournful he didn't recognize. But when she saw him she had started screaming, throwing her bedding around and cursing, looking more like an enraged animal in a cage than his beautiful wife of twelve years.

He had always known Celia was high spirited – his father would say high strung. Peevish and prone to rages, as a young man he had found her unpredictable moods intoxicating and somewhat endearing. But now he was older, he was holding on to one of the only good paying jobs in town, and he had two daughters to raise. He had grown up. Celia hadn't. Underneath all the trappings of a woman she was still that fifteen-year-old girl who once ran naked as a jaybird across the high school football field at homecoming. But this, this was different. Celia wasn't just being her usual mareish self. Like her song, she was something alien and unrecognizable.

When the lights went out, she had retreated into the darkness shrouding her cell, squatting on the bench and staring at him. He couldn't see her eyes, but he could feel them burning into him through the blackness. He had told her he would be back, to see what was wrong before stepping out into the lobby of the Sheriff's station to find the room empty. Buck Petty was standing in the middle of Catman Street just outside the front door staring upwards. James had walked out and followed his gaze to see the most incredible lightshow twisting through the sky.

Their wonderment at the beauty of the aurora was cut short by a plume of black smoke lifting from behind the Trapper Hotel. James jumped in his truck, the Sheriff in his patrol Jeep, but neither would start. They hadn't the time to wonder at this strange turn of events as his Aunt Sissy's voice, shrill and harsh, came echoing up the frozen streets. They had run, dashing around stalled vehicles and the side of the hotel, through the RV lot to where Len Hall's tiny trailer stood, ablaze. Daisy was holding Sissy back with all the strength she could muster as inhuman howls filled the sky from inside the flames.

James had run around the back of the singlewide where he stood on a rotted tree stump and the trailer hitch trying to kick in the back window, but the acrylic sheet made flexible with the heat just absorbed the blows as the flames spread to the little tuff shed just against the outer wall, nearly exploding as cans of gasoline and oil went up.

"Len!" Sissy had wailed, her voice harsh as she collapsed into the dirt, her fingers clawing at the sand as if she were afraid of falling off the earth into outer space. Friends and neighbors up and down the long lone circle of Pinefare came running, their hand-held extinguishers, arriving too late as Len's screams of pain and fear finally fell silent.

James returned to his seat outside Celia's cell, inwardly reeling. Len Hall - the man who had taken him fishing as a kid while his father managed the hotel; the one person who would drive out to wherever you were to fix a heater in the dead of winter or climb up on a roof to patch a leak in the middle of a downpour asking nothing but a handshake and good company in return – was dead. When he walked in she was singing again, turning her face to the window and crooning to the bands of light twisting overhead.

He didn't tell her Len was gone. Even at her best Celia wouldn't care.

The silence that filled the room as night fell was as

much a prisoner to Celia's madness as he was. Brilliant light from outside poured in through every opening in the building like shimmering jade and ruby water, and for a moment James whished it would drown them both. Celia's mind would finally be at peace, and he could finally rest knowing she was at peace. When his father walked into the room the silence was broken, shattered into a million pieces as Celia started to laugh. It was a wild, evil thing – her laughter. It pounced on him from the walls and ceiling, clawing and tearing at his flesh, ripping at his heart. His father dropped a firm hand to his shoulder pulling him from its grip.

"Come on, son." Morgan said. "There's no good you can do here." He nodded and stood up, leaving the lockup again, letting the door slam shut behind them. They walked out into the night, the frosty air stinging his lungs, the lights in the sky illuminating the town as if it were day.

"Len's dead." James finally said.

"I know." His father sighed deeply. "We have Sissy in a room at the Trapper. Doc McAbe gave her a valium. She's comfortable for now."

"The power's out." James looked to his father. "To everything. Cars, phones, streetlights…"

"The computer in my office." Morgan nodded. "We're using spirit lamps in the hotel. Daisy bought about a million of them for the ghost walk thing she did last Halloween. By the time I got here she had already put one in every room. She has them on the tables at the bar too. It's going to be a bitch managing the Trapper without Len." Morgan choked on the end of his sentence. "We should have made him the mayor of this damn town. Put him up in a better house. That way he wouldn't spend the last moments of his life dying like a dog in the back of some garbage trailer. He was…" Morgan's mouth opened, but no words would come out. "He was the best of us."

"I know, Dad." James nodded. They walked in silence the rest of the way to the Trapper, the snowflakes falling around them picking up the colors of the aurora and shimmering like a million pieces of a shattered rainbow cascading down.

There was hot food at the hotel. And warm light. Besides the boiler in the basement Daisy had a large fire in each of the hotel's two massive hearths and he was fairly certain she had both wood burning ovens going in the kitchen. Daisy had been obsessed with retaining what she had called the hotel's soul during the renovation. When the engineer from Billings had come in and suggested that she have the coal run boiler removed in favor of something more modern, instead she convinced him to research units made in Europe which would burn wood efficiently enough to heat the entire building.

When the kitchen was remodeled, Daisy installed wood burning commercial stoves as well – pulling the original large cast iron cooking range out of the basement and sending it to a specialist in New Jersey to be restored to full working order. By the time Daisy had finished she had spent nearly every dime of her daddy's life insurance policy reshoring the structure and renovating the conveniences, so the hotel could operate as it had when it was rebuilt from the ashes of a 1912 logging fire that had ravaged the entire town. If there was a single building in the State of Montana which would welcome a snowy night during a power outage without a hint of a complaint, it was The Trapper.

And by the look of the crowd of people gathered around the tables in the bar, everyone in town knew it.

The conversations were hushed to begin with, but they lowered to whispers when Morgan and James walked in. He was aware of the town gossip, most of it surrounding Daisy's pregnancy. When it had slipped out that she was expecting twins, they didn't need to witness Celia attempting to kill his father's young business partner to confirm their suspicions. He had shielded the girls from the talk as best as he could, but there would be no escape from it now. Not unless he planned on ripping them out of school and holding them hostage in their home up on Bear Reach. There was other talk too – questions about the loss of the electricity, and sad whispers from those who had watched Len Hall die. James sat down at the bar, hanging his wide brimmed hat over his knee and sinking his head into his hands, elbows resting against the bar.

"I forgot to ask, Dad." He finally said lifting his face from his palms. "How'd you get into town?"

"I borrowed Smokey." Morgan answered, then asked Daisy for a whiskey as she swept by. She nodded and pulled out three shot glasses and filled two of them from a bottle of Roughstock single malt, the third she poured only halfway and filled the rest from a bottle of soda water. "You're pregnant!" Morgan protested as she raised the third glass.

"Morgan, there's more booze in the apple pie than there is in this shot." She said with a sorrowful smile on her tearstained face. "To Len."

"To Len." James lifted his glass, watching his father nod and join the toast. Daisy tossed her drink back and went on with her work pouring behind the bar and walking dinner tickets back into the kitchen where Mamie Blackman was busy filling plates from the ovens and cooktops.

"How did Smokey handle the ride into town?" James both loved and hated that horse. He was snotty and full of himself, and stupid enough to charge a bear even if he would spook at a butterfly. That said he was the cowiest damn horse James had ever been on, damn near psychic when it came to moving a herd.

"Oh, he was fine." Morgan turned in his barstool to face his son as Daisy dropped off a small loaf of fresh baked bread, a large black handled knife, and a ramekin of butter. "Kind of a shit when it came to skirting the creek, but he was fine. I've got him in your aunt's stables for the night. Your mother is going to stay with the girls until you can get back out there. She had a fire going and most of your icebox packed out into the snow before I even had the horse tacked up. She sends her love and would like to know just what the heck is going on."

James laughed at this. "Yea. I would too. I thought I had left my lights on in the truck until I looked over and saw that Buck was having the same problem. Tried to call after … the fire… and every damn line was down. Even that piece of crap cell phone I carry around. Nothing new, not having reception. But usually it at least turns on."

His dad furrowed his brow. "Let me see."

"Can't."

"I can't see your phone?"

"Nope."

"I'll give it back."

"You can't see it," James said as he buttered a piece of bread, "because I chucked it into Mule Wash."

"You!" Morgan nearly sprayed bread out his nose as he snorted in surprise. "You chucked it in the wash?"

James pushed his hand out in an arch making a low whistle. "Right off the bridge and into the water. Glad to see the back of it. I hated that thing."

"Daisy." Morgan put his head in his hand, chuckling. "Can I see your phone?"

"Sure." She said, pulling the slim device from her apron pocket and sliding it across the bar to him. "It's not working right now though. I must not have charged it and it died on me. I'll plug it back in when the power's back on."

Morgan's face fell into a thoughtful scowl as he stood up from the bar. "Excuse me folks." He said over the top of the conversations. "I have kind of a strange question to ask. Do any of you have a cell phone in your pocket right now?" The change in the atmosphere of the room was instant. A handful of people looked to their neighbors and then nodded slowly. "Are they working?"

"No." Nate Petty, a local logger and the sheriff's son called from the back near the door to the patio. "It stopped working at the same time my truck did."

"Same with mine." Lodi Blackman who was seated next to Morgan at the bar held up his iPhone. "I was on it at the time, had a full charge. It got hot and then it just died."

"What do you think happened?" A younger woman with long black hair, one of the few winter campers staying at Sissy's RV Park spoke up. "I tried calling 911 when I saw the fire and my phone wouldn't turn on. Nothing in my camper works either. Not even my laptop and I know for a fact it was well charged."

"Did Daisy give you a room yet?" Morgan asked and when she shook her head Daisy nodded and went out to the reception desk to grab one of the room keys. "We'll help you pack your gear in after dinner. Anyone else have anything that isn't working."

"My backup generator is fried." Cody Barret, a long-haul trucker who kept a winter cabin off the western end of the national park spoke up. "I was trying to get ahold of Pete to ask him about the lights – the northern lights – I've only seen them this bright in Alaska. But the HAM wouldn't come on. And when I went to turn over the generator, I couldn't even get it to click for me."

A horrible thought struck Morgan. Pete Sanders, the local ranger, was stationed in a fire watch tower at the top of Grizzly Peak with only his HAM radio for company and a little electric stove for heat. Both were run off a natural gas-powered generator at the base of the tower. "Has anyone seen Pete in town today?"

"My pop headed up there with a couple of horses." Nate said. "Right after… Len."

Morgan nodded, the weight of Len's name hanging over the room. "Ok. Well Nate if there's anyone who can bring him back into the fold it would be your dad. If we don't see him by daybreak James and I will take a couple horses up and see if we can't find them. With the lights as bright as they are it shouldn't be too hard finding their way back into town.

In the meantime, everyone enjoy your dinner as best you can. If you're stuck here because your place is too far out or too cold, we'll set you up for the night. We have clean sheets and hot water and plenty for breakfast in the morning. If some of you who are heading home tonight could go through the RV park and check to see if we have winter campers trying to cowboy through – let them know we have space for them if they want it. And make sure to check on your neighbors tonight. See if they need firewood, make sure they've shut their gas off at the tank if they need to. Let's all just go that extra mile tonight."

The door to the front of the hotel by the reception desk swung open letting in a cold blast of air as Verdi Groger half walked half staggered in from the cold. "My power is out." She announced shivering. "The entire marina is dark. No phones."

"Where's your son, Verdi?" Morgan looked at her, trying in vain to hide his disgust.

"My…son?" Verdi sounded incredulous. "I've come out here to find out which one of you people dropped their bug zapper into the snow and shorted out my power and you want to know where my son is?"

"As you can see, the power is out here too." Morgan leaned against the bar, trying to keep himself from marching over to Verdi and throttling her within an inch of her life. "And unless you've put in a fireplace or you have him in your jacket pocket you've just walked five miles in freezing weather while leaving your kid alone with no way of keeping warm."

"He has blankets." She spit back as she pulled a pack of cigarettes from her inner pocket. "Fuck it's like a funeral parlor in here. Nice place you're running, Morgan."

"James." Morgan growled without turning to look at his son.

"Yup." James stood up and put his hat on, thanked Daisy for the service, asked her to keep something warm for him when he got back, then walked past Verdi to the door. It took him just a few moments to get Smokey tacked up, one more to find the duster his father had stuffed in the bags, quite a few more to convince that somebitch of a horse that yes, he was going back out into the cold, and another forty to backtrack Verdi's trail in the snow. He was thankful for the lights over head as he moved Smoky into a fast walk following the county highway from the center of town to the Inch Lake Marina through the still night air and rolling dunes of snow.

When he arrived, the dock house was dark and there was no answer to his knock at the door. He couldn't remember what Verdi had named her boy, so he just knocked again and said, "Kid? You ok in there?" When there was still no response he took a deep breath, and booted in the door.

He found the boy curled up on a couch in the front room, his skin pale and chilled to the touch but he was alive, his little quivering breaths coming out in snorts of steam around his mouth and nose.

"God damn it." James muttered and scooped the kid up blankets and all. The boy was shaking too hard to sit in the saddle alone, so James had to lay him over the front like a calf as he climbed back on top of Smoky. The horse snorted a little but otherwise held perfectly still as James turned the boy around to lean against his chest, then wrapped his leather duster around them both to share his heat, plugging any gaps with the thin cotton quilt Verdi had left him wrapped in. He took the road back to town at a slower pace, letting Smoky find his footing as they followed the highway winding past the wide Flatbow river back to town. The boy groaned a couple of times, but the shaking had stopped and though it was hard to tell in the bright green light some color looked like it was returning to his face.

When they made it back to the hotel James handed the kid down to Nate Petty who had just been leaving with his wife Rose carrying their three-year-old son. They rushed him back inside while James wheeled Smoky back up Catman Road to the Sheriff's station to check the cast iron stove there. The logs he had thrown in just a few hours earlier had smoldered down to glowing coals but there was still a good amount of heat in the brick-built building. It was the second oldest in town, built within a year of the Trapper and made to withstand long harsh winter storms blowing in from Canada. He paused for a moment listening to Celia in the back still singing softly to the lights, then putting another two fat quarters onto the coals waited for the fire to jump to life before walking back out to where he had left Smoky standing in the snow. He would need to see him bedded back down, clean the snow from his feet and hair before he could go back into the hotel for a bite to eat. Then he would walk a plate back for Celia and make himself as comfortable as he could on the floor beside the front desk, tending the stove through the night and fighting back the cold.

CHAPTER 19

1024 Blackjack Oak Parkway - Baptiste, Idaho

Abigail fumed as she stomped up the drive, her hands tucked in her coat pockets for warmth. This place had gone to absolute shit. Fucking yanks! Not even the successful ones could have nice things without eventually turning it into bloody Brixton. The door slammed behind her as she stripped herself of her jacket and scarf, pulling a Kleenex from her pocket to dab her nose before she entered the den where Travis and Joanna were sitting beside their small ornate fireplace. "Well," she grunted as she pulled off her fleece lined boots, placing them next to the hearth to dry, "I found out where the other Walker boy got off to yesterday. And what all that racket was. You will never guess what they have done!" She slumped into a chair, looking first to Travis and then Joanna. "They've pushed their cars into the street along the curb."

"Well," Joanna was choosing her words carefully, "considering what happened to Lex Donati's place maybe that isn't such a bad idea right now. Are we really sure he wasn't home?"

"Oh no." Abigail waved her off. "He never winters here. He's a snowbird. I believe he was in New Mexico this year. Anyway, that's not my point. It's why… *why!*…they moved them to the curb that just bloody disgusts me. They've torn down the garage doors. I don't know how they did it without electric tools, probably bashed them down with rocks like bleeding monkeys. They've stolen some of the lumber off the jobsite at Lot 50, I have to assume with the blessing of Bruce Tolman - he's over there – *helping!* Does he live in this neighborhood?"

"No." Travis looked thoughtful. "He and his family

own the little sheep ranch back behind the end of the golf course." He turned to his wife, "You know the one, when you turn off of Kentucky Bar past the club house and you take that funky little road past the water tank…"

"Swallow Fork." Joanna said looking back down at the magazine in her lap.

"That's the one." Travis stretched out his legs, enjoying the warmth of the fire. "Anyway. The Tolmans have like a hundred acres up there. They raise sheep and I think have a couple head of cattle."

"Yes. Bloody noisy things, those sheep." Abigail sighed. "I can hear them all night during the summer. Why summer? Anyway, that explains the horses."

"Horses?" Joanna looked up, startled.

"Yes, Joanna." Abigail draped her hand over her eyes, the tips of her fingers massaging her lids. "That's what I'm trying to tell you. They have horses down there. Bruce is using his to drag lumber from Lot 50 through the green ways to the Walker place and they're building stables in their garage! It's a bleeding barnyard now. Oh! And the Zhous? They've left the garage doors on. Small mercy. But they've ripped the motors and tracks off the ceiling - those they've tossed in the yard! - and now their garage is stacked from floor to rafters with bales of hay!"

"What?" Joanna gasped.

"Yes!" Abigail sat up to look at her. "The slightest loss of a modern convenience, a flickering of the lights, and the Walkers seize on this like some golden opportunity to go back to chopping wood and shooting squirrels. Well. When the electric is restored the very first thing I am going to do is call my bloody attorney. I am going to sue the hell out of their little cult – you know they're all living communally now. It's like a horror movie. I am going to sue them for loss of property values. Travis, you're in federal law enforcement. Is there nothing you can do to stop this assault on our civility?"

She looked up at him, but there was nothing about his

body language or the look on his face that she liked. He had sat forward on the couch, a grim expression on his face as he rubbed the palms of his hands together. "Joanna." He said finally. "How much food do we have in the house?"

"Oh, I don't know." She replied, flipping the page of her magazine "We ate the last of the soup last night. Oh Abigail, it was so romantic. Travis pulled his camp stove out of our third room. We had dinner by firelight. It was like we were on a date. But then we ran out of propane. Travis, I was thinking we could bundle up and walk down to that little market in town. I'm sure they're open. They're always open. Even when the snow is deep."

"Joanna." The seriousness in Travis' voice stopped her cold. "How much food is in the house?"

She gave him an irritated look as she got up, slapping her magazine down on the kitchen counter and searching their cupboards, calling out an inventory as she did. "A box of Kashi – well half a box. But there's no milk. I tossed it and everything in the fridge after the power went out. We'll have to replace it. We have some crackers. Some dry pasta, a can of tomato paste – oh! No make that two cans of tomato paste! A five-pound bag of almond flour – don't remember why I bought that - those corn bread mixes you like, a can of chili, half a loaf of bread, some Jell-O packets, your protein shakes, three cans of tuna, and about a third of a bag of Dove chocolates."

"That's it?" His eyes went wide.

"Well, the spice rack is full." She looked at him impatiently. "I told you. I tossed a bunch out. The freezer was defrosting all over the floor. So we have to do some shopping. So what?"

"Where did you toss it?"

"In the dumpster, down the sink…" She looked at him and laughed nervously, "Travis, what's the big deal?"

Without saying a word, he walked out of the room, going down the hall to the single car garage they stored their dumpsters in. He flipped the light switch, cursing when nothing happened. Then, using the pale blue-green light streaming in from the paneled windows at the head of the garage, he found the red cord at the base of the motor and pulled it to disconnect the arm from the bay door so he could roll it upward. Joanna and Abigail stood in the doorway as he pulled the heavy plastic bin into the light and lifted the lid. What his eyes didn't tell him, his nose did as the smell of mold and wet rot came up from the pile of food half puddling half freezing at the bottom.

"How about you Abigail?" He said closing the lid.

"I'm in the same boat." She said slowly, not quite liking where he was going with this. Then with a little sniff she added, "I eat nothing but fresh foods. They all went in the skip when the power went out. I'm down to one tin of potted meat and a bag of crisps."

Travis took a deep breath and rolled down the garage door. Then went upstairs to change into his uniform.

1002 Yellow Jack Place – Baptiste, Idaho

Zia burst through the front door panting; the tips of her wet hair frosted with small beads of ice. Bruce Tolman had ridden across the golf course this morning to check on the job site and after a small conversation with the residents gathered between the only two houses with fireplaces on Yellow Jack, had agreed to help them modify their homes for better functionality. It had taken him an hour to ride home and return with a large acetylene welder and some tools dragging through the snow behind his mount strapped to his kid's toboggan. He then used it to construct a larger skid out of a couple car doors that Beau Walker could pull behind his own gelding through the wooded area between the back edge of the houses to the equestrian center across Highway 95 from the head of Buster Jigs Road.

"You're sure he's going to be okay?" He had said to Jennifer Walker as the young man clicked to the tall gelding he called Tubbs, pushing him into a walk through the snow. When she answered to the affirmative Bruce had shrugged and then set to work dragging his own sled over to the Pratt house to see about fixing the valve on their hot water heater. Most of the homes on the block had opted for electric heaters, Derik Pratt through pure felicity had opted for gas – as had the Walkers though it seemed now like that had been a deliberate choice. Jennifer had provided him with two new manual valves still in their packaging asking him to swap them out for the electronic ones which had stopped working. In a matter of hours both houses had their hot water capabilities restored. Seizing on the opportunity for a bath, Zia had returned to her home while Bruce oversaw the conversion of some of the Walker's and all of Teagan Booker's wide garage spaces into usable stables.

But now Zia had returned, freshly scrubbed and panicked searching frantically for Jennifer. She was upstairs in her family room beside her wood burning stove talking with Derik, Ferris, and Mary Beth about modifications which could be made to the houses in an effort to return them to working order as well. Bruce was standing over Jennifer's shoulder as they poured over the building plans he had taken from the office for each lot, baby Aaron asleep in her arms.

"The man." Zia gasped in broken English, her high emotions making it almost impossible to find the words outside her native tongue. "He comes. The one in the brown shirt."

Alla came in from the bedroom across the hall where she had been reading fairy tales to the younger children to keep them occupied and out of the way of construction. She rattled off a couple of lines in flowing Ukrainian, listening intently as Zia exploded with information her hands waving expressively as she spoke. Alla nodded and then translated to the group.

"It's Travis." She sighed. "He's going door to door collecting food. He says he is starting a ..." she paused, searching for the right words, "community food storage. For the whole neighborhood."

"He had gun." Zia broke in, calming slightly but still rattled. "And the English woman she is pulling the wagon."

"They made Zia give up her food supplies." Alla said angrily. "The ones we have buried in the snow. And everything in the pantry. They took it all. He's going to ration it out to us."

"I wait." Zia burst into tears, Derik immediately rising from the couch to comfort her, moving her to sit beside Jennifer on the sofa as she spoke. "I was scared. He had gun. I show him everything. He took it and I waited, he went to Tammy - and then Mary Beth."

"My house?" Mary Beth's eyes went wide.

"I'm sorry." Zia was shaken and sobbing. "I gave up the food."

Mary Beth had risen to the window, watching Travis exit her back gate with the two large trash bags of perishables she had packed into a crudely built igloo off her back porch. "That son of a bitch has my turkey!" she growled.

"Zia." Jenifer patted the young woman's arm and smiled thinly. "I want you to take a deep breath. It's ok. You did what you had to do."

"He's coming over." Mary Beth turned from the window. Jen bent down and kissed little Aaron's forehead and handed him over to Zia, then standing she strode down the hall into her master bedroom.

Travis pounded at the door with the side of his fist,

then stood back with his hands crossed just at the buckle of his duty belt, the pale rays of green light glinting off the polished brass of his badge. At first he thought Jennifer might not answer. He had no idea how many of the neighborhood women she had in there with her but it was high time Jenifer Walker learned to submit to rule of law. He looked to where Abigail and Joanna stood on the sidewalk with Jo's little green garden wagon brimming with confiscated food, the long shadow of Noah's Gadsden flag billowing over their faces. That would be the next thing to come down. He would burn it in the street in front of their house.

The door swung open and Jenifer appeared, her left arm crooked at a strange angle above the deadbolt as she held the door firm against her side so he couldn't see into the room behind her. "Travis." She said calmly. "I thought I told you not to come back here. You aren't welcome."

"It's Officer Ross." He said, expanding the width of his shoulders as he pointed to his name tag. "I'm taking over leadership of this area until we can get in touch with FEMA for them to provide relief. At this time, I'm collecting all private food stores to form a community bank which will be housed at my residence. We will ration the food communally, so we can be certain everyone eats while order is being restored."

"That's a nice speech, Travis." A taunting look came into Jennifer's eyes. "But my private food stores are just that, private. I'm not giving them to you."

Travis's eyes flicked to where her arm was concealed behind the door, then he stepped forward to take command of the porch. "I am going to search your home and I will be leaving with all food stores you have. And all your weapons, just to make sure we can maintain neighborhood peace."

He was so busy watching her left hand holding the dish cloth behind the door he never registered the Winchester Defender in her right. In one swift move she pivoted the barrel up from where it pointed at her entry way tile to the hollow of his hip and fired. Joanna screamed from the sidewalk as he staggered backwards reaching for the gun holstered on his belt, his expression twisted in confusion as his hand came away empty and slick with blood. His duty belt, shredded from the close-range shot, dangled behind him at the belt-loop as his sidearm danced around the back of his knees like a weight on a string. He tried to recover it and Jenifer fired from the door again, the shot scattering across his shoulder and face spinning him around to fall into the snow outside her walk. She pumped the shotgun, expelling the smoking cartridge and emptied another round into the back of his head before pumping again and leveling it to where Joanna was racing towards her husband lying in the yard. Abigail stood frozen in place at the sidewalk as a pool of hot urine spread across the front of her designer jeans.

"Stop!" Jennifer barked as Joanna froze, nonsensical words tumbling hysterically from her mouth as she crumbled to her knees. A flash of movement from the woods behind Janice Wheeler's home caught Jenifer's eye, she looked up to see her son Beau pushing Tubbs at near breakneck speed across the frozen lawns, his father's 9mm in his hand. He must have been on his way home with another bale of hay and had ditched the sled in the woods when he heard the gunfire. "Don't move Abigail!" Jenifer turned her focus back to where Joanna lay in the snow sobbing. "He can't miss you at this range!"

She turned over her shoulder and called back to the house for Zia, the young woman walking out into the yard holding two small backpacks in her shaking hands. At the same time Fang Zhou came around from behind her house leading her husband's big boned stallion Templar, his daughters Amy and Heather trailing just behind their almond shaped eyes wide taking everything in. They had been watching their father cutting boards in Jenifer's back yard when she had come to the slider and whispered her plan to him. Behind them walked their mother, her face stony and expressionless. Zia dropped the packs into the snow at Joanna's knees, her cousin Alla holding baby Aaron at the open door. Across the street Lisa, Tammy and Ashley stood on the porch of the Zhou house, expressions of horror on their face.

Jennifer took Templar's reigns and climbed into the saddle, keeping the Defender trained on Joanna the entire time, her eyes flicking to where Beau had moved Tubbs behind Abigail. The English woman held her hands up in the air above her head, sensing rather than seeing the gun he held on her. "Pick up the packs." Jennifer commanded as Ferris walked out of the house, a four-pound hammer and a long length of chain in his hand.

"Please." Abigail whimpered, "I'm unarmed."

"How about you?" Jenifer asked Joanna, who had fallen into silence as she watched Ferris taking the sidearm off Travis' body. "Are you unarmed?" Joanna looked up at her, rage and hatred twisting her narrow features, but she remained silent. "Fine." Jennifer nodded. "On your feet. Hand that other pack to Abigail." Joanna rose from the ground, dusting the snow from her jeans then turning she crossed the yard to do as she had been ordered, Jennifer trailing behind on Templar, the barrel of the shotgun never wavering.

The neighborhood formed a procession, Abigail and Joanna leading their armed guards down Blackjack Oak first to Abigail's house where she was instructed to change clothes. "Something practical." Jenifer said watching the woman like a hawk while Beau stood guard over Joanna in the front yard. "No cotton. No denim. Something meant for snow."

"There's no food here." Feng announced to the crowd of neighbors standing on the driveway after making a complete inspection of the house. Abigail emerged from the front door dressed in a neon green ski-suit and boots. They followed the pair back to Joanna's where the same process was repeated, this time Ashley joining Feng in his inspection while Joanna changed into her husband's kaki gortex jumpsuit, the triangular patch of the BLM emblazoned on the shoulders.

"Very little food." Ashley announced coldly, as Joanna's hateful gaze scanned her neighbor's faces defiantly. "They would have been completely empty by the end of the day. And their wood pile in the garage is thin. It would have been gone by the end of the week."

The procession continued down the greenway planted with young walnut and locust trees beyond the Lindon's house towards the heavy iron gates spanning the end of Blackjack Oak Parkway. The gates had remained closed on their mechanical arms but opened freely when pulled. They stopped at the end of the road where Ferris walked the larger gate open while Derik used the small sledge hammer to smash the face of the electronic lock holding a pedestrian gate on the left-hand side. Once through the keypad and into the box he could manipulate the heavy bolt built into the back, so the smaller gate could be opened as well.

"Go." Jennifer said flatly as Ferris handed Joanna her husband's gun.

"Go?" Abigail wheeled, her eyes wide. "Go where?"

"Anywhere but here." Jennifer shrugged slightly. "You are not welcome here anymore."

"But this is my home!" Abigail insisted. "I own that house! It is my property!"

"Property you forfeited when you attempted to murder your neighbors." It was Mary Beth who spoke, her fisted hands trembling at her side. "Taking our food to restock your own? We have children here!"

"Murder is a bit dramatic, don't you think?" Abigail sighed. "We were simply organizing a communal bank. Managing the resources until rescue arrived."

"No one asked you to do that Abigail!" Tammy shouted. "No one told you to come into our homes and take what we had."

"What? You wanted us to go get a warrant? It's

existential circumstances!" Abigail screamed back. "Travis was a duly appointed federal officer and you shot him down in cold blood."

"Go now." Jenifer's voice was level as she put the Defender to her shoulder. "Or I will shoot you both right here, right now. This horse won't even shuffle his feet, and I'll sleep like a baby after."

Joanna spit into the snow then turned, her husband's sidearm in her clinched fist, the sack which Zia had given her slung over her arm. Abigail stammered in protest until Heather Zhou picked up a wad of snow and lobbed it, striking the dark haired woman square in the face. She sputtered and spit, but soon another snowball was flung, and another until she was forced to retreat under a hail of snow, ice, sometimes rocks or cold wet horse dung - anything and everything the crowd of angry neighbors could get their hands on. Ferris closed the gate behind them, wrapping the chain he carried around the center pillar so both the main gate and the pedestrian one could be secured separately with two locks. They watched the two women disappear around the outer wall of the neighborhood down Kentucky Bar Boulevard heading away from the golf course in the general direction of town.

"What was in the packs?" Jenifer looked down to where Bruce Tolman had come to stand at Templar's flank, his eyes watching the two women as they disappeared into the drifting snow.

"Some MREs." Jenifer said as she expelled the unused shell from the rifle into her hand. "Basic gear. Just enough to get them by if they have the will to use it."

"That's a risk, you know." He said, after taking a long deep breath. "Letting them live. It just gives them a chance to come back and try to hurt you again."

Jennifer looked down at him, a sad smile on her face. "I know." She said, "But I'm not at the point yet where I feel like building gallows in the park at the end of the street." Then turning to the group of neighbors who had gathered around her, their faces expectant. She turned to her son, a weary look on her face. "Beau, go with Ferris and Derik and get more chain out of your father's den. Chain up the gates at the end of Buster Jigs Road and Roundup Camp Drive same as you did here. Make sure to use only the C group locks so everyone can get a copy of the key. We want to keep people out, not lock them in. Zia and Alla, you two go with Mary Beth, Tammy and Ashley - make sure all the food gets back to where it belongs. Get it buried. This time let's run a hose over it, lock it in ice to make it harder to steal. It will mean more work at meal times but at least it will be there. Lisa and Teagan – would you mind watching the children while Bruce, Feng, Bi and I go for a ride?"

The two women nodded but Bi's eyes went wide at this, and she shook her head. "My mother doesn't ride." twelve-year-old Amy Zhou said. "She's afraid of horses. But I'm part of the saddle club."

Jennifer turned to Feng, "Do you keep horses over at the stables?"

"No." He shook his head. "We were going to buy her and her sister horses for their New Year's gifts. But it looks like that might be harder than we expected now."

"Maybe not." Jenifer looked back to Beau. "And you're certain no one is at the center feeding the animals?"

He shook his head. "The troughs were all empty last night. And again this morning. The main building is locked up tight."

"They're a commercial operation." Bruce said. "If they aren't being paid no one shows up."

"Do you think she can handle a string of ponies?" Jennifer asked Feng.

"Oh yes." He nodded, "She is very good."

"Well, when we get there have her pick out her favorite, then one for you and her sister." Jenifer said. "Then we'll pony over the school horses, so everyone who wants one can have a mount. We'll just have to take over more garage spaces from the empty houses."

"We can handle the gates." Derik said, slinging the hammer over his shoulder. "If you need Beau."

"Ok." Jennifer collected her thoughts. "Beau you let Mr. Zhou double up with you. Amy, you come up here with me. Bruce… if we can borrow you for another couple of hours I promise to make it worth your time."

"You mean other than the valves I have in my pack?" He cocked his wide brimmed hat a bit with his thumb wondering what other surprises Jenifer Walker had up her sleeve. When she nodded, he shook her hand. "You need me, you got me."

Everyone broke off to their respective tasks. Teagan happily herded the flock of children upstairs into the warmth of the Walker family room to color and tell stories after Jenifer gave her instructions as to warming the small supply of breast milk buried in mason jars in the back yard snow. Bruce climbed up on his gelding Skyline to lead the way out of the neighborhood. As they headed towards the gates at Buster Jiggs, Jennifer caught sight of the makeshift sled in the woods between the houses and the heavy block wall encircling the entire neighborhood. She made a mental note to remind Beau to pick it up on his way back and to finish the task of clearing out the equestrian center hay barn. Ferris let them out the main gate, promising to come back after they had finished securing the third to let Beau and Amy in with the rest of the horses.

"Your sister has quite an arm." Jennifer remarked to Amy as they crossed the empty highway.

"She hates Abigail." Amy said matter-of-factly. "Hǔ hasn't been back since Abigail chased him out of the yard."

"Who?" Jennifer looked to Feng who was riding double ahead of Beau beside them.

"No." Amy laughed. "Hǔ. It means tiger. He's the big fluffy cat she had been feeding. He looks like our cats Simoji and Long. She loved him and now she's worried he won't ever come back."

When they arrived at the center, letting themselves into the big pole gate at the front of the property and making their way to where the stables were lined up behind the hill. She was proud to see that Beau had spent his morning mucking stalls and feeding, and left instructions for him to take the neighborhood mounts first and then make a second trip for all the school mounts – five of those in total. "We'll leave the others, but I want you to keep coming back and doing the feeding. If no one comes to claim them by the end of the week, we'll pull them over with us just to keep a better eye on them. When you get back, I want you to set the American flag at half-mast."

"What do I do about Mr. Ross?" Beau asked a bit squeamishly. They had draped him in a sheet before leaving to screen the little children from the sight, but otherwise he remained.

"I'll deal with him when I get back." She said. "Now tack up Scout for Mr. Zhou."

Scout was Jefferson's gelding, a bit shorter than Tubbs but strong and capable for the task at hand. Soon the three adults were on their way south on Highway 95 where it skimmed along the eastern banks of the Snake River heading towards the little mini storage just across the street from Kentucky Bar Road. Climbing down from the saddle Jennifer knocked on the door of the little two-story house which served as both manager's residence and office. She waved through the window to the manager who peered suspiciously through the upstairs window, and after speaking with him a moment convinced him to unlock the gates he had chained from the inside.

"You're looking pale, John." She remarked as the older gentleman limped over to open the gate, an automatic rifle slung over his shoulder. "Is everything ok?"

He gave her a weary look, "Patsey's sick. She ran out of her albuterol two days ago, and her Altace is really low. We're worried that if the lights don't come back on soon, things are just going to get worse."

"Have you been to town?"

"Can't make it. It's too far to walk, and I can't ride."
He chuckled a little pointing to Templar, "We're just holed up
here waiting it out."

Jen thanked him and said goodbye, promising to lock
up when she was done, then led Templar by the reigns down
a long row of storage units while Bruce and Feng followed
behind. "It's going to get worse." She remarked to the two
men. "It's only been two and a half days, but when the reality
of the situation sinks in it's going to get much worse."

"You mean in the neighborhood?" Feng gave her a
serious look. "I was thinking that too. What are we going to
do when Tammy or Ashley run low on food? It's going to be
a couple of months before we can plant what seeds we have,
and another few months to let them grow. And even then,
what we have in the garden shed isn't going to feed the
neighborhood. If a couple of childless adults are already
stealing to fill their own pantries, what will a mother do when
it comes time to feed their kids?"

"Well, that's why we're here." Jennifer took out a set
of keys from her pocket and opened one of the storage lockers.
It was a big one, eighteen feet by twelve feet stacked floor to
corrugated ceiling with boxes of meals ready to eat, canned
goods, five-gallon buckets marked flour, eggs, soup base,
barley, rye, cornmeal, and powdered milk. Mylar bags lined a
shelf on the wall filled with dried beans, split peas, freeze
dried vegetables and meat, dehydrated fruit, and potato
shreds. She opened a foot locker that had been stacked atop
three buckets labeled sugar revealing rows upon rows of
neatly categorized seeds – all heirloom varieties of nearly
every vegetable imaginable.

"Where did this all come from?" Bruce asked, his jaw
falling to his chest.

"We've been squirreling it away little by little."
Jenifer smiled sadly. "Noah and I. We think that feeding just

our family – we should have about a five-year supply by now. If we share it around, stock people up. If everyone is careful… it should get the neighborhood through at least the middle of spring. The pain in the ass is going to be moving it. I think we can make another two sleds out of those pallets. What do you think Bruce?"

"Yea." He nodded. "I can do that."

"Good. I'll open the one next door." Jennifer said sorting through the keys on the ring. "It's mostly food but some other supplies as well that might come in handy. The bottles of alcohol aren't for drinking though, make that clear when you go back. That and the tobacco are for barter. They'll be worth their weight in gold in a couple of weeks."

"They're worth it now." Bruce shifted his weight a bit uncomfortably. "You wouldn't happen to have any Skoal wintergreen, would you?"

"I might." Jennifer paused at the door, the lock in her hand. "And we certainly owe you for the work you've done today. But I'm not going to lie Bruce. If we're going to survive and thrive, we can't be looking for the government to try and run to our rescue. We need to be making ten, even twenty-year plans."

He sighed, leaning against the wall of the unit as she rolled up the door. "How many lambs are we talking here Jennifer?"

"How many will you give me for six logs and a box of cartridges for your .30-30?"

"I actually prefer my 30.06." He crossed his arms.

"Well," Jennifer smiled as she rolled up the second storage bay door to reveal the family arsenal. "we've got that too."

CHAPTER 20

Huffman Island on the Snake River – Oregon / Idaho Border

They woke with the sun and the sound of the river sliding by the little sandy bar where they had moored the two boats, Whiskey and Tango already yelping and chasing one another through the ice crusting the edge of the water. After camping on the banks of Fox Creek they had hiked the few miles to the Snake River, following the water south along the shore. By noon they found themselves on the porch of a small ranch house facing the business end of a Henry style Mare's Leg .45 explaining their situation to a grizzly faced old man not wanting anything to do with strangers and their damn big dogs but eyeing the pelts wrapped on their packs just the same. As it turned out he did happen to have a couple of canoes in the barn he was willing to part with - for the right price. Once Rob had confirmed they were in good working order and could transport all six plus gear and hounds the haggling began. Yes, he would take the whiskey, thank you kindly, and the cougar meat, and a couple of those skins too. He had a niece up in Boswell could do beadwork on catskin like you wouldn't believe, make a darn fine jacket outta catskin.

"He can have mine, Dad." Jefferson offered pulling his pack from his back ready to cut it and the meat loose for trade.

"That your first tom, boy?" The man had gruffed through a missing tooth eyeing Jefferson and tapping his finger on the hickory stalk of the gun.

"Yes sir."

"Don't never give up your first tom, boy. You keep that. It's your right. You smoke it for two three days over a green pine fire and it will keep forever." So, no not the boy's tom, but two other catskins and tobacco if they had it. In the end he got the skins, the whiskey, two packs of Marlboros, half the meat, a takedown bow from Bear – with the arrows, an E-tool, two MREs – oh oars? You wanted those too? Wool socks. And just to sweeten the deal, the spot on the map where they had abandoned their vehicles. He could be over that hill and back on mules in a day, see what else they had left behind that would be of any use. Noah sighed as he handed over the keys to his rig, knowing what a stash of treasure he had left behind simply because he couldn't carry it all out. But it had gotten them two long canoes in good working order – with oars – and saved them from having to walk all the way south to Annex just to find a bridge across the Snake. This moved them significantly faster than snowshoes over rough ground.

They fried up the rest of the cougar meat for breakfast, ate as they listened to the dogs running a rabbit to ground somewhere in the brush. They returned when Noah let out a low whistle, their muzzles bloody but their bellies full. The men would have to rely on the MREs in their packs for lunch and by the time the swirling rainbow of colors in the sky had faded with the sun to a more gently rolling aqua streaked with yellow and pink they were on their way. By about 9am the little cross river communities of Annex and Weiser had come into view and by just after 10 they were slipping away behind them again.

They paused on Smith Island around noon to rest their arms and stretch their legs a bit and to eat. They talked little, as easy conversations were dampened by worry for their women and families at home. How were they holding up? Was everyone all right? How were they making it through without heat and more snow blowing in from the North? All these things weighed heavily on them, especially Dave, Dan, and Rob who knew how little prepared their families had been.

To make matters worse nothing looked familiar from the river. Towns and communities they might have recognized on a map or from the road glided past with little to no acknowledgement as they steered the canoes towards home. There was a moment of panic when the narrow craft holding Dave, Jefferson, Whiskey and Bear nearly capsized in the freezing water as they drifted over some unseen obstacle lodged on a submerged rock or a sand bar but they acted quickly to rebalance and remained upright for the remainder of the journey. Then just before 3pm Bear let out a howling whoop that made the men in both boats jump as he held his oar aloft in victory. They were gliding past some unnamed unremarkable finger of land, more a half-frozen marsh than really an island but to the burly former sailor in the back of the second canoe it might as well have been a banner welcoming him home. He explained that this was his preferred place to hunt snow geese, just a quick fifteen-minute drive from his own front door. His excitement became contagious then, spreading across them like a warming blanket of hope as they guided the canoes to shore howling with him like a demented pack of wolves, Whiskey and Tango adding their yodeling to the song.

Making land they put on their snowshoes at double-time pace, leaving their packs in the boats and lashing themselves like sled-dogs to the handles in the stern. The canoes skimmed over the surface of the snow almost as easily as they had the water, struggling only when they came to long stretches of barbed wire fence where they had to be lifted and handed overhead. It took them twenty minutes to reach the 95, and another two hours to make out the edge of the golf course in the snow ahead.

The sun was setting as they rounded a bend in the highway, something in the distance stopping Noah in his tracks, his two dogs instinctively laying down in the snow at his feet. He dug through his pack retrieving his Bushnells – momentarily grinning as he imagined the old codger's face when he found a twin pair in the back of the rig – then lifting them to his eyes scanned the neighborhood ahead of them, first the block walls and the trampled down area in the snow on Buster Jiggs. There had been a lot of activity recently back and forth across the highway. That was to be expected as he didn't for one minute believe Jenny would sit quietly on her hands where there was work to be done. Then he lifted the binoculars to his flagpole and grimaced.

"Well, that was faster than I thought it would be." He handed the glasses to Jefferson who looked for the same clues while Noah translated what he had seen. "Our flag is at half-mast." He said. "Just the American flag. Which means there's been a run in of some sort with a government official, something nasty but it's done now. I didn't think they would be able to organize this well and so far out when there are larger populations to subdue."

"Unless." Bear offered pointedly "Unless it was something internal."

The men didn't say what they were thinking but one name immediately leapt to mind. Noah double checked his rifle, as did the others, then moving it to the low and ready he pushed down hill towards Buster Jigs. The sun had set by the time they had reached the gates, they were surprised to find them bound with chains, the locks so far on the other side of the monument pillar they couldn't reach them through the bars. Noah pressed his back to the block wall and forming a cradle with his hands boosted Jefferson up and over the gate to dangle then drop to the opposite side.

"It's Mom." He said flatly as Noah handed his remaining keys through the bars of the gate, Jefferson trying one and then the other until the padlock came open in his hand.

"Was it the A?" Noah asked as Jefferson opened the pedestrian gate to let the men and the boats inside.

"C." Jefferson stated closing the gate behind them and locking it again.

"So... things are generally ok." Noah let the tension in his neck release as he shifted his rifle on its sling to his back. "She's handed out keys, we're at a state of watchful peace."

They walked up Buster Jigs past the single home which served as both construction office and sales model then turned right onto Blackjack Oak past the darkened faces of the houses. Dan was the first to come past his house, opening the door to find nothing but cold blackness inside. Next, they tried Dave's house but when Ashley didn't answer his call from the doorstep he shrugged and rejoined the other men across the street at Rob's house as they found room in his shop to stow the boats. That task finished they walked down Yellowjack Oak, finally noticing the first signs of life as they rounded the bend and headed downhill. Whiskey, bounding ahead excited to be home, was taken by surprise by a bugling snort and a stamp coming from the long row of garages that jutted out from the house. The black mouth-cur bitch yelped like she had been scalded and running away, wheeled in the trampled snow outside the house to bay viciously at the darkness inside the open garage, her mate Tango rushing down the hill to join in her raised hackle song.

"What the hell?" Noah stopped. He hadn't expected Jenny to take the end of the world lying down – but he also hadn't expected his big blue roan stallion to be stabled in the garage. He called the dogs to heel and they obeyed, but reluctantly.

"This is new." Bear gave Noah a bemused look as they walked across the yard to calm his blowing horse. From inside the house Scotus was barking, his growls of alarm sounding feral even to Bear. Jefferson was just kicking over a darkened patch of snow, inspecting it in the brilliant jade light when the door to the house flew open, golden firelight stretching out like a pool over his boot.

"Hold there!" A woman's voice so full of steel he barely recognized it barked out from the open door as the sound of a shotgun ratcheting froze the blood in his veins. "Hands up where I can see them!" He raised his hands, slowly, turning his hooded face towards the warm light.

"Jefferson?" his mother breathed as he heard the Defender's safety click into place. "Jefferson!" She was crying now as she dashed down the steps to throw her arms around him, smothering him in tears and kisses as if he were a small child. "Noah!" She sobbed. He stepped away from her as she fell into his father's arms both laughing and crying at once.

"Bear!" Lisa's strangled cry echoed through the neighborhood as she came running from the Zhou's house down the street. Soon families were pouring out of the two homes to greet their men with hugs and tears... all the while Jefferson was staring at the pool of blood lying frozen in the snow outside his front door.

Red Rim Ranch – Outskirts of Ivins, Utah

At first, he didn't feel any pain. Which worried him. When you fall to the ground from six miles in the sky it should hurt. Unless you're dead. But he wasn't dead. And then the pain came flooding in. From every nook and cranny of his body, every joint, every muscle, every cell felt as if it had been run over on the freeway by a fleet of eighteen-wheelers.

"Hey there mister. Welcome back." a woman's voice came out of the darkness to him, her hand smoothing over his brow gently. He murmured something, and she laughed a little, "No. I'm not your mother." He opened his eyes and looked into the narrow features of an olive-skinned woman with wavy chestnut hair and bright green eyes.

"How is he?" Steven McCrory's voice came from somewhere in the room but Hunter couldn't focus his eyes beyond a few feet from his face to see where the doctor was.

"Well enough to be slightly embarrassed." The woman said stepping away from the bed he was lying on.

"He'll live."

"Good." Steven said. "Because I'm going to kill him."

"Kill me?" Hunter struggled to sit up. "Why? I'm not the one that crashed the plane. It was working just fine until you got on it."

"Hey! Easy." The woman scolded, helping him up. "You got a good knock on the noggin there. You've been in and out for a few days."

"A few days?" Hunter looked around the room, his eyes suddenly focusing as he took in the medical bed, the wide window, the shitty art on the wall. "What hospital is this?"

The woman laughed. "This is my grandfather's old room. You're in my home Mr. Church." She smiled sweetly at him and then picking up a tray of bandages in one hand, handed him an open bottle of water with the other and motioning for him to drink brushed past Steven McCrory leaning in the door.

"Who was that?" He asked as Steven came to sit on the side of his bed, crossing his arms.

"Her name is Myra Kitchener." He smiled. "She's a hellova cook."

"How are you?" Hunter took a sip off the bottle, closing his eyes against the dry pain in his throat as he swallowed.

"A few scrapes and bruises." Steve shrugged. "If you're going to be in a plane crash the Challenger is the one to do it in. The pilots might have even made it had we not smacked into the cliff wall. Myra saw us go down, came out with some horses, helped me pull everyone out. The copilot held on there for a few hours but in the end, there was nothing I could do for him." He let out a deep breath.

Hunter sighed, "I need my phone." He patted the pockets of his slacks. "Have you seen it? I gotta call my wife, my boss, Mr. Goodwin… we got to get a benefits package out to their families ASAP."

"It won't do you any good." Steve said.

"Shit." He sighed, laying back down on the pillow. "It got totaled in the crash."

"I'm fairly certain it was totaled before that."

Hunter looked intently at Steve as he thought over the events leading up to their plummet from the sky. "Why aren't we in a hospital?"

"Well Hunter." Steve looked at him seriously. "Let's get you up, see if you can walk, feed you some rabbit, fill in some of those blanks." It took the doctor only five minutes explaining all that had happened for Hunter to realize what had gone wrong. Steve was surprised when Hunter explained to him some of the basic concepts behind both the appearance of the light and crippling of the grid.

"I've come across some literature that would suggest small generators can be rebuilt now, after the fact." He said "The basic physics of how they work haven't changed in any fundamental way. But new resources of lodestone will need to be recovered to do it because the plasma burst demagnetized everything exposed to the surface. But that isn't going to happen any time soon. Our reliance on electronic devices is the chink in our armor. They're in everything. Our mining equipment, our cars, our appliances. Computers all but make executive decisions running our economy. Without a paycheck coming in miners don't go to work to gather new loadstone, to make the magnets at a factory – also managed by electronic devices and machinery. It's the tiny pinholes across the hull of the Titanic basically."

"You are ridiculously well versed in this." Steve gave him an odd look.

"Where exactly are we?"

Steve looked at him seriously, "You just dodged that. Let's feed you. But we are coming back to it."

Steve helped Hunter to his feet, provided him a shoulder to lean on as Hunter gained his balance, helped him to stand in front of a small mirror to inspect the line of stitches

Steve had put through his scalp running in a nearly straight line from the corner of his eye to behind his left ear. The doctor explained how the craft had skidded along the sandy floor of the canyon, the left wing sheering off against the wall turning the Challenger's nose to impact into the rock. "The pilot was dead by the time I climbed up into the cockpit, he must have taken the full force of the hit. A piece of the paneling is what got you. We had to pull it out and sew you back up. It missed your eye by just a fraction of an inch. Which is fortunate, really." Steve made a comically over exaggerated face of disgust. "I would have been hard pressed to have a serious conversation with you wearing a pirate patch."

He led Hunter down a narrow hallway to a small kitchen warmed by kerosene lamps. Myra was just coming in from outside holding a large cast iron Dutch oven with potholders and placing it down on a cold electric stove smiled as she closed the door. "Good. You're up. I was certain you were going to die but Doc here was holding out for you."

Steve helped him to sit at a simple wooden table while Myra dished out the food, placing in front of him a plate of chili with pieces of what could be chicken floating in the sauce. What the dish lacked in visual aesthetics, it more than made up for in taste and after Myra said a simple grace over their meal – thanking God for their health and provision – Hunter ate with more than a little enthusiasm. "Careful there, mister." Myra laughed after serving him a second helping. "You're about to lick the flowers off the plate."

When they had finished Steve stared at Hunter expectantly while Myra washed up. "My client." He finally said, watching as she scrubbed the dishes in a large plastic tub and rinsed them in another. "He's kind of an eccentric billionaire. The facility we were going to is only part resort."

"What part?"

"The part I convinced him was necessary, so he wouldn't be an eccentric hundredaire." Hunter sighed. "It's part resort, part personal doomsday bunker. We've prepared for almost every natural disaster imaginable, and several political ones. Coronal mass ejections – CME events - was on our radar, we researched it. We talked to a few experts. They assured us that the odds of it happening were … well it wasn't going to happen. Not with the kind of power which would do anything more than interrupt some social media, some communications, it wasn't a real systemic threat. We were more concerned with localized political threats – an electromagnetic pulse set off by some terrorist group or someone hacking the grid. Things which would leave the system intact but still would affect basic living conditions for long enough that it would be prudent to be prepared."

"So how do you know it's not?" Myra sat down at the table, her dishes dripping dry on the counter.

"The lights." Hunter pointed to the window above her sink. "That's plasma from the sun – super charged particles – that haven't been absorbed yet. How long have they been going?"

"The past three days." Myra answered while Steve just sat in thoughtful silence.

"The longer they go, the bigger the charge, the more extreme the effect on the earth." Hunter looked at Steve, wanting him to say something. "We didn't lead with this information when we called you for the interview because…" he opened his hands at a loss for words.

"Because," Steve sighed, finishing Hunter's thought for him, "calling up a stranger and saying 'hey, what are you doing with your life in the event of the end of the world' sounds crazy?"

"That and – honestly - what were the odds?" Hunter nodded. "The viral events were more likely, you're a doctor, you know that. And you know there are national contingency plans to deal with those so – again – the odds of us sheltering underground to survive the next great plague was slim to none. I was humoring a client who paid me well to find a doctor for concierge service. I was hoping to help him build it into something productive. And it was working. The more I pulled him out of his seclusion, the more optimistic he became. The more days that went by with him feeling secure in his plans to survive a collapsed society, the more comfortable he became in a fully functioning one."

"So where is this place?" Myra asked. "This doomsday bunker?"

Hunter was silent for a long moment and then deciding that at this point what harm would come from letting the cat out of the bag said, "It's inside the Snow Canyon State Park, on the western end, overlooking Hell Hole."

Myra gave Steve a significant look, then asked "So what are your plans now?"

"I have to get home to Phoenix." He put his head in his hands, wincing as his fingertips brushed against the stitches. "My wife, she's not up to the task of figuring out life without modern conveniences. And my daughter is only five. And we have to get Steve home."

Steve put up his hand and shook his head. "I was in Vegas on a job interview. I had no real ties to Kansas City, had a nice apartment but that was about it. I didn't even have a dog and I really don't care if no one is watering my ferns. We can take care of getting your family to safety first."

"That's a big trip." Myra leaned on her elbow. "Any idea how you plan on making it without a car?"

"I don't." Hunter shook his head.

"You'll need transportation." She got up and poured a glass of water from a pitcher on the counter, then sliding it in front of Hunter sat back down. "You'll need food, and a way to filter water so you don't crap yourself to death on the way. Phoenix was a big dangerous city three weeks ago. I don't imagine turning the lights off improved it any. You'll need a way to defend yourself. Any idea where to find that stuff?"

"That actually won't be as big a problem if we're

anywhere near Saint George." Hunter sighed.

"Because that's where this bunker is." He nodded, noting the pointed tone in Myra's statement. "And that's where all the doomsday stuff is." She sat still for a moment, weighing her options, then finally said, "Ok. I'll take you up there. And from there to Phoenix." It was said so lightly Hunter had to laugh.

"Like we'll just hop in the car and away we go?"

"Oh no." Myra got up and poured herself a glass of water, offering one to Steve who declined. "It's going to be a long grueling journey. It's going to be hot and dusty and that's the fun parts. But sure, I'll do it. But there's a condition. When we get your family, when we find them and carry them off to safety, I get to come with you wherever you end up. This bunker of yours or some small town, wherever that is we all gang up and stick together until life returns to normal." When he looked at her like he was going to protest she set her cup down and crossed her arms. "I have over two-hundred acres here. We used to grow cotton, but then my grandfather got sick now all we grow is sand and bills. The well pump is out, which is a horrible thing to happen in the desert. All the water you've been drinking – it comes from a seasonal creek that is going to run dry come July. If I don't go with you, I'm going to have to go somewhere anyway. I would rather not do it alone, but the only person I had left in the world was my grandfather and he's been buried out on the ridge for a year. He now has your pilots to keep him company. That makes me a free agent.

"Now you two head cases want to go traipsing off into the desert on your own and I'm not going to stop you. And even though Doc here looks like he can handle himself it's almost three hundred miles as the crow flies to Phoenix. Being as you haven't wings, you're going to have to follow the rivers. That's an added two hundred miles just so you don't leave a pile of dried bones in the desert. Normally people only walk about eight miles a day before they have to tap out, it's closer to five over hard terrain, three if you aren't used to it. One if you're really *really* not used to it. Which means you aren't making it to Phoenix for a couple of months. Or..." she cocked her head. "We can take my horses. They're in excellent condition, used to the trail and the elements, can bump that up to about fifteen miles a day – that reduces the trip to about twenty-six days depending upon conditions. Can ether of you two ride?"

Hunter gave her a dubious look. "I haven't been on a horse in years – not since I was a kid."

"I'll put you on my beginner mounts. They're mule-steady and aren't overly interested in doing much but following the others. You'll be surprised how quick it comes back." She looked to Steve. "How about you Doc?"

"Just when I was a kid." He reached up and ran his hand through his hair. "And if I remember correctly, I fell off a lot."

"Ok. So same for you. I can work with this. You guys need me. And if I'm making it out of life alive, I need you guys too." She looked from one man to the other. "Do we have a deal?"

Hunter looked to Steve who shrugged. "We have to make it to the Acropolis first. That's where all the supplies are."

Myra gave him a little smile and then crooking her finger for him to follow her into the living room she pointed out a large plate window. The desert rolled away from the porch of her adobe style cabin, the bright rainbow-colored lights in the heaven reflecting over the blood red earth. Looming in the near distance, seemingly just past the corrals in her yard were the Red Mountains and the ridgeline overlooking Hell Hole.

"Drink up." She said handing him another glass of water. "And get some sleep. We'll want to skirt the peak and be on the trail before the sun rises."

CHAPTER 21

Wolfe Homestead – Outside Orein, Nevada

Becca cursed softly under her breath as she warded off the doe's stamping hind leg with one hand while rescuing her bucket from underneath the swollen udder with the other. She had been doing fine until Comet – the fluffy little Aussie Shepherd she had taken home on a whim from the feed store – got it into his head that barking loudly and repetitively at the goat was definitely helping. The doe had lifted her long grey and black snout out of the bucket of cob attached to the milking stand and had looked at the puppy with an expression of contempt before bleating back at him and threatening to kick over the milk.

"Mike!" Becca yelled to the barn where he and Jake Sanders had been hiding from the blowing wind, working on something – lord knows what – for the past hour. "Mike! Call your damn dog!"

Mike poked his head out of the barn, a crooked smile on his face as he let out a short whistle which jerked Comet's head around like a ball on a string, the pup taking off in a streak of fur to clamor around Mike's ankles "Why is it," he asked, "he's your dog when he's sleeping, the kid's dog when it's time to feed him, and my dog when he's barking at the goat?"

"Because," she grunted putting the pail back down and turning back to milking. "He's your dog when he's pissing me off."

"Good to know." Mike shot her a wink then disappeared back into the barn.

She finished stripping down the udder and set the bucket aside on a fence post before unlatching the neck bar of the stanchion and shooing the goat away to bury her face into the grass filled manger beside her sister. Becca carried the milk into the house to filter through a square of clean cheesecloth. When the last of it had dripped into a jar she screwed on the lid and took it back outside to sink into a bucket submerged in the creek running through the back yard behind their kitchen. It had been a trying three days without power, even with Mike home to help it was a full-time job just keeping the food from spoiling, milking, and chopping wood for the fireplace inside the house.

Most of the things she was trying out to keep her house managed were things she remembered her grandmother telling her as a child, how to keep food refrigerated in a creek, how to wash clothes in a tub… they were running out of soap. She would have to try her hand at making that. But she would need potash lye and pig fat. They didn't even keep a pig and the grime was collecting in the corners. It was getting to be a lot. Ranching was hard work anyway – but without the machines to do most of the lifting for her she was at her wits end.

So were the kids.

They had already been complaining there was no television. The added chores pushed them close to open mutiny. It had been really hard last night when the Ynekos had ridden over, Max dropping it into casual conversation that he didn't think the grid would ever come back up, citing the lack of traffic in the air since the aurora had appeared. Hearing this Louise had stormed up to her room, refusing to come down to even say goodbye. When Becca had gone up to tuck her in, she could tell from her daughter's red rimmed eyes that Louise had been crying. "What if Mr. Yneko is right?" Louise had moaned. "What about Felicity? What about us, Mom? What are we going to do?"

She had been thinking about Felicity ever since, wondering how her oldest daughter was faring. And the worry had made her angry. And the anger had made her tired. She had exploded on Mike this morning when Jake had shown up at the door, yelling that she was stuck doing all the work while he played with his friends. She knelt there at the creek for a long minute, thinking as the water babbled around the thin layer of ice skimming the sides. She thought about Felicity. What a huge change coming to the ranch had been after spending most of her younger years bouncing from one military base to the next as Mike got transferred. How small life here must have seemed, and how very small her parent's dreams had been. How limited her social life had felt. They watched as she turned her frustration inward, they thought she would snap out of it. And then came her problems with the law.

The first time Max Yneko had caught her drunk in Thunder Bar he had brought her home. They didn't fault him – or Tom Bishop, she wasn't one of the local kids the big man had seen around town and the California driver's license Max had taken from her said Felicity was twenty-two, not seventeen. Tom hadn't let her back in afterwards and had made it a point to come all the way out to their place to sincerely apologize for serving their daughter against his better judgement. Rebecca knew well what an accomplished liar Felicity could be. The second time Max caught Felicity drinking – this time shoulder tapping in the parking lot of a gas station for a bottle of Wild Turkey – he had issued her a ticket and she had been ordered by the court to complete a substance abuse program. The third time he locked her up and threatened to issue Mike a citation for "neglect of an incorrigible minor".

They had let her do her two-month stint in juvenile hall with little to no contact from her family, hoping a little tough love would help her pull her head out of her ass. When she came home, she wasn't grateful. She hadn't changed her attitude. If anything, she was worse. The day she wrapped Mike's work truck around a transmission pole had been the final straw. She was physically okay, but her relationship with them was a tangled mess of love and worry and anger. After a long talk with Felicity about her wants and needs in life degraded into a knockdown screaming match between herself and her mother, Mike took out a large personal loan and sent Felicity off to an all-girls boarding school in Boise. At the time Rebecca had been in agreement with the plan. In many ways it was a relief to have Felicity out of the house. But at the same time the rupture in the family had been an anchor around Rebecca's heart dragging her deep below a sea of pain.

Rebecca walked over to the barn, watching Mike and Jake tinkering under her suburban. They had rolled the big vehicle in there this morning after having a hushed conversation on the porch. Rebecca blinked as she saw they had drained the engine of its oil and the tank of its gas and were in the process of removing the transmission. Her engine sat on a large hay tarp, the floor crane they had used to remove it rolled over to the side next to some bags of rock salt and a bucket of cob.

"Even if we strip everything – the tranny, the exhaust, the seats, – we still have a weight issue to deal with." Mike was saying. "It's not just the chassis and the body – it's the payload."

"This is going to work." Jake retorted. "Trust me. We just need the right amount of horse power."

"What's going on?" Rebecca crossed her arms as Mike rolled out from under the suburban to give her a sheepish grin.

"We… uh…" Mike looked to Jake for help. The younger man just shrugged, giving Mike a look that said *What do you want from me? She's your wife.* "We're building a wagon.

"A wagon." She said flatly looking over the truck, trying to visualize something that would make sense.

"Yea… see, Jake he says that when he was in Iraq the local farmers would hook their donkeys up to detached truck beds." Mike stood up wiping his hands on a shop rag. "They use those to transport just about anything. I figured we might as well be mobile… for as long as this lasts." He wasn't telling her the whole story, she could tell. Mike was managing the flow of information and that pissed her off. Becca gave him a withering look but said nothing. "Anyway, we thought that with enough power ahead of it we could haul just about anything. At least that's what we're hoping."

"Did you walk over here, Jake?" Becca turned from her husband to his accomplice.

"Yes ma'am." He looked nervously from her to Mike and back again.

"Must have been something really important to have you walking three hours from town to be on our doorstep by daybreak." She turned back to Mike, her voice sour. "You boys hungry?"

Mike cursed under his breath and then confessed. "Look. Don't tell anyone. Not the kids. Not Ane Yneko. No one. But right before the power went out Jake and a couple of the guys were digging an entry down into the mine. They hit a couple of ore vugs. It's in the back of his rig parked in the equipment yard right now. The other guys didn't notice. They get to running those buckets and it's just in and out for them. Jake says he wouldn't have seen it either if he hadn't been out of the cab finishing the dig logs."

"The light caught it just right." Jake said taking a rock out of his shirt pocket and handing it to Rebecca. She turned it over in her hand, watching its dalmatian like spots glint even in the low light of the barn. "One of the guys looked at it and said something about lead in the water. He didn't even know what he was looking at."

"But you did." She said, eyeing him seriously as he nodded. She was silent, thinking. Then finally she said, "You both know who keeps Clydesdales. Other than trained oxen – which no one has – they're the only animal that will have the strength to pull your wagon. You two are going to have to cut Calvin Schertz in to your little bonanza. I'll make lunch while you clean up. Then I'll pull some of those canned peaches out of the pantry and make a cobbler. You can ride over there after you eat and discuss percentages over dessert." She looked at Mike's astonished face, tossing him the stone as she pointed to the engine on the barn floor. "Not one drop of oil in my feed, Mike Wolfe."

She would talk to Mike later about Felicity, she decided. Tonight, when they were alone, she would tell him her plan to bring their daughter home.

Boulder Golf Club and Marina – Henderson, Nevada

"It could have been worse." Dex smiled at his brother. "They could all have been like this."

Bobby gave his twin an annoyed look, but then laughed despite himself. Their assault on the water tower hadn't gone as planned. They had scaled the hillside and cut through the chain-link fence just fine, had even gotten through the chain padlocked around the pressure relief valve in a matter of moments. The first sign of trouble came when they turned the massive wheel valve and not so much as a drop of water came out. They had looked back down the hill to where the rest of their crew were driving their thirsty mooing herd in their direction. While Devin backtracked, the massive pipes leading over the top of the hill towards the marina, Dex and Bobby had gotten the chain-link surrounding the golf course rolled back enough to let the herd in only to face their second disappointment. The water hazards where they had planned to stakeout the herd while they flooded the plain below the tower, rather than having sloped sides like a pond several had been cut out and lined by concrete in much the same way as a swimming pool. While the cows could easily lean in to drink the water, the animal's predisposition to soak their hooves while they were drinking turned the blue green ponds into drowning pools waiting to happen. They had spent the night standing guard over these hazards shooing horses and cattle back to the more gently sloping water sources and by day break were thirsty, hungry, and ready to drop from exhaustion.

The livestock did, however, seem to be enjoying the plush green grass.

Devin came riding up from the direction of the club house a sheepish grin on his face. "So, I talked to the course manager.... He's been stranded here since, you know... anyway he says the tank is an overfill basin. It's meant to store water that comes out of the ground that they aren't using for the course and the marina. It was a requirement put on them by the EPA, but as this place actively uses every last drop it can get – it's basically a three-million-dollar piece of window dressing. Oh – also these guys, between the caddies and the golfers and the staff – they've eaten through every last scrap in the kitchens and broken open the vending machines. They're pretty bad off.... A few are dead."

"They starved to death in a matter of days?" Dex gave Devin a horrified look.

"No... a few of them just dropped down clutching their chests when the light show came on." Devin rubbed the back of his neck. "Older guys, mostly. The caddies seem to think they had implants, like pacemakers, they know at least two of them had insulin pumps – those guys lasted about a day before having seizures and slipping away. The bodies are in the equipment shed. It's like a Bolivian morgue in there."

"So, they aren't too upset about the cows." Bobby grimaced, imagining the horror of watching people around you drop like flies.

"Nope." Devin said. "But they are willing to trade."

"Trade?"

"One of the kids who works there says he knows how to get the water flowing out of the wells." Devin jerked his head towards the building behind him. "He says if his plan doesn't work, we don't owe him anything. But if he can get the water flowing again, he wants a couple of head of cattle to feed them all. And – his words, not mine – safe passage through our lands." He laughed at the brothers' expressions. "The kid is kind of a nerd. Basically, he wants to walk through our property towards town."

Dex turned to Bobby with a look of bewilderment that said *He could have done that anyway*.

Flatlanders. Bobby rolled his eyes in response. "How many of them are there?"

"Maybe twenty." Devin looked at them. "And just so you know… when you two do that twin communication thing. It's creepy. Anyway, I'll put up one of the head if you do the other."

"Done." Bobby wheeled his horse and whistled to Laura who, from the distance of about a green, looked like she was sleeping in the saddle. She came over from the water hazard she had been guarding, rubbing her eyes.

"Yes, Boss Man?" She yawned.

Dex flashed his brother a wolfish grin that said *Does she call you that in bed?*

"Shut-up." Bobby spit at him, then turning to Laura asked her to take over watching this hazard while he and Devin went back to the ranch to check on their guests and grab the buckboard. Devin hunted down his crew picking three of his strongest men while Dex and Bobby cut out the driving team from a small herd of mares munching on the deep rye grass in a rough between holes three and five. They did not come willingly, but they came just the same.

As they rode back to Big Stakes, Bobby went over the plan in his mind. Hitch up the team to the buckboard while Devin's guys found the odds and ends the golf kid said he would need in their maintenance barn. If the plan worked, they would drive the herd back to the ranch and fix the barbed wire fence between their property and the golf course to keep the animals from trying to return. Then he would drive the golf refugees over to Devin's where they could repeat their magic trick. After which Bobby would drive the team home, unhitch them, feed them, and finally drop bone tired into one of the available beds.

Three hours and some confusing welding directions later Bobby and Devin were dragging up the useless ag pump from the uncapped well head and tossing it into the back of the buckboard while Devin's guys were wrapping what was essentially a U-shaped pipe with a rounded cap in the remains of a bike innertube to help it stay level inside a wider section of pipe. At the top of the cap the golf course kid had used a little pipe glue to attach a small pvc T-joint with the bottom of the T sticking up through the hole.

"See, the air gets trapped in the top of the jar and vents up the pvc pipe." He pointed to the long rows of sprinkler piping Kip and Brody had harvested from the course after digging graves for the dead in the green of the 18th hole. Laying the bodies to rest there felt appropriate. All told they had about two hundred feet. They listened as Dex put the finishing touches on a corresponding metal pipe they had in the back of the barn for corral repairs, welding the ends together until they had a 200-foot shaft that would connect to the u-joint. The kid picked up a cap he had constructed for the PVC line which had the valve from the bicycle tube glued into it, so the mouth of the valve came through a hole he had made using a nail and a zippo lighter from the gift shop. "We use the bike pump on the cap to push air pressure back down into the bell, this forces the water over the edge of the u joint and up the metal pipe where you can connect it to really anything you want. If the water stops flowing, just adjust the air pressure. If you hear the air bubbling over the edge of the bell you have too much pressure. If you don't there's not enough."

"How do you know this?" Dex asked flipping up the shield of the welding helmet he was wearing.

"The Romans used these to run their fountains. So did Louis the Fourteenth." The kid shrugged. "Also, I grow hydroponic weed in my mom's basement."

Dex laughed as Bobby shook his head, both of them nodding as Devin muttered something about hippies. They stood the makeshift pump on end and slowly, hand over hand, lowered it down the wide ag well until they felt the resistance of the water below.

"Ok," the kid said placing his ear near the pipes, "be quiet so I can hear. Lower it some more. Keep going." The top of the metal pipe made a hollow gargling sound and rattled a little as they pushed the pipe bit by bit into the water leaving about a five-foot piece at the top were Dex had attached a steel plate that would serve as both a well cap and a catch to stop either pipe from falling over or into the bottom of the well. The kid put his ear to the top of the metal pipe signaling to Devin to start using the bicycle pump to pressurize the air line. As he did the gurgling noises grew louder.

"That's good." The kid said, stepping back. It took a few minutes but soon the pipe was gushing water nearly ten feet in the air over the top of the pipe. "Gentlemen… I give you life!" The kid announced taking large stage bows as Dex, Devin and Bobby took turns washing their hands and face in the cold water.

"You're a goofy little shit." Bobby said, holding out his hand to give the kid a hardy shake. "But damn if you aren't a Godsend!" The kid didn't look like he quite knew how to handle the compliment suddenly growing shy, but he managed to mumble out a man-sized yea, no problem, any time. "Dex! Take this young man out to pick his favorite steer. Help him find a juicy one. Kip, Brody – get this attached to the ag lines and then set up the other two bells on the house lines. With any luck we can actually take showers tonight. Devin, are you going to need my guys?"

"It seems pretty straight forward." Devin shook his head. "You go get Laura and move the stock back this way and I'll run the wagon. We'll get it and the team back to you in the morning." Bobby's shoulders sank in relief as he thanked Devin for his help.

"Get some rest Bobby." Devin smiled. "You look like death warmed over."

CHAPTER 22

The Trapper Hotel – Pinefare, Montana

Sheriff Buck Petty and Pete Sanders came dragging in around one in the morning, Buck saw Sanders set up with a room at the Trapper before swinging by his own home to kiss his worried wife Marie hello, and then seeing the smoke rising from the office chimney stabled his weary horse and kissed her goodnight again. He walked in to find James French lying uncomfortably on the floor of his office and Celia snoring away like a drunken logger in her cell. He gently kicked James's booted foot, shaking the younger man awake before shooing him off to the hotel for the night promising to keep the lock up room warm. James walked over to the Trapper where his father was still awake from letting Pete Sanders in.

Unlocking the big double doors Morgan jerked his head towards the reception desk and the stairwell behind the small office that led to the manager's quarters above the bar. James took the stairs two at a time to the top landing, a narrow Victorian hallway with only one of Daisy's spirit lamps on a table at the end of the walk to illuminate the ornate scroll work around the top of the walls and over the doors. He leaned heavily against the door to the right, turning the knob as the door behind him swung open. Daisy stood in the doorway wrapped in her old cotton robe and a nightgown, her very pregnant belly rounding out ahead of her making her look like over ripe fruit ready to split.

"Hi." James leaned in the doorway, his back aching.

"Hi yourself." Daisy said quietly. "I woke up when your dad let Steve in." She explained. "I figured you would be over soon, so I waited up. We haven't had a lot of time…. well, any time, at all to talk."

"I don't know what we're going to do about Celia."
He said abruptly. "But I promise she won't be bothering you
again."

"That's not what I wanted to talk to you about." Daisy
held up her hand to quiet him. "You don't have to explain your
wife's reaction. And the only thing she hurt was the
dumpster... well, and the car. I just wanted to tell you how
sorry I am to have caused you so much trouble. I know people
are talking. I know what they are saying – that these babies
are yours. And if I deny it too loudly, it will just make it
worse." James smiled at this. She was right, the more they
insisted there was nothing between them the faster the tongues
would wag. "But James, I am just heartsick over this. I never
wanted to be the cause of anything that would hurt you or your
family. Or your relationship with Celia."

"You didn't do anything to hurt me and Celia." James
said quietly. "That bridge has been burning for years now."
They stood there for a while in silence before he finally
stepped back into his father's apartment. "Get some sleep,
Daisy."

"Good night. James."

He heard Daisy leave her apartment in the morning,
as she made her way down the narrow stairs to the kitchens to
light the stoves and open the doors for the small staff that
relied on the Trapper for employment. He looked around the
little room, no bigger than a closet really, which had been his
for his whole life. He, Daisy, and Mack had all been born at
the Trapper, had grown up here together playing in the halls
and rooms as tots and when they got older the woods and lake
outside. Daisy had been the tag-a-long he and his twin brother
had loved as well as they could have any natural born sister.
When Mack had died it was Daisy who had held James
together. And when he had brought Celia home to meet his
parents it was Daisy who had worked extra hard to make
certain his mother and aunt didn't have to do anything around
the hotel and café other than enjoy having company. Daisy

was a giver, he had always known that, that she would give up her left leg if she thought it would benefit his family. But there was a gulf between them now and only one way to keep her from risking her reputation and that of the hotel on him.

He didn't fault Daisy for her fling, or the fallout. She wasn't a reckless woman. She had been pretty enough in High School to have married any one of the jokers in this town, but never gave the time of day to any of them. After her mother had died, she only had eyes for the hotel. And when her father followed his wife to the grave just two years later, she lost herself in the restoration to stem the grief. He had seen her dancing with the young buckaroo on the Fourth of July. James had bristled because he knew the type; rough stock rider, cocksure, used to the adoration of women, a real sonovabitch. But he didn't interfere because he knew how lonely Daisy's life had become despite the swirl of people around her and didn't want to step on her good time. He had caught the guy's name on a Whitefish Rodeo program when he took the girls to watch the next day. He hadn't done very well. Guys like him rarely do. Too much booze and good-timin' the night before always made for a shitty ride.

He pulled his boots from under the bed, slipping them on one at a time knowing what he had to do and hating himself for it.

He stopped into his Aunt Sissy's room, sitting on the side of the bed as she lay staring at the wall. He didn't know if it was her grief or the sedatives but no matter how he tried he couldn't get her to speak. It broke his heart to see her like this. Growing up he had always thought his aunt to be unsinkable. Finally giving up he said goodbye and kissed her temple as he left. He walked down to the bar, glad to see that the sheriff was there as well ordering breakfast for himself and for Celia.

"James." Buck stood up to shake his hand. "How did you rest?"

"Better." He lied, then looking to his father behind the

bar. "I've been wanting to talk to you both, might as well do that now." His father held up a finger to say *one minute* then placed the sheriff's order and one for James as well – biscuits and gravy, with a side of skillet sausage burnt to a crisp – with whichever Blackman happened to be working the kitchen that morning.

"Alright son." Morgan threw a bar towel over his shoulder. "Shoot."

"We can't have Buck sleeping in his office all night. It was different before when he had a full rotation of deputies in the county to mind the lockup. And let's face it, if the world were upright, Celia would have been transferred to the Whitefish mental facility by now."

"I don't know…" Buck broke in, but James shook his head.

"You saw her last night. She's out of her head." He sighed. "But I can't take her to Whitefish now. They wouldn't have the wherewithal to deal with her, the world the way it is right now. But we can't dominate Buck's time either. He's the closest thing to government we have right now and there are others here who are going to need his time and attention. I'm going to grab a few horses off the Mule Wash then ride out to the frontier museum. Take that old buckboard they use for the rodeo parade. They're closed for the season anyway so there shouldn't be anyone up there."

"You sure you want to conspire theft with the Sheriff right here son?" Morgan leaned in on the bar, James offering him a weary smile. They stopped talking for a moment while Mamie Blackman brought out the two plates of breakfast, knowing which one to set in front of James without even asking. She smiled at his thanks and bustled back off into the kitchen. The Trapper had been a full house the night before and Daisy was moving in the background like a bee going from table to table, the kitchen orders flooding in.

"I'm going to use it to move the girls off Bear Reach and onto the Mule Wash with me." He continued taking a bit of the food, eating as he talked. "Then I'll bring Mom into town and take Celia up to the Reach. I can keep an eye on her up there and it's too far out for her to bother anyone. I won't leave her a horse, so she'll be on foot. I know Celia. She wouldn't walk this far out, not even over some grudge. She's at her core a woman of leisure so I'm confident that if she's kept on foot, she won't brave the snow. If you would release her to me, Buck I can promise she won't be a burden on this town again."

"I could do that." The sheriff said, sensing there was still another boot in this fire, "Sounds like you would have your hands full though James. Running back and forth between the two properties."

"Yup. That would be true." He nodded, avoiding the realization in his father's eyes. "I have the Wash to manage. It won't be long until the food stores run thin around here anyway so fewer mouths to feed in town will help everyone out. I figure while I'm up there I can use at least some of my time to build some wagons, using the buckboard as a pattern. You can sell them down here for me, Dad. People will be wanting them, and they'll bring in some money or dry goods if they are to be had. Anyway, I won't be in town much. At least for the rest of the winter."

"You can't just lock yourself away from people up there, son." Morgan's voice was gruff.

"It's just better this way, Dad." James sighed as he caught sight of Daisy pouring out coffee from a percolating pot, smiling as her customers paid in cash, the smile never fading as those who could rely on their debit and credit cards just days before offered to pay in work or barter. "If I'm out at the Wash, with Celia, there's no way anyone can say I packed her off to make room for a love affair and eventually people will just let Daisy be. Come spring, when the roads are clear, if the power is still down, I'll ride out to Whitefish and see about the hospital, see what kind of shape it's in, see if they've recovered enough to take her on and if they will trade a head or two of beef as payment for her care."

"If that's the way you want it son." Morgan's voice was resigned. He hated this plan. But James was right. It was the only way to protect Daisy – both physically and socially – without keeping Celia locked up like a rabid dog.

"It's not the way I want it." He admitted. "But it is the way it has to be."

Mamie Blackman bustled out with Celia's to-go order, prepared the same way as James' but wrapped in aluminum foil. She placed it on the bar in front of Buck, hurrying back off. "I'm not going to tell Celia about this." He said. "But I'll release her to you when you get back."

"Thank you." James set his knife and fork down. He sadly shook both men's hands, let his father pull him in for a massive bear hug, then walked out the front door towards the RV camp stables to collect Smoky without so much as lifting his hand to wave Daisy a goodbye.

"God damn rodeo bums." Morgan gruffed, blinking back emotion as he watched his son leave. "Roll into town from parts unknown, break up hearts and families just for fun. If that damn Dex Barring steps so much as a toe in this county again, I'm gonna meet him with a short rope and a tall tree."

"Yup." Sheriff Petty looked to where Daisy was standing, rubbing the small of her back where the ache of hours on her feet had started to sink in. "I might just help you with that." He pulled a five-dollar bill from his wallet and laid it on the bar. "It's all I have left in cash, Morgan." he said a little embarrassed. "And I'm thinking the automatic deposit is going to be a trifle late next week."

"Keep it, Buck." Morgan said handing the small bill back. "You perform a service to the community. Let's just call your care and keeping taxes paid."

South Cove - Bartlett Reservoir, Arizona

"It's too cold." Bella stood at the edge of the boat launch, her toes in the sand just a foot from the water. Her wide hazel eyes flitting to the rainbow-streaked clouds. "It's gonna rain. You shouldn't swim when it rains."

"Come on sweetheart." Sarah coaxed as she stood shin deep in the water. Of all the supplies she had packed, bathing suits weren't on her mind when she had been stuffing clothes into the bag. But after paying for their campsite – the ranger in the booth at the head of the park unconcerned about the end of the world, fees were fees – and setting the hammock tent up by laying it flat on the ground to form a barrier between themselves and the sand before stringing the cover tight between two piles of red granite she was hot and sore and ready to get clean. She took Bella by the hand, not bothering to lock up her supplies. Other than a couple of abandoned cars near the dock, there was no signs of life anywhere. The ranger said all the campers had left when the power went out – most of them walking down the banks of the Verdi River heading towards Phoenix to see what had become of their families when the HAM radio in the station had gone dead.

"You're the first people I've seen in four days." The round-faced native woman had said as she handed Sarah a slip to be displayed on the post of her campsite."

"So, do we get a discount?" Sarah said hopefully, causing the ranger to look up – a hint of a smile in her otherwise stony expression.

"Nope."

Not seeing the ranger at the desk Sarah knocked on the side of the little hut until she appeared. "Sorry. No turn down service." *Ah,* Sarah thought. *We have a comedian.*

"How about a gift shop or a snack bar?"

The ranger looked at her seriously, pretending to check her uniform pockets before feigning regret. "Not on me."

"Thanks anyway." Sarah sighed.

"If you need charcoal and fluid, you can have mine." The ranger called after her.

"Got any towels?" Sarah had asked as she turned around.

In twenty minutes, they were both stripped to their underpants, Bella's little feet slapping across the warm pavement towards the water, a thin white terry cloth towel draped around the back of her tiny neck like a limp anaconda. She had paused at the edge of the water however as doubt and fear mounted in her eyes. In all her five years of life Bella hadn't been in any water deeper than her bathtub at home, not even the rooftop pool her mother had loved to sun herself beside.

"Bella." Sarah was tired and trying hard to be patient. "You want to be clean, don't you? Get all that yucky sweat off your face?" Bella turned her eyes down to her grubby toes, twiddling them in the sand. She nodded but didn't budge. "I promise, this is as far out as we will go, and I will hold onto you the entire time."

"You promise, Sarah?" She wouldn't look up from her toes.

"I promise. Bella."

There was a moment when Sarah wondered if she would have to walk out of the water and carry Bella in. She wanted so bad to be clean and she knew Bella would feel so much better when she was too. Finally, the little girl slumped her shoulders, letting the towel fall to the sand as she took tentative steps into the cool water of the lake. She had a moment of panic as the sand slipped under her feet and she clung to Sarah's leg like she was drowning, but as soon as she realized she could sit in the water and it wouldn't pass her chest she began to laugh, running and splashing back and forth from the shore. She leaned back, letting Sarah wash her auburn hair with the little bottle of shampoo Jim had put into their packs then giggled as Sarah used the soap to wash between her toes. Sarah made Bella wait up on the beach while she washed her own hair and face, going further out but never taking her eyes off the little girl as she dipped down letting the cool water heal her aching muscles.

When she was done, she encouraged Bella back out, careful to stay away from the drastic drop of the shelf of red stone and sand they were standing on but letting Bella attempt something between a dog paddle and a landed fish flop, experiencing buoyancy for the first time. "I'm doing it." Bella gasped as the water splashed over her tightly closed eyes, her little nose wrinkling with the strain of keeping her face out of the water. "I'm doing it!"

For all her hesitation to get in, Bella cried when it was time to go back to their camp, sitting morosely on the nylon hammock while Sarah ran a comb through her drying hair. They shared the main course of one of the Humanitarian Daily Rations, a sticky ricey tomatoish glob that reminded Sarah a little of Chef Boyardee. Bella gobbled hers down and begged for more, crying when all that was left were the crackers. Then sullenly, she rolled over and fell asleep.

"She needs protein." Sara looked up to see the ranger standing at the foot of her campsite in the shimmering green and purple light, two fishing poles over her shoulder. "I have a blanket she can sleep on. Come fish."

"I don't have a license." Sarah said wryly.

The woman shrugged before turning towards the dock. "Neither do I."

Sarah thought for a minute, then scooping Bella up from the top of the bedroll she carried the sleeping toddler to the water. The ranger already had the blanket laid out, a puffy soft quilt that looked like it might have been fifty years old, it's ragged edge up against the corrugated wall of an empty bait shop ensuring Bella couldn't roll off the wide dock in her sleep and into the water.

"Here, no... not like that." The ranger took the pole from Sarah as she tried to cast. "Haven't you ever been fishing before?"

"No." Sarah laughed a little. "My dad always wanted to take me when I was a kid, but I didn't want to touch the worms."

"Like this." The ranger demonstrated a cast with her own rod, and then after Sarah repeated the motion, "Good. You want to get it out without hooking your friend behind you."

They sat in silence for the longest time, casting then rolling the lures through the water slowly, the ranger showing Sarah how to make the painted minnow on the end of her line dance as if it were wounded. Across the lake a massive bonfire was lit – it was too far away for Sarah to make out the features of the people moving back and forth across the front of the fire, their shadows dancing like dark spirits against its bright orange flames. She could hear them, their voices echoing snatches of conversation that only added to the haunting effect.

"They aren't going to make it." The ranger said after what felt like hours, heaving a heavy sigh. "You're going up river?" then to Sarah's nod. "Stay away from them. They won't make it. You'll do ok if you keep up like you do. They'll be dead in a week."

"Are you psychic?" Sarah joked, her smile withering under the woman's intent gaze.

"No." She sat there, silent, then, "I've had this job for thirteen years. I've seen groups like that ... had to pull them out of the canyons and the lake. They're stupid. They have a death wish. It's hard enough to keep them alive when they come on good days. If they aren't all dead in a week, I will be very surprised."

"Are you going?" Sarah asked. "Somewhere else? Up river?"

The woman shrugged. "Why go? I have shelter. It's warm. I have water. It's good. I have fish. Some nights I have people to talk to." Sarah smiled at this.

They stayed there for hours, watching the lights slip across the surface of the water and skimming their lures in its depths.

When Bella woke up, she was back on the bedroll, the only sign she had moved the four largemouth bass frying on the flat rocks thrust into the coals of a small sage wood fire. They ate with their hands, Bella sucking the flaky white meat from the tips of her fingers. Then they washed off in the reservoir, filling their canteen and a couple of empty Fiji water bottles before Sarah packed up their camp, smothering the fire in wet sand. As she peddled up to the front of the campground, she handed over a hand-written note to the ranger along with a twenty-dollar bill – "for her fishing permit."

"If a man comes behind us, looking for us. Will you give him that?" She asked. "His name is on the outside."

The ranger took the note without even a nod, or a wave goodbye as Sarah peddled up the asphalt road.

CHAPTER 23

1002 Yellow Jack Place – Baptiste, Idaho

Noah stepped out on to his front porch and into the street to watch the sun rise up over his house, the pale gold light melting the ribbons of rainbow from the sky. He wondered how long the aurora would be there. If it was now a permanent fixture or if he would someday be telling little grandbabies on his knee about the day the skies shimmered like fireworks and the entire world changed. Templar whickered to him from the garage, wanting to get out and go for a ride. He stepped back into the yard, kicking the snow that fell overnight away from the patch of blood and ice and ... was that brain? Poor Travis. If Noah had known the solid titanium Jennifer had hidden in her soul under all that sweet soft satin exterior, he would have proposed the moment he met her rather than waiting a whole six months to be turned down – the first time.

As if she could sense he was thinking about her, Jenny stepped from the house wearing sweats and one of his old T-Shirts, an afghan thrown over her shoulders like a shawl and a cup of coffee in her hand. All that flowing beautiful hair unbound and bouncing around her face like a halo. She handed him the mug and kissed him softly on the cheek, the toe of the snow boots she had pulled on at the door smoothing the snow back over the blackened stain.

The door slammed behind them as Jefferson stalked out of the house, the sides of his head still pink with the heat of the water he had used to shave, the remaining hair forming a low mohawk. Otherwise, he was dressed in a pair of snow pants and his hooded coat, a pack slung over his back and an axe in his hand. "

"Jefferson." Jenny's voice was soft but insistent.

"Where are you going?"

He wheeled in the driveway his face betraying a flash of anger as he struggled to control his emotions, "There's stalls to muck across the street." He said with a deep sigh. "Beau already beat me to these ones. And I have stuff to do."

"Hey." How she could sound both stern and wounded at the same time was a mystery to Noah. That was the edges of the titanium showing through the satin. "Kiss your mother goodbye." Noah cocked an eyebrow at his son who sighed again but leaned in to give Jenny a hug as she planted a kiss on his cheek. "Ok." She smiled. "Go do stuff."

He moved to stand next to her and she took the coffee from his hand, her eyes never leaving Jefferson's back as she took a sip and handed it back. "The hair is new." She said with a little amusement, then, "Did something happen on the trip? I mean other than..." her voice trailed off as she pointed towards the sky.

"No." Noah took a deep breath, knowing he was about to tangle with a mother bear over her cub. "He wants to go."

"He just got back." She didn't raise her voice, didn't even change the tone, but what she meant was *No*.

"Someone has to go and row the other canoe." Noah waited for her to answer him, but she stood there solid on her *No*. "Rob can't. He put everything he had into getting home and really needs the rest or he'll be no use to the neighborhood. Dave and Bear can't go. Feng says that cough sounds wrong, like it could develop into pneumonia and has them both on a strict diet of sleeping indoors until it clears up. Feng can't go, he's the closest thing to a doctor we have – so here he stays. And Bruce is sticking around to finish building whatever big plans you have for this place."

"He's just a boy." She insisted. "He's *my* boy."

Noah thought for a minute, and finally played his last card. "I guess I could go..."

"No!" She wheeled on him, her eyes alive with fire

"No, Noah! Do you have any idea what I was going through? Not knowing when you were coming home. *If* you were coming home? You are not going."

"Then it has to be the boy." She glared at him, her eyes made even more bright and beautiful by the tears welling up in them. "You would want it to be him if it was your daughter, Jenny. You would want it to be a friend who she could trust, who would make careful prudent decisions and had her best interests at heart. Right now, there is a fifteen-year-old girl stranded away from her heartsick mother and all your son wants to do is help. Let him." She turned on her heels and stormed back into the house, slamming the door behind her. Noah smiled to himself and turned to watch the sunrise just a little longer before he followed her inside.

Jefferson stabbed the apple picker into the matted bedding, turning to toss the woodchips and manure into the wheelbarrow behind him before turning back for another load. He knew what he was asking was dangerous, not like the trip off of the mountain and a clear shot down river to home. There had been time for the hunger to set into the city by now, he had listened to every word his parents had taught him about the desperate instincts inborn in humanity as they climbed over one another to survive. He knew that they might have to stay in the city a few days trying to find where the girls had moved too, where they were hiding. They might have to backtrack along the river, or leave the river for major roads if they had tried to find some way back home. But just because it would be difficult didn't mean he couldn't handle it. He could hear Beau on the other side of the stables emptying a new bag of shavings into the last stall.

"You're going to want to put more greenwood on that fire." His father's voice behind him made him jump. He looked to the outdoor arena where he had tented his cougar skin over a tripod of cut saplings, the low fire just below burning down to ash instead of smoking the inside of the hide like he wanted. Jefferson nodded as he set down the rake and walked to the pole fence forming the arena to pile a couple more bows on the coals, being careful not to stoke the flames high enough to scorch the skin. He looked to where his father was standing, holding Templar's reigns as the big stallion pawed the ground impatiently.

"Thanks."

"Sure." Noah nodded as he leaned against the stall door. "Your mother and Beau brought in the storage units."

"Yup." Jefferson said bitterly as he walked back to the stall, working fast to finish the job. "Beau told me. Told me about how they ran off Abigail and Joanna too."

His father chuckled at this. "Apparently Ashley has started a new painting. Had Feng ride out with her to her studio to bring back her art supplies. She's got a picture of the whole thing in her head, is going to put it down on canvas."

Jefferson smiled, "Can hardly wait to see it."

"You know, son, there was a lot of food in that unit. But it's all freeze-dried shelf stable things." Noah watched as Jefferson tossed another pile of manure into the wheelbarrow. "Which is good, but it's lacking in one thing."

Jefferson tossed the last pile of chips, then setting the apple picker aside with a confused scowl hoisted a large open bag of wood shavings into the stall and tipped it over spilling out about a quarter of its contents. "What's that?" he asked using his boot to kick the shavings around to form an even level of clean bedding.

"Fresh meat." Noah fiddled with his reigns absent mindedly, "We got a lot of mouths to feed. We could use some deer or even elk if you can find it."

Jefferson stopped kicking the shavings and looked at his father, the scowl on his face lifting, "Yea. Ok." He nodded. "I can do that."

"Good." Noah said. "Now what are the rules."

"No does till fall."

"And how do you know it's a buck or a doe?"

"Check the bush twice."

"Good." Noah sighed. "It's a big job but I know you can handle it. You can leave tomorrow. Your mom wants a day to get a good look at you, and gather up some stuff for your trip. Though I'm not certain how much hunting you'll have down in Boise."

Jefferson blinked, "Boise?"

"Yep. Take the bow with you. Bag us something good."

"I'm going to Boise?"

"Your mother gave her blessing this morning." Noah smiled, throwing his son a wink. "Oh, and she said to tell you she loves the new hairstyle. Never change it. She even suggested you get a tattoo to match." Jefferson gave his father a sheepish look as he ran his hand over his freshly shaved scalp. "She thought maybe a big ole screaming eagle with fireworks. Or an anchor with a heart that says *MOM*."

"I want to go." They looked up to where Beau was standing at the corner of the line of stalls, a hopeful expression on his face. "Please? Can I go?"

"Nope." Noah winced a little at his son's crestfallen expression. "Beauregard, if I even think about asking your mother if you can go, she'll have my hide smoking out there with your brother's cat and then go bake a pie … Besides, I need you here."

"For what?" Beau's disappointment turned to curiosity.

"Well, as it turns out we have some night raiding to do. Mary Beth is low on some medication she needs, Feng gave me a list of stuff he would like to have around, and we need to hit up the fireplace showroom so Bruce can put stoves into the neighbor's houses and we can get our floorspace back. Then we need to find a home improvement center, bring home some water heaters that will run off the gas to replace the electric ones, so everyone can have hot water. And more of those manual valves so we don't blow the place up." He could see from Beau's face that none of that sounded as fun as a hundred and sixty mile maybe weeks long rescue mission. "C'mon kid. Knock over a couple pharmacies with your old man."

The Acropolis – Red Mountains, Utah

"So now what?" Steve shifted uncomfortably in the saddle. It had taken them an hour to skirt the base of the cliffs from the ranch and another three to climb the thin slip of the trail to the peak, following the edge of the rise to the long dusty road used by the Land Rovers to shuttle people and supplies up and down the hill. He had been using muscles which had not gotten this much of his attention since officer training. They were stopped at the outer gate staring up at the solid twelve-foot surface at a loss after Hunter had half climbed and half fallen off of his horse, walking stiffly – almost comically bowlegged in his black silk Prada slacks and Berluti dress shoes – to the gate. He had, just taking a risk, tried stuffing the tips of his fingers into the metal jam to pull at the gate, but with the solar power out they refused to move on their hinges.

He looked to where Steve - dressed every bit the Utah wrangler in the wardrobe Myra had pulled from her grandfather's closet - sat mounted on Pico, one of the string of nine ponies they had brought with them. Myra had spent a good part of the morning riding to neighboring ranches to find a buyer for her other horses and had returned with a roll of cash and three gold Krugerrands in her hip pocket to find Steve well outfitted and Hunter – just a bit too small in the shoulder and long in the foot -still dressed like a rumpled dusty GQ catalog but wearing her grandfather's favorite Stetson straw hat.

"Don't worry." Hunter said pulling a set of keys from

his pocket. "There's another way in." He led them around the wall to where the empty stables were built opening the breezeway and listening as Myra instructed them in the proper methods of stabling a horse, removing all the tack even if they were just leaving the animals unattended for a moment. Hunter lifted the handle of the red yard hydrant, waiting as the pipes made a dry humming noise followed by a sudden outburst of water from the attached hose into the troughs and waited while Steve filled all the basins for the horses. Once the animals were taken care of Hunter led them into the tack room, and moving the large bags of grain from a pallet in front of the false wall worked with Steve to break it down while Myra helped herself and the horses to a bit of feed.

"This is good stuff." She pointed to the bags. "We should put three of them on the pack horses before we go. It's just going to go to waste up here."

He nodded as he caught his breath, swinging a hickory handled ax into the wall with another massive thud. When the sheetrock was finally down Myra inspected the palms of his hands. "Keep the ax." She said. "But we'll need to get you some gloves, and some sandpaper to take the lacquer off the handle or your hands will be hamburger before we're even a day in." He pointed to the massive metal door behind the wall, panting and handing her the key. "Nope." She said with a small smile. "Sorry Buckaroo. You do your own heavy lifting from here on out."

Hunter gave her a dirty look but pushed himself off the pile of grain sacks to unlock the door. The long tunnel beyond leading to his garage was pitch black and they had to feel the wall as they walked just to keep oriented forward. Hunter felt rather than saw the single garage bay gliding by him to his left as his toes banged against the steps leading up to his office. He turned the knob above the keypad, glad none of the internal doors had the security lock down features of the gates. He pressed the door as almost blinding daylight filled the garage then stepping through into his office, nearly jumping out of his skin as a woman screamed.

"Eldora?" He looked to where the cleaning lady had been lying on his office couch, a blanket pulled up over her shoulders now clutched up under her nose. "Eldora! Calm down. Its ok!" Then as he made out the word the woman was screaming repeatedly, "No! God damn it, I'm not a ghost!"

"You died!" She shrieked, "We saw the crash." Then her eyes darting to the door where Steve and Myra were walking into the room. "The door." She breathed. "The door is unlocked!" and then without another word she leaped up from the couch and shouldering past Steve dashed down the tunnel towards the light at the other end.

"That was Eldora." Hunter said to Steve's questioning gaze. "She's usually very nice."

Steve just made an 'oh' noise as Hunter rose from where he had been crouching in front of the couch and led the way through his private salon towards the gallery staircase to the main part of the building. Myra was almost speechless at the sheer size of it. "How? How did you build this place without anyone knowing about it?"

"My client." Hunter sighed. "He followed strict protocols when it came to security." They turned towards a clanging noise as a man wearing an ill-fitting, rather expensive looking three-piece suit had dropped the massive can of peaches he had been eating from in the kitchen doorway.

"Tim." Hunter greeted the man casually. "Hey, is that my Armani?"

"The door!" Tim stammered then dashed past them up the gallery stairs to disappear into Hunter's private quarters.

"So...you've met all the staff." Hunter smiled at Steve. "Everyone except..." there was a shriek from the kitchen as the door flew open and a young blond stepped into the room. "Everyone, this is Angie."

"You're alive!" Angie was crying. "We were all standing on the balcony to watch you come in. And then the plane went down!"

"I know." Hunter held up his hand. "And now the door is open."

"The door is open!" Angie did a little dance as she kissed him on the cheek then waving to Myra as she sprinted past to the gallery.

"They better not steal those horses." Myra sighed.

"Maybe go check." Hunter looked at the door, Myra nodding to follow them out to the barn.

"They were excited to get out of here." Steve chuckled, then grew serious as something dawned on him. "That sheetrock could have been easily taken down from the inside. They hadn't done it themselves because the lock was double sided."

Hunter nodded thoughtfully. "What bothers me is the elevator hasn't been uncovered. You would think Goodwin would have at least tried it."

"What elevator?"

"It's a long story." Hunter said as Myra came back into the room.

"They didn't even look at the horses." She called coming down the gallery stair. "Just dashed off into the desert heading for the trail. Nice place. But it doesn't look like a bunker."

"The Acropolis has hidden charms." Hunter quipped, "Let's see if we can't find Goodwin."

They found him lying in bed wearing his silk monogramed pajamas, his skin mottled and blue, his eyes closed and the rancid stink of urine and death hanging in the upstairs bedroom. Myra gagged against the back of her fist as she rushed across the bedroom to open a large set of French doors leading to a private veranda, throwing them open to let some air into the room. Steve, a bandana pulled up over his mouth and nose looked closely at the body. Then finding a half empty bottle of pills on the bedside table opened the top to inspect a few of them in his hand before dropping them back in, putting the cap back on and tossing the bottle to Hunter.

"Benzos." He said. "Not something I would have prescribed to anyone. They're meant for surgery."

"He must have gotten them from the med bay." Hunter looked down at the unlabeled pill bottle. "We have a fully stocked pharmacy down there."

"I don't like this guy." Steve said walking away from the bed. "If he got this from a supply bottle, he took the time to read up on the dosage in a PDR. There's just enough pills in there to do him and the three people we let out."

"No wonder they were spooked." Myra said following the two men out into the outer den, Hunter closing the door softly behind him. "He was expecting them to eventually give up and join him."

Hunter crossed his arms thoughtfully, thinking about Luke Goodwin, about how there were no signs of even an attempt to open the lower floors of the shelter to feed the three members of the staff there with him. This was a side of Goodwin Hunter would have never guessed at. He had worked so hard to make this place a beacon of hope, a refuge. Why would he turn it into a tomb? He looked up into Steve's steely expression and just opened his hands at a total loss for words.

"Right." Myra said looking at him narrowly. "You said there would be supplies."

"Let's clean out this room first." His voice was shaking as the enormity of Goodwin's suicide weighed on him. "I don't want to come back in here." He stepped behind the desk of the den and finding the latch hidden in a panel on the side of the bookshelf built into the wall rolled the massive oak cabinet on its hidden track to reveal the ten-by-five bank style vault door behind. Hunter turned the dial of the lock, the numbers clicking as they whizzed by, then turning the massive wheel to move the steel bars behind the door out of the frame pulled it open.

"Holy shit." Myra murmured as her eyes went wide at the gold and jewels horded inside. Hunter pulled an empty canvas cash bag from a stack in a bin on the wall and handed it to her.

"Take whatever you want." He said then stepped out to sit back on the desk.

"Yea." Steve moved to sit beside him. "I don't like this guy. I don't think I'll take this job."

"You're still coming to Phoenix?" Hunter considered the pills and the vault, and wouldn't fault Steve if he didn't.

"Yes." The bigger man answered. "But someday, you're going to tell me that deep down you saw this place for what it was. What he was really building."

"Let's finish up here" Hunter said thoughtfully. "Because you really aren't going to like the basement."

"Hey guys." Myra sounded excited as she pulled a large flat felt lined tray from the vault, showing off a selection of pocket watches on chains, letting them pick their favorites before taking one for herself. "We'll have to wait for noon to wind them but at least now we can tell time."

They left the larger bars, taking only the gold that was readily transportable – mostly coins they stripped of their protective packaging, and jewelry. In a tray filled with rings Hunter found a sapphire and diamond engagement set that he knew Lucy would love and rather than dropping it into the bag tucked the set into his shirt pocket along with a small ruby encrusted locket for Bella. Ever practical, Steve opened a bin and finding stacks of cash inside filled a second bag up to the top. "We'll use this first." He said. "And we should be very cautious flashing it around. Put some cash in your wallet, we'll refill as we go but don't carry a lot on your person."

When they had finished Hunter locked the vault back behind its shelf while Steve stepped back into the bedroom securing the windows and placing the bottle of pills back on the bedside table before shutting the bedroom door.

"It's going to be ripe in there by dinner." Myra said.

"Yup." Steve nodded picking up his sacks of cash and jewels. "And hopefully if anyone gets in here, they'll be distracted by the dead body on the bed."

"You plan on coming back?" Hunter was surprised.

"Depends on what's in the basement that I'm not going to like."

Hunter nodded, and then moving aside a piece of wainscoting at the front of the desk opened a hidden door in the wall. Steve narrowed his eyes. "Servant's passage."

"You know, towards the end there I got him to call them *staff*." Hunter said helplessly as he led them through the darkened passage finding his way to the stairs in the inky blackness. He had to guide them by memory, one hand against the wall, walking past the wide empty openings side passages which would take him downstairs beneath the staff quarters. Halfway through, Myra fumbled through her pockets finally producing a zippo lighter she used to illuminate the space around them.

"Here." she said handing it to him. "I forgot I had it on me." He continued leading them down a flight of stairs which ran under the salon to the stairwell behind the elevator shaft at the front of the house. They descended in what felt like a never-ending spiral, and as they did Myra leaned her head over the railing to look down. "Hey!" she panted. "There's light down there!"

Hunter nodded. "The shelter is on a separate power system. The backup generators must have kicked on."

"But how are they working?" She asked as the dim light below them came closer with each step like water rising in a well.

"It's the depth." Steve answered from the back. "By the time we get to it we'll be down low enough to survive an atomic blast."

"Wow." Myra shook her head in the dark. "You guys were really prepared for anything."

They walked in silence the remainder of the way,

Steve taking in the full tour with quiet but growing anger. He lost his cool when he saw the armory. Myra reduced to sullen silence when she saw the cistern. "Do you realize," she said leveling her green gaze hotly on Hunter, "the number of farms and ranches which have gone dry in this valley? How many people you have put out of their homes – some of them farms built by their great grandparents – how many family businesses you've shut down hording this much water for one eccentric old man and his paranoia? They told us it was a drought!"

"I wasn't here for the construction." Hunter knew how lame his defense sounded. "He brought me on after all this was built. I was just trying to manage it, maybe turn it into a resort eventually. Bring jobs."

"We didn't want to mow your lawn, Hunter!" She shouted "We wanted to work our own land. Our. Land! How did he even get the rights to build up here? It's a state park. You can't even graze a few head of sheep up here without jackboot thugs in uniform showing up to kill your stock and take you to prison!"

Hunter offered her a weak smile. "His...uh... brother is a congressman."

"Well now." Myra threw her hands up in the air. "Don't that shit just figure."

"It's done now." Steve stepped in to make peace. "There's no going back to change it. And from the looks of that armory and the barracks behind it this valley dodged a major bullet."

Hunter looked at him in confusion. "You mean the staff room? That's up a floor. There's no rooms down here except for storage and Goodwin's private quarters."

"No sir." Steve shook his head. "I mean the barracks on the other side of the armory." Steve crooked his finger leading Hunter past the utility room and back towards the armory pointing to a cheap wooden door at the end of a long locker bristling with guns.

"That's just a closet. It holds cleaning supplies."

"Look again, chief." Steve said gently. Hunter walked over and opened the door, stepping into a long concrete room that stretched the length of a football field into the bedrock and filled with neat orderly rows of metal bunks, each with a cheap closet style wardrobe at the head and drab green footlockers stored underneath. "So," Steve crossed his arms in the doorway, "We have a congressman's brother who built a palace in the desert, removed resources from the original residents while building servant's quarters and a garrison hall. This guy wasn't looking to rescue people. He was looking to rule over them. And when none of his plans to do so worked out, rather than sheltering the few he had with him – who would eventually ask to be treated as peers rather than servants – he opted to kill himself."

Hunter stood in stunned silence for the longest time. When he could finely speak all, he could say was: "That lying son of a bitch!"

CHAPTER 24

Thunder Bar – Orein, Nevada

The little plastic spout started to hiss, a thick lather of foam building up around the rim of the glass as the keg ran dry. "Well. That's the last of it." Tom Bishop said with a hint of sadness as he placed the half full pint glass on the bar, then looked at Ceciliee. "Pass these around. I'll take this one."

He looked at the small gathering of people in the bar, Mike and Rebecca Wolfe were there, as were Tim and Cathy Barring along with their daughter Maggie and her husband Josh. Jake Sanders sat with Calvin and Mary Schertz – an adorable little couple well in their seventies who had lived in the valley all their lives and remembered when most of the small cluster of homes in and around the ruins of Bridge Street was open farmland. The Garza's had found their way back into the valley, brought by an uncle who kept mules on the outskirts of Sparks presumably to clean out the remains of their house in the condemned area of town though Dalisay spoke more and more of staying.

The Thurstons – Wally and Kat – sat by themselves in a corner booth, mostly because they had in the past few days taken on a smell most of their neighbors found objectionable. Kat smiled, showing a row of yellow teeth as she took her glass in her grimy hand, making Tom shudder. It was still the middle of January, that wasn't garden dirt under her nails. The Lowery Family sat in the center – Jacob, Gertie, and sixteen-year-old Josh. If Thunder Bar was closing, Jacob was determined to have at least one beer in here with his boy. Sitting in a side booth with Ane and Max Yneko was Linda Lane. Her husband Ely would not be making it tonight. Or any night after.

Tom came out from behind the bar. He stood still in

the middle of the room for a long moment holding his half pint and staring into it. Then raising it, he choked a little as he met their expectant gazes. "Thank you." He said, forcing a smile. "For coming to drink a beer with me. It's been a great ride. It really has. And I am so thankful for your business and your friendship." They were all quiet, unaccustomed to such a show of emotion from the man who had more than earned the reputation as the town's resident curmudgeon. They raised their glasses silently and drank.

Max, setting his glass aside stood up and addressed the group. "I guess I better get started." He said. "I have a letter here to read to you all from Ely. Linda took the time to write it down for him before he passed. And I think, maybe, we should take a moment of silence and drink in his memory." He ignored Kat Thurston's disapproving hiss, as he counted out a moment in memory of his employer – a man who hadn't stopped working to keep the community on its feet after the mine collapse, the loss of the grid, and finally the end of his supply of medicines keeping his kidneys from failing. Max picked up a slip of folded paper from the table and begin to read.

"To my friends and neighbors of Orein, I cannot tell you the sadness I feel knowing I am not going to see you rise from these ashes. But rise I know you will. You are the sons and daughters of frontiersmen, prospectors, cattlemen and cavalrymen and it has been my great pleasure to have spent this time with you. It has been an honor serving as your sheriff. You have made my life full. I leave you now in the capable hands" - Max's voice broke a bit at this - "of my Deputy Max Yneko. I bequeath to him my badge and the mantel of responsibility for your care and keeping. In our new charter..."

"Excuse me." Kat Thurston broke in. "Sheriff is not a title to be inherited. It's an electoral position that..."

"All in favor of electing Max as Sheriff." Tim Barring shouted over her, more than a little annoyed. Everyone present, with the exception of Kat and Wally, lifted their hands. "There, you're elected. Please continue without further interruption."

Max nodded then cleared his throat, "In our new charter …"

"Imperialistic charter!" Kat broke in again.

"You two." Tom hiked his thumb towards the door. "Out. Now."

"This is a town meeting. We have a right to be here." Walter chimed in, his voice a rasping whine. Tom crossed his arms, the look on his face promising the beating of a lifetime if they didn't leave. Grumbling they got up and walked out the door, Kat screaming something about racism from the street as they turned down Red-Light Row towards home.

"In our new charter," Max gave Tom a wry smile, "we have stated our faith in the continuation of our community, and it is to this end I would like to advise you one final time. Cut the fences between yourselves and the abandoned properties beside you. Do it without fear and without resignation. By the time the corporate offices are on their feet in China, D.C., or the Midwest you may claim them as your own. Jealously guard this land as it is the inheritance you will give to your children. Though it seems hard, though it looks like an impossible task… plant. Plant seeds for the future you all are clinging to. Tell the Schertzs and the Barrings they must be our library now. They're the only ones who remember this valley before cars came, they must now teach us how to live that way again. Tell Mike in answer to his question that yes, he may buy the forge materials. They're in the back of my old shed. Tell him he thinks he's slick but I know what he is up too and as payment for these things, he is to take care of my Linda. I leave her to him to treat as one of his own." Mike lowered his eyes to avoid the curious gazes of his neighbors, Rebecca did not. "Max, you are probably reading this. You may have all the gear in my locker. Throw out my dirty magazines and don't show them to my sweet wife." The room burst out in chuckles, the loudest of which came from Linda who had to dry her eyes.

"I love you all." Max continued when he could. "And I will see you all on the other side. Sincerely, Ely Henry Lane."

"To Ely." Tom raised his glass, and they all toasted with him.

"Where are you going?" Max asked the big bartender, who shrugged.

"Not quite sure." He said. "North maybe. Someone has to leave this valley, find out what's going on. Try to see who else has their feet under them. The Sheriff said to plant. We're going to need seed to do that. I'm going to need something to brew beer in if I hope to open this place back up. That isn't just equipment, that's people who are able and willing to sell grain. I toured a place last year in Wyoming when I was on my way to Sturges – a Hutterite community that had set up a water powered grain mill like you see back east. I might find my way out there; see how they're doing. But first I'm going to make my way up to Palomino, check on the mustangs they keep out there. Make sure those federal boys didn't just walk off and leave them penned."

Max nodded, taking this in. "We're gonna miss you, Tom." He said at last. "We'll keep this place upright for you, make sure it's ready for you to come home to."

Tom's eyes watered a little at this, but he finished his drink and pulling a sharpie from behind the bar picked up the two glasses of beer the Thurstons had left on the table. There was a general chuckle as he wrote their names on the side of the glasses, and without dumping them set the glasses up on the back wall. It was a tradition of his since he opened the bar to write the names of the people permanently banned from the premises on the glasses they were drinking when he kicked them out, placing them on a shelf above the bar to form a wall of shame.

Tom collected each glass from his final patrons as

they finished, washing them in a tub behind the bar, carefully drying them and writing their names on the glasses placed them on a serving tray beside the register. "When I come home, you all are to come back here for your next glass of beer."

They shook his hand, filing out one by one. Ane pulled him into a tight hug, pressing a little New Testament for Bikers into his hand. As Rebecca left, she handed him a little velvet bag – inside he found two hundred dollars cash, a set of gold earrings, and a gold watch that looked like it had stopped working well before the aurora had come. Then she handed him a photograph of her oldest daughter. "If you make it up to Boise." Her voice was choked. "Please, try and find Felicity for me. Please bring her home if you can."

"Becca. You don't have to pay me to go looking for your girl."

"No." She pushed the pouch he was trying to hand back to her into his hand, her eyes pleading. "No. You keep that. You might need it." He looked down at her. Mike Wolfe had been a damn good friend, but that didn't stop Tom from thinking Rebecca was about the most beautiful woman he had ever seen. He saw the worry and wear around the edges of her face, then nodded placing the pouch in his hip pocket.

He finished saying his goodbyes, moved a couple of boxes to the basement for storage, then walked upstairs picking up his hunting bow from where he had left it on a back table, put on his winter jacket, and locked the doors to his bar. Max Yneko was waiting for him outside, a bay Mustang mare with the scrawling Alpha Angle symbols of the government coded across her neck just below the ridge of her mane.

"She got a name?" Tom asked as he exchanged the keys for the reigns.

"Not really." Max said. "Tim just kept calling her that one behind the other one. He says she's solid. You going to be ok on her?"

Tom nodded. "Yup. Tim taught me to cowboy when

I was a kid. Still help him once in a while, now and then. I'll be good."

"Alright." Max shook his hand. "You got hard tack and beans in the bags, just like in the movies."

"Where the hell did you find hard tack?" Tom laughed.

"Well as it turns out hardtack is French for flour and water smashed together and baked." Max shrugged. "Who knew?"

They waved goodbye and Max watched as Tom rode off through the snow along the shuttered line of businesses, heading north and out of town.

Wagner Café - Pinefare, Montana

"I've got about three hundred pounds of flour in the back." Sissy sat down at the counter running her hand over the smooth surface of the bar. "You know my mamma built this place. All my eggs are either gone or broken. I have some leaf lard. On the second day we filled up some buckets with snow and stuck them in the walk in, that helped but I'm sure the ham is off now. And the chicken will have to be tossed. Same with that beef." She sighed as she looked at Daisy. "You're welcome to all of it. Lock stock and barrel. Can't cook anything with the propane out. Can't keep anything with the power out."

"Come over to the hotel with me." Daisy gave her a pleading look. "I'll move into my old room. You can have my daddy's."

"No ma'am." Sissy shook her head. "You're going to need that room with the babies coming. Besides, I can't stay in town. I keep looking out there at Len's place and it's just this big gaping hole. And I can't look at it anymore." She sniffed. "Besides. I'm needed out at the Mule Wash. We got two little girls out there with no idea why their mamma isn't coming home, and James has his hands full just keeping the place running through the winter. Without guests coming in the food supplies are good, but James can't cook worth a damn. Besides. With all these people stranded here and no money or supplies coming in – one less mouth to feed is better." She paused. "Daisy... you get to the bottom of your food stores. You listen to Morgan. You put your ass on a horse and you go with him and my sister out to the Wash. That hotel ain't worth dying for."

"Well." She crossed her hands over her belly. "We aren't there yet. And we're losing people already. Had a couple of the winter campers wake up this morning and decide to hike out of here towards Whitefish. And there was the woman we found in the bathtub." Her eyes went wide as she tried to push out the horrible image in her mind of the woman, her eyes closed as if in sleep, lying naked in the tub, the water around her cold and scarlet with blood.

"It's cabin fever." Sissy patted her hand. "They don't have anything to do here. They're scared. They're fenced in. They don't see any hope at the end of the tunnel. This too will pass."

"I know." Daisy couldn't help but let a few tears trail down her cheeks. "I better go. The ice we have in the lockup in the basement will need to be changed."

"I don't like you doing all that heavy lifting." Sissy said with a rueful look on her face.

"Well, someone has to." Daisy sighed. "Morgan's still down at the marina helping Nate Petty put in that woodburning stove they commandeered from the vacation cabins out towards Lodi's place."

"Having Verdi Groger out of your hair." Sissy sighed. "That's worth its weight in gold."

"I feel sorry for her boy." Daisy frowned. "Out there without any company or anyone really but himself to look out for him."

"You'll learn as you get older, Daisy." Sissy looked at her. "Some women just weren't meant to breed. C'mon honey. I'll shovel that snow for you. You got a clean patch picked out?" Daisy shook her head. "Oh well. We'll figure it out. You can talk to me while I work."

They walked out of the darkened café, locking the door up behind them as they went. Sissy took a peek into the little row of stables she kept behind the RV office just to make sure everything was still copacetic in there; one never knew when horses were involved. She came out with a questioning look on her face. "I thought you said Morgan was still gone?"

"I thought he was." Daisy looked to the barn. "Is he not?"

"Rodeo is in there, eyeballs deep in his feed." Sissy turned back towards the hotel. "He must be inside."

They hadn't gotten five steps towards the back-patio door of the bar when Morgan came out into the snow to greet them. "You won't believe it."

"What?" Sissy called back.

"Boats." He smiled widely. "Three of them at the marina right now. They'll be coming up to the bar behind Catman in about an hour. You won't believe what they have on them."

"Jesus Morgan. Would you just tell us?" Sissy had very little patience for him just this moment.

"Eggs."

"Eggs?" Daisy looked at him confused.

"Eggs and milk and cheese. And flour! A whole pallet. And canned goods stacked up like cord wood!"

The boats turned out to be makeshift barges which had been hastily made from bits and pieces of scrap, the main body constructed from a cut down shipping container soldered on top of commercial sized natural gas tanks to serve as pontoons. Sheriff Petty came riding down to the water's edge holding a stack of cash that looked suspiciously like it had been "liberated" from some unguarded ATM, waiting for the last of the individual families to finish their bartering and then buying the remainder of the stock to refill the Trapper's dwindling storerooms.

While the men on the "boat" and shore unpacked the goods, Daisy talked to an older gentleman who was manning the long poll at the rear of his cobbled together barge. He and the other men on the boat had been working an oilfield down in Beaver when the lights had gone out. Without the company food truck coming in they had capped off their work and struck out for civilization. Happening upon a line of trucks stalled on the side of a highway outside of Jennings, they didn't just see the end to some very empty bellies but a means of commerce. Fair pricing only, they weren't gonna gouge.

Sending a couple men back for welding equipment out of the yard they put the sweat and muscle into building their boats, stacked them high, and were going to see how far up the Flatbow they could get before coming back down to raid the highways and byways for more supplies, and yes they would be happy to take trade goods when the paper money ran out. Daisy trudged back to the hotel for a pad of paper and a pen, there were things she needed – badly. Maple syrup, kerosene for the lamps, whiskey and beer for the bar, coffee, tea, as many bags of sugar as they could get their hands on, soap – oh god they needed soap, shampoo, conditioner, and did he think he could get a couple of pigs? Live pigs for bacon and ham. And salt. All the salt he could carry. And was he meeting others up and down the river who were also striking out? Could he maybe find someone who could find someone who was heading into the deserts of Nevada? There was someone she needed to get a letter to.

"We need to build a smokehouse." She said to Morgan as they stood on the shores watching the men on the empty barge pole away north to join their sister ships still stocked with perishables and goods. "We need a way to keep meat through the summer too."

"Yup." He said. "I'll get right on that as soon as I get back."

"Are you going back to Verdi's?"

"Nope." He smiled. "These boys have given Buck and I a brainstorm. We're taking Lodi and Nate and going up to the wash to collect James and that buckboard. We know where the restaurant distribution center is, James and I toured it when we set up the food contract. There are highways filled with goods that are going to go to waste if they aren't used and this little town is maybe a week from running through what we just bought. We're going to go and bring as much back as we can."

"You sure the weather is going to hold out for that?"

"What choice do we have Daisy?" He gave her a serious look. "We can sit here and starve. Or cut our wrists in the bathtub. Or, the men of this town can decide it's worth saving and go out there and do something about the hunger issue."

"Seeds." She said. "We're going to need seeds."

Near Devils Hole – Verdi River, Arizona

She hadn't noticed the flat tire because the bike had been dragging through the soft sand for hours now. At first, she just thought that the weight of the trailer was slowing her down. Or that she was getting tired. But the more effort she put into pedaling the slower she seemed to go. She spread the hammock out on the ground using the tent cover as a shade for Bella then unpacking the trailer turned the bike on its side discovering that not only had the tire gone flat but attempting to continue pedaling had bent the rim hopelessly out of shape. She sat there for a minute feeling helpless, tears stinging her eyes. Even if she had the means of fixing the tire – which she didn't – there was no way to hammer the rim back where it belonged.

"Idiot fines." She muttered. "For not finding spare parts for the bike." She looked over the pile of supplies she had been pulling on the trailer. They had eaten most of the food out of the Saks 5th bag. She didn't want to lose the extra bottles of Fiji. She definitely couldn't lose the boots or the meal packs. Then she looked down the trail to where it sloped toward the edge of the river. She had lost a lot of time following a wash away from the water where there were no real trails or marked roads on her map and was trying to circle back around to find its banks. Working quickly, she released the safety strap and the hitch from the bike thankful it was just a matter of releasing a few levers rather than needing any sort of tools which she didn't have.

Using her nylon twine, she tied the hitch of the trailer to the bottom of the frame of her hiking pack then reloaded her gear, then Bella, then rerolled the tent hammock into its vinyl bag and stuffed it inside. It took her all of thirty minutes of pulling, her feet sinking into the deep sand as the wheels of the trailer became stuck on buried rocks and sage roots, to realize that this method of travel would slow them to a crawl. More trouble came when she pulled the trailer through a puddle of water near the bank of the river and noticed a slight bubbling hiss. She stopped, this time leaving everything on the trailer, and inspected the tires finding the slow leak where the trailer frame had been bent far enough back from the small tire to allow the obstacles in her way access to the soft innertube inside.

The trailer would be unusable in a matter of hours. She checked her map. She had three more miles to go before the river looped back around towards a road, and another four after that until she found the next reservoir where she could camp. To make matters worse the novelty of their trip had worn thin, and as the speed of the expedition slowed and the path became rocky Bella had started to fuss. She wanted to go home. She hated camping. She was wet. It was hot. She was hungry. She was bored. No, she didn't want her fairytale book. She wanted to watch Curious George. She had to go to the bathroom. Why was there no toilet paper? Using binder paper from Sarah's notebook was scratchy. Bella returned to the trailer unwillingly. Strained her little body in resistance to the safety straps. Kicked and screamed in full tantrum mode jerking the entire trailer, pulling Sarah off balance as she tried to trudge on.

Idiot fines.

There always is one.

For not following the roads.

For not having replacement parts.

For not being prepared.

The sun had been down for over an hour by the time they made it to Horseshoe Lake. Sarah was exhausted, had never been so sore in her life – even taking into account that first mad dash across the city to Bella's home and the climb up to the penthouse. The trailer wobbled on its now completely flat and bent tire and Sarah still had to set up camp. Finding nothing but short scrub and brush they once again slept in the sand on top of the hammock rather than in it, and this time without the benefit of the tent cover. Sarah had just enough energy to stash the gun inside the trailer by her head, remind Bella for the millionth time to never ever touch it, then feed the crabby little girl another humanitarian ration - this one a lentil-based meal with a flavor that would have made Sarah's toes curl if she wasn't so hungry.

They were just about to settle into bed when Bella threw up.

Don't cry. Don't do that. Big Jim's words echoed in her head. *Your baby is looking to you now. Don't cry. Don't cry. Don't cry.* But as Bella heaved her dinner and possibly parts of her lunch into the sand just outside their bedroll Sarah cried. When the vomiting turned to gassy diarrhea, she cried. When Bella collapsed into feverish sleep she cried. When the light of the aurora began to fade from the sky, leaving her alone under the stars with no one around to hear her she tucked her knees up under her chin and cried.

It took two days for Bella's fever to break. Two days of carrying the little girl down to the water to wash her and cool her. Two days of boiling water over a smoky sage wood fire and mixing in the last of the breakfast cereal and some cooked fish to make a warm gruel so Bella could get at least a little nutrition when she could keep food down. Two days of washing and scrubbing their clothing and sleeping bag in the lake and placing it out on rocks to dry in the warm winter sun. For that, Sarah could be grateful. That it was winter and warm instead of summer and baking. She was certain if it were summer Bella would have died. Bella was alert on the third day and ate without trouble. They sat on the shore of the river and watched a small band of people hiking along the opposite shore. Sarah kept Bella from waving, wary that this may be the same group she had seen around their campfire while fishing with the ranger. On the fourth day Bella was well enough to play. And by the fifth, Sarah determined she was ready to travel.

She presented Bella with her very own pack made from the now useless trailer held together with duct tape and fishing line. The safety harness became shoulder straps and by warming the PVC posts of the canopy over the campfire Sarah was able to shape them into a small frame. Bella carried her fairy tale book and the extra rations; an empty tin can that had held fruit cocktail for a cup, the sharp edges the opener left behind on the rim painstakingly ground down smooth with a rock; and two rolls of toilet paper Sarah had found in a utility closet at the back of an empty ranger hut which she had searched thoroughly for medical supplies. It had been locked but as it turns out door handles – even heavy metal ones – are little match for a woman armed with a rock and desperation. Properly outfitted, Sarah leaned down to kiss Bella's cool little brow and they walked off leaving nothing behind in the sand but the bent trailer tires twirling in the wind on their axel, a ring of campfire stones, and sickness drying into the sand.

CHAPTER 25

Banks of the Boise River – Outside Notus, Idaho

The first sign they had of trouble outside their little enclave were the pillars of black smoke rising in the distance over the city of Nyssa. They had only been in the water for about two hours, Jefferson's mother holding him as if she would never let go before tearfully saying goodbye and handing him a pillowcase stuffed with rations, a spare hunting knife, and a bag of peanut M&Ms she had scrounged from the back of the pantry. They were his favorite and he had resolved not to touch them until he was home again.

It had been a challenge learning on the go to pilot the canoe on his and Dan was refusing to slow down to give him much time to learn. He had the hang of it just as they passed a group of men in an inflatable boat draped over in camouflage like a duck blind. They exchanged pleasantries but little information. Dan told the men they had come from "upriver a-ways", the men didn't speak of hunger in their town but warned Jefferson and Dan not to land and to especially avoid the sugar mill on the river. They weren't inhospitable, but they weren't sharing either. A commercial airliner had come down in a field near the high school on the first day. That fire had burned itself out, these fires were from the city hall when their mayor and chief of police attempted a gun confiscation program "until order was restored". The canoes slipped past the two men's bodies hanging from the main street bridge over the river, placards bearing the word "TRAITOR" fluttering in the breeze from the nooses around their necks.

They ate lunch in the boat, waiting until they turned off the Snake on to the Boise about a half hour south of Apple Valley, the tiny village dotted on their map invisible from the river and the exchange between the two waterways wholly unremarkable had it not been for the ragged fingers of sandy islands on their left marking the way. They paddled in silence, their breath coming in plumes of steam as they sweated into their heavy coats, the palms of their hands aching against the oars. Dan cursed as the sun set, but otherwise said little as they made land alongside an open field and built a small fire for warmth.

They hadn't quite had the tent set up when the ratcheting of a shotgun swiveled their attention to a middle-aged man standing just in the lengthening shadows of a cottonwood growing against the shoreline demanding to know just what the hell they thought they were doing on his land. Hands raised Dan kept his attention while Jefferson slowly unholstered his mother's Glock 17 from his hip, ready for trouble. Dan explained their mission, promised they would only stay until first light, had no intention of approaching the house.

The man looked skeptical until Dan produced the parent information packet Danielle's teacher had sent home detailing his daughter's itinerary and where he planned to look for her. The man knew the school, but not the hotel, warned them of several places where they would need to be careful of rapids up river – advised dragging the canoes overland rather than risk life and limb in the cold waters– then said a gruff goodnight and disappeared back into the field over the ridge.

They were gone before sunrise, taking the farmer's advice and sledding the canoes behind them down empty roads, weaving around abandoned vehicles and launching into calmer waters four miles downstream. They spent the rest of the day in this manner, sometimes rowing, sometime trudging, most of the time losing speed as the flow of the waters changed direction with the terrain. Four hours into the journey the river ran shallow, the bottoms of the canoes dragging over icy rock and sand until they were forced back onto shore to pull on.

Dan said little. Ate little. The further down river they got the deeper the lines of worry etching his face became and Jefferson was certain Dan would look a hundred years older by the time they made camp again. Around one in the afternoon they drifted past Star where a group of women filling buckets from the river fled from the water's edge like a flock of startled geese. Half an hour later a group of mounted men with rifles forming a guard on either side of the shore waited for them. No words were exchanged as Dan and Jefferson stroked past keeping their eyes on the horizon ahead. Just after this encounter the river became a maze of swamp and sand. They pulled out onto land again, dragging across the bend of a meander into a small lake then paddled back to the river finally making camp beside a darkened house above a small levy. They slept restlessly trying to ignore the stench of death seeping out around the frozen pains of the windows from inside.

The final twelve miles of the journey became a confusing mishmash of suburban neighborhoods and snow draped trees. There were more boats on the river, their passengers bundled against the cold as they crossed the waters or attempted to fish in the center. They were women and children, men with hungry haggard faces, cold suspicion gleamed in their eyes as the two canoes slid through the water beside them. When they found a stretch which wasn't populated by other boats Dan pulled up onto the banks under a stand of aspen and oak where they did their best to conceal the canoes under piles of snow and leafless branches.

"Ok." Dan said with a deep breath. "We walk from here."

Jefferson nodded as he shouldered his pack then picked up the compound bow his father had given him last Christmas. They crossed a wide-open park then between a couple of apartment complexes to West Royal Boulevard, walking past the cold blackened remains of a bonfire outside the broken glass doors of an empty lobby. Under a thin layer of top snow were beer cans and bottles, and several tailgate style propane stoves, but otherwise the street was empty. They crossed South Capitol where a small group of men were working to unload an open semi-trailer, tossing a majority of the contents into the street.

"Hey kid." One of them called to him while his buddies cackled, "Need a new laptop? It's still in the box."

Dan warned him to stop, but Jefferson walked over to them looking over the contents of the truck. Most of it appeared to be merchandise intended for the university bookstore. "Got any sweaters?"

"Maybe." The man eyed Jefferson a moment. "Why? What do you have?"

Jefferson dropped his pack and reaching in produced a bag of Jack Links Jerky. The man's eyes went wide. "Well kid, do you want it in orange or blue?"

He made the exchange and stuffed the hooded sweater – grey, with a blaze orange and blue bronco embroidered across the chest – into his pack while the men, stopping their labors to rip open the bag of jerky, stuffed their mouths and squabbled over the crumbs while Jefferson fell back into line behind Dan. The older man was studying for the millionth time Danielle's trip itinerary and the map of campus that had come with the parent information pack. They started with the engineering building on University Drive but when they found the doors firmly secured and no movement or lights in the lower windows, they moved across Bronco Lane to the sports stadium.

It was empty as well but there were signs of the chaos which must have reigned over the past week. Security gates had been torn down and inside the doors to the concession areas teetered on their hinges where someone had used an axe to get at the meager food stores behind the locked grates. They moved on to the dorms behind the stadium where they found a man in his twenties huddled over a small campfire he had built on the steps, cooking something that looked suspiciously like cat. Dan showed him a picture of Dannie, he didn't recognize her, but in exchange for a Gatorade he was willing to share some details as to what happened on campus after the lights went out – a story which consisted mostly of buildings being closed by security and a two-day frat-party in the quad that turned desperate after the booze and lunchmeat ran out. Dan gave him the Gatorade even though his information was nearly useless.

"She won't be here." Dan said leading the way back through the massive stadium parking lot to West Caesar Chavez Lane which skirted the river. "She was with a group of teachers and parents. They wouldn't have stayed on campus for that. They would have gone back to the hotel."

They passed over the river at Friendship Bridge, stepping over the body of a young man lying face up in the snow his empty eyes staring into the pale blue sky, the contents of the backpack he had been carrying strewn out on the ground around his head. Jefferson tried not to notice how close in age the young man was with himself. When they got to the zoo, he noted the enclosures and cages had been pried open and Dan remarked how that was most likely not the handiwork of PETA. They crossed Myrtle Street ignoring the broken glass and sooty scorch marks smearing the face of the supermarket to the east as they walked west to the Hampton Inn on the corner of Capitol. There they found a small cluster of people wrapped in blankets over their winter clothes who looked like they had been sleeping rough the past week. One of the women remembered the students but not Danielle, they and their teachers had walked up Capitol Boulevard towards City Hall looking for information. Dan thanked her and pressed a small package of cookies into her hand that she promptly shared with the others around the fire.

Jefferson and Dan hadn't gotten to the end of the hotel when a little old man came limping up behind them – begging them to wait. He knew where the students had been taken. There was an emergency camp at the High School. He had been there. Dan showed him the picture of Danielle, yes, he remembered her there. Sweet girl. She had been such a comfort to his wife who had been scared. There might still be people there. About three days ago the food and medical supplies had run low, many of the people sheltering there had left after the volunteers had gone home. Dan thanked him. Jefferson pulled out the MRE he had opened for the crackers that morning, happily handing over the main course. The old man was shocked at first, then looking around hurriedly stuffed the meal into the waistline of his jeans under his jacket then limped back off in the direction of the hotel.

Dan and Jefferson followed Capitol Boulevard all the way to where the state building stood at the top of a slight rise. There had been lightweight chain link security fences put up surrounding the steps, but they had been torn down and discarded into bent heaps still lying in the street. Police jackets, empty gas canisters, and bloodied riot gear were strewn across the ground as the smoke of what must have been a massive blaze still poured from the broken windows of the large domed building ahead of them. The red scrawl of spray paint over the stairs read "FEED YOUR PEOPLE" and beside the message lay the scorched remains of an American Flag.

They turned left here following the old man's directions from Jefferson to 11th dodging overturned and burned-out vehicles, broken storefront windows and more than a few dead bodies. At the corner of State and 12th a scrawny man with a junkie's twitch immerged from a ground level parking garage calling to them like a carnival barker – hey fellas, you want a good time, the food might be low but the times were high! No? He had girls. Oh, that's got your attention. Yea. Pretty little things, hungry too. Ready to do just about anything if they happened to have some Dinty Moore or potato chips.

The man's sales pitch ended in a squawk and a stream of blood as Dan's fist slammed him square in the mouth. Recovering from the blow the man showed himself to be surprisingly strong as he wrestled Dan to the ground. Using the element of surprise might have given him the upper hand but Dan was angry, the kind of angry Jefferson had never seen. The younger man pulled out his handgun, pointing it at two other men who came running to their friend's aid from the garage, stopping them in their tracks while Dan rolled him onto the ground and continued punching him over and over again until his face was a hamburgered mess of blood and flesh, all the while Dan screamed his insensible rage.

"The girls." He growled, standing up from the lifeless body streaming blood into the gutter outside the garage. "Where are they?"

When they didn't answer fast enough Dan pulled his own gun and shot the one closest to him in the head. Jefferson jumped at the bark of the gun but didn't lower his own as the remaining man hit his knees begging for his life, pointing to the back of the garage where a couple of fires were burning at a makeshift camp. Dan tied him up with his own shoestrings then stalked to the back of the structure with Jefferson in tow, checking the faces of each of the twelve women huddling near the fires. They weren't pretty, they weren't young, but they certainly promised to do whatever the two men wanted if they had any food to spare. More importantly none of them was Danielle. They left the garage, Dan giving the remaining pimp a well-placed kick on his way by, ignoring him as he crumpled over on his side, hands still bound behind him.

At the front of the school they were met by a group of men in Neighborhood Watch T-shirts and ordered to stop in their tracks. Dan held up his hands, and knelt on the ground pulling Jefferson down beside him. The men took their sidearms, and Danielle's picture, telling them not to make a move as one of them disappeared into the High School. Moments later Danielle came rushing down the front steps. She fell into her father's arms sobbing as the Neighborhood Watch helped Jefferson to his feet, returning his gun.

"Sorry man." One of them said with a not so sorry

shrug as Dan wiped tears from his eyes and stood up. "We've had some unsavory characters roaming the streets lately and there's nothing but kids and old people in there."

"Where's the rest of your class, Dannie?" Dan asked his daughter. "We can get you all home."

His daughter gave him a sad smile. "Come inside, Dad."

She led him into the gymnasium, a wide-open space filled with emergency cots piled with sleeping bodies while she told them about the lights going out in the engineering building, how at first Ms. Pree and Mr. Mays had been organized, taking the parents and the students back to the hotel where there was food and water but no heat. They had all camped out in the lobby, sleeping close to each other for warmth. The following morning, they had packed up their things and walked to the shelter at the high school where they were promised emergency services would get them home. It was a plan which never came through, and slowly the school's emergency supply of rations had run out. About the same time, riots had broken out at the capitol building. They had gone with their teachers thinking it would just be a meeting of emergency personnel, information as to who would be providing food and shelter, instead the governor had stood up on the steps surrounded by state police telling the people that no federal aid would be coming in as no one could get ahold of FEMA or any other federal service – and they didn't have any more answers than anyone else. Danielle said the riot started when a woman threw an empty can of soup in the governor's direction.

"It was insane, Dad! There was just this horrible feeling of anger and hatred in the crowd. They started ripping up chunks of sidewalk and garbage cans, they threw whatever they could get their hands on." She and a couple of the girls from her class had managed to get separated from the parents and teachers, but when the mob refused to disperse with the teargas a deputy had lost his footing and gone down. Danielle sat on the edge of her cot, her eyes wide and vacant as she spoke. "We had climbed up on the statue across the street from the capitol building, trying to see if we could see Mr. Mays or anyone from our group. They grabbed the officer, the people in the crowd, and they just kept kicking him. After that the state police stopped using the beanbags. They shot Mr. Mays; we were able to get him back here but he died. They put his body out in the football field. We didn't have any shovels or anything so we couldn't bury him.

"A few of the others made it back with Ms. Pree, but a lot of them just didn't. We noticed it was mainly the kids who had their folks on the trip. Ms. Pree said they saw an opportunity to go and took it." She gave a thin smile. "Ms. Pree stayed a couple days after that. She told one of the aid workers she was going outside for a cigarette, but she took her bag and never came back. After that the aid workers left one after another. They just kind of dissolved. You would look up and notice another one gone. Then some guys came through with knives. They took a lot of the food we had left; Mandy Maker, June Biggs and I hid under the bleachers against the wall but they took Lonny Frank and Katlin Harp with them too. After they left we just sat here, the rest of us.

"When the Watch showed up, we were scared. We threw things. I hit Mr. Allen in the head with a flagpole." She pointed to the man who seemed to be in charge, who looked at her and waved from across the room then went back to talking to a couple of his men. "It took us a while to realize they were here to help. They've been bringing what food they could, what supplies they could. They're working on a plan to get everyone somewhere safe. Mr. Allen's church is taking refugees out of town but it's a long trip. We don't expect the guides to be back for another group for about a week. And not everyone here wants to go. I would have gone, but Mandy got sick and couldn't make the trip. I stayed here to take care of her." Danielle's jaw began to quiver as fresh tears filled her eyes. "When she died, we put her next to Mr. Mays."

"That's ok, sweetheart." Dan said on the verge of tears himself. "You don't have to tell us everything right now." She nodded and pressed her face into his chest, silent sobs racking her frame. A movement out of the corner of Jefferson's eye caught his attention and he looked to see Mr. Allen waving for him to come over. He got up, leaving Dan and his daughter at the cot and joined Mr. Allen in the hall.

"Hey, earlier. I am sorry." He said. "We see people coming up here, armed, we've had some security problems. There have been men poking around at night. They know we have young girls in here. I have to tell you man, it's the island of misfit toys around here anymore. I can't keep them safe much longer. You're taking Danielle home, that's great. But I have to ask do you have room for any more?"

"What?" Jefferson asked as the man shifted his weight uncomfortably.

"Right now, I have seven young ladies in need of protection." He hedged his words, until Jefferson told them about the pimps in the parking garage a block away. "Yea, that's Ricky. He's small potatoes. Neighborhood asshole, sometime dope dealer. Those girls he has in there are all customers of his. Not that I don't feel sorry for them, but you can't rescue someone from themselves. The guys I'm talking about are organized. We can see them sometimes on the rooftops at night. They're the ones that kidnapped the two girls that came in with Danielle. We still haven't been able to find out what happened to them, we have runners that meet up with other watches, but no one has seen them. It's just a matter of time before they hit this place again. They only took three things – food, water, and women. And as long as we have more girls in here, we're just daring them to come back. So, my question to you is – how many of them can you take with you?"

Jefferson thought for a moment. He thought about the food supplies stashed in his bag, those they had back home, about the number of people they had come here after, and how many seats they had in the canoes. "We can take all seven." He said finally. "But they have to be ready to go right now. No rolling bags, nothing that will slow us down. They take only what they can carry."

Mr. Allen nodded then held open the gymnasium door as he and Jefferson split off, him to organize the girls, Jefferson to explain the situation to Dan. In minutes they were by the door, lined up and ready to go. A young mother caught Jefferson by the sleeve as he walked by. "Please." She said pushing her toddler forward. "Please you have to take him too."

"You don't want to come with him?" Dan looked at her in disbelief.

"My mother." She pointed to the cot beside her where an elderly woman was laying. "She's sick and can't travel. I can't leave her. Please.... *please!*"

"He's too little to walk to the boats." Jefferson said to Dan under his breath. "And if these guys are watching this place like Mr. Allen says we might have to fight."

"I'll carry him." A young woman about Jefferson's age who had joined the line ready to go said. "I'm good with little kids and I promise I'll keep up."

"Ok." Dan said. "Pick him up and stay in the middle of the group. Girls, if we get into trouble you all find a place to hide together, keep this little man with you." They all nodded.

"Hi sweetheart." The girl said scooping up the little boy. "You come with me, ok?"

"We'll be in Baptiste." Dan told the mother who was fighting back tears. "When you get a chance follow us out. We'll take care of him until you come. Alright girls, let's go."

The watch followed them as far as the capitol building. Dan was surprised to see another group of men waiting for them on the steps, some of them wearing T-Shirts and caps that read City of Boise PD. While they had been organizing the girls, Mr. Allen had sent a runner out to the other Neighborhood Watch Units to arrange an escort all the way to the University. He shook Dan and Jefferson's hands, wishing them Godspeed and giving each of the girls a fatherly hug as they passed. The PD crew saw them as far as The Grove Hotel where they were handed over to a group of men who looked very much like militia – Dan starting to get a picture of the fragmentation and politics of public safety rising to fill the power vacuum in the city. Each group seemed to have its own turf, and knew how to best navigate the threats and passages of their own territories.

This new group led them west avoiding a string of grocery stores and a mall. When they reached American Boulevard one of the bigger men to the side of the group shouted. "Contact left!" and immediately his men gathered behind an overturned truck as bullets began to pop off the buildings over their heads. The girls screamed and ducked as the militia men returned fire – somewhere over the top of the din Dan heard a man yelling at the end of the alley "Don't none you assholes hit any my hoes!"

"Go!" The leader of the watch yelled at Jefferson who had fired his Glock down the street hitting a man wearing a black hoodie with a red bandana tied tv sitcom outlaw style over his mouth and nose. Jefferson nodded then started dragging the girls to their feet to make a run for the bridge. On the other side there was a small group of men not much older than he was, all wearing Boise State ROTC shirts.

"Where are the Minute Men?" one of the young men shouted as Jefferson and Dan shooed the group of girls past him over the bridge.

"Up the street." Dan panted pointing behind them.

"Persky! Daniels!" The young man shouted. "You are package escort. The rest of you fall in on me!"

Persky and Daniels led the way down the banks of the bridge where Dan and Jefferson were surprised to find their canoes waiting in the water.

"Your camouflage game is shit, guy." Perskey said to

their shocked faces. "Took us all of two minutes to find them. Now get out of here and do better next time."

It took them a little time to organize the girls in the boats, making sure they were evenly loaded, handing out oars. As Perskey pushed the trailing canoe off the banks and paddled away Jefferson looked back to see Daniels running across the bridge eager to join the fight as the sound of gunfire clacked and echoed from the streets behind them. They rowed as far as they could, skimming the canoes as fast as possible, hugging the shoreline and crossing on land over levies and dams, loading and unloading their passengers as fast as they could. They were still in the tangle of homes and open spaces when the sun began to set. Jefferson shouted ahead to Dan if they should make camp for the night. Dan just shook his head, shouting back that they weren't going to stop until they were clear of the city. He slowed his canoe enough for Jefferson to pull alongside.

"Remember that lake we spilled out into?" he asked, Jefferson nodded. "There's a little island in the middle of it. We'll camp there. Sleep just a little bit. We'll deal with the swamp and Star in the morning."

"You don't think those guys are following us, do you?"

"I don't know." Dan said, huffing with each stroke. "But until we are sure they aren't we have to act like they are."

CHAPTER 26

Hemenway Harbor – Lake Mead, Nevada / Arizona Border

Myra pushed her way through the crowd at the water's edge looking for her string of ponies. Behind her boatmen called and hawked while the ragged mob moved towards the boat launch. "Step up! Step up! Next ferry leaves in fifteen minutes. Smoothest ride down the Colorado to the Yuma Trains! Only steam trains in operation heading east and west! Cash only – No chips!" She spotted the men up away from the press and throng. They had finally found Hunter some decent trail clothes in Bloomington and given the last week in the saddle pushing twenty miles a day, he was starting to almost look like a real horseman. She walked up to them shaking her head – it was a no go.

"They won't take livestock." She sighed. "And we aren't making it through that desert on foot. We have to have the horses. We need to stop over somewhere. See if we can't pick up another pony just to carry water. Then we'll cut back to the Colorado. Take it down to Alamo Lake. There's a little slip of blue on the map called Date Creek, we can hopscotch there before heading for Wickenburg, but you know how little I trust blue streaks in the desert."

"So where are we going to get extra horses?" Steve adjusted himself in the saddle. "Because that won't be here. We've been here – what? Half an hour? Already been offered bundles of cash for the ones we're sitting on."

"Seems like a bit of a seller's market." Hunter quipped as Myra pulled herself up into the saddle.

"There's a reason for that." She said, and then to their questioning gazes, "Look around. You see much of anything here on four legs beside our animals? These folks want two things – a fast trip out of Sin City and a meal."

"What now trail boss?" Steve asked as she stepped up into the saddle.

"I heard about a place from one of the guys selling boots." She said leading the two men and their string of backup mounts south west away from the water. "Dude ranch that's made a big power play down here, raided one of the dry lots outside south Vegas and have gone full cattle. They might have a few horses that haven't been eaten or ridden away."

They rode for about an hour through the ruins of upscale suburban neighborhoods and industrial parks of what had once been Boulder City, burnt out and looted with the exception of a few lingering shops and booths springing up along the portions of the grid fed by gravity wells rather than the solar powered pump systems that had extended construction into more arid reaches. From the looks of the holes dug through the corners of doors and fences the local coyotes and foxes didn't mind walking over hot asphalt onto dead and dying lawns any more than they cared about walking over the burning sand. They followed the 93 past the rolling greens of a golf course that looked a bit dry and singed around the edges till they came to a massive gate with the words "Big Stakes Ranch" cutout in iron across the top post.

"I get it." Steve chuckled while Myra rolled her eyes. "Oh c'mon, that's funny." They let themselves into the gate and rode up to the massive ranch style inn ahead, coming into the courtyard just as two men, wearing different shirts but the same face, walked out of a large arena style barn.

"Hello." The neatly shaved one greeted them. "If you're looking for rooms, we're full."

"We aren't." Myra nodded towards the barn. "We need horses. Something sturdy to haul water for us. And barrels if you got them. We can pay in cash."

"We quit taking cash three days ago." The rough saddle worn one said. "Fiat paper not being what it used to be."

"I'm Bobby." The clean shaven of the two said as

Myra, Steve, and Hunter swung down to introduce themselves. "That ass over there is Dex. We might have something for you, but the ass is right. We aren't taking cash."

"What are you taking?" Hunter asked, his eyes flicking to Steve.

"Food." Bobby said. "Or something we can use to buy food. The casinos are still able to get in some vegetables and canned stuff. We've been pulling stray head out of homesteads and ranches that are folding up, but you don't make market beef by eating the herd. Or seed. Enough seed packets could get you some tack. But not the horse to go under it. Or casino chips, those will work too. And we take propane or firewood. Neither of which I see on your packs."

"They aren't taking chips down at the doc." Myra pointed out.

"It's more of a regional currency now." Dex crossed his arms and leaned against the side of the barn. "We live here where the casinos still stand by their marks. Boatmen make runs to places where casino money doesn't hold any more value than the plastic they're printed on."

"How about gold?" Steve asked and the two brothers exchanged glances.

"Yup." Bobby nodded. "Casinos still trade in that."

"How much gold?" Hunter asked. "For two sturdy horses, the tack, the barrels, and to let us pitch our tents in the courtyard here to give these horses a rest."

Dex looked to Bobby, who was staring at Hunter. "Say five grams?"

"And if we wanted baths." Steve asked. "And feed for these animals?"

"That would be included." Bobby nodded. "Though I have to warn you, the baths won't be hot. None of our water heaters work in this place anymore."

"Do you have a place we can wash our clothes?" Myra said pulling her shirt away from her skin. "I'm about ripe enough for pickin'."

"We do." Bobby nodded. "And a line to hang them on. For five grams of gold, you'll find us rather accommodating."

Hunter nodded, then moving to his saddle pack pulled out a single gold ingot marked Credit Suisse on one side and emblazoned with a stylized rendering of Fortuna on the other. He tossed it to Bobby who studied it a moment, cupping it in his hands to inspect its luster before tapping it thoughtfully into his palm. "Dex will take your horses and tack. Let me show you where you can get cleaned up. Then we'll get your tents squared away and look over the stock. See what we can't find for you." They nodded and pulling their saddle bags and the rifles they had taken from the Acropolis armory from their horses, followed Bobby inside.

He led them into the reception lobby, handing the bar over to a pretty blond behind the counter then up a flight of stairs to a few rooms with curtains draped across their open doors. "There's not really much in the way of privacy. Other than the curtains." He explained. "These rooms were being remodeled when the grid went down, but the tubs work as do the showers. No beds so we just use them as the community bathroom. We have just enough water pressure for the toilets and the tubs up here so people who stay in the other rooms know to stay out when the curtain is closed. We have fresh towels in the closet and you're on the honor system to take them down stairs to be cleaned when you're done, and there's soap and toiletries on the sink. We do our laundry out behind the kitchen. There's a little better water pressure out of the hose there, and there is laundry soap. Dinner is served around sundown if you're hungry. It's quiet right now as most of the people who stay are trading work for supper, but you'll get to meet a lot of them then. Where did you folks come in from?"

"We just rode in from Saint George." Myra said stepping into the first room and drawing the curtain, her eyes glittering at the sight of the walk-in shower.

"You two will have to take turns over here." Bobby

led them further down the hall to another room, where Hunter motioned for Steve to go ahead while Bobby pointed to a wooden chair at the end of the hall.

"Do you have anyone from the Phoenix area who has come in recently?" He asked pulling his wallet from his back pocket to show Bobby a photo of himself, Lucy, and Bella. "Specifically, these two?"

"I'm sorry. I haven't." Bobby said after studying the photo for a moment. "It's a long trek to Phoenix, especially for a little one. Even with the ferries running."

"Thanks anyway." Hunter put his wallet away while Bobby left him to wait. It was a long shot, Lucy looking for him. Before the outage he couldn't imagine her crossing a mall to find him in a different store, but things had changed. Maybe she had changed with them. She loved him. He loved her. It wasn't completely unreasonable to think she might come looking for him in Vegas. He sat down in the chair trying to remember the last words he spoke to Lucy and Bella. Did he tell them he loved them? He couldn't remember.

He was thinking about Bella, excited for her new telescope, bouncing around the house playing fairy godmother, asking him why. Why is the sky always blue? Why do dinosaurs like bubble baths? Why did he have to go to work again? Why daddy? Steve rudely interrupted her by shaking him awake.

"Hey buddy." He said as Hunter stretched the stiffness out of his back. "Shower time."

Hunter nodded and entered the room, pulling the curtain across the door. Stripping he piled his clothes and saddlebags in a corner and turned on the shower, tensing for a moment as the cold water hit him then relaxing as it spilled over his skin rinsing off miles of dust and sweat and pain. He had to get home. He had to find his family. He had spent so much time away from them; at the office, on client needs trips, sometimes just to be away, he had missed Bella's first steps, her first words. To be fair Lucy had missed those as well. He thinks her first word might have been abuela – Lucy got a new nanny after that one - but that didn't matter now. What mattered was he was going to find them and never leave them again.

It took three passes with the shampoo to get all the grit out of his hair, then a full minute to kick all the grime down the drain. The low water pressure wasn't helping. Just as he was wrapping himself in a clean towel there was a knock on the door frame. He pulled back the curtain to let in Steve caring two bowls and a small aluminum pail of steaming water. "Talked the kitchen into giving us the tools for a hot shave." He said putting the bucket down and pulling a couple of safety razors from his back pocket. "

"How much did it cost?" Hunter asked dryly.

"Not much extra." Steve said stepping up to the mirror and filling his bowl from the pail. "That little blond running the front is shrewd, but not heartless. I bought some casino marks at the docks, so we have a little petty cash. Don't have to go flashing the gold. And while you were in there a couple of cowhands brought in a wild hog. They're butchering it in the yard and that Dex fellow has a fire going. Not that I'm not loving the rabbit, and that coyote wasn't a treat, but fresh fire roasted pig meat sounds great right about now."

Hunter nodded as he filled up his bowl, wondering what Bella and Lucy were having for dinner.

Circle B / Barring Ranch – Orein, Nevada

"Now that the Schertzs have a use for those big horses of theirs they don't seem so eccentric." Ceciliee Goya was sitting down at the Barring's kitchen table carefully transcribing the *USDA Guide to Home Canning* into a five subject notebook that had been scavenged from the shuttered

Dollar General on Bridge Street. Each of the women around the table had their own book to copy taken from Cathy's personal library and had been meeting every Saturday evening to transcribe the pages for their own home. Ane was working on the *Reader's Digest Back to Basics: How to Learn and Enjoy Traditional American Skills*, Becca was more reading than copying the brittle pages of *Board of Agriculture and Fisheries: Leaflets Numbers 1 to 100* printed in 1912, while Gertie and Dalisay shared *Ten Acres Enough: The Classic 1864 Guide to Independent Farming*. Just to be helpful, Mrs. Barring was copying out *Homemade Contrivances and How to Make Them: 1001 Labor-Saving Devices for Farm, Garden, Dairy, and Workshop* to be passed around from one home to the next until each house had a copy.

"Oh, we never thought them eccentric dear." Cathy smiled over her work. "They grew up in a world without laptops and cell phones. When those things came, they felt like distractions rather than luxuries. So the Schertzs just kept on keeping on the way they knew how."

"I wouldn't mind a little distraction right now." Dalisay sighed, putting down her pen to flex her hand.

"You know Old Man Schertz, Calvin's great grandfather?" Cathy reached across the table as she spoke, taking Dalisay's hand and massaging it in her strong grip. "He used to run the stagecoaches between Truckee and Winnemucca and back. He was a pony express rider before that as a younger man. Growing up we always saw a lot of his pap in Calvin. Mary says she's not seen him so happy to get up and get going in the morning since the eighties. Now that Mike and Jake are hanging on his every word, he feels like he's part of the community again. Here she thought he was ready to pack it in and head to the old folks' home and instead he's springing out of bed like a young man."

Gertie squinted at her page, then getting up to grab another candle from the side table against the wall paused. "There's only four left."

"It's fine dear." Cathy released Dalisay's hand letting her get back to work. "I've been braiding some strips of denim I made off an old pair of jeans no one wears anymore. I plan on making tallow candles next Monday, and maybe some soap – if you ladies have the time and the materials, I would be happy to show you how it's done."

"Ane, you can bring your little ones over to have Louise watch them." Becca looked up from her work, thinking about how little contact the two families had prior to the outage and the way they had come to rely on one another over the past few weeks. Ane crinkled her brow, but nodded, then took a deep breath.

"I think I might be pregnant." She blurted out as the other women looked up at her, stunned. "I've been meaning to ask Max to grab one of those home pregnancy tests from the pharmacy but between him being so busy helping the other men search the highway for supplies and trying to keep an accurate record of the land we've taken over; I don't want him worrying."

Becca scooted her chair over to be closer to Ane, knowing the stress she must be under. "Well," Cathy said moving to Ane's other side. "There is something we can try. My mother told me about it, but I've never done it myself. Dalisay, would you go get my sugar jar? Ane, I'm going to need you to give me a sample."

Ten minutes later they all gathered around a small bowl on the table, the flicker of the candles giving the room the air of a séance or a tea leaf reading rather than a pregnancy test. "This seems like a waste of good sugar." Ane groused as she pushed a little cup of urine towards Cathy. "And a bit unsanitary."

Cathy shushed her as she spooned a little bit of sugar into the bowl, followed by a tablespoon of urine. They all peered over the rim of the bowl, "So we're looking for clumps?" Ane asked finally.

"Yes. The hormones don't let the sugar absorb."

Cathy said as she looked into the bowl. "Or so my mother would say."

"Well, it's not dissolving." Dalisay said hopefully.

"But it's not really clumping either." Ane said. "It's just sitting there. Like wet sugar and pee."

Cathy looked into the dish, disappointed. "Well, so much for that. I'll clean this up."

"I'll ride out to the Dollar General tomorrow, see if any of the pharmacy supplies are still there and worth saving." Becca said. "Mike's so caught up in this new project he'll not even notice I'm gone."

"What are they working on, anyway?" Ane asked, "And don't say wagons. We know the wagons part. But that isn't all they're working on."

"Is there something wrong at the mine?" Ceciliee asked nervously. "Something they aren't telling us? Because I'm still in The Ruby Boot. Alone with my kid and my mom now that Mike's mine guys have wandered off."

"Wait, you haven't claimed a farm yet?" Dalisay gasped.

"What, you have?" Ceciliee spat back. "Whatever happened to forget this place, move to Reno?"

"Oh no!" Dalisay shuddered. "I'm never going back there. It was spooky with the lights out. Those people are heathens, probably already eating each other. Nope. Not me."

Becca took a deep breath, hoping the two women would keep arguing until Mike showed up in the wagon to take her and Ane back home.

French Homestead – Bear Reach north of Pinefare, Montana

James stepped into the kitchen from the side door, carrying plastic grocery bags from the wagon. He looked into the living room where Celia sat in her rocking chair staring at the fireplace. She looked thinner than usual, gaunt and haggard. She hadn't been bathing and he could smell her from the dining area. He placed the bags on the kitchen table, they contained the odds and ends which he had claimed from the run to the distribution center that lay along the highway between Pinefare and Whitefish.

They hadn't been the first people to break in and found the security gates pulled down from their hinges and the loading bay doors unlocked. This made loading their wagon and driving the horses back and forth from town and back again the hardest part of the three trips they had made in as many days. He stocked the shelves of the pantry, then walking outside opened up the narrow root cellar under the house where he stored a small wooden crate filled with apples and carrots and a second one with potatoes. Some of the fresh produce had kept rather well in the unheated warehouse and had been treated like bricks of gold in town. Picking up an apple he walked upstairs, kneeling beside Celia trying to look into her eyes. She just stared unblinking into the flames of the fire.

"Hey." He said smoothing a strand of her hair behind her ear. "We've been to find food. Just a few more trips and we should make it through the rest of winter. All of us. Even the winter-overs in town. Why don't you get up and see what I brought?"

When she didn't move, or even acknowledge him speaking to her he pressed the apple into her hands, his fingers pressing hers gently around it then recoiling at the sticky slick mess he felt there. He looked down to see her fingers a mangled mess of blood and flesh, the nails nearly ripped off to the quick. For a moment he thought maybe rats had been chewing at them until she turned to look at him, her eyes wide and expressionless as she spit out a nail tip from between her blood-streaked lips.

"Celia, this has to stop." He said, standing up in

disgust. "You can't hurt yourself like this. What if these get infected? What then? Don't you realize you could die?"

"James." She said quietly, turning back to the fire. "I was watching Oprah. I didn't hear you come in. The pilot light is out."

He sighed heavily as he took hydrogen peroxide, ointment, and bandages from a cupboard over the kitchen stove then returning to his wife said, "I know Celia. Let's get your hands fixed and I'll help you into a bath. Does that sound ok?"

She didn't respond. She simply stared into the fire. He was nearly finished with the bandages when Celia burst out in laughter, a high-pitched cackling that made James jump as his skin began to crawl. Then, just as suddenly as she started laughing, she stopped, her mouth snapping shut so tightly James could hear her teeth clack together. The silence which followed was even more unsettling, filling the cabin like something alive and malevolent inhabiting the air around her. It watched him from the windows with invisible eyes as he filled an aluminum bucket with fresh snow from the yard though she remained in her chair, looming over him as he set the bucket to melt on their iron stove.

When he had managed to fill the acrylic tub in their master bath, she was as cooperative as a baby. She just sat limp and staring as he helped her in and washed her skin and hair. He took his time combing the tangles out of her long caramel-colored locks. Celia had always the most sensitive scalp, he remembered nights when they were newly married when she would come to bed crying because of the pain caused by a hairbrush or pulling her ponytail out. If Celia experienced hurt, James never wanted it to be by his hand. He toweled her dry before dressing her in a clean nightgown, then boiling more water he made her a bowl of instant oatmeal. When she refused to feed herself, he sat her down on the edge of the bed, spooning the warm cereal into her mouth before tucking her in.

"Get some sleep." He said closing the shades against the afternoon sun. "I'm going to restoke the fire, don't let it go out."

"James." She rolled over to face him as he walked to the door, for a moment her face seeming completely lucid. "What day is it?"

"Wednesday." He said, "The third of February. It will be the girl's birthday soon. Maybe you could bake a cake, I brought some mixes. I thought it might be nice to bring them by to see you. If you feel up for company."

She stared at him and began to cackle again, his shoulders slumping as the thick smell of urine wafted up from the bed. She would have to be washed again, and her sheets changed, he would take her soiled bedding back to the Mule Wash to be cleaned along with her other clothing. No longer compliant she fought him through her second washing, punching and screaming, biting him as he attempted to restrain her and rinse her clean. Flopping to the floor she kicked and slapped at him as he struggled to put her into a clean set of pajamas. He pushed her into Brynne's room, forcing her down onto the little bed, his eyes and hands hot with anger,

"Now lay down!" he barked. "And if you piss this one, you'll just have to sleep in it!"

She chased him up the hall as he pulled the soiled blankets from their bed, shrieking and railing at him. Calling him everything under the sun but his name. She threw a vase which narrowly missed the side of his head as it shattered against the kitchen wall. Then, squatting over the living room rug, Celia urinated through her cotton pants onto the floor. James just watched; his face curled in disgust before slamming the door to stomp out into the snow. Tossing the bedclothes into the back of the wagon and climbing up into the seat he picked up the long driving lines and clucked to his team, driving them away from where she stood on the cabin porch shrieking his name, her voice fading with every hoof fall.

CHAPTER 27

Hot Springs on the Verde River, Arizona

They had been hiking for three and a half days and Sarah was surprised at the distances they had traveled. They rested when Bella was tired but for the most part the little girl treated walking along the river like play, skipping along ahead of Sarah to explore rocks and fallen trees. The first night after leaving the lake Sarah finally found a stand of trees that would hold their weight and they slept up off the ground. Bella helped to gather firewood, sat quietly after dinner as Sarah read parts of the field guide and the bible to her – though Sarah wasn't exactly sure if they were the good or helpful parts.

The next morning along the way Bella sang-song back portions of the reading the night before. *Never put your hand under rocks or trees, snakes live there and will bite you. It was a snake in the garden who tricked Adam and Eve. We should always be careful of snakes and check areas where they might live with sticks.* When Bella's feet were tired, they would soak them in the cold river and read fairy tales over crackers with peanut butter and jelly. In the evening Sarah would stop to make camp and to fish for their evening meal. Even with the rests and the exploring they were averaging about fifteen miles a day.

When they came upon a rock wall built into the edge of the mountain above them Sarah pointed it out to Bella who eagerly clambered up the side of the hill, moving as easily over the terrain as a baby mountain goat. Sarah barely kept up as they crested the wall to find two pools of hot mineral water in concrete basins, one in a little cavernous room and the other built between a concrete walkway and the hillside. Sarah looked inside the room, then guided Bella to the outdoor pool as someone had painted some rather anatomically accurate pictures on the walls. They were older paintings, crude not just in content but in execution – deliberately made to be shocking.

As she shooed Bella away, Sarah's mind drifted back to her freshman fall semester when she had taken a philosophy of art course and the professor explained the difference between nude figures and pornography. Nudes were a study in the human form – a research into the construction of mankind the creature or a commentary on his state of being. As such, even a postmodern primitive could express the tasteful conversation of one's naked flesh. Pornography, on the other hand, was a deliberate insult, a sort of blasphemy against man and his convictions or creation which narrowed a whole human being into the sum of his or her sexual parts reducing them to nothing more exalted than a butter churn and nothing higher than a dirty Kleenex. As such, even renaissance masters could create porn. As with music and literature, art was less about medium and execution and more about message and intent. While there was a feeble attempt at stylization in the paintings on the wall, they were certainly artless and pornographic in their depictions.

When the temperature of the outdoor pool met with Bella's approval, they settled in for a long soak. Bella's swimming skills had much improved over their journey; she had become bolder and more confident, launching herself from one wall to the next using pure speed to keep her little body afloat her face rarely going under. She giggled excitedly while Sarah washed her toes and behind her ears, slipping away to jump from the bench into the middle of the water and dog paddling back. The delicate little china doll with the soft auburn curls had broken during her sickness beside the lake. Bella was no longer pale and thin; her skin had taken on an almost copper colored glow as little freckles dotted her button nose. She was stronger, healthier, less wary of the world around her – almost feral in her enthusiasm to reach the next hill, the next bend in the river, the next thing to learn.

As much as Sarah wanted to stay at the mineral pools, she knew they would need to press on. There were no more reservoirs to keep them separated from the other band of people who had been shadowing their journey along the water's edge. As a matter of fact, there were places so calm and narrow that even Bella could easily bound over the river from one bank to the next. And they still had such a long way to go, though she remained unsure as to where her ultimate destination should be. Should she try to reach her parents in McCoy, Colorado or Bella's grandparents in Baptiste, Idaho? Either way they would be forced to leave the comforting banks of the Verde for those of Oak Creek, and after that make the eleven-mile overland march to the outskirts of Flagstaff, and from there another fifty miles with no real natural water sources to the muddy banks of the Little Colorado. Though there may be manmade ones. Which came hand in hand with manmade dangers.

Bella fussed a bit when told it was time to leave, but Sarah pointed to the sun overhead reminding her how good it felt to sleep up off the ground. Progress on the trail had become Bella's new obsession and when she heard that they might be able to get another five miles of trail under their belt while they looked for sturdy trees she immediately climbed out of the large pool and began to dry her feet so her socks could be easily pulled back on. They hiked wet, letting their skin dry as they walked, Sarah handing out bits of food as they went. Bella had also become insistent that she carry her own water canteen – per the instructions in the survival guide. Sarah had finally made her one using the duct tape and nylon cord to wrap one of the empty Fiji bottles. A serious look on her little face, Bella fitted the mouth of the bottle with a carbon filter from Sarah's pack and refilled her drinking water from the fastest flowing water she could find.

Not far up the river they climbed a steep rise that had formed in the hollow of a meander, then scaling it down again forded the river at a shallow bend maintaining a direct path of travel. Sarah would not allow Bella to do so on her own power because the river had deepened enough she was worried the little girl would lose her footing and be swept downstream. Bella pouted and huffed in her arms as she crossed through the swiftly flowing water, first once then twice. The third time Bella stamped her foot in anger as Sarah swept her up, going limp in Sarah's arms as a form of protest, threatening to pull them both off balance. As they stopped for Sarah to catch her breath from wrestling both packs and a surly child to the opposite bank, she noticed a long line of tracks sinking deep into the sandy mud running alongside the Verdi. It was the first sign of the band of strangers following the river ahead of them they had seen in days. As best as she could tell they had come down the slope of the hillside at a fairly fast clip, one of them running onto the shoreline to turn and follow the rest further north.

On a little fish shaped island nearly three miles further upstream Sarah noticed the wrappers of sterile medical supplies and the ripped edges of bandages lying around. Picking up one of the wrappers she read it – Epinephrine .3mg – the packaging not unlike those of the preloaded syringes Officer Merris had slipped in her pack back in Phoenix. When she came upon the blowing wrapper of a snake venom extraction kit just a few feet away she was certain the strangers couldn't be too far ahead. She sat Bella down on a fallen log, checking in and around it twice for snakes first before backtracking the marks left in the sand of the island. She didn't know exactly how many people there were, though she counted more than four variations of shoeprints coming onto the island from the river. They had set their companion down near the log where Bella's little shoes were swinging rhythmically into the bark, then they had all gotten up and walked further upriver around the bend.

"What's the matter Sarah?" Bella asked sweetly, the cloudiness of her earlier tantrums rolling away. Whenever Sarah was worried, even though she tried to hide her

306

emotions, Bella would sense something amiss and try to comfort her nanny in much the same way Sarah would soothe the little girl after a nightmare. As if fear and uncertainty could be kissed away like a scraped knee. Sarah looked at the sky, the sun would be down soon. It was probably best to stay put for the night rather than risk coming onto the strangers' camp so close to dark. She strung up the hammock between two ironwood trees just at the water's edge then spent the rest of her time building up brush, rocks, logs, whatever she could find to block the light of her campfire from shining up the canyon in the direction the strangers had gone.

By the time she sat down to boil water to warm their barley stew dinner in its mylar package the howls started. At first it was a low moan that seemed to be coming from the rocks, and for a moment Sarah was prepared to grab Bella and her open pack to race up the mountainside abandoning their gear fearing it may be the first signs of a flash flood. But when the sound came again, this time louder, she recognized it as a man's voice. She couldn't make out what he was saying, if he was saying anything. But as the cries became more panicked, more insistent, rolling high overhead and twisting with pain into an almost animal like shrieking, Sarah felt the hair on the back of her neck stand up. Bella, terrified, clung to Sarah's leg refusing to let go until Sarah sat down in the tent rocking the little girl in her lap.

"It's a ghost." She whimpered burying her face in Sarah's chest as the floor of the riverbed grew black, the sun dipping down behind the tall hills on the western side of the canyon. "It's a ghost and he's going to eat us."

"No baby." Sarah kissed the top of her head. "No one is going to eat you. Someone is hurt very badly, and I need to go and see who it is. I need you to stay here and be brave."

"No." Bella shook her head and clung to Sarah even tighter, starting to cry. "No. Don't go. Don't leave me here."

Sarah smoothed her hair, rocking Bella and speaking with a gentle voice, "Bella you have to be quiet. I don't want them to hear you or see you. Ok?" Sarah peeled Bella off her chest and reached into her pack. "Here." she said pulling out a chemlight and breaking it in half shook it to life. "See? This is a magic wand. You sit here in the tent and you hold onto this light. You eat your dinner and you don't move. I need you to be very brave sweetheart. I'm just going to go up the river a little way so I can see who these people are and what's wrong. Ok? Can you be my big brave girl?" It took some more convincing but eventually Bella agreed to stay quiet and hidden. As Sarah left her little camp, she thought of all the millions of things that could go wrong. What if there *was* a flash flood? What if a wild animal wandered into their camp? What if these people were circling back in the darkness and came upon Bella alone?

Sara walked as quietly as she could in the darkness around the rocky sandbar on the inside of the bend and was surprised to see the light of a massive fire flickering off the canyon walls not even a mile ahead. They were closer to her camp than she had thought, and that made her very nervous. She and Bella had spent the past week alone and this sudden intrusion into the privacy of their lives was unwelcome. As she stole further down the right bank, she realized the strangers' camp was on the left behind a cluster of rocks stacked up like a natural pillar against the water's edge. Shedding her hiking boots and socks she left them behind on the sand and, slipping into the river, used the current at the bend to float herself across silently, catching hold of the rocks on the other side and lifting herself onto a ledge where she could peek across towards the camp.

She counted four of them, no six – one had just immerged from the brush outside the ring of light and the prone figure laying in front of the flames was actually two people, a man and a woman. He was the one howling with pain and she was doing her best to comfort him. She watched as the figure which came from the bushes walked around the fire to each individual – there was something familiar in the way he moved but Sarah couldn't quite place it. She held her breath as the figure walked directly towards her, dropping her hand to the holster on her side wondering if the gun would fire after being submerged. If it didn't, if something went wrong, the idiot fine could be more than she could afford.

The figure stopped just feet from her hiding place. "We need to talk." It said grimly, sending a chill down her spine as she reached into her memory trying to place where she had heard it before. It wasn't until Lance answered back from where he had been sitting with his back against the rocks just out of her view that she knew exactly who these strangers were.

"We don't need to talk." Lance retorted. "I already know what you are going to say."

"He's going to slow us down." Matt's voice was an insistent whisper. "Do you want that? Do you want to die?"

"No, I don't want to die." Lance wasn't shouting, or angry, but there was a dark resignation in his voice.

"Look." Matt's tone was reasonable, even conciliatory. "I know you two are close. But his hand, it's swollen up like a balloon and it's just getting worse. He's throwing up everywhere." There was a measure of disgust in Matt's voice at this. "At this point we have to think of the good of the group. Are the needs of the group served best by throwing medical attention at someone who is going to die anyway?"

"Well maybe if our chief medical officer didn't spend half her day in a bottle of whiskey." Now Lance sounded bitter.

"What Lottie does with her free time is …" Matt sighed. "Look, no away team can survive without its blue shirt, ok? Besides, the whiskey will be gone in a couple of days. And it's a rattlesnake bite. Those are deadly even with perfect conditions."

"It's just this feels a lot like Mae Lu all over again." Lance gave a dark chuckle. "It's Mae Lu déjà vu."

"Mae Lu was a walking corpse there at the end." Matt insisted. "She was shitting her pants, vomiting everywhere…"

"You caving her head in with a rock didn't help things."

"What was I supposed to do, Lance?" Matt hissed. "What was I supposed to do? Just leave her there to suffer? Let her die alone instead of among friends? She was sick, and we had to move on."

Lance shifted below her, rising to be a looming black shadow above the rock pile blocking the light from the fire. "We should have just stayed at the bath house. Things were fine there."

"Yes, I agree." Matt sighed. "If you want, we can backtrack in the morning, spend another couple of nights. But let's get this very necessary public good done first."

"What about Leia?" Sarah did not like the tone in Lance's voice.

"What about her?" Matt turned his back to Sarah, moving to stand beside Lance. "If she gets in the way she can stay here with her boyfriend. But we need those supplies she's carrying… so make this quick." Sarah's eyes widened in horror as Lance pulled a hatchet from his belt and stepped towards the man lying in the rocky sand beside the fire.

There was the sound of a struggle and Leia screaming for Lance to stop, but Sarah didn't watch. She pushed herself back into the water as silently as possible, swimming as best as she could against the current to the right bank of the river. Leia's shrieks echoed around her as she frantically pulled her dry socks over her wet feet, but by the time she got her boots on the screaming had stopped. Sarah ran through the darkness, the scrub and the brush slapping across her face and hands. She had to get back to Bella, back to her child – *her* child. The one Lance had abandoned in Phoenix, the one who was sick at the lake for four days, the one she had risked everything to protect and care for and feed – *her child the one that she loved*. She jumped across the thin slip of water dividing the island from the mountainside. Tripping over the log and stumbling past her fire.

"Bella, don't scream." She said regaining her balance and approaching the tent. "Bella it's me, don't scream. Ok?"

"Sarah?" Bella's voice sounded a little sleepy.

"Yes baby. Its me." She opened the flap of the tent, grabbing up Bella's little pack and pushing it inside shivering as a breeze whipped down the canyon pressing her dripping clothing into her skin. "I need you to put your shoes on as fast as you can."

"Why?" Bella rubbed her eyes. "Is the man ok?"

Sarah froze, thinking about the horrible screams and the wet thuds echoing across the rocks around her. She held Bella close to her chest, kissing her on the forehead. "Please. Bella. No questions. I need you to put your shoes on as fast as you can while I smother the fire. We have to walk now and we have to do it very quietly. We can't speak. We can't make any noises with our feet. We have to be silent little mice, okay?" Bella nodded. "Okay. Good girl. I'll be back. I'm just going to get some wet sand."

Sarah smothered the flames quickly, thinking about the river and the walls of the mountain ahead. Bella would never make the climb on the right bank; they would have to cross at the tail of the island and climb up out of the narrow valley from there. It put her on the same side of the river as Lance and his band of crazies – but it was the only escape she and Bella had. She hurried to untie the hammock, when she couldn't work the knots in the dark, she cut the lines and stuffed the tent into the top of her bag. "Bella, baby, your light. I need your light!" She said, the little girl whimpering as that too went into the bag "I'll give it back baby, I promise. Do you have absolutely everything? Yes? Let's go."

Sarah pulled her hiking boots off again, and tying the laces together stuffed her socks into the toes and hung them over the rail of her pack. Scooping Bella up off the ground she crossed the Verde at the tail of the fish, then wrenched the socks back over her toes jerking them up painfully before putting her boots back on. "Listen to me Bella." She said holding the little girl's face in her palms. "We have to climb this mountain. It's going to be hard. We have to do it in the dark. But you can't get upset. And you can't talk. Not until we get back to the river. Do you understand?" Bella nodded.

Sarah pushed Bella ahead of her up the mountain, sometimes walking sometimes crawling on all fours as the angle of the hill steepened. More than once Bella or Sarah lost their footing sliding backwards, the rocks and sand shifting and clinking in little avalanches down to the banks of the river below. When they finally reached the crest Bella sat down, refusing to budge. To her credit, she didn't make a sound. Sarah picked her up, held her close, then guessing which direction to move in the dark started walking along the top of the hill. She had gone maybe a quarter of a mile before Bella started to squirm, wanting down. Sarah set her on her feet, taking her hand and leading her over a gentle rise then stopping as the other side seemed to drop further down than they had climbed. She was terrified to have put in all that work getting Bella up the hill to only come hiking down into the middle of Lance's camp so she turned towards what she hoped was west, walking out away from the sound of the water.

As they went over a saddle Sarah realized she had been cliffed-out, and now would not be able to walk any further west without backtracking. Doing so risked getting lost too far from the river to find it again, and losing the river meant losing the life sustaining resources of food and water it brought. Carefully she led Bella down, back towards the water, back towards danger. They walked for an hour before they found the river again. Sarah looked for signs they were followed or had come down to the river too close to the other camp. When she was satisfied there was no light from the bonfire, or loud voices, or footfalls behind them in the dark she turned her attention to the river itself. The thin slip of moonlight rising in the sky wouldn't reveal the direction of the flow, it just shimmered dimly across the dark surface in obscure ripples of light. Sarah stopped to think, then praying she hadn't been too turned around in the dark, turned left and walked on.

"Sarah." Bella whispered. "We're back at the river. Can I talk now?"

"I don't know, Bella." Sarah whispered back.

"I'm really sleepy." Bella whimpered.

"I know." Sarah patted her hand. "I am too."

It was midnight before the moon had risen enough to light their path, and when it did Sarah noticed a thin sandy trail heading up away from the water's edge through a stand of trees and brush. Hoping for a campground or some secure place out of the path of Lance and Matt and the others she pulled Bella away from the river, back up hill, but not as steep of a climb. They walked for another hour before the trail widened into a grassy pasture, the light of the moon glimmering off the roof of a darkened building. As they came closer Sarah saw it was a wooden barn, built in the same style as was in every one of Bella's picture books. Big, red, gambrel roofed, double doors, with a hayloft. She pushed hard sliding open the door – it stank inside, something was rotting somewhere in the back, but that didn't matter. It had walls, it had a roof, there was clean hay in one of the stalls.

Too tired to do anything else she spread out the bedroll, pulled off their shoes, and climbed in tucking Bella in beside her.

CHAPTER 28

1918 Main Street – Orein, Nevada

One of the biggest inconveniences about life now, Rebecca thought, is the lack of proper hitching posts in front of large buildings. It was a hilarious thought really. Just a month ago she had been worried that the kids were watching too much tv while she got the work done outside, or that there would be too long a line at her favorite coffee place which would make her late stopping by the grocery store for a gallon of milk, or that she wouldn't get a sitter for a night out with Mike. And now her biggest problems were how many hours it would take her to warm up the oven and keep it hot enough to bake the daily bread and that there was no decent place to tether her horse. She finally decided the bumper of a Volkswagen bug abandoned in the parking lot was as good a place as any and walked inside the doors Max Yneko had pried open so the residents could scavenge what little they could find in times of need.

The food aisles had been picked clean as had all the bottled water, though the dairy case still had a rancid smell from the weeks the ice cream had been left to melt and sour inside. She picked up some plastic bags from the register and started in the personal health area – easily finding the EPT test Ane would need and then on a whim grabbed a bottle of Flintstones Vitamins for the kids before making her way to the stationary isle for more notebooks and crayons and a few coloring books. She wondered if Louise would like a copy of People Magazine even if it was a month old, but then thought it would probably be a cruel reminder of the world they would not see again for a very long time. She found a mug down one of the isles with a little painted horse on it and dropped it in her bag instead. She was looking over the laundry isle, debating whether she should just take an extra bag of clothes pins and line home or if she should do the neighborly thing and leave them for the next scavenger when Kat Thurston walked in.

"Hello Rebecca." Kat said with her usual tone of forced politeness and contempt, then doubled over coughing into her sleeve.

"You ok Kat?" Rebecca asked, noticing the older woman was extremely thin and pale beneath her heavy layers of clothing and dirt, and she felt a pang of guilt. Yes, it was difficult to be civil to the Thurstons, likeable was not a word someone would use to describe them, but they were obviously suffering more under the pressures of surviving than anyone else who still remained in town. They weren't necessarily alone on their thirty-acre parcel. Jake had told them over lunch the other day that there were several people who had joined them on their farm in the past week. Most of whom seemed to be refugees from Reno.

"I'm fine." Kat waived her off, before a second coughing fit stole her breath nearly sending her to the floor had Rebecca not caught her by the elbow.

"Here." Becca moved her over to the end of the isle, pulling out a mop bucket from the bottom shelf and turning it over sat the older woman down, placing her hand on Kat's forehead. "My God you're burning up. Let me go see if there's any Tylenol left."

"No." Kat gasped between coughs, but when she couldn't catch her breath again Rebecca searched the isle anyway, returning with a bottle of Robitussin Cough, Cold, and Flu.

"Take this." She said breaking open the bottle on the spot and using the little cup over the cap to measure out the correct dose.

"This stuff is poison." Kat looked at her ruefully but took it anyway. "I'll be glad when all this petrochemical garbage has been consumed and we move on to more homeopathic methods of dealing with illness. You can't take a pill for your soul, Rebecca."

"No." She nodded at this. "That is true. Kat, if you don't mind me asking – don't you have anyone else to come all the way out here to do your shopping for you? Your place is at least seven miles away, and you are obviously unwell. You shouldn't be trudging through the snow like this."

"Ah!" Kat sat back with a triumphant grin. "You people have finally noticed our counter community. We're going to take Orein back, you know."

"Not with that cough you aren't." Rebecca gave her a little smile. "I'm serious. If you have people, they should have come for you. You should be in bed."

"Everyone is down with this." Kat wheezed. "We'll be fine as soon as our immune systems kick in. I just came to see if there were any vitamins that might help us along. Could you check for me? I need the organic C vitamins and if it's here elderberry tea."

"I'll be right back." Rebecca brought what was on the shelf, going back and forth as Kat read the labels on the boxes to make certain they were vegan friendly, cruelty free, and in the process told Rebecca all about the new community they had started. They were mostly people Kat and Wally had met at Burning Man. Yes, most of them were from Reno but there was a couple from Sacramento who had hiked the entire way to their farm with everything they owned on their backs.

They were all Facebook friends who had always discussed building the perfect new world, and when the old one collapsed it seemed the perfect opportunity. They planned to become migratory, traversing the plains as the ancestors had, following the sky from the Thurstons' farm maybe all the way up into Canada and back again just as the ancient ones had done. Sure, it was difficult dealing with the politics of all the people involved, but nothing a drum circle and an authentic sweat ceremony couldn't fix. Part of the problem was accommodating everyone's animals; most were pets and not accustomed to the cold.

"Right now, we have a scarlet macaw sharing our bedroom." Kat cleared her throat as she pulled a water bottle from her hip. "He was a rescue, would never make it in the wild poor thing, so release is just simply not an option. Even if someone were to hike down to Mexico with him. He didn't get along well with the chickens at first but they are learning tolerance and acceptance."

"You're keeping chickens in your bedroom?" Rebecca tried not to let her disgust show on her face.

"Oh yes." Kat said in a sage voice. "If it's too cold for us to stay outdoors, who are we to deny shelter and warmth for the animals we have imprisoned? You know the ancient Celts would all share a one room house with their livestock during the winter. We mustn't discount the wisdom of the ages my dear. You'll learn that, eventually. When you let go of your conquering mindset and work with nature instead of against her. She's a bad bitch. Look what she has done to your temples, your edifices of stone, your power structure. She has laid them all low." The woman coughed again into her sleeve but stood to go despite the fit. "I will see you again Rebecca Wolfe. When you are tired of struggling. You will come to us and we will accept you with open arms. … oh! Did I mention… Dandelion, the woman from Sacramento, she's a fire dancer. Very exciting. We aren't without our thrills."

Rebecca smiled to herself, shaking her head as Kat strode out the door. Then looking down at the grime which had transferred onto her hands trading bottles and boxes between herself and Kat, got up to see if there was any hand sanitizer left on the shelves. The sanitizer was gone but she did find a bottle of prenatal vitamins and some children's ibuprofen. Rebecca dropped them in her bag and wiping her filthy hands on the leg of her jeans left the store to head back home.

By the time she got home she was cold to the bone. Rebecca was almost too tired to ride out to the Ynekos' ranch to give Ane the pregnancy test, and almost asleep in the saddle by the time she circled back again to reach her own barn. Mike was in there, tinkering with the little farrier's forge he had gotten from Ely Lane. He and Jake had spent the week trying to make it run on a tank of gasoline fumes he had pressurized with a bike pump with little success, forcing him to go back to the drawing board when it came to fuel sources. He looked at her as she led her mount in, concern furrowing his brow. "I'll be fine." She told him when he insisted, she go to bed. There was still so much to do and her trip into town had taken time away from her work.

She still had to milk the cow Mike had "liberated" from a local commercial dairy after the workers had walked away to leave the animals in a dry lot, the feed piled up in a separate enclosure. Everyone in town picked their favorites and the rest had been released to maverick, the contents of the large hay barn distributed among the remaining families. There was also the goats and the new lambs Mike had purchased from a neighboring ranch that needed feeding and their pen cleaned. By the time she got to mucking the horse stalls she was dead on her feet. Mike took the rake from her and they had a fight, she had been handling this place on her own for years -thank you very much- and could you please make your goddamn dog shut up. He put his hand to her forehead, she felt it slip across the beads of sweat that had raised there – of course she was sweating, did he not see the work she had been doing while he futzed around with the forge? But when he lifted her into his arms and carried her into the house, she didn't fight him.

It just felt so good to be off her feet. And he was so warm.

She shivered as he helped her undress, complained when he put her in one of his old t-shirts instead of her flannels like she wanted. Could he stoke the fire? Their room was freezing. He ordered the children out, mommy needed to sleep, but as soon as Mike went out to finish the chores little

Sammy came toddling back in. She climbed up into bed beside her mother where she planted little baby kisses on Becca's brow, singing nursery rhymes over her like prayers. When Mike came in from the barn, they were both fast asleep.

When Rebecca wasn't better the following day, Mike began to worry. He was also worried about the cough she had developed overnight, hacking and barking like she was drowning. He organized Louise to take over her mother's chores and spent time outside teaching eight-year-old Jack how to muck stalls warning him, twice, to stay out of the cow pens without an adult present before he rode into town to Jake's little five-acre parcel down a dirt road behind the Thurston place.

He was shocked at the number of people crowded in the yard around Wally and Kat Thurston's farmhouse. He counted at least twenty living in tents around the little square building with a gabled roof, just a typical 1940's craftsman home which had been painted in psychedelic colors shortly after the Thurstons had purchased it. There was some sort of sculpture in the center of the row of tents that looked like garbage piled together in a heap. A nude woman streaked with blue and yellow mud walked from one of the tents, waving to him as he passed the fence line, and behind her came a chorus of all too familiar coughs. He found Jake sitting on his porch in his long thermal underwear, a wool throw blanket over his shoulders, his face pale and greasy with sweat.

"I can't figure out if I'm hot or cold." Jake chuckled, self-consciously covering the end of his missing leg with the edge of the blanket.

"You been like this all night?" Mike asked.

"Nope." Jake shook his head. "I was fine last night. Woke up sick this morning." Then he smiled. "Sorry boss, but I don't think I'm going to make it into work today."

When the sound of Max Yneko's Tobiano mare running up the drive came from behind him, Mike knew they had a serious problem. "Great minds think alike." Max said gruffly, then looking at Jake he cursed under his breath.

"Yea." Mike nodded. "I was going to send him out looking for a doc in Carson City or even Dayton, but it doesn't look like Jake's going anywhere but to bed."

"Ane's sick." Max said. "She woke up this morning with a headache, and the chills. I wanted to stay home to take care of her... Mike... she's pregnant."

They put their heads together, Ane must have caught it from Rebecca, Jake from talking over the fence to Wally. When Jake mentioned Kat had told him about running into Becca at the DG it all started to make sense. "We have to get ahold of this thing." Mike said. "Whatever it is, it's going through people like wildfire. Max, you ride from house to house – keep your distance at the gate but make sure no one comes near the Thurstons until they've beat this thing. Jake, you need care and quarantine. I've been exposed through Rebecca -so have all my kids. Get on your horse if you can and ride out to my place to keep an eye on things."

"Where are you going?" Jake asked.

"I have to find a doctor." He said. "See if we can't get people well."

They helped Jake into his clothes, the cough racking his body making dressing nearly impossible, then put him on the search and rescue roan Jake had taken over from Mike for his personal use. He was decent in the saddle but still rode slow, the cough choking his lungs with almost every breath. Mike stopped at the gas station on his way out of town, grabbing the few bags of chips he could find on the shelves there and stuffing them in his jacket pocket. It was a two day ride out of Orein Valley to Dayton even if he took the Ormsby cutoff through the hills. He walked his horse, stopping only for water at guzzlers that had melted snow in the sun, following the traces of deer trails over the sage and hills. He rode into the night even though his horse wanted to rest, at times using a bit more spur than carrot to urge his pony on. By midnight he had broken into chills that couldn't be explained just by the wind driving the snow ahead of him. Dawn found him hacking against his burning lungs and the Dayton Valley laying out beneath him like a smoky ribbon along the Carson River, his horse tired and mutiny minded.

He got off to lead his mount into town on foot, stopping first at a small medical center he had gone to once when a loader had blown a pneumatic valve and sprayed his arms with hot fluid burning him slightly. The building was closed, locked up tight, but a woman digging through the dumpster in the parking lot directed him towards the veteran's clinic down on Pike. Mike walked the two miles along the highway before he reached the older section of town. Turning right onto Main Street away from the bridge he led his pony to the old Union Hotel. Waving hello to a middle-aged woman sweeping the concrete walk outside he asked her for the address for the Veteran's Hall. She pointed down the street to a small iron sign across from a saloon. "But if you're looking for Doc," she offered, "he's not at work yet. He's having his breakfast, but I don't mind going to get him." Mike thanked her then leaned heavily against the posts holding up an upstairs balcony, worry and exhaustion weighing on him like a bag of bricks.

The Doc turned out to be a baby-faced young man who barely finished medical school at UNR and had been in the middle of residency training at Carson Hospital. He had been working as a volunteer for a flu shot sponsored by the Dayton Valley Lion's Club in the Vet Rec Hall when the lights had gone out. Over the following weeks his nurses and colleagues had drifted away to check on loved ones, and he had remained doing his damnedest to keep the residents of the valley healthy.

"Stay right where you are, Doc." Mike called from across the street. "We don't know what this is, but it's contagious." He explained the symptoms, the headaches, the chilled fever, the cough – the doctor said it sounded like some variant of the flu and almost wouldn't come to Orein until

Mike told him about Ane Yneko – pregnant, and little Sammy barely two years old and hacking so badly by the time he left, Mike was worried she might not live to be three.

"I have to stop by the pharmacy." The young doctor said. "Let me grab my coat and bag."

The "pharmacy" the doctor needed to visit was actually a small locked closet in the basement of the county courthouse on Cemetery Road. After two days of looting following the blackout, the senior ranking deputies stranded in Dayton had organized a complete audit of all medical supplies and controlled substances in town. Collecting anything of value to the doctors and nurses volunteering to help their community, they emptied all pharmacies within riding distance into the basement where they kept the medicines and other miscellaneous goods under armored guard. One deputy, a barrel-chested mountain of a sergeant named Chris Hunting, tossed Mike a respirator mask before asking after Ely Lane. He was visibly saddened to hear of Lane's passing and promised to make it into Orein to pay his respects to Mrs. Lane. The doctor immerged from the courthouse moments later and asked Hunting for a horse.

"You keep an eye on him." The deputy cocked his head towards the young doctor who was walking to a makeshift paddock across the street. "He doesn't quite have his seat yet." Mike responded with a coughing "will do" then mounted up to lead the way back over the highway towards the Ormsby trail through the Opal Range.

The Banks of the Boise River - Notus, Idaho

They would have put back into the water around their old campsite had the farmer with the shotgun not met them at his fence line, waiving the struggling band of refugees into his open gates. The girls, thankful for a path that had been trampled down so the snow was no longer knee and at times hip deep stamped the cold from their feet and broke into laughing conversation heading in the direction the farmer had pointed like a gossiping flock of geese.

"You best come up to the house." The man said shaking Jefferson and Dan's hands. "I have news from upriver."

At first the two Baptisteans were worried it was news from home, reaching them somehow down the course of the waters, but as the farmer put a pot of coffee and a large pot of canned stew on his wood burning stove he explained. No, he hadn't heard from Baptiste, but there was trouble on the border with Oregon. "A band of misfits, most likely out of Portland, have been attacking homes and towns up and down the Snake." The farmer sighed, pulling out a set of bowls from the cupboard. "Young men mostly, though they do have some girls. They've been stealing what they can. Burning houses. There have been stories of ..." He looked into the living room where the girls had clustered around his fireplace and lowered his voice, "rapes. Murders. All sorts of God-awful things. They dress all in black and paddle those big inflatable white water crafts. They killed a lawman in Fruitland, raped his wife and kid. Painted a massive red flag across the barn before they stole his livestock and set fire to the house. You would hear stories of this sort of thing in major cities, but it seems that with the leashes off there are just more dogs that need to be put down than those that deserve to live.

"Nyssa and Ontario have shut down the waterways they control. No one gets up or down without their permission, and they are very much shoot first ask questions later. I've been watching for you two since you left, hoping you wouldn't get by during the night." The farmer sighed running a calloused hand through his hair, "I'm not too concerned about the watchmen on the river, two canoes full of women and children should be able to pass but there's a lot of wildlands on the Snake, places for these animals to hide. I've been talking to the neighbors too. They're worried for you. Got a buddy by the name of Phil Perry down the road says he can help you folks get home by taking the highway overland through Sand Hallow. We're not going to force a thing on you, but we would like to help if we can."

"We would appreciate that." Dan said. "But we haven't really any money to pay."

"You just help Perry through the winter." the farmer said. "That will be payment enough. He's a tough kid, can hold his own so he'll be an asset to you and yours. Then come spring time we can talk about furthering communication between our two towns. It seems to me we've spent so much time crop specializing around here we won't do well without a larger community. I'll have sixty-five acres standing fallow if I don't find a use for it, and a barn full of wheat seed that's going to go to waste if it doesn't get planted. Most of the neighbors are in the same boat. It's been long enough if this power issue were an easy fix, it would have been done already. We've come to the conclusion we have to muster on our own. Which means we have to send someone out to find farm hands and marketplaces, and Perry's our best damn shot. He's not just your chauffeur, he's our ambassador."

When Dan and Jefferson agreed, the farmer looked relieved. "Good then. Eat up. The stew is by Kroger, but the bread is by Muriel Jones – she baked a bunch after you folks left hoping you'd be back through soon. She's extremely excited. Hasn't been up to Baptiste in a few years, knows your town from when she was a little girl though. If it's ok by you, we'll feed the girls and take them over to the Jones'. They're off the river and Muriel is a dead eye with a Winchester in her hand – no one will get to them with her standing mother hen. You two and a couple of the bigger girls– however – have a little work to do. A learning curve to overcome. Perry says he can give you a quick lesson and the rest you can learn on the trail."

"That's good." Dan said. "I know Jefferson can ride, but I haven't been on a horse in a long time."

The farmer laughed, "Oh son. You won't be riding horses. Not in this snow. Nope. Perry's got something much better." But he didn't say much more as they finished eating. They walked the girls over to the Jones farm, saw them seated comfortably in the living room and then pulling Danielle and the blond who had taken charge of the little boy back at the high school aside explained to them their help would be needed. The blond, who called herself Lessy, nodded then went to tell the young boy Tyler to stay put and she would be back in a little while before meeting them outside. They walked for about an hour in the snow, across the Notus bridge and through the town, the farmer waving hello to several people who had come to their doors and windows to stare curiously at the little group. "We're pretty tight knit around here. Most people are related by blood or marriage. Strange faces stick out, and that was before you couldn't turn the TV on."

They noticed the barking about the time they passed the fire station, a chorus of yips and howls that filled the air for miles. As they hiked to the top of a gentle rise they looked down at a little farm, the yard dotted with about seventy tiny huts in neat rows and attached to each hut – a wriggling bounding barking dog. The sign on the gate read *Phillip Perry Sledding – Iditarod Championship or Bust*.

"Everyone thought he was crazy when he moved to town." The farmer laughed as he led the way to the gate. "Said it was a shameful waste of good sugar beet land. But Perry, he just took it. Made friends with the neighbors. Who's laughing now? Huh? He is. That's who." Perry turned out to be much younger than Dan had expected – a dark haired man in his early thirties who dressed like a longshoreman, carried himself with the air of an experienced golf instructor, and had a mouth like a Mormon missionary.

"Shoot yes we can take you up there. Won't be a big

thing." Perry offered them some coffee which they declined still warm from the pot shared over lunch. "Biggest hiccup will be teaching you how to guide the dogs. I have a flat I can put the canoes and gear on, that won't be a problem – but you said there are ten of you? I'll have you men take on two passengers each that's six, you look like you have some muscle," he pointed to Lessy, "you can haul the food, and you," to Danielle, "you will drive the other two with the little one on someone's lap. All in all, we can get you home in one piece. Let's show you how to hook up and do basic commands, see which team fits you best. That's going to take the rest of the day though. When do your people expect you home?"

"We'll be overdue in a week." Dan responded.

"Oh, so we have some time. That will work out good." Perry's eyebrows shot up, then turning to the farmer. "Ben, if you could have the others here by noon? I think I'll keep these folks overnight. And we'll leave about one, it's Baptiste you said?" He looked down at the map he held in his hand. "We avoid all the cities – leave by noon. Make camp by one. Then get an early start the next day – barring any real problems, we could have you home by about lunch?"

"That soon?" Dan looked skeptical. "That can't be right."

"Well, we'll be taking it slow." Perry said seriously. "Being as you are beginners and all. But top speeds, these kids can get up to twenty miles an hour, run for about an hour at that speed with breaks to keep them on their line. They're spooky efficient! Leave a lot more time to do camp set up and takedown. My only regret is you can't use them in the summer. It's a top-notch ride. You're gonna love it. Oh, and Ben. Thanks for sticking around and feeding the teams I'm not taking. I moved their food to the root cellar and doused it with water. All you got to do is take the pick to it – one fish per dog per day. And I've got full cupboards and a good woodpile. I even ran to the library and found some of those

Louis Lamour you like so that's all stocked up. You should be good till I see you next? I think? Oh, I forgot to ask… can you all whistle? You're going to need to be able to whistle."

They spent the rest of the day getting to know the teams, Perry seemed to be watching them closely to see who got along best with each dog. He was quiet for a while just watching them interact finally giving Jefferson a big yellow and cream male named Cooper for his lead dog, and Dan a shaggy black and white female named Foxy. Lessy looked like she was a little afraid of the dogs, which bothered Perry since he said they could sense it but he liked the way a little grey husky named Snorri would circle her feet like living velcro so he left them alone to get used to each other. Danielle was the easiest to match with a lead dog as she seemed to get along well with all of them, making the teams interchangeable pieces for her. She ended up with a solid black bitch named Lark and the team that listened best with her in the lead. Perry taught them to stop, go, and turn as well as how to slow the team with commands and to use the break in the back of the sled, how to watch the team for signs they needed to rest, and how to move them back into position when the lines got crossed.

"Don't be afraid to stop." He told them. "Just whistle to the other sleds and we'll wait for you. It's better to look out for the team than to worry too much about distance. These dogs can camp anywhere you can camp and some places you can't so long as you keep them in one piece."

1011 Yellow Jack Place – Baptiste, Idaho

Beau slipped in the snow, struggling to maintain his balance without using his arms as they were busy wrapped around his chest holding something tightly bundled against his body. He walked past Teagan Booker's house, watching his dad and Mr. Tolman up on the roof putting the finishing touches of flashing around her new stovepipe. He smiled to himself feeling pride at having helped in the night raids, holding the horses while his dad and Mr. Zhou broke down the big bay doors at the back of the warehouse in Payette, even helped to load up the stoves they had taken from the showroom to put into the houses. Beau had also been the one who found the correct valves in the back of the ACE Hardware – so now every home had not just running water but hot water for showers and cooking. They had even changed out the valves and added a fireplace to Mrs. Wheeler's house in case she someday came back, and had swapped out the electrical hot water tank in the Ross house for a gas model so it could serve as a meeting house where everyone could talk about the neighborhood and plans for the coming spring.

He stopped short as something stabbed him through his shirt, "Ow!" he hissed as he walked up the drive to Mr. Zhou's house, then shaking the bundle under his jacket whispered, "Cut that out."

He knocked on the door and waited as there was a little commotion inside before looking up into the round but slim face of Mrs. Zhou. "Is Heather home?" he asked.

"Where do you think she would be?" Mrs. Zhou asked with a half-smile. "Disneyland?" He stammered for an answer while Mrs. Zhou called her daughter to the door. "Chu! Get down here."

Heather came to the door wearing a pair of white snow pants and boots and a fluffy pink sweater covered in hearts, behind her Amy came to the door as well wearing a turtleneck and jeans with wool socks. Beau stared at Amy a minute before the lump under his jacket stabbed him again. "Ow!" he grimaced opening the coat at the collar, allowing the furry hissing bundle inside to poke out its mangy head. "I think I found him this time."

"Hǔ!" Heather cried clapping her hands and reaching

for the squirming yowling cat, ripping him from Beau's shirt like a patch of thorns. "Where was he?"

"Hunting mice in the barn across the street." He said. "We'll be moving the rest of the horses over here in a couple of days, so I wanted to make sure he made it here first." Heather dashed into the house with the cat to show her mother, leaving her older sister to stand awkwardly at the door.

"Thank you." Amy said with a shy smile. "That means a lot to her."

"Yea, sure." He nodded.

"Well… bye I guess?" Amy waved a little as she closed the door.

"Bye." Beau could feel his face turning red as he walked across the street to his own house.

"That boy." Her mother said as she walked into the kitchen. "He must have brought your sister every stray cat in Idaho just to make you smile."

"Mom!" Amy sunk down into a chair beside the kitchen table.

"Well, it's true. Now go wash your hands and help me with lunch." Amy stepped to the sink, happy for the trickle of heat that came from the pipes, when the sudden sound of barking and baying came from outside.

"What on earth?" Her mother said stepping back into the living room to open the door just as four sleds each pulled by a team of bounding, singing dogs turned the corner off of Blackjack Oak and came racing down the street. "Lian! Chu!" Her mother shouted from the door, "Come look outside!"

Amy crowded the doorway behind her mother, ignoring the bump on her arm as Heather elbowed her way to the front. Outside, Jefferson Walker had come streaking into view, leading the way for five other sleds each pulled by a team of dogs. His passengers, bundled up like royalty in furs, laughed as the sled skidded to a halt. There were shouts of excitement from the street as families were reunited and newcomers were greeted with hospitable curiosity. Jefferson turned to look at her and flashed her a smile, the sides of his freshly shaved head now tan as he brushed a little snow from his sandy brown mohawk. Her mother was urging her to come and see this miracle, to put on her snow boots and join the neighbors around the Walker's flagpole. But her mother's excited instructions were drowned out by the sound of her own heart pounding in her ears.

CHAPTER 29

Oxbow Ranch – Off the Verde River, Arizona

She woke up around noon to the sound of thunder clapping overhead, rattling the rafters of the barn. Something in the loft – probably the outer door – was banging and bumping with the wind. A second peel of thunder followed by a brilliant crack of lightening filled the world outside with dazzling blue light, making Bella scream as the furious rattle of hail pelted the walls and the roof, bouncing into the earth like flung gravel. As the wind picked up the barn groaned and Bella clinging to Sarah begged for someplace else to hide.

"Stay here sweetheart." Sarah said crawling out of the sleeping bag and zipping it back up.

"You leave!" Bella shouted back over the din of the storm. "Every time I'm scared you leave!"

Sarah knelt and kissed Bella's forehead, holding her close. "I only leave so I can see if you should be scared or not. Ok? I'm going up into the loft to shut the door upstairs. That's all. I'll be right back. I promise."

She tucked Bella back in and climbed the ladder one step at a time, gripping the rungs tightly as another clap of thunder shook the posts. As her head came even with the loft floor she looked around for the open door – and screamed. Swinging in the wind, hanging by the neck from the rafters, was the body of a large man, the loft door banging in the wind behind him. Downstairs Bella shrieked, burrowing into the sleeping bag. Sarah took a deep breath and lied. "It's ok Bella. I'm sorry. I didn't mean to scare you."

"What was it?" Bella whimpered; her voice barely audible above the howling wind.

"It was a drop of water." Sarah forced a laugh, her eyes never leaving the swinging body. "A big drop of water fell from the roof and down my shirt. It was really cold and it surprised me. Everything is fine baby. I'll be right back."

"Hurry!" Bella wailed. "I don't want to be here by myself."

The body had been there so long there was hardly any smell, though she had been hoping the rotting scent she had noticed coming into the barn had only been a dead rat or a bird. He was an older man, wearing brown coveralls, a note pinned to his chest.

To Whom It May Concern,

I can't do this if the meds run out. Please understand the pain is too much. Take care of Addie and Baker. They like to be together.

She left him to walk over to where the door was swinging wildly on its hinges, looking out across the widening valley above the barn. There were houses out there, real houses. She hadn't seen them in the dark, nor had she seen the row of fruit trees lining a long grassy pasture where two horses were running the painted white fence line panicking in the flashing storm. Forgetting the door, Sarah scrambled down the ladder and pulled Bella out of the sleeping bag and their packs out of the straw.

"Hold this up over your head!" She told Bella folding the sleeping bag in half and helping the little girl to lift it up. "There's a house not too far from here. We're going to run." Bella baulked at the door as another thunderclap rolled across the sky, but Sarah dragged her out and towards the white clapboard building at the end of a long gravel drive leading to the barn as the hail rattled on the ground around them. Sarah prayed the entire time that the lightning that followed would strike somewhere else, as she watched the electric lights inside the house ahead of them glow dimly as it flashed across the boiling sky, spotting their vision and filling the air with the smell of ozone. When they reached the house, Sarah looked back at the barn, at the twisting hanging figure just visible in the shadows of the loft, then turned and walked the wrap around porch looking for a door. The one on the side of the house which looked like it led into a kitchen of some sort was locked, but the main door around the front was open.

Sarah stepped in cautiously. She wouldn't think someone who was sheltering inside would have left the body in the barn, but she didn't want any surprises. She sat Bella down on a ragged couch just as the lights gently warmed again and lightning cracked into the trees swaying in the yard. "It's going to hit!" Bella sobbed into the sopping sleeping bag which she was clutching like a security blanket. "It's going to hit."

"It's not going to hit us." Sarah patted her back then walked into the kitchen looking for the electrical panel. She found it in the back of a pantry, flipping the main breaker to the off position – not knowing if that would stop the lights from glowing as the particles in the air charged ahead of the lightning but hoped maybe it would. She unlocked and opened the back door and finding a woodpile behind the house, Sarah grabbed an armload and hurriedly built a fire in the potbelly stove in the corner of the living room.

"There, see?" She asked Bella after finally getting the old newspaper she had used for kindling to light using a box of matches she had found on a shelf in the kitchen. "This is a nice place. Honey – I have to go and check the river. Make sure it isn't going to rise up here. And I left something in the barn. Do you feel safe here?" Bella nodded. "Good. You stay right here and read your book. Don't touch the stove. I know you can't see the fire behind the door, but that stove is going to get very hot, don't go near it." Bella nodded again. Sarah checked the flue to make sure smoke wouldn't suddenly come flooding in while she was gone, then made a quick search of the four bedrooms upstairs, reassuring herself there was no one hiding under the Victorian beds or in the miniscule closets. Coming back down stairs she kissed Bella on the forehead, lay the sleeping bag out in front of the stove to dry, and then walked out the front door and back towards the barn.

She didn't feel the same urgency now that Bella was safe, or the same need to run from the storm. In fact, she felt more relaxed than she ever had since the lights went out. She had a woodpile. An actual wood pile. There was water in the river. She had only looked briefly at the pantry in her search for the breaker panel – but it had been stocked full of food. Real food. Mac and cheese, Life cereal, cans of soup, vegetables, fruit cocktail. There were bags of beans and rice. She had never cooked beans and hoped there would be instructions on the packaging, but there had also been a can of Crisco and a bag of flour. And a trap door in the bottom of the pantry that led beneath the house. She didn't know what was down there, but she had faith that the presence of a root cellar meant even more food.

She walked past the barn just as the hail rattled the earth around her, forcing herself not to look up into the open door of the loft, the swinging body calling to her mind's eye and beckoning her gaze. She walked a little swifter, fearing she wouldn't be able to resist the call. Leaving the yard around the barn she found the trail, it seemed so much shorter in the light than it had in the dead of night. She could see where the waters of the Verdi had risen, rushing rapidly at the base of the trees surging in almost breath like movements up and down the bottom of the hill. She couldn't be certain, but she thought the path she had led Bella up was now a good five feet into the water where rapids were starting to form.

Sarah heard shouting down by the water, someone barking orders and someone begging to stop. She stepped away from the hill blocking her view of the river path. There she saw Matt clinging to the long thick arm of a cottonwood tree, trying to push his way through the edge of the muddy river, the water surging up around his waist, Lance just steps behind on a rapidly disappearing trail. She couldn't see the others, but she could hear them further down the stream begging Matt to turn around, to head back the way they had come until the flood was over.

"You guys are such pussies." He said looking back at them. "There's a trail head right here."

He looked up, his eyes opening wide in surprise when he saw her standing there, cool, calm, collected, and holding her pistol in her hand. She lifted it and fired, ignoring the floret of blood that opened in his shoulder. He screamed and fell into the water, his leg pinned against a crook in the tree branches, his head bobbing and sinking over and over again into the brackish flow. Lance looked to where she was standing, moving closer to the water but still holding firm footing on the trail. "Sarah?" he stammered. "You found us."

"I saw what you did, Lance." He at least had the decency to look ashamed. "This is my place. My shelter. You and your pack of wolves are not welcome here."

"Sarah." He watched, pale faced, as Matt's body finally went limp. "Please."

"You need to go back." Her words became punctuated by a desperate shrieking. As if in agreement the water had surged snatching Lottie from where she had been clinging to the crumbling mountainside in the rear and pulling her into the main body of the river, carried her screaming down towards the teeth of the churning rapids. Lance wheeled towards her, leaping from the trail to the tree where Matt's body still bobbed, the force of the water bending it grotesquely at the knee where he was caught in the limbs. Lance stood on the branches, pulling his axe from his belt.

"We will take it from you if we have to!" He snarled. And she fired. This time she didn't miss, the bullet striking the young man square in the chest knocking him back into the water. He bobbed back up nearly twenty yards downstream, feebly gasping for air as he disappeared around a bend. She pointed the pistol at the remaining two members of the group,

Kennedy and Jessie.

"You have a choice." She shouted above the torrent. "You can take your chances with the river or you can die right here on this trail. If I were you, I would jump into the center. Let the flow carry you back down to the bathhouse. If I see you again. I will kill you. If I even think I feel you behind me, I will find you and I will gun you down like any other predator on the trail." She looked directly at Kennedy, who seemed to be weighing his options, pointing the gun right at his chest.

"Do it." She hissed. "Give me a reason to shoot you."

He looked from her to the river and back again, then jumped. She didn't even have to watch Jessie. He had made his decision when Kennedy took his leap. She holstered her gun and walked back up to the barn. Calmly Sarah climbed into the loft and taking the knife from her pocket, she cut the rope holding the man's body from the rafters. He dropped to the wooden floor with a dry thump that would have made her wince had she not so firmly set her resolve. Sarah cut open a bale of straw beside him, covering him gently in the dry grass as she shook out each leaf. She whispered a small prayer for him as she drew the straw up over his swollen face, promising to dig him a proper grave when the weather to cleared.

She would. She cared that he was laid to rest with a little bit of human dignity. But right now, she would need to go back inside and make sure Bella was okay. She crossed the field as the hail turned to heavy feathers of falling snow, watching it melt as it touched the wet earth. They would get a light dusting tonight. It would make the world look like it had been sprinkled with powdered sugar. It would be gone by eleven the next morning, but the river would still be up. The thunder rolled somewhere further south as the front of the storm headed out into the desert, leaving the world peaceful in the wake of its rage.

"I heard something." Bella said as Sarah came in, kissing her on the forehead and checking to see if the sink in the kitchen was working. The water came out a little muddy at first but soon ran clear and cold. "There was a lot of big bangs."

"It was just thunder sweetheart." Sarah turned to where Bella stood in the doorway, her little eyes wide and apprehensive. "Now. What would you like to eat? Do you want soup, or mac n cheese?"

There could have been a tornado outside, but Bella wouldn't have cared as she danced in the kitchen chanting "Mac and cheese! Mac and cheese!"

Wolfe Homestead – Orein, Nevada

The doctor came ten hours too late to save Rebecca. She died in her bedroom while Louise, clutching her mother's fevered hand, begged her not to go. Jake hadn't been able to do much to help, sick as he was, but he was able to tell Louise to push fluids to little Sammy and read the packaging on the children's ibuprofen which helped to keep the fever down. The doctor said that babies were amazing, had little immune systems that seemed to take hits and keep chugging. He agreed that Louise keep up on the fluids but to keep the ibuprofen doses low, even suggested she not use it. When neither Jack nor Louise showed signs of infection, he handed Mike a packet of Tamiflu suggesting he actually not take any and let his body develop immunity, then asked directions to Yneko Ranch.

He did arrive in time to help Ane, but not the baby. Her body stricken with sickness and burning like fire let loose in a flood of blood and pain. Andrew and Colt couldn't keep any fluids down, Max watched helplessly as they lay on the floor of the living room shivering and sweating through their cotton pajamas while the young doctor watched Ane to be certain the hemorrhaging would stop. He did advise Max that he give his children the Tamiflu, worry about building immunity later on in life. Max was left alone, the only healthy body in his house.

Mike rode with the doctor to the Thurston's home, where he banged on the door demanding entry. Donning masks and gloves they broke down the door finding fifteen people laying on the floor, too weak to stop the men from coming into the house. They found Walley dead in his back bedroom, his body being kept company by a flock of chickens – some of whom were dead - and a scabby molting macaw parrot. At first, they couldn't tell if the parrot was coughing or mimicking the sounds of illness from the other room, but when it started to wheeze and struggle to breathe, with clear mucus foaming at the edges of its nostrils, the doctor was fairly certain the parrot was sick.

"Get out!" Kat had screamed as she staggered into the house from the camp outside, leaning in the doorway while she coughed, the hacking getting so hard Mike had no idea how she was able to keep her legs under her. "Get out! This is tribal land you are trespassing on. You are desecrating the burial chamber of our chief!"

"The fever." The doctor said as he stood up from the bed. "It's making her delirious."

"Nope." Mike said. "She's always been like that."

They were met at the door by an angry but weak and coughing mob, demanding they leave, screaming for them to keep their poisoned medicines to themselves. They rode back to Max Yneko's house, the doctor advising Max to set up a quarantine around the Thurston farm. In the end the sickness - the doctor naming it "Parrot Flu" for lack of a better description in his notes - took a little under a week to move out of the Orein Valley. With it went Rebecca Wolfe, Jacob and Gertie Lowery, Mary Schertz, Dalisay Gaza with her five-year-old daughter Izzy, and Ceciliee Goya's mother. They were buried together on the little hill where Linda Lane had laid her husband to rest. Louise refused to cry as her mother was lowered into the ground, she held Sammy in her arms while Jack leaned against their father for support.

Her mother's last words were "Be strong." And Louise was an obedient child. They read some words from Rebecca's Bible; the entire time Mike silently staring through red rimmed eyes at her grave. Then he took his children home.

That night he tucked Sammy and Jack into bed, then kissed his daughter Louise on the forehead and told her to keep an eye on the kids. Louise watched her father from the window; he paused just outside the barn door then disappearing inside let out a wail that seemed to shake the foundations of the house. She listed to him for a long time, pressing her forehead into the cold window glass and letting fiery tears trace down her cheeks as she listed to her father's animal like sobs coming from the cavernous blackness filling their barn. Then the crying stopped, and a horrible silence filled the air over the Wolfe Homestead. Louise watched her father walk out of the blackness, leading his saddled his horse, and heading towards the road.

Mike left his homestead just as the light of the sun faded from the sky. He met Max Yneko on the road, nodded to him as the Sheriff wheeled his horse to follow Mike back into town. They rode in silence, their knowing eyes asking no questions when Lander Lowery spurred his little bay pony up from the riverbed to fall in line, followed by Calvin Schertz and Robert Garza. Jake Sanders was already waiting on the corner of Main Street and Bridge, along with Tim Barring and Josh Masters. All men were armed. All possessed by the same dark purpose.

"You sure about this?" Tim alone asked of Max Yneko. He didn't need to ask Mike. The man's eyes never left the end of Main where the empty dealerships and coffee shops gave way to pasture and open land. They burned like fire and brimstone beneath the rim of his dark hat.

"And we are certain they have no children in the camp?" Josh adjusted his lariat, putting it at the ready.

"I've been watching from the roof of the dealership all week." Jake said, pulling on his gloves. "They've placed their dead inside the house and only Kat comes in or out. No children in the tents, very few women survived."

"The doc said not to let the virus leave town." Max responded, pulling on his own leather gloves, "We have a duty to the other communities these people will try to sponge off next. Their food stores are nearly gone and their starting to pack up to go. If they leave, they take the virus with them. More innocent people will die." His tone was flat as he pulled his wild rag up over his face, covering his mouth and nose. The others did the same, pulling the rifles from the leather scabbards tied to the fenders of their saddles and riding off in the dark along Main Street using only the light of the silver dollar moon above to guide them.

They lifted the gate of the Thurston Farm off its hinges first, and while the other men worked Jake slipped up the road on his roan to watch the back. Once the gate was down Tim Barring would take the opposite corner behind a coin-op laundry mat to make certain no one could jump the fence in that direction. There were still portions of the property shrouded in darkness where the Thurstonites could slip by but when put to panicked flight, figuring out ideal routes of escape would take up precious seconds the men of Orein had no intention of giving them.

They started from the front, descending on the tents and the house like a rolling clap of thunder, the light from the muzzle of their rifles flashing like the judgement fires of God. Mounted and at full speed they cut through the tents and people like grass. A couple of men in ragged pants, their hair bushy rats' nests above mud-streaked faces, tried to pull Yneko out of the saddle. He had been dazed when a woman threw a rock that hit him in the side of the face, and these Thurstonites planned to capitalize. Mike ran one down beneath his horse, reaching over Max's saddle to fire into the second.

"I'm good." Max shouted, shaking his head then taking aim at a cluster making their way to the barn he squeezed the trigger, dropping them like sacks of grain. Mike left him to join Josh at a stock pen taking special care to shoot everything that moved inside. They worked the fleeing, screaming crowd like cattle, bunching them up to mow them down.

From his porch Jake caught sight of a couple trying to slip through the barbed wire fence in the back and he opened fire. From the western corner of the property the bark of Tim Barring's .30-30 told him the old rancher was holding up his end of the work. A shout of pain pulled Jake's attention to the long dirt road running alongside the Thurston farm to the front of his house. A single man, naked below the waist, his skin painted in multicolored zigzag designs, was tangled in the fence and hanging by a leg. Jake shot first the woman who had left him there, then ended the man's suffering with a decisive bark from his gun. When Kat Thurston came to the door screaming, her long red and silver hair a tangle of sweat and beads and feathers, seemed to dance like snakes made of flame. She shrieked that they were murderers, killers, slaughterers of an unarmed and peaceful people who only wished to live in harmony with Gaia and the new order that nature had provided. She died in a hail of bullets on her front porch, her body falling back into the house become tomb. When they were done the remaining men of Orein stacked the bodies in the house, men on top of women, with dogs and pigs and goats. Mike searched for the parrot inside, but the reek of death forced him out. Wally still lay on the bed, his lips skinned back from his teeth in a bloated black smile, the bodies of the chickens arranged with crystals and handmade trinkets around him.

"It's not here." He shouted stepping out of the porch while Robert Garza poured cans of gasoline on the bodies inside.

"It's a parrot." Max said stripping off his gloves and

tossing them into the house while all the others did the same. "If it's not already dead it will die of cold in the night. Some coyote will find it, eat it, and if we're lucky that's the end of it."

When all the gloves and ropes and wild rags had been collected and tossed inside, Tim Barring lit a wad of hay he had taken from the barn and threw it into the house. Behind him Jake was holding his roan steady as he tossed a gas lantern into the barn. The hurricane glass shattered into the baggage and feed inside, racing up a wooden beam before catching the straw inside the stalls. They left as silently as they had come, the house and barn blazing like torches behind them. When they reached the river at Bridge Street, they waded into the near freezing water to wash their horses and bodies in harsh lye soap.

Changing clothes, they burned the ones they had worn on the raid in the middle of the broken concrete bridge pointing like a crooked finger towards the sunken crater which was once their town. They watched the pile of clothing burn for a while, then one by one each man slipped away on his mount towards home. Mike was the last to go, waiting until the jeans he had worn were nothing more than red hot ash blowing out into the snow. By dawn the only sign of Parrot Flu and the Thurstonites left on their town were two large black scorch marks in the bloody trampled snow and the freshly dug but not yet marked graves of the Orein loved ones on Ely hill.

CHAPTER 30

The banks of the Hassayampa River – South of Allah, Arizona

They had not gone far from Big Stakes Ranch when they realized why the boats at Lake Mead Marina had refused the horses. Besides being a cobbled together fleet of repurposed party pontoons built for tourist booze cruising and fishing, structurally unfit for large animals to share with passengers, as it turned out the fleet simply carried the throng across the lake to the head of a narrow and treacherous trail skimming down the cliff face on the Arizona side of Hoover Dam. From there, passengers were expected to brave the climb along the thin, nearly invisible slip of a trail to the rocky crags at the foot of the spillway where they could be loaded into large inflatable rafts to face rapids, hard nights camped on the shore, and there were even stories of bandit attacks along the more difficult passages.

"They're charging two hundred at the top for a nasty hump down to where its only one hundred per seat." Steve had said after speaking to one of the raft guides as his party refilled canteens and barrels in the bottom of White Rock Canyon.

"Vegas mentality." Myra had remarked. "Somethings will never change."

The cliffs standing between them and the river slowed their pace as they shadowed the water from the peaks, spending half their time moving forward and the other half finding paths to the water's edge to camp before backtracking out of the canyons to continue on their way. It had taken them three days to find a place with enough shoreline for the horses to stick to the river's edge and another eight to reach Alamo Lake – a rattlesnake and scorpion infested marshy rimmed reservoir that dropped off into lukewarm green water skimmed with duckweed. The two mules from Henderson had challenges fitting in with the string of horses that had made the trip from Utah along the Virgin River, but when they left the banks of the Colorado striking out through the saguaro stippled wilderness following the ghostly footsteps of the Santa Maria, they were more than happy to have them. They traveled a day and a half before they found the 93, and by nightfall they made camp in a rest area with no running water.

When morning came, Hunter didn't waste time musing about the final moments of a couple entombed in their BMW just ten feet from where he had slept. What was there to know? The blackout had come. The car had stopped. With little shelter and no water and nothing but the desert around them, they had waited for a rescue that never came. He could not dwell sentimentally on the lives of two strangers when he had nothing but dust driven road and heat ahead of him.

Eight miles further, the horses pricked their ears, straining against their bits towards a pit of water fenced off from the side of the road. It smelled like rotten eggs and was the color of antifreeze, but it still took more than a little spur to move the horses on so strong was their need for water. A mile further they came upon the burnt-out ruins of a gas station with water gushing from a ruptured pipe. They filled their hats from the spray raining down around the geyser, as happy as if it had been an oil strike, letting the mounts drink their fill from the brims before wetting their own dry throats and moving on. By nightfall they had reached an abandoned golf course, one built without water hazards but plenty of large stucco houses. They pulled the garage door off one and dragging it onto the fading green used the door as a lean-to blocking the sand and wind. They let the animals graze what they could, refilling their water barrels from a garden hose attached to the clubhouse.

"How is the water still running here," Hunter asked as he pulled the hose from the barrel. "when everywhere else the desert is coming back in with a vengeance?"

Myra pointed up into the hills to a massive white municipal water tank rising from the rock and juniper. "We're lucky. Those larger ones are typically over the top of a deep water well. Use down here in the valley pulls water out of the earth into the tank like a siphon. It won't run the whole valley." She paused, gasping then took a long drink from the hose. "But this section of the line should be constantly fed."

At dawn they found another dry riverbed, the sun-bleached skeletal remains of the Hassayampa. They rested their animals in a low spot where what water remained had pooled, changing mounts to give their weary horses a break. It was here that Hunter first noticed the closeness growing between Myra and Steven. He must have been blind to not have seen it before. The tender way she laughed when the doctor joked with her, the extra duties Steve would take on to try and please her. Perhaps the fact that Hunter was almost home, so close he would count the distance on the map with a single finger length, that made him finally see the light in their eyes when they spoke to one another. He put his map away, not mentioning his excitement but allowing them to have this moment splashing in the muddy and not quite cool waters.

It was outside of Whitman that they lost their first mount. Ranger, the sturdy appaloosa Steve had been riding, stopped dead in his tracks refusing to budge. Steve climbed down from the saddle to try and coax him forward, or at least off the heated asphalt when Ranger dropped to his knees. The doctor tried to help him up, pull him to his feet, but even Hunter could see the horse was fading as it lay on the highway flailing.

"Get away from there!" Myra shouted as she jumped down, trying to pull him away but as he tried to help his horse, a wildly flailing hoof caught Steve in the thigh knocking him to the pavement. Hunter cursed trying to get to his friend but did not make it before the horse rolled over onto Steve's prone form pinning him against a concrete curb. Hunter could hear the bone in Steve's leg crack like dry wood echoing through the nothing that surrounded them. Finding his breath in pain Steve screamed, looking down at where the twelve-hundred-pound animal had finally given up the ghost on top of him.

"Steve!" Myra was crying as she knelt at his side. "What do I do? Tell me what to do!"

It took the rest of the afternoon trying to free their friend from where he was pinned beneath the dead horse. Unable to roll Ranger off without causing any more agony they had tried pulling up on the cinch together to let Steve drag himself out. "There's nothing doing." He had panted right around sundown.

"Steve, if you ask me to cut off your leg," Hunter looked at him seriously, "or to just leave you here for the coyotes, I'm going to punch you square in the face."

"No." Steve had laughed a little at this, as he accepted a sip of water from Myra's canteen. "You're just going to have to drag Ranger off no matter how badly it hurts." He had been sweating against the pain for nearly an hour and was starting to lose focus. "Let's get him up so I can see how bad it is. Once we're at that point – Myra, you're going to have to follow my instructions exactly while Hunter gives me a shot of morphine. I have some in my bag."

She nodded with tears stinging her eyes, as they tied their ropes around Ranger's legs and wrapping the other ends around their saddle horns managed to drag the limp animal off Steve's lower body. He howled the entire time as shattered bone cut through his skin under the pressure of the horse. "My saddlebag!" he panted as Myra rushed it to his side then fumbled through it looking for something.

"He's going into shock!" She shouted as Hunter rushed to join them leaving their horses tied off to Ranger.

"What do you need buddy?" Hunter said opening up the medical kit Steve had taken from the Acropolis.

"The tourniquet straps." He said, his fingers grasping at the bag. "Have to stop the bleeding. Not too tight. Just enough to slow the flow."

Hunter found the strap and pulled it across Steve's thigh just where his friend showed him. "My boot." Steve gasped motioning franticly with a pointed finger away from his foot. "Off." He clinched his teeth, growling against the pain as they drug the boot away from his heel and cut a line up the side of his jeans to expose the sharp edge of bone poking up just under the skin of his shin. "You have …to …set it." He panted gripping Myra's hand.

"Ok, but morphine first."

"No." Steve shook his head. "Set it. Wrap it. Take off the tourniquet. Check for leaks. Then morphine."

"I can't." Myra wiped the tears from her eyes. "I've only watched other people do it. We've always called 911."

"Today, you are 911." Steve grimaced breathlessly as he lay back against the asphalt. "Feel where the bones are. Then have Hunter lift on my heal and stretch it, slowly, to push them back in. Try not to cut me."

She nodded. Then turning to Hunter, she ran her hands along the shin feeling the spaces where the bone was out of alignment. "Ok." She said with a gasp. "Pull." He did, Steve took in a deep breath of air trying to fight the urge to move away from the pain while Myra pushed the bone back down into position."

"The splint!" He wheezed. "Wrap it and put on the splint! Wrap it tight!"

Myra grabbed the rolled bandage from the pack and bound the bone in place, then taking an EMT splint from the bag she packed the bleeding wound in Steve's shin where the bone had stabbed through, strapping it down as tightly as she could with shaking hands. "Good." Steve murmured as his head lolled back and forth on the pavement, as his trembling fingers released the catch of the tourniquet. "No morphine. I'll pass out. If I start to balloon… it's a problem."

"Should we have let him do that?" Hunter asked Myra quietly.

"I don't know!" She half hissed, half sobbed.

"Will one of you please bring me my blanket?" Steve chuckled darkly. "I'm a little tired."

"Are we supposed to keep him awake?" She asked but Hunter had no answers for her.

They stayed there on the highway just outside Wittman overnight, neither Myra nor Hunter able to sleep as Steve moaned fretfully in his. By morning his toes had turned a deep shade of purple that made Hunter afraid they had wrapped the bandages too tight or he was bleeding internally. But when Steve woke and sat up to inspect his leg, he didn't seem that concerned.

"We have to move him." Myra said around seven. "It's only going to get hotter and we'll run out of water if we don't move soon." It took every ounce of strength they had to pull Steve up onto his good leg and every dirty word Myra knew to wake him up enough to get him into the saddle. With Myra holding Steve's backup mount Bandit steady and Hunter supporting his broken leg at the thigh, Steve half climbed half drug himself into the seat. Myra tied her horses off to one another then handed the entire string to Hunter as she climbed up behind Steve to keep him in the saddle.

"You have to lead." She said. "I can't see over his shoulders. Take it real slow."

Hunter nodded, then pulling himself up onto his horse towed Myra's string behind, praying the mules were smart enough to follow on their own. They went slow through the abandoned neighborhoods of Wittman coming down into Surprise. As they plodded on Hunter watched the desert hills along the skyline gradually replaced by wide set concrete buildings and open equipment yards until soon there were no more cactus running over limestone and shale ridges but instead well maintained streets leading to the termite mazes of suburban neighborhoods.

"Stop!" Myra called from behind Steve's hunched shoulders. Hunter drew up on the reins and turned in the saddle to see her pointing at a small blue sign beside her on the road.

"A hospital?" He looked around at the empty streets, the heat shimmering off of their black surfaces. He rubbed his chin, considering the sign. "They're probably not even open."

"We won't know if we don't go see!" She called back, desperation in her voice. Hunter nodded at this and guiding Bandit as gently as he could to behind his own mount, turned to the right up a wide four lane road. As they came around a wide curve in the street, he pointed to a string of wrecked cars lined up in the far-left lane.

"That's promising!" He called back as they passed a pickup truck crammed sideways between two smaller sedans. "It looks like someone cleared the road. Why they would need these lanes open without vehicles running I have no idea…"

"They might have done it just as the lights went out." Myra called back. "In case they were blocking emergency vehicles not knowing that nothing is running." They took another turn, this one uphill to the left, the pony bearing both Steve and Myra snorting at the strain as Myra used her spurs to encourage it to follow Hunter into the parking lot of a massive medical center.

"You pay up front." The orderly that met them at the open door crossed his arms, his dingy scrubs wrinkling across his massive chest making him look more like a bouncer at a biker bar than a medical professional. "You pay or you take a hike. We got to keep the lights on."

"What lights?" Hunter gave him an incredulous look as he peered over the man's shoulder. "It looks like you've moved the operating tables to the lobby because you're no better off in there than we are out here."

"It's a figure of speech." The orderly gruffed. "Thirty dollars to see the doctor, ten to see the nurse. Cash. No casino tokens."

"I have fifty right here right now if you grab a doctor and get my friend set up." Hunter said pulling his wallet from his back pocket. The orderly snatched the bill from Hunter's hand then gave a sharp whistle as a team of nurses pulling a gurney helped Steve out of the saddle and onto the surprisingly crisp white sheets.

"Horses stay outside." The orderly stated pointedly. "Surprise Regional Medical Center is not responsible for any lost or stolen items while you are here." Hunter climbed down out of the saddle and took Bandit by the reigns.

"Go." He said to Myra who was giving the orderly a confused look. "I'll take the horses over to that stand of trees and set up camp."

"Camping is extra." The orderly cut in. Hunter gave the man a dirty look handing Myra his wallet.

"She'll take care of it." He said, then walked away towards the edge of a golf course – this one with full but algae skimmed water hazards and a dying lawn. He staked out their tents in the rough and hobbled the horses on the fairway, giving them just enough play to reach the edge of a pond with a spouting water feature in the center. Myra didn't show up until one in the afternoon. By that time Hunter had let the horses graze, removing their hobbles one at a time to let them have a good roll before tying them to a remuda line and taking a nap stretched out over their gear like a human hammock. Myra woke him with a gentle kick to the boot and he started upright immediately.

"How is he?" were the first words out of his mouth.

"Crabby. Spiteful. He called his doctor a quack and then got into a degree measuring contest." She sighed. "But he gets to keep the leg. They're putting a cast on him right now. His hip where he took that first kick is bruised all to hell, but they don't think anything is broken there. They should be done in a couple of hours and then he's free to go. You know, I can't believe he's being such an ass right now. They have nurses in there taking temperature by candlelight, they won't put anyone on the second floor because the elevator is out, obviously, and they don't know how they would evacuate in case of fire." She fixed Hunter with an exasperated glance,

"You know, these people could just go home and forget about trying to keep an actual hospital open and running. No one would think any less of them. But they keep coming back just trying to lend a hand."

Hunter looked up at the darkened building, taking that information in. "They don't want to keep him overnight?"

"They suggested it. But he wants to get down the road." She looked at Hunter seriously. "Getting you back in touch with your wife and little girl is his everything right now."

"Well." Hunter lay back down against the saddle he had been napping on and tipped his hat back over his eyes. "You tell him we've already lost the day and the only thing he's missing out on is sleeping on the golf course and taking a piss on their green." When she didn't move, he pushed the brim of his hat back up. "I'm serious Myra. You march back in there and make him stay. And then you throw a little cash around and have them wheel you in a bed right there next to him. I'll swing by and pick you two up in the morning."

"You know." Myra said, turning around. "I think I might. But you're sure you're ok resting here for the night?"

"Myra…"

"Yes Hunter?"

"You're ruining my beauty sleep."

She was quiet for a long moment before saying, "Sleep all you like, it ain't going to help."

Hunter laughed as he listened to her walk away through the grass, then listened to the sounds of the animals ripping up the delicate roots of the green as they grazed. He was glad that Steve was doing well. Happy the two of them would finally get a moments rest when they weren't worried about making camp or setting watch or pushing to get back into the saddle at first light. But he was worried too. He had spent so much time trying to get home, so much of his energy imagining walking through those doors and finding Lucy and Bella sitting on the couches – happy, alive, and well – that he hadn't considered that maybe none of that was true.

What would he do if they were gone?

He didn't sleep much of the night considering just this.

He took extra time over his breakfast to give his friends an added break, and the horses an extra hour of petty revenge on the hospital golf course. He brushed them out, checked their feet, packed out the mules, and saddled the horses then walked them slowly back across the course to the emergency room doors.

"No horses." A new orderly with the same attitude said as he approached.

"Yea, I know." Hunter sighed. "I'm here to pick up my friends."

"Where the hell have you been?" Steve came out of the door on a pair of crutches, Myra walking behind looking rested and clean. "I've been waiting there so long I was afraid this asshole was going to charge me a sitting-in-the-chair fee."

"That will be twenty dollars for the crutches." The orderly cut in.

"Keep'em." Steve had changed into a clean shirt, looked like he had washed, but was wearing the same jeans with one leg of the fabric cut off just at the knee above his shiny new plaster cast. He pushed the crutches at the large man as Hunter supported his weight under his thigh, so he could get back up into the saddle. "I don't need 'em." His tone was slightly taunting as he sat up tall on Bandit, his busted leg riding outside of his stirrup. "I got a perfectly good set of legs right here."

"You gonna be able to ride in that thing?" Hunter asked, genuinely concerned for his friend's safety.

"I'll be fine." Steve said. "I just won't post." Then he muttered, "Let's get the outta this duckpond." and clicking to Bandit walked the horse off making quacking noises as Myra double checked her own saddle and climbed up on her own.

"They gave him some meds." She shrugged. "He's

going to be a little loopy."

"Come on!" Steve shouted back to them. "Let's get on the road."

They weren't a mile on their trip when Hunter started to really take in the silence around him. The open desert had been quiet, but in a different way. There was always something - something scurrying, something scuttling, something alive. But the closer they came to the edges of the urban landscape the less alive the world seemed. Everywhere he looked there were signs that life had existed, even after the blackout; bikes, piles of personal belongings along the road, even the occasional corpse spoke of exodus, violence, and thirst in the great city's final days – but there was little sound save the howling of desert winds past broken windows and the dead watchful eyes of buildings. It was unnerving, like they were traveling through a city of ghosts.

Taking point, Hunter led them from the freeway onto Bell Street through Peoria hoping to find the canal system which had been the life-giving artery of civilization in the Arizona desert. They passed the burnt out remains of commercial airliners jutting out of the crumbled faces of warehouses; shopping centers with electronics, clothing, furniture, and toys strewn like rocks from a volcanic blast in parking lots and roads. Each stage of lawlessness and social breakdown had left its mark as first consumer goods were looted, then grocery stores picked clean, and finally the artificial lakes and streams of parks and public pools drained as a population of over two million sought to quench their thirst.

They smelled the ballpark before they saw it, the warm winds of winter picking up the scent of death and decay and carrying it past their faces while glossy well-fed vultures circled in massive flocks overhead. From the trail following the canal they glimpsed the ragged city of tents, canvas and nylon torn from their poles and blowing in the breeze like ragged flags. Ahead of them a coyote trotted down into the concrete embankments of the dry canal bed, pausing to consider them before continuing unworried on its path, a sneaker clad foot dangling from its jaws. Across the canal they passed a small orchard, the trees stripped bare of leaves and bark by starving people until they were little more than skeletal hands reaching towards pitiless clouds. Along the canal there was still some life as little shanty camps had sprung up beneath overpasses and bridges where dirty children played in antifreeze colored puddles, their weary guardians watching the horses pass with hungry gleaming eyes.

"Let's get out of here." Myra had whispered when an older man in a business suit and a Rolex watch shuffled over to poke at one of the animals as it walked past. They left the canal and set up camp in the open parking lot of a post office sleeping in shifts and keeping watch over their mounts. They left before dawn when the footsteps of unseen people seemed to surround them, the horses tossing their heads and whickering in fear. They shadowed the 17 through Alhambra, stopping only for a moment to talk with a passing caravan of camels, their riders pausing to take in the unusual sight of cowboys crossing this urban wasteland. The woman in the lead asked where they had come from, then hearing of their disquiet in the night pulled out a map and recalculated her own path to avoid the canals and advised them to do the same.

"Stay away from the water until you reach the edge of the city." She said then pointing back the way they came. "It's a little less savage in the burbs but even those people won't stop at eating your horses." There were still pockets of life downtown she said, they had just come from there where they had traded water and military rations for gold and jewels, but if the Peorians were on the warpath they would need to divert through Tolleson just to be safe. "Don't linger after dark." She said waving goodbye and pulling her grunting beast east onto McDowell. "And if you have to, sleep with one eye open and one hand on those rifles. They're most likely the only reason you aren't in a soup pot already."

"She means the horses, right?" Steve asked to which the other two could only shrug.

South of the 10 they saw the first signs of flooding, stopping to water their horses in the rushing banks of a stream flowing through what might have been a church or a school, it was hard to tell from the footprint left behind. They forded the stream walking through it as it flowed towards Van Buren, turning east towards the glistening high rises of downtown.

"You lived here?" Myra asked as they turned onto 1st, her eyes following the rise of the building into the sky, letting out a low whistle. "Swanky."

"Yup." Hunter said, climbing down from his horse and handing the reigns to her. "I would ask you up, but I don't think we can valet the horses and it's on the forty-second floor."

"Yea, I'm not making that climb." Steve shifted in the saddle, Hunter could see the pain starting to sweat through the pills as he helped the big man to the ground, making him as comfortable as he possibly could in the wide-open lobby. "We'll stay here and guard the horses from thieves and cannibals."

Hunter nodded, telling them that if there was trouble to fire at least one shot up the elevator shaft. Sometime in his absence it had been pried open, the cables exposed beside the empty doorman's desk. He would hear it wherever he was in the building and chances were if someone were trapped in the elevator box, they were already dead and wouldn't mind the slug. He felt a genuine pang at leaving them on the sidewalk as he walked inside, they had become like family for him. It seemed wrong not to have them up, offer them a cocktail, then later call the car service to take them to dinner – someplace nice with an excellent wine list. When this was over, when he had Bella and Lucy safe in his arms, he would have to find some way to thank them for all they had sacrificed to get him to this point.

He stepped up on the first stair then stopped, listening to the jingle of his spurs echo through the cavernous lobby, struck suddenly how different a person he was today from who he had been leaving.

"What's wrong?" Myra called from the doorway.

"I've actually never taken the stairs here." He threw her a weak smile.

As he climbed the stairs, his spurs jangled, the sound echoing like temple bells around him. He passed a door on the tenth floor that looked like it had been caved in with a sledgehammer. Bullet holes stippled the concrete on the opposite wall. He ignored both as he continued his climb, weeks in the saddle and the hope in his heart making the stairs light work. Somewhere around the thirtieth floor he passed a man with a shaven head covered in tattoos, he was buttoning a long flannel shirt as he came down.

"Hey man." The man said simply, "Unless you also found a way to make bottled water cold, she's not taking any more clients for the day." Then looking Hunter up and down he gave a little smirk and pressed past continuing his trip down. "Fuckin' vaquero. Don't know that only luxury items get luxury coño?"

Hunter stood there puzzling over what the man had said, then shrugging the encounter off he continued climbing. It took him half an hour to reach his penthouse on the top floor, even taking the stairs two at a time. Hunter paused outside the door leading to his floor, part of him dreading opening it and finding his family gone. Then taking a deep breath he swung it wide leaving the stairwell and sliding his key into the apartment door.

CHAPTER 31

Mule Wash Ranch – Outside Pinefare, Montana

"Dad!" Becky came running into the barn, her sister Brynne hot on her heels, both girls held a look of horror on their young faces. "The Reach!" She pointed north over the snow-covered tree line, panting. "There's a fire."

He left the barn looking up over the hills at the narrow column of smoke rising against the morning sky. "Dad," Brynne sounded like she was on the verge of tears. "Is Mom okay?"

"Girls, go in the house. Get your Aunt Sissy." He turned towards the barn, opening Smokey's stall door while grabbing the horse's halter. By the time he had the horse tacked up and ready to ride his aunt and daughters were standing in the yard watching the smoke curling over the trees.

"James." Sissy gulped, fear tinting her voice. "Don't go out there."

"I need you to get the girls ready to ride to town." He said. "I have to go see how bad it is. Don't wait for me to get back. I'll meet you all at the Trapper."

He clicked Smoky into gear heading up the service road which would take him to Bear Reach, taking the trail slowly so the horse could find his footing. A warm snap had melted some of the snow followed by a long week of near artic winds, together they had blanketed the world around the Mule Wash in a thick layer of ice making navigating the roads and highways far more difficult. Two days ago his father had ridden in from town to check on everyone, make sure they were still alive. A lot had happened, most notably Gyp Masters had broken his arm when his horse had slipped on the ice along the riverbanks. Never mind Gyp was most likely drunk off his ass when the accident happened but he was laid up and unable to work until the bone healed. An accident like that in town was bad. One like that out here could be fatal. James prayed the smoke was coming from somewhere other than his home although he knew better.

When he reached the clearing outside his cabin this knowledge was confirmed. His home and barn were engulfed in flame; the light reflected off the ice in the trees funneling the heat up the road where it hit him like a furnace blast. He turned his head as the beams supporting the roof buckled, caving into the mouth of the fire, and as he did he noticed something glinting in the melting snow. Smoky tossed his head, pacing nervously against the roar of the flames as James slid to the ground, tying the horse to a tree before walking closer to where a smaller fire had been started in the walkway outside. The heat and the smoke stung his eyes as he kicked a pile of snow onto the smaller fire, somewhat unsurprised when parts of it stubbornly refused to be put out – most likely it had been started with a match put to motor oil.

But he was able to kick free one of the items piled on the tiny pyre. It was a picture frame, one of the larger ones from the wall in the living room where they had hung the family portraits. James had taken them all down a couple of days ago and placed them in the root cellar when he came in to find that Celia had gone from room to room with a shard of broken glass, scouring all the faces from the photos except for her own. There had been something ominous about looking at the pictures hanging on the wall, the soft sweet faces of his little girls scratched away into white formless masses streaked with blood from Celia's fingertips. He had managed to rescue their baby albums, tearing them from his wife's cursing grasp, barely dodging the long dagger of glass she had clutched in her fist as she punched wildly at his face. Those he had taken up to Mule Wash with him, but he had left the wedding album which now lay in the snow, its plastic sheeted pages curled upward in the heat like the legs of a dead cockroach.

Standing up from where he knelt over the frame James looked to the woods beyond the burning house. Smokey wouldn't walk between the blazing house and barn, so he circled the horse around off the road, weaving through the pine and ash between his property and the banks of the Flatbow River. He picked up Celia's tracks in the snow just beyond the line of trees.

She was barefoot.

She walked on with no sign of caring for the cuts on her feet, the blood filling her prints like frozen syrup splattering the snow.

She was heading for town.

He looked up along the river, watching the prints weaving along the water's edge, indecision weighing on him like a landslide. If he anticipated her and went directly to the Trapper, he would arrive with plenty of time to interrupt whatever plans Celia had. But she was hurt, bleeding, and improperly dressed – the cold might just stop her before she was able to make the ten-mile hike into town. If he followed her, he might be able to save her life before she died of exposure. Take her back to the Mule Wash, doctor her feet, lock her away from the girls. He mounted Smoky, careful not to move the horse too fast over the sheets of ice, following Celia's bloody prints towards town.

It had taken the two girls and their great aunt almost three hours to get to town, Biscuits and Bobtail the girl's two horses slipping and sliding on the frozen highway making Sissy gasp as the mounts threatened to tumble ass over teakettle into the snowy banks leading down the rocky face of the mountain towards the frozen river below. At several places Sissy insisted they dismount, leading the horses on foot until she felt the road was safe enough to ride. They entered

Pinefare exhausted and emotionally spent, the girls practically collapsing in Morgan's arms when he came out of the hotel to greet them. They told him about the fire out on The Reach, about their father leaving them to check on the cabin, he stopped them as they began to vocalize their worst fears and ordered them – all three – into the Trapper while he stabled the horses. They sat down in the lobby beside the cast iron stove, ignoring the mugs of cocoa Daisy had brought them, too sick with worry to eat or drink. They waited there watching the shadows outside grow long in the street.

When the sun went down with still no sign of their father, their grandmother Sassy shooed them upstairs to bed telling her twin sister Sissy to make herself at home in her own room. Sassy joined Morgan on the front walk of the Trapper. Her husband had lost sight of the pillar of smoke in the darkness just as it had turned from black to white, but he still craned his eyes towards the northern tree line knowing just how dangerous for horse and rider the trails had become.

"You think Dad is okay?" Becky left the window of their father's old bedroom overlooking the Flatbow as it coiled around the back end of town to climb into bed beside her sister.

"Do you think Mom is okay?" Brynne stated rhetorically. Their father had explained a little of their mother's condition, but they both knew he had been holding details back to protect them. Becky was silent at this for a long while, then started to cry softly burying her face into her sister's back to muffle her sobs so they wouldn't wake Aunt Sissy in the other room. Brynne reached back behind her, grasping her sister's hand as her own tears silently fell.

As the hours past the girls finally fell asleep, the unfamiliar sounds of the hotel settling in for the night echoing through the narrow hallways around them. Sometime around midnight Brynne sat up in the dark, the round disk of the moon spilling silvery light in through the drawn curtains to run in jagged streaks across the carpet. She shook Becky awake, signing in the darkness that her sister should be quiet. Somewhere in the blackness a door had creaked open, shutting again now with a gentle thud.

"Where was that?" Becky whispered.

"I don't know." Brynne whispered back. "It could have been anywhere."

The girls waited in silence as the stairs coming up to the manager's landing creaked beneath some slow invisible weight. "It's probably Aunt Daisy going to bed." Becky whispered laying back down.

"It's not." Brynne insisted. "I heard her go in just after sundown."

"Then she got up to go pee." Becky sounded grumpy, her face hidden in the veil of night falling across the pillow. "Go back to sleep."

"Becky." Brynne's whisper sounded hollow. "There's someone standing outside our room." Becky sat up to stare into the shifting field of black where the open door led into a small living space that formed the rest of their grandparent's apartment. There was a steady tapping, like the dripping of a leak into the floorboards as something slid across the doorframe shifting the depth of the shadows that gathered at the door. Downstairs they could hear their grandfather's voice filtering up through the ceiling from the bar below.

"Is it gone?" Becky whispered after a long tense silence broken only by the tapping, her voice little more than a breath.

Brynne shook her head, her soft blond curls bouncing in the midnight moonlight reflecting off the snow outside, her wide eyes never leaving the open door and the void inside the room beyond. "It's watching us."

"Is it a ghost?" Becky buried her face into her sister's shoulder.

There was a sudden commotion downstairs in the bar which made the girls jump to their feet on the bed like a pair of startled rabbits. Their grandfather shouted as the bang of heavy boots sounded on the landing outside, all the while the thing watching them from the doorway slithered further into the room. The girls shrieked as the door to the apartment from the landing crashed open, then winced as the light of the spirit lamp on the table outside came spilling in. Becky gripped her sister and covered her eyes but Brynne couldn't look away from the dark outline of a woman, blood dripping from the ribbons of flesh across her hands and beading against the polished floorboards with a tap-tap-tap.

There was a struggle in the doorway, a crash in the other room as the woman shrieked in high-pitched nonsensical wailing. The girls sobbed as hands grabbed at them, screaming and slapping them away until they realized their Aunt Sissy was standing beside their bed urging them to follow her. The older woman drug them from the room, their feet skipping across the wood planked floor as Sissy pulled the girls out to the landing while the shadowy figure of the woman rolled and tumbled in a shrieking mass in the pitch-black living room. They passed their grandfather and the sheriff on the landing, Sissy never stopping as they rushed down the stairs past Aunt Daisy's open door, the pregnant woman standing in her doorway with an expression of stony shock across her face. Aunt Sissy snatched a set of keys from the reception desk then drug them up the guest stairs, finally coming to the second floor where she unlocked the door of a room and pushed the girls inside.

"Stay here." She panted tossing Brynne the set of keys. "And lock this door. Don't open it for anyone except for me."

There was a wailing that filled the hotel, rising like smoke through the passageways as doors banged open and curious guests ran down the stairs towards the commotion. The woman was shrieking, her voice seeming to come from the very walls of the hotel itself. And then, it began to drift away, outside into the frozen night. The girls ran to the window, following the sound as it bounced off the buildings outside. In the street below, they saw their father holding the thrashing wraith around the midsection as she flailed and keened in the moonlight. Ahead of him walked the sheriff, heading towards the jail holding a spirit lamp high to light the way.

In the morning they returned to the Mule Wash with their aunt, shaken and numb from more than the cold. Becky would later regale friends and neighbors with the story of the bloody woman who haunts her grandfather's hotel seeking revenge on the lover who wronged her. Brynne would never speak to anyone, not even her sister, of the moments when the woman had entered the room – the silvery streak of moonlight falling across her mother's twisted features, her eyes glittering with hatred, the long shard of broken glass she had held above her head like a knife. The girls wouldn't see their father for a week. He had business in town. They later got their Aunt Sissy to reveal that he had ridden into Whitefish but would not tell them why. When he returned to the Mule Wash he looked tired, older – as if somewhere between Pinefare and Whitefish he had aged ten years. They spoke in hushed tones about a hospital but clammed up when they found the girls listening from the other room.

"Go muck the stalls." James said looking down at his two daughters with a stern expression they barely recognized. "There's too much work to be done around here for you girls to be loafing indoors."

Downtown – Phoenix, Arizona

Lucy was lying on the couch, the crisp white linen of her sundress billowing around her in the breeze blowing in from the open patio door while she slept. She looked like an angel – or a fairy tale princess asleep in her tower waiting for her true love to wake her. A bottle of water sat on the table beside her, the heat from the light coming in from the open curtains making the liquid steam and bead against the smooth curve of the glass bottleneck. He knelt beside her, smoothing her corn silk colored hair, ignoring the auburn roots which had grown out against her scalp. Her long soft lashes fluttered like rolling caterpillars against her porcelain cheek as she blinked open those eyes, the same clear hue of green as the bottle on the table. She looked at him, confused, then sat up looking at the room around her.

"Hunter?" She breathed as her eyes flew in a strange expression of panic towards the bedroom beyond the kitchen. "You're here."

"I'm here." He smiled, kissing her dewy brow gently taking in the salty flowery scent of her skin mingling with her makeup and shampoo. "Get up. I need you to pack some things."

"Pack?" Lucy stretched like a cat, rising slowly to her feet. "Oh! Hunter. We're going to Barcelona. Finally." She sighed then walked to the closet in her room pulling out a rolling suitcase and placing it on the bed, chittering as she worked. "I'll need a new bathing suit, of course. And heels. You know I think there might be some things missing from this closet. I swear I'm missing that cashmere stole you bought me. Sarah probably took it. She's always thieving things from my closet. Did you know she's quitting? Maybe we can hire someone who doesn't rob us blind. Hunter..." She sighed, then, "Hunter! Are you even listening to me?"

He came into the bedroom behind her, his spurs jingling slightly as his boots crossed the apartment from his daughter's room.

"Hunter." Lucy looked at him for the first time and gave a disgusted laugh. "What the fuck are you wearing?"

"Lucy." His voice was cold and serious. "Where's Bella?"

She gave him a puckered, disdainful look then sighed.

"Hunter, seriously. You can't go to the airport like that. You need to change."

"Lucy!" His voice was desperate as he crossed the space between them in two long strides, "Where is Bella? Where's Bella, Lucy?"

"Oh. Her." Lucy turned away from him with an annoyed expression on her face. "She's gone."

"She's gone?" Hunter was dumbstruck at this. "Gone how Lucy?" When she didn't answer he grabbed her and spun her around to face him, shaking her a little. "Lucy! How is Bella gone?"

"Ouch, Hunter. Jesus." Lucy pulled away, her face flushing with anger.

"How is Bella gone?"

"I don't know." Lucy said turning back to her suitcase. "She's gone. Sarah came in here, upset, screaming something about the end of the world, and she took Bella. I think they went camping or something. Or for a bike ride. I don't know."

"How long ago, Lucy."

Lucy sighed, irritated. "A few weeks ago? They haven't been back since the lights wouldn't come on. And by the way, you can lose the attitude. You know, life hasn't been easy here while you've been out playing in Vegas. Maybe someday you'll understand how difficult it's been around here. How hard I have had to work just to keep Perrier in the house and Prada in the closet. You really don't appreciate me."

"Sarah was here."

"Yes. She took Bella on a camping trip, and now you and I are going to Barcelona. Get dressed."

"A camping trip where?"

"Oh, for fuck's sake."

"A camping trip *where*, Lucy?"

"I don't know." Lucy snapped, pushing him away from her. "And honestly I don't care. This is why we hire

365

people, Hunter! So, they can come in here, steal clothes from the closet, and take Bella on long camping trips and we don't have to care. She's with Sarah. That's all that is important. Now get dressed in something other than that ridiculous cowboy costume or so help me you are not sitting next to me on the plane."

Hunter stared at Lucy, her clean white dress and her perfect makeup, her shimmering clean hair, the bottle of Perrier fizzing on the side table beside the leather couch. He looked at her perfect, graceful, white swan like neck.

Then he grabbed it.

And squeezed.

Steve finally took another of the Vicodin he was given from the hospital. He hated them. They made him fuzzy and cranky, he hated not being his best self around Myra. But the pain from his broken leg was finally starting to edge through and he didn't want her to see him fall apart in a screaming, sobbing mess. They hadn't seen anyone since the man in the flannel shirt came down from somewhere in the building, it had been a couple of hours and the street outside the skyrise apartment building had remained empty. Myra was about to suggest she go up after Hunter to make sure everything was alright when she heard the clink of his spurs on the stairs. He strode out of the building a strange expression on his face, Steve looked at her, then to the stairs – there was no one following him.

"Hey," Steve said quietly, pulling himself up from the floor as Hunter stepped past him outside to his horse, taking a long pull off the canteen looped around his saddle horn. "Man I'm… I'm so sorry."

"Bella wasn't here." Hunter said plainly, his tone a little more even than the expression on his face. "The nanny took her out of the city on the first day. She took food, some cash, and my gun. And she left me a note."

"She could still be alive." Myra stepped down to hug him but stopped dead when she noticed the cold anger in his eyes. She offered instead. "Go get your wife and let's find them."

"Lucy's not coming." Hunter put his canteen away, then walked over to Steve to help the bigger man hobble over to his horse. "You two don't have to come, we can take you back to the hospital, I'll leave you the gold. Then you can figure out where you want to go from there."

"Hunter." He turned at the weight in Myra's voice. "We signed on to find your wife and daughter. We aren't leaving you until that job is done. Was Lucy up there?"

She shuddered at the expression that flitted across his face, there was something about it that made Myra uneasy. Steve noticed it too and looked to her questioningly as Hunter pushed him into the saddle. "Yes." Hunter fixed her with eyes as cold as a rattlesnake's "Lucy was up there. She won't be coming down. I have to find my daughter."

"Well then." Myra said, stepping to her horse and climbing up beside Steve. "Which direction are we heading? Because you aren't going to be rid of us, so you might as well speak up."

Hunter stared at her for a moment, then shrugged as if to say to them *suit yourself.* Then stepping into the saddle on top of Nighthawk, the glossy black horse he had purchased with the mules at Big Stakes Ranch, he pulled the reigns and clicked the horse into a jog heading north on 1st Avenue to turn east on Van Buren.

CHAPTER 32

Mr. Church,
I hope you are alive to read this. Everything is dead and I'm
scared. I have Bella and a group of friends; we're leaving the
city. I only know we will be following the Verde River. I don't
know where we will go after that. I asked Lucy to come too
but she didn't want to leave. I have some of Bella's sidewalk
chalk and some paper. Wherever we rest I will draw this cross
as a sign we have been there and will try to leave you a note.

If you can, please find us.
I'm so sorry for causing you this worry but I had to protect
Bella.
~Sarah

Oxbow Ranch – Off the Verde River, Arizona

Sarah stood back from the door, inspecting the cross
and four dots she had drawn there in baby blue chalk. There
was another symbol like it painted in white on the rocks beside
the river with an arrow pointing upward to the trail. She had
found the can of paint in the cellar beside boxes and boxes of
trail mix and jerky meant for the snack bar at the front of the
Oxbow Ranch Historical Park. She had buried Rudy, the man
she found in the barn, and had painted his name into a wooden
board taken from a storage shed to use as a marker. He had
been the caretaker here, was dying of cancer, and she had

spent the past three days combing through his personal journal. He had hung himself the day before the lights went out, deciding that the pain was just too much for him to bear.

She felt a little sad he hadn't lived to see the auroras. The man she got to know through his writings would have loved them. She also found a .308 semiautomatic rifle with a cleaning kit in the back closet and a copy of the *Shooter's Bible* on the shelf in the study. She emptied the pantry into a set of saddle packs she found in the barn after spending an afternoon catching Addie and Baker the two sturdy trail horses in the pasture outside. Slipping her latest letter to Bella's father into the mailbox, she turned to where the horses were tied, their packs on Baker's back the saddle on Addie. "Come on baby. Time to go."

"Why?" Bella pouted, looking at the two horses warily. "Why can't we just stay here?"

"Because baby, food and wood run out." Sarah picked the little girl up to hoist her into the saddle. "And we still need to get out of the desert before it really gets hot."

Bella teetered there for a moment, clinging to the saddle horn stiffly as Addie shifted her feet while Sarah pulled herself up as well. "Are you sure you know how to do this?" Bella asked as Sarah arranged the reigns in front of her.

"Yes, I do." Sarah said. "I grew up on a little horse ranch in Colorado. I can handle horses better than I can handle a bike."

"I liked the bike better." Bella groused as Sarah clicked Addie into a walk, pulling the reigns towards the trailhead heading north through the mountains away from the white clapboard house.

"You'll learn to love this." Sarah said with a thin-lipped smile. "You'll be surprised how quickly you'll forget about the bike."

... To Be Continued

Plunged into darkness in the dead of winter, communities of the American West have had to rely on their courage and each other in order to survive. With Spring comes hope, and new opportunities to rebuild at least a portion of the lives they have lost. But in the North, melting snow and ice bring black clad raiders from the coast while the South must face a deadly new wind which brings sickness and death.

Coming soon: Ash on the Vale of Canaan

CPSIA information can be obtained
at www.ICGtesting.com
Printed in the USA
BVHW030228230821
615006BV00005B/289

9 780578 937113